LADY MAIGREY'S PRAYER

The Scimitar smashed into *Phoenix's* hull, exploded.

To die in a ball of fire.

Maigrey pressed her lips tightly together. She had to keep her attention focused on her own flying.

Veering away from the Corasian ship, she tried to get a fix on *Defiant*. The destroyer was out of visual range, Sagan must have warned it off. But Maigrey located it on her scanner and, after some difficulty with the computer, managed to set her course.

Now all she had to do was hang on and fly.

"Creator," she whispered, shivering in the cold that was creeping through the hole in her flight suit, "give me the major who sent that kid to die. That's all I ask. Give him to me."

STAR OF THE GUARDIANS

Volume Two

KING'S TEST

BY

MARGARET WEIS

BANTAM BOOKS
NEW YORK · TORONTO · LONDON · SYDNEY · AUCKLAND

KING'S TEST

A Bantam Spectra Book / April 1991

To Raoul and the Little One

*I've been waiting at these damn
RR tracks since midnight!
Where are you?*

And then, I said, we must try them with enchantments—that is the sort of test—and see what will be their behavior; like those who take colts amid noise and tumult to see if they are of a timid nature, so must we take our youth amid terrors of some kind, and again pass them into pleasures, and prove them more thoroughly than gold is proved in the furnace. . . . And he who at every age, as a boy and youth and in mature life, has come out of the trial victorious and pure, shall be appointed a ruler and guardian of the State. . . .

But him who fails, we must reject.

Plato, *The Republic*

Book I

Avenging Angel

Proud, art thou met? Thy hope was to have
   reached
The height of thy aspiring unopposed
The throne of God unguarded, and his side
Abandoned at the terror of thy power
. . . Fool! . . .

John Milton, *Paradise Lost*

Chapter ···❦··· One

All of the above.
One possible answer, multiple-choice test, circa 1990

Outside, in the passageway that ran parallel to the hangar deck, the Warlord waited—silent, patient. The corridor was dark; he'd ordered the lights shut down. It was empty. He'd sent his retinue about their business, relayed a soothing message to the admiral to the effect that he, at least, was back aboard.

The Warlord was needed on the bridge, needed desperately. *Phoenix* had sustained heavy damage in her battle with the Corasian fleet. Concern was growing over the continued safety and effectiveness of the ship's nuclear reactor. Aks was receiving garbled reports that another Corasian vessel had been sighted coming out of hyperspace. And he'd been repeatedly harassed by hysterical transmissions from the Adonian weapons dealer, demanding to speak to the Warlord and no one else.

Sagan leaned up against a wall, crossed his arms over his chest, counseled patience, and waited.

A door leading from the hangar deck opened noiselessly; a lithe figure was briefly outlined against the light behind her. Pale hair gleamed with an almost hallowed radiance.

Quiet as the shadows around him, the Warlord strode across the corridor.

Maigrey was aware of him. Her hand went to the blood-sword, but Sagan's was faster. His fingers closed over her forearm with a crushing grip and he shoved her back hard against the steel wall.

"So, my lady, you gave the boy his courage. Dion is gone?"

The light of the starjewel was the only light in the corridor. The bluish white brilliance illuminated Maigrey's face. The

3

skin was translucent, lifeless, the gray eyes dark and empty, sighted in on a battle with him to death.

Her eyes narrowed. "Yes, he's gone," she said warily.

"To *Defiant*, to warn John Dixter of my treachery?" Sagan almost smiled.

"I'm not certain. I hope so." Maigrey stared at him in sudden understanding. "There was nothing wrong with the communications aboard the spaceplane, was there, my lord?"

"Nothing that I couldn't have fixed, my lady."

Sagan could faintly see blood pulse in the livid scar on her cheek. The tense muscles in her arm that held the bloodsword relaxed in his grip.

"Naturally, since you were the one who broke it. The message about the mercenaries being held prisoner on *Defiant* was a ruse."

"Not exactly, my lady." Sagan reached out his hand, touched the scar on her cheek with his fingers. He felt her tremble at his touch. She tried to draw away from him, but there was nowhere to go. He had her backed up against the wall. "Captain Williams has these orders, given before I left: If the Corasians are defeated, John Dixter is to be taken prisoner and immediately executed. The mercenaries who survived the battle with the Corasians are to be killed the moment they return— So help me, lady, try that again and I'll break your arm!"

Maigrey, breathing heavily, subsided. The Warlord regarded her grimly, intently, and when certain that she was once more under control—if not his control, then at least her own—he continued.

"You will be pleased to know, Maigrey, that Williams bungled those orders. Dixter has escaped and joined his people. The mercenaries have barricaded themselves on two hangar decks. They are currently under siege."

Maigrey jerked her arm free of his grip. "You've sent Dion headlong into a raging battle! You knew that when you baited him!"

"The bloodiest kind of battle, my lady. Men trapped, cornered, fighting for their lives."

"What is this, my lord, another test? This one could get him killed!"

"Yes, my lady, another test. But not for Dion."

Sagan continued to regard her gravely, opening his mind,

opening his heart. Maigrey listened and understood, stared at
him in bewildered disbelief.

"You're testing God!"

"If this boy is truly the Lord's anointed"—Sagan's lip curled
slightly—"then He will watch out for him." Wincing in pain,
the Warlord flexed his arms, reached around to massage the
back of his neck.

"Come, now, my lord! I didn't hit you that hard." But she
knew how he felt. Every bone, every muscle in her body
ached. We're getting old, she thought. Wearily, she returned
the bloodsword to its scabbard. But she kept her eyes on him.

The two stood in silence, watching each other, wary of the
least move, the indrawn breath, the flicker of an eyelid.

"You're going to try to go after him, aren't you?" Sagan
reached out his hand, took hold of the starjewel she wore
around her neck, studied it with a contemptuous air. "You're
going to play Guardian. . . ."

He was near, too near, as near as he'd been to her aboard
the Corasian vessel. What had happened there had been a
mistake, but a natural one. They'd both been in danger, they'd
depended on each other, they'd defeated their enemies,
triumphed, as they had triumphed together so long ago. She
remembered the heat of his body, the flame of the shared
power. He was so close to her now, she could feel the
vibrations of the steady, strong beating of his heart.

Closing her eyes to him, Maigrey wrenched the starjewel,
the Star of the Guardians, from his grasp, held it clasped fast
in her hand.

His breath was warm on her chilled skin. She pressed back
against the wall, averted her face. His hand touched her
cheek, the terrible scar slashing down from her temple to the
corner of her lip.

"You're going to try to get away from me, mother that
sniveling boy, rescue an old lover, when—together—we could
have so much. . . ."

Red emergency lights flooded the chamber. Drum rolls
broke the silence, beating the tattoo, sounding the call to man
battle stations.

A centurion, one of Sagan's own personal guard, came
clattering down the corridor. Finding his lord and the lady in
extremely close proximity, the guard skidded to a halt,
coughed in embarrassment, and looked as if he wished the
ship's hull would crack open, suck him into deepspace.

"Well, what is it?" the Warlord snapped, turning away from Maigrey.

She sighed, held on to the jewel tightly, its eight sharp points piercing the flesh of her palm.

The centurion kept his eyes fixed firmly on the bulkheads. "A Corasian warship is bearing down on us, my lord. Admiral Aks respectfully requests your presence on the bridge."

"I'll inform the admiral that I am coming. You escort my lady back to her prison cell."

The Warlord started down the corridor, checked his stride. Glancing back, he put his hand to his bruised neck. "No, my lady. On second thought, I'll be damned if I let you out of my sight. Ever again." He held out his hand. "My lady?"

Maigrey slowly let go of the jewel. She would find a way to escape. In the confusion of the forthcoming battle, with Sagan's attention necessarily elsewhere, escape would be easy.

It was the leaving that would be difficult.

She laid her hand in his. They walked together down the corridor, walked calmly through the red flaring light, the drumbeat warning of approaching peril, battle, death.

Perhaps, she thought, suddenly chilled, Dion is God's way of testing us!

Chapter ❦ Two

This is servitude,
To serve the unwise, or him who hath rebelled . . .
John Milton, *Paradise Lost*

Peter Robes, duly elected President of the Galactic Democratic Republic, entered his private office, located behind his public one. The office was dark, shades closed against the early morning sun, and smelled of leather and polished wood and old books. His secretarial 'bot trailed behind him, murmuring reminders of appointments in its soft and calming voice. Robes nodded, making mental notes of each.

"First meeting, military chiefs of staff," the 'bot informed him.

An emergency session called to deal with the Corasian threat to the galaxy. That meeting won't be difficult, mere dissimulation, Robes told himself. I'll have to exhibit concern, of course, but not too much. Concern alleviated by . . . confidence. Yes, that will do nicely. Concern to keep them on their toes. Confidence to show that I trust them to protect the fair citizens of the republic.

"Next!" he snapped.

"Top economic advisers," the 'bot replied.

Robes sighed, frowned. This one would be more difficult. The galactic economy was in shambles. The deficit was larger than the number of inhabited planets, the people rebelling at the mind-boggling tax rate. But that isn't my fault, he reassured himself. What am I supposed to do about it? The Congress blocks me at every turn. Mindless bunch of idiots!

Fortunately, this threat of war should settle *them* nicely. I'll ask for emergency powers to deal with the current alarming situation. As for those fools threatening to secede over the tax

7

issue, we'll see how fast the sheep run from the fold when they hear the wolf's prowling about!

"When have you scheduled the press conference?"

"1200 hours, Mr. President. The major networks are carrying it live . . ."

The media ate this stuff up—vids of ghastly aliens flaming across the screens of billions of terrified galactic viewers. Voters, who would be more than happy to give their President anything he wanted. . . .

Pausing in front of a large mirror that hung just inside the office doorway, the President flicked a switch marked INTERIOR LIGHTING. Bulbs surrounding the mirror flared. Robes studied his tie and his facial expression at the same time, wondering whether to change either for the day's business.

He wanted to reflect worry, but not anxiety. A slight wrinkling of the forehead, therefore, and a touch of puffiness beneath the eyes would do nicely. He tightened the corners of his lips to indicate he was giving the problem serious attention, then allowed the lips to relax slightly to exhibit absolute confidence in his chosen leaders. Neatly combed hair would represent discipline and authority to the military chiefs of staff and the economic advisers. He would have to remember to tousle his hair slightly for the press conference, to prove he was merely one of the people.

The President pressed a button, turned from the mirror to a vidscreen to see himself as he would look on camera. The face was fine. The tie wouldn't do. It was too dark, too somber for the vids. Yanking it off, he tossed it over his shoulder to the 'bot.

"Bring me something in a subdued purple, with a very fine gold thread running through it. Keep this one for tomorrow, when I announce the news of Citizen General Sagan's death."

"Wishful thinking," came a soft voice.

The voice startled the President, startled the 'bot. Its clawlike hands, grasping a lasgun, were lining up on its target.

The thought crossed Robes's mind that all he had to do was allow the 'bot to carry out its programmed response and he would be rid of that soft voice forever. He quashed the temptation frantically, with a fearful glance at the source of the soft voice.

"Halt!" he shouted, more loudly than he'd intended. His voice cracked.

The 'bot obeyed instantly, lowering the weapon. Gliding

near Robes, it murmured officiously, "This meeting is not on your schedule, Mr. President."

"I know," Robes returned irritably, to cover his fright. "I—I won't be long."

"Security will have to be informed—"

"No! That won't be necessary. That is"—forestalling the 'bot's response—"I'll handle security myself."

"Very good, Mr. President."

The 'bot continued on about its duties. It smoothed out and hung the discarded necktie on a tie rack inside a small dressing room attached to the office. Whirring to the desk, it touched a button on a hidden panel. Vertical blinds parted, flooding the room with sunlight.

Robes could now see his visitor, who had seated himself near the window. Magenta robes, fancifully decorated by a streak of black lightning, were, at first glance, all that captured the attention. The man inside the robes, being old, of small stature, and fragile-boned, was nearly swallowed alive by the folds of fabric, the vibrant color. The eyes—too large for the old man's bulbous head—were so widely open they seemingly had no lids against the dazzling light.

The 'bot continued its duties. It exchanged yesterday's wilted flowers for today's fresh ones, started the coffee maker, switched on soothing music. Robes remained standing by the mirror, finding comfort in the solid reality of his own reflection. He tugged nervously at his shirtsleeves.

"Send it away," said the soft voice.

"That will be all for now," said the President.

The 'bot instantly turned and headed for the door.

"I will wait outside," it said.

Robes cast a glance at the magenta-clad figure, saw the head move slightly.

"No, I have other tasks for you to perform. Go to the war room and bring me the updated reports—"

"I could call them up for you on the computer—"

"Damn it! I don't like repeating my words and I don't like being contradicted! I instructed you to go to the war room. Now do so!"

"I wasn't being contradictory, Mr. President. I was merely acting as I have been programmed, offering you the most efficient method of obtaining information—"

"Yes, yes." Robes discovered he was sweating. Now he'd have to change his shirt! "I'm sorry I raised my voice. The military edit everything that goes into my file. I want the reports directly as they come in."

"I will need to use your clearance code, sir."

"Then use it, damn—" Robes caught himself. He was swearing at a machine. Extremely bad form. And this was being recorded for posterity. The 'bot whirred out the door. "Thank you," the President said, rather lamely.

"Don't forget the press conference, Mr. President. 1200 hours. Excuse me, I have neglected to bring you your tie, sir." The 'bot switched direction. Pivoting on its wheels, it headed for the dressing room.

"I've changed my mind," Robes said hastily. "I want one that is . . . blue on the edges, deepening to purple down the middle."

The 'bot whirled. "You don't have one like that in your collection, sir."

"No? Then you'll have to stop and pick one up. There's a haberdashery on the corner of Freedom and Fifth—"

"Very good, Mr. President."

The 'bot slid out of the room, the door closing behind it. Robes placed his hand over a control panel and the door sealed shut. He now had complete privacy—at least as complete as a highly placed public figure was allowed. His bodyguards could always get inside, of course. Which reminded him.

Crossing over to his desk, not without an uneasy glance at the motionless magenta figure by the window, Robes sat down in his leather chair and summoned security. An image of a uniformed, grim-faced woman appeared on his vidphone.

"Yes, Mr. President?"

"I'm having a meeting in my office. I've activated the seal. I'm not to be disturbed."

The woman's eyes shifted away from his, glancing at a screen to her right. "We have no record of anyone entering your office, Mr. President." A muscle in her jaw twitched, her eyes shifted again, she began moving a hand stealthily across her desk. "I trust all is well, sir."

"Everything's fine! I—I mean, all is well that ends well." He remembered in time to give the correct code response. Otherwise, in the next ten seconds, he would have been surrounded by a S.W.A.T. team. Taking a handkerchief from his pocket, he mopped his forehead. He'd have to redo his makeup. "I'll explain later. Thank you."

"Yes, Mr. President."

The vidphone image faded with the woman's voice. Robes stared at the blank screen, avoided lifting his gaze for as long as possible. "You did that on purpose!" he spoke in hollow tones. "That and the way you're dressed! Why do you do this to me?" His fists clenched on the top of the desk.

"Only the harmless amusements of an old man, my dear. So little pleasure is left to me these days. Surely you won't deny me the occasional, harmless practical joke?"

"A joke that nearly got you shot!" Robes felt suddenly rebellious. He had three difficult meetings to face today, and now, in addition, he would have to manufacture some lie to placate security.

"Oh, I hardly think so." The old man shifted position in his chair, turned to face Robes directly.

The President raised his head, determined to stare the old man down, assert some authority. But the sunlight was too bright. Robes couldn't see the old man's face for the radiance surrounding him. The brilliance made his eyes water, and he looked back at his clenched fists.

"Peter, Peter, I understand," the old man said solicitously. "You always tend to exaggeration when you're under stress. I make allowances. That fleeting thought you had—allowing the 'bot to kill me? Stress, of course. I assure you, my dear, I'm not in the least offended."

Robes's fists suddenly unclenched, his hands went limp. "I—I'm sorry, Abdiel. It's this damn invasion—"

"—which both you and I know is not really an invasion at all. More of an invitation, wouldn't you say? I trust this conversation isn't being recorded."

"God forbid!" Robes shivered.

"He has more important matters on His mind. If you will allow me . . ." Abdiel raised his right hand. The light bulbs in the mirror went out, the desk lamp went dark. The coffee maker shut off in mid-cycle, the music ceased.

"What have you done?" Robes looked around in alarm.

"Disrupted the flow of electricity into the room."

"That *will* bring security!" The President was on his feet.

"No, no, my dear. Don't be so jumpy. They are under the illusion that all is well. That ends well." Abdiel smirked at his little joke. "I do hope this ends well, don't you, Peter? Please sit down."

The President resumed his seat, noticed that his hands had

left sweaty marks on the polished wood. "What was that crack you made when you first came in?"

"I don't recall." Abdiel's voice was bland. "The forgetfulness of old age. Refresh my memory."

Robes cast him a bitter glance. "You've never forgotten a thing in your life. What do you want from me? Why are you here?"

"Don't skip from subject to subject, Peter. It makes you appear insecure."

Robes drew a seething breath. He took care, however, to let it out slowly, trying to remain calm. "I was saying something to the 'bot about announcing Sagan's death and you said—"

"Ah, yes. It comes back to me. 'Wishful thinking,' or words to that effect."

"What did you mean?" Robes demanded.

"That Sagan isn't dead, my dear. He's very far from being dead, in fact."

Robes picked up a pen, began tapping it on the desk blotter. "Then it's only a matter of time. I've seen the battle reports. The Corasians outnumber him almost two hundred to one. No one—not even Derek Sagan—can win against those odds!"

"As usual, you have been misinformed. Or rather, you have not seen the updated information. Sagan was able, at the last minute, to ally himself with a group of mercenaries under the leadership of one John Dixter."

"Dixter?" Robes's mouth jerked in a nervous grin. He twiddled the pen. "It's you who have been misinformed, Abdiel. Dixter and Sagan are bitter enemies. They have been since before the revolution. Dixter's a royalist. Sagan was a traitor, leader of the rebellion that murdered Dixter's beloved king. Then there was that woman, that Guardian. Morianna. Maigrey Morianna. A love triangle—"

"A triangle, certainly. But not necessarily one of love. You forget, my dear, I know both Sagan and the Lady Maigrey well. Very well, indeed." Smiling, Abdiel began to massage the palm of his left hand, an absent motion, habitual.

"Not as well as you'd like," Robes said, but he muttered the words to himself.

Abdiel either heard or divined the thought. "You are jealous, my dear, because you succumbed and they did not. But then, they were very young, in their teens. That was my mistake. Youth is naturally rebellious, independent. One has nothing to offer youth, because it has everything. Or thinks it has. I should have tried again when they were older, but I had you and I thought that would be enough." Abdiel sighed, appeared almost wistful.

"What do you mean, 'succumbed'?" Robes almost shouted. "I may have joined with you now and then, but that was to share thoughts, mental stimulation! You don't control me like you do those wretched disciples of yours—"

"Calm, Peter, calm," Abdiel admonished.

Robes snapped the pen in two. "And why are you blaming me for this mess, anyway?"

"Because you should have dealt with Sagan long ago, as I advised. He helped you gain the presidency. But I foresaw—and I was correct—a time when he would become disillusioned with 'democracy.' The Blood Royal would burn in his veins. And, as I predicted, he has become a dangerous foe."

"I needed him! You know that! Sagan was the only one who had a chance of finding the true heir—"

"Stop whining, Peter! It doesn't become you. And now that you've found the true heir to the throne, my dear, what in the name of all that is holy do you intend to do with him? If anything, he is more dangerous than Sagan!

"No, my dear," Abdiel continued, "you've bungled it badly. If you had taken my advice, this self-styled Warlord would be dead by now. The upstart prince Starfire would have faded into obscurity, lived a humdrum ordinary life, never knowing, never dreaming he could lay claim to the galactic throne." The old man rose from his chair and started forward.

Robes watched him, unable to take his eyes off him. The old man seemed always to slither rather than walk.

"But no. You knew best, didn't you, my dear? You refused to listen to Abdiel. You—the professor. Peter Robes, Ph.D., renowned for your knowledge of political science. Peter, Robes, leader of the revolution. Peter Robes, President of the Galactic Democratic Republic. Peter Robes, fool."

Abdiel came to stand beside the desk. A motion of his hand and the vertical blinds revolved, closed, shut out the sunlight. The room grew dark. Robes had the eerie impression that Abdiel had blotted out the sun itself.

The President hunched over his desk, his hands curled, the fingers twitching like the legs of a dying spider.

"The Creator moves against you, Peter," Abdiel said softly.

"I feel His anger. He lifts His rod to chastise you. Derek Sagan has made contact with one Snaga Ohme, a genius when it comes to designing engines of destruction. You know. You've read the reports of your late and unlamented spy, Captain Nada. But do you know, my dear, that the space-rotation bomb's manufacture has been completed? It is ready for use. And if Sagan succeeds in laying his hands on it, you had best start hoping that some university has a job for you in their political science department. Because that's what you'll be doing. If you live that long."

Robes lifted a haggard face. "What do you mean *if* Sagan succeeds? He doesn't have the bomb yet?"

"No, my dear. The obstacle you threw in his path has at least accomplished that much. Though I have no doubt such a brilliant move was inadvertent on your part."

"Then we can get the bomb! We can steal it!"

"From Snaga Ohme?" Abdiel laughed derisively. "My dear Peter, a gnat couldn't fly undetected through the Adonian's security field!"

"Maybe not a gnat!" Robes switched on a desk lamp, looked directly into the old man's face. He was confident now, self-assured, business as usual. "But a mind-seizer could get inside. A mind-seizer could 'persuade' Ohme to turn over the bomb!"

"So now you come to me at last, do you, Peter, my dear? When everything is falling apart around you, you expect me to pick up the pieces."

Robes swallowed, mopped his forehead again. His makeup was leaving large pink-colored patches on the white linen; he might truly have been sweating blood. He was suddenly sorry he'd turned on the light.

"Very well. What do you what?"

Abdiel drew near Peter Robes, the magenta robes brushed against the man's arm. The President jumped, hurriedly pulled away. He tried to stand up from the chair but felt a hand on his shoulder, gently pressing him down. Robes, quivering, remained seated.

"What do you want?" he repeated hoarsely.

"You, my dear." Abdiel began to pull the flesh from the palm of his left hand, peeling it off in strips.

A tremor shook Robes's body, he shrank back in the chair.

The flesh wasn't flesh at all, but plastic designed to resemble skin. Abdiel removed it. Five steel needles, surgically implanted in the old man's palm, glittered in the light that seemed to emanate, not from the lamp, but from the old man's bright eyes.

Robes gazed at the needles in a horrible fascination. His own right hand trembled. He moved it, slid it down surreptitiously beneath the desk, but Abdiel's hand snaked out, caught hold of him. Gently, caressingly, the old man stroked the hand he held in his.

"I am the only one who can save you, Peter, my dear."

Robes shivered; his teeth ground together. Sweat trickled down his face; his muscles were stiff, rigid. He made a choked, swallowing sound. The hand in the old man's clenched tightly into a ball, a fist.

Abdiel continued patiently stroking the fingers and slowly Robes relaxed, his hand opened, revealing the palm. Abdiel studied the palm's smooth surface a moment, then delicately began stripping away the plastic flesh, laying bare five red puncture marks. The marks were old, the scars healed over, seeming not to have been used in a long time.

"You, Peter, will put yourself 'in my hands,' if you'll forgive my little joke." Abdiel laughed, a dry chuckle. "You will give yourself to me, completely, unreservedly. You will become my 'disciple.' In return, my dear . . ."

"Yes!" Robes cried out in a ghastly voice. "What do I get in return?"

"Whatever you desire, my dear. You can continue to be President of this galaxy. Or, if you are growing tired of putting up with the nonsense of these senators and representatives, you can proclaim yourself dictator, king, emperor. With my guidance, my wisdom, my power, you can become anything you want." Abdiel drew the hand near him, pressed it against the soft magenta robes. "Or you can continue as you are, without my help. You can deal with Derek Sagan. You can handle the upstart prince. You can prevent the civil war that will tear the galaxy apart and end your political career forever!" Abdiel gently patted the hand he held. "You do see clearly, don't you, my dear, the divergent paths before you?"

Robes closed his eyes. He was shivering as with a fever. His right hand had closed again over the marks on the palm—the marks that designated him, in reality, one of the Blood Royal. The marks that had once been a badge of honor. The blood-sword, the weapon of the Blood Royal, inserted its needles into those marks, injected a genetically coded virus and a flood of micromachines into the body that aligned the weapon directly with the brain, allowing the user to control the sword with his or her own mental processes. It gave the user heightened mental powers, as well. And it let two people, connected through the use of the bloodsword, share their minds with each other.

Once marks of honor, the scars on my palm have become marks of shame! Robes thought. I should break his grip on me, order the old man out of my office. He's given me the choice! A choice.

But the defiance drained from the President; his shoulders slumped in despair. Abdiel always gives you a choice, Robes realized. It makes you more surely his when you come to him of your own free will.

The President kept his hand shut fast. Too much was going wrong, too fast. The situation was bad and growing worse. Systems—wealthy, powerful systems—threatening secession. The opposition party swelling in strength and numbers. His own popularity slipping. His advisers had told him, only last week, that, unless the situation changed, he couldn't win another election. That was why he'd started this war—destroy Sagan, bring everyone running home to their President in panic.

But the only one running in panic was Peter Robes.

Slowly, trembling, the President bowed his head, opened the palm of his right hand. Abdiel aligned the five needles in his left palm to the five red wounds on Robes's right.

The President did not lift his head, did not look up.

Smiling, Abdiel inserted the needles into the man's flesh.

Robes cried out with the pain; his body jerked convulsively as the virus, the micromachines flowed, not from a bloodsword, but from the body of the old man, giving his mind direct access to Robes's, to the brain, to the conscious, to the subconscious.

Abdiel probed and penetrated, plunging deeper and deeper into the President's mind, learning its secrets, learning what caused pleasure . . . what caused pain. Though he had given in, Robes's mind fought instinctively, struggled to defend itself against invasion, but wherever Abdiel encountered resistance, he pressed harder. The old man now knew too much. The punishment for defiance was terrible, arising as it did from Robes's own inner being.

Eventually, Peter Robes gave in. He surrendered himself utterly.

Abdiel sucked the man's mind dry. From now on, whenever he wanted, he would be able to manipulate Robes. The man was under his complete and total control. Gently, Abdiel withdrew the needles. Five small pools of blood on the President's palm glistened in lamplight.

Robes had long ago lost consciousness. Abdiel rested the President's limp and unresisting head back against the chair.

"You are mine," Abdiel said, running his fingers along the sweat-dampened forehead, "my dear."

Chapter ··❦·· Three

We took him for a coward . . .
> William Shakespeare,
> *Two Gentlemen of Verona*, Act V, Scene 1

The battle against the Corasians was straggling to its inglorious end. Abdiel's awarding of the victory to Warlord Sagan was perhaps a bit premature. One giant enemy mothership had been destroyed, but another had come out of nowhere (or hyperspace, which amounted to the same thing) and had launched an attack against Sagan's command ship, *Phoenix*.

Dion, from his vantage point in space, could see that *Phoenix* was taking heavy damage. The other ships of the line hovered near but had not been called to assist. Dion wondered why, then concluded that Sagan undoubtedly wanted the honor of destroying the enemy himself.

Dion knew why one ship wasn't fighting the Corasians. *Defiant* was no longer a hunter. It had been turned into a trap, whose jaws were set to close over Dion's friends—by orders of Lord Derek Sagan.

"Sir," the irritatingly calm voice of the shipboard computer broke in on the young man's thoughts, "your bodily function signs are registering a debilitating level of stress—"

"Shut up," Dion said.

Whoever was winning or losing this battle, the young man knew that he, personally, had lost.

Sagan despised him. Not that what the Warlord thought mattered. The feeling was mutual. Dion despised Sagan with a hatred all the more bitter for being tangled up with admiration.

But this time, at least, I managed to outsmart him, the young man thought in gloomy satisfaction. My coward act

18

fooled him completely. I can't take any of the credit, though.
Sagan's already convinced I'm worthless. I merely confirmed
his faith in me. Yeah, I fooled him good!

Who am I kidding? I didn't fool Sagan. I only fooled myself.
The cowardice wasn't an act. This . . . *this* is the act. And I
didn't escape. He tossed me aside. He let me go because I
don't matter anymore. Who wants a king who leads his people
into battle, gets scared and runs away?

"Enemy approaching," the computer announced. "Locking
on to target—"

"No!" Dion jerked the controls, wrenched the spaceplane in
a steep climb. He looked around frantically, peering out the
viewscreen. He couldn't see any enemy plane! Was it coming
up on him from behind? "Where is it?" he demanded, voice
cracking in panic.

"Now out of range and not following in pursuit. Is your
targeting scanner malfunctioning, sir? You should be able to
locate the blip—"

Dion felt a hot flush suffuse his skin. "No, th-the scanner
is . . . functioning . . . just fine." I'm the one who's not!

"Sir, perhaps you are not aware of the most current data we
have received on the enemy. Most of the Corasian central
computer systems have been knocked out, leaving the small,
individual enemy planes operating on their own without
guidance from their commanders. Since Corasians are almost
totally dependent on computerized guidance, these small
planes, such as the one we just *fled* from"—was it Dion's
imagination, or was the computer actually putting a sneering
emphasis on the word—"are practically helpless—"

"Obey your orders." Dion licked his dry, cracked lips. "I
don't have time to swat flies." That sounded well, it would
sound well to anyone listening in on him. Sagan would be, of
course. Probably the Warlord was laughing, remarking to
Admiral Aks right now, "The boy's a coward. What can you
expect?"

"Maintain course to *Defiant*," Dion instructed. I have to
warn my friends, he added to himself. Warn them that a man
they trusted, a man they admired and believed in, is nothing
but a treacherous, despicable liar!

"Sir, your heart rate is at an extremely dangerous level—"

"The hell with my heart rate!" Dion didn't need to see the
flashing digital readouts to know he was falling apart, crum-
bling inside. He counseled calm, recalled Maigrey's advice.

Think about his friends. Their danger. They were the ones who mattered. He had to reach them in time, warn them of Sagan's plan to capture them, execute John Dixter.

"Computer, when we reach *Defiant*, broadcast the emergency landing signal—"

"Begging your pardon, sir, but there's no need for that. Simply utilize the standard transmission—"

"What do you mean, no need? The transmitter's not working! Sagan tried using it to contact . . ." Dion's voice died.

The computer didn't respond; its lights flickered.

"The transmitter *is* working," Dion said, stunned. "It's been working all along!"

"There was a malfunction, sir. But it has now been corrected."

"Malfunction, huh? Just what was the nature of the malfunction?"

"Highly technical, sir. You wouldn't understand."

"You're right there. I don't understand. . . ."

He could hear the voice. *Lord Derek Sagan to Captain Michael Williams. Battle won. You may proceed with the extermination of the mercenaries as planned. Take no prisoners. . . .*

And the computer's response. *Transmission failed, sir.*

It was a setup! Sagan had known Dion would respond to any threat to his friends, to John Dixter, Tusk, Link, Nola . . . The Warlord had conned him with a phony message! No such order had really been transmitted. What was this? Another one of Sagan's little tests?

Dion sagged over the control panel, shaking with anger, disappointment.

I'll probably arrive on *Defiant*, find Dixter and Tusk guzzling beer and laughing at me, he thought. *Well, well, kid. You passed the test. You were going to come to our rescue. You're not a coward, after all. Not a complete coward, anyway. I'll bet your ego feels a whole lot better, doesn't it, son? A hearty slap on the back. We're real proud of you, boy. Now, run along back home. . . .*

I have to find out the truth! I have to know what's going on! Dion reached for the water bottle, drank, spit it out on the deck. The water tasted stale, like blood.

This is the Warlord's private plane I stole! Dion realized

suddenly. He sat bolt upright. The communications must tie in with Sagan's own personal channel.

"Open the Warlord's channel," he commanded.

The computer's lights flared. "Sir, I—"

"I don't want to talk on it," Dion said in mollifying tones. "I just want to listen. You've been ordered to obey me, haven't you? Just in case I had guts enough to play in his game?"

"The channel is now open, sir."

"Keep quiet!" Dion whispered. He clamped his lips shut, silencing even his breathing, cursing the background noises of the spaceplane that he hadn't noticed until this moment. It occurred to him that maybe some sort of indicator would flash aboard *Phoenix*, alert the Warlord that he had an eavesdropper. Dion half-expected at any moment to hear Sagan's baritone, irritably commanding him to stop interfering in the affairs of the adults.

Gradually, after listening several moments to an appalling level of noise, Dion realized that no one aboard *Phoenix* was likely to hear him breathing. They wouldn't be likely to hear him if he shouted. The channel was dead, silent, when suddenly a voice came on.

"This is Captain Williams. I want to speak to Lord Sagan."

The voice sounded strange, high, tense, agitated. Dion had trouble recognizing the young, personable, and highly ambitious captain of *Defiant*.

"His lordship is not available, Captain Williams. I will transfer you to the admiral."

"Aks here."

"I must speak to Lord Sagan!"

"Captain Williams"—Admiral Aks's voice didn't sound much better than that of his junior officer—"*Phoenix* is under fire from a Corasian destroyer. We've taken a direct hit. Our situation is critical. What the hell is your problem?"

Captain Williams was silent long moments. When he spoke, his voice was carefully modulated. "This is my problem. As you are aware, John Dixter managed to escape detention. He and his people have barricaded themselves on two hangar decks. I am currently fighting a full-scale pitched battle against a force of well-trained mercenaries who are quite prepared to die and take my ship and my crew with them!"

"We are aware of the situation, Captain. Lord Sagan was informed of your unfortunate blunder before he left on his mission to rescue young Starfire. He presumed, Captain Williams, that you were capable of repairing your error—"

"Begging your pardon, Admiral," Williams cut in, "but I have no time right now to listen to criticism of my actions. My report will be made in full to yourself and Lord Sagan, provided we live through this. I am essentially being forced to fight a land battle aboard a starship, and we are not equipped to handle this sort of action. I repeat: I need reinforcements, I need brain-gas—"

"Your requests have been logged, Captain. Advise me of your current status."

Dion heard voices in the background, Williams's included, as if he had turned away to confer with someone else aboard his own ship. The boy waited, tense, to hear the response.

Williams returned.

"The mercenaries have barricaded themselves with their spaceplanes on hangar decks Charlie and Delta. The hangar bay doors are sealed shut, but the mercenaries managed to capture the controls on Charlie deck. It will be only a matter of time, according to our computer experts, before they override the system, wrest control away from the computers, and operate the doors by the emergency manual devices. I have been told that there is nothing we can do to prevent them . . . something about safety regulations—"

"Yes, yes." Aks sounded impatient. "Go on, Captain."

"We retain control of the hangar bay doors on Delta. The mercenaries are trapped there with no way out. Given reinforcements, we could retake the controls on Charlie deck and end the fighting with an all-out assault. As it is, my numbers are too few. My forces are divided, split in half. We're just barely holding our own."

"Thank you, Captain. I will relay your report to Lord Sagan."

The transmission ended, cut off from the admiral's end. Dion heard Williams attempt several times to reestablish contact. At length, using language suited neither to the captain's rank nor to his normally cool demeanor, Williams broke off.

Dion stared blankly out at the stars wheeling beneath him. Dixter . . . his friends . . . cornered! Fighting for their lives. Dying. . . .

My fault! Dion said to himself in bitter realization. I was the one who talked them into joining us! I led them into this trap! What do I do? What *can* I do?

His heart raced; his hands began to sweat and he wiped them on his flight suit. He forgot about the Warlord, forgot to wonder why Sagan had gone through that charade, pretending the transmitter was broken, relaying a false message.

Tusk, Nola, John Dixter . . . dying. Maybe already dead, all because of me.

"Did you say something, sir?"

"Yes, is that *Defiant* I can see out there now?"

"Yes, sir. *Defiant* confirmed."

The destroyer glimmered white in the eternal night of deepspace. Dion could see dogfights raging around it—probably some of the mercenaries who still had their freedom, attacking Sagan's forces, trying to aid the captives trapped inside the ship. Dion stared at the destroyer, swore bitterly beneath his breath. This wasn't going to be easy.

First, I have to find a way to get on board, he thought. That shouldn't prove too difficult. But once I'm on board, I have to reach the hangar decks without getting myself killed or captured in the process.

"Call up a blueprint of that destroyer," he ordered the computer.

"I beg your pardon, sir?"

"A blueprint! A diagram. You know, what the ship looks like if it's sliced open."

"Yes, sir," the computer murmured. A short interval passed and then an image appeared on the screen. "Is this what you want, sir?"

"Yes." Dion studied it. "Next shot. Quickly. I want to see the entire ship."

"Yes, sir."

Diagrams flashed on and off. He absorbed each one, the images imprinted on his photographic memory.

A voice came over his commlink.

"We have you in our sights, spaceplane. Identify yourself, and approach no closer."

"This is Eagle One," stated the computer with some asperity. "Lord Sagan's private plane. Please be so good as to—"

"We have received a report that Eagle One has been stolen. You have thirty seconds to identify yourself."

The computer sounded baffled, unable to cope with the

situation. "Stolen! That report is completely false and errone-
ous. I would know if my ship had been stolen or not and it has
not. I repeat, *Defiant*, this is Eagle One, Lord Sagan's
private—"

"Fifteen seconds and counting, spaceplane."

Dion could see, or imagined he could see, one of the
gigantic lascannons swiveling around to his direction. So this is
Sagan's plan . . . get rid of me. No fuss. No muss. Nothing
left behind except a few little specks of dust.

Dion drew a deep breath.

"Thank the Creator!" he screeched. Fortunately, he didn't
have to pretend to be frightened. "I didn't think anyone was
going to notice me! I—I got chased by one of the Corasians and
I'm lost. I'm trying to get back to *Phoenix*."

Silence on the commlink, voices in the background, talking
to each other.

"Who the hell is that?"

"Dunno. Sounds like some kid."

"Who the hell is this?" The voice returned to him.

"Dion. Dion Starfire." The young man paused, waiting.
Sweat trickled down his neck into his flight suit.

The voices were conferring again. "Starfire? Isn't that—"

"Yeah. That's the kid. The one who might be king, if you
believe—"

"King? Shit! What in the name of Lucifer is he doing
wandering around out there in the middle of a battle? And we
received a report that that plane was stolen!"

"Hell, remember when you were sixteen and took daddy's
floater without permission? What did your old man do?"

"Turned me over to the cops. Taught me a lesson, I guess.
At least the next time I stole it I took it off-world. Hey, kid.
Starfire."

"I'm here. Say, can you tell me what it means when a red
light starts flashing above a dial marked FUEL?"

Silence.

The voice returned and was very calm, very soothing. "I
think it might be a good idea if you skipped going back to
Phoenix. Come and visit us for a while, kid."

"Is there a problem?"

"No! No. Let us check that gauge for you. Probably a
malfunctioning indicator switch. Happens all the time in those
new prototype planes. We're gonna lock a tractor beam on to
you. There, that's gotcha, kid. Just take it easy. Cut your
engines. Relax."

And in the background, "Raise *Phoenix*. Tell Lord Sagan we're bringing the kid into *Defiant*, safe and sound. Maybe there'll be a promotion in this!"

Dion grinned, settled back comfortably in the pilot's seat. "Don't count on it!" he said softly.

Chapter ·✦◦◯◦✦· *Four*

I am fire and air . . .

William Shakespeare,
Antony and Cleopatra, Act V, Scene 2

Aboard *Phoenix*, the fragile lives encased in the warship's megagrams of zero-grav fused steel endured the enemy bombardment with the stolid fortitude and iron discipline drilled into them by their commanders. Each man performed the tasks demanded of him to keep *Phoenix* alive and functioning or to inflict damage on the enemy. Each kept his duty uppermost in his mind, attempting to override the deep, inner knowledge that he was trapped inside these metal walls with no escape, no way out, and that a million mischances could end his life, either swiftly, before he might be able to take that next breath, or slowly, dying alone in horrible, agonizing terror.

"My lord." Admiral Aks straightened from leaning over an instrument panel, where he had been almost pleading with the computer to change its verdict. The admiral was gray with fatigue, looked his age and ten years older. "The damage to the reactor is irreversible. An explosion is imminent. We must evacuate."

A muscle at the side of Sagan's eye twitched. The dark eyes narrowed. "How long?"

"An hour, perhaps, my lord. Unless we take additional damage."

A thud, the ship rocked. Maigrey reached out, steadied herself on the control panel. The shields blocked a direct view outside *Phoenix*, but the vidscreen was providing excellent coverage of the Corasian vessel looming near, the fiery tracers of the ongoing barrage.

"Shields on the port side are damaged but holding. It was

the shields for'ard that gave. We've got the port side to her now, my lord—"

"Yes." Sagan cast a glance at Maigrey.

I can give you nothing, my lord, she answered him silently. Neither encouragement in your hour of need . . . nor triumph over your defeat. I'm too tired. I don't care anymore.

Maigrey wondered if she looked as bad as he did. She must. The Warlord seemed to think it safe to shift his attention away from her. "Put me through to the reactor's engineers."

A vidscreen came to life, portraying a scene of death. Bodies lay unheeded on the deck, the living stepping over the dead, who after all had no more concerns. Smoke hung in the air; twisted and tangled metal could be seen in the background. Maigrey saw the warning lights flash, heard the Klaxons bleat. A man stood before the screen, his protective suit ripped and torn.

Whatever Sagan's thoughts might have been, they didn't show on his face. Maigrey could have read them—as tired as he was, his guard was down—but she didn't want to. Biting her lip, she turned away from him, kept her eyes on the screen.

"What is your status?" Sagan asked, voice calm as if this were a routine exercise.

"Not good, my lord. The blast doors held, the contamination's been contained to this area, according to reports—"

"That's confirmed, my lord," Aks murmured.

"—and we've slowed the meltdown, but there's no way we can halt it."

"How long?"

"If we stay with it, we can give you an extra hour in addition to the original estimate, my lord. Maybe longer; but after that, I can't guarantee it."

Sagan paused, involuntarily turned his gaze away to the Corasian vessel. Its giant bulk filled the screen. The man in the reactor room saw him, perhaps guessed his thoughts.

"You can use that extra hour, my lord?"

"Yes, but I won't order you to stay. In fact, I order you to leave, right now."

The man glanced down at his torn suit, at the badge that measured radiation level. He smiled wearily. "We respectfully decline to obey, my lord. We're dead men, anyway. We'll give you the time you need."

"You will be recorded in my personal log as heroes. Your families will be compensated. I will see to it personally."

"Thank you, my lord."

That was standard procedure. The men all knew it. But the engineer's strained face relaxed. He must have been thinking of a wife somewhere, children. This eased his burden. He could go to his men, too, and have something to tell them . . . besides the fact that they were going to end in a ball of fire.

A tear slid down Maigrey's cheek. It was stupid to cry. She'd seen men die. They were dying now on *Defiant*. John Dixter. Maybe Dion. . . . She should try to escape, try to help them, but she stood here crying like a child. She wiped the tear away, but another came after it, and another.

"Stop sniveling!" Sagan snapped, adding beneath his breath, "You were a Guardian once! Try to act like it!"

I was a Guardian once, Maigrey thought. I was twenty once. I was going to live forever . . . or so I imagined. Now I'm forty-one and my body aches. I'm sick of watching good men die. I'm sick of the fighting. Let the damn ship blow up. Let it all end right here, right now. There are worse ways to go than in a ball of fire. For one brief moment, we'll shine as brightly as the stars.

". . . evacuate all personnel except those absolutely necessary to the ship's function. Fly off all planes, including those that are damaged if they're at all spaceworthy. A bounty to any pilot who brings in a damaged plane. And I want to make a course change. Cease fire. Bring *Phoenix* in nearer the Corasian—"

"Nearer, my lord?" Aks stared. "Cease fire?"

Oh, get with it, Admiral! Maigrey silently advised him. A child of six could figure out this strategy. She wiped the back of her hand across her eyes. The Warlord checked an irritated sigh, patiently explained his plan to his admiral.

Aks protested. "But, my lord, that's far too dangerous! You should leave now. I have your shuttle standing by—"

"Tell Giesk to send some of the wounded in my shuttle. I'll fly my plane out. The lady will accompany me."

Maigrey was shivering. The bridge was icy cold. All systems not absolutely essential to the sustaining of life had been either shut down or moderated. That, apparently, included heat.

I have to get away from here, away from him! she prodded herself.

Why bother? she answered herself dully, despairingly. He'll only find you again. Your minds are too closely linked.

He's become like death. There's noplace to run, noplace to hide.

Death *is* the one place, she reminded herself, sighing. But that is forbidden me.

I am a Guardian. My life is pledged to my king. As long as Dion lives . . .

As long as he lives. What good am I to him now? What good am I to anybody? She had heard Aks repeating Captain Williams's report to the Warlord. She had heard the mercenaries were trapped, fighting for their lives. John Dixter, who came into this war for love of her.

The tears began to come in earnest now; she couldn't stop crying. Sagan would be furious. Let him.

". . . Snaga Ohme," Admiral Aks was saying to the Warlord in a low voice. "He insists on speaking to you."

Maigrey gulped, caught Sagan's swift, penetrating glance, and changed her startled reaction to a hiccup. Her tears ceased with a suddenness that made her eyes sting and burn. *Snaga Ohme*. The Adonian weapons dealer, the genius who had been in secret contact with Derek Sagan. John Dixter had stumbled across the information, and now, Maigrey guessed, Dixter was paying for his knowledge with his life.

Her proclivity to burst into tears paid off for her now; gave her an excuse to keep her face hidden. The mind-link between herself and the Warlord was now broken. Sagan erected mental barriers the moment the Adonian's name had been mentioned. And the Warlord, angered at her giving way to her weakness, was paying scant attention to her. Maigrey let her body sag down into a nearby chair, slumped on the console, hid her face in her arms, and strained to hear the almost inaudible conversation.

"I don't have time to talk to that fool—"

"My lord, he insists." Aks lowered his voice further. "He has heard about our . . . um . . . danger, my lord. He wants . . . his money."

"Money!" Sagan exploded. Drawing a seething breath, he managed to regain control of himself, but it was with difficulty. "Very well, Admiral. I will speak to him. In my private quarters."

Maigrey felt the Warlord's attention turn again to her. He was staring at her, wondering what to do with her. He was the only one aboard this ship whose powers were equal to hers, who could stop her if she chose to use her phenomenal, inbred abilities. But she was undoubtedly the last person he wanted around while he was talking to this Snaga Ohme. Quite a quandary.

"Leave her in my care, my lord," Aks said, voice softened. The admiral was of the old school, obtuse, but chivalrous. "You can see, she's exhausted, harmless—"

"My lady will be harmless only when she's dead. And somehow I don't think I will trust her even then." Sagan heaved an exasperated sigh. "But I have no choice, it seems."

Maigrey raised her tear-streaked face, watched the Warlord warily. He had said he would never allow her out of his sight. . . .

Sagan gestured to his personal bodyguards, who had been standing at a discreet distance during his conversation with the admiral. The men obeyed with alacrity. The Warlord reached out, took the lasgun from one guard's holster.

Maigrey was too dazed with fatigue to think what he was doing. She recognized his intent only when he turned, pointed the lasgun at her, and fired.

··◀■ ■▶··

"I trust your weapon was set on stun?" Sagan handed the lasgun back to the shaken guard.

"Y-yes, my lord," the man stammered. "As you command, when we are aboard ship."

"Very good." The Warlord glanced down at the motionless body lying on the deck. "Stay with her."

Bending down, he put his hand on the woman's neck, felt the pulse, then gently brushed a strand of wet hair from her face. "After all, my lady, you did complain of being tired. The rest will do you good." Straightening, he involuntarily put his hands to his lower back, but was careful to keep his face expressionless, careful to keep from wincing in pain. "Aks, carry out your orders. I will be in my quarters."

Derek Sagan was a tall man; his strides were normally long and powerful. He walked swiftly through the ship, making certain he moved no faster than usual, though the seconds ticked away inside him like the pumping of his heart. Men caught dashing through the corridors in panicked haste came upon their commander strolling purposefully, with measured stride, and slowed their pace.

The Honor Guard were at their posts outside the double

doors, which were splendidly decorated with a golden phoenix rising from flames. The phoenix was about to fall again, would have to rise again. Sagan wondered briefly if he had the strength.

"I'm not to be disturbed," he told the captain of the guard, who wasted no words in replying but nodded once and placed his men at the door, weapons ready. The Warlord, seeing all was satisfactory, entered his quarters and sealed the door shut behind him.

He paused for a moment, glancing around his rooms. He had few personal objects. He preferred to live a Spartan existence. Those objects he did own were valuable, priceless, rare. His hand lingered fondly on a breastplate supposed to have belonged to Alexander, a helm that had been Caesar's. All would be destroyed. There wasn't time to save them, room to pack them. Evac ships were notoriously unfit to handle a complete evacuation. Whatever space these took up might mean a man left behind.

All but one. Sagan's hand passed swiftly over the valuable artifacts, stopped at a glass case in which were placed several curious objects, including one that most observers would have overlooked or—if they noticed—wondered why it was here at all. It was given no special prominence. Indeed, it seemed almost to have been placed here by accident.

The Warlord doubled his fist, smashed it through the glass. Shards cut his flesh; he didn't flinch or appear to notice. Impatiently, he brushed aside precious jewels that had been gifts of a long-dead king. Sagan's fingers closed over a battered, shapeless, well-worn leather scrip—plain, without marking, and obviously ancient. Reverently, he drew it forth, smoothed it out with his hand. Blood from the cuts on his flesh smeared across the leather. Sagan ignored it. His blood had fallen on it before, sanctified it.

The vidscreen beeped persistently; a lighted button flickered in the darkness of his quarters. Snaga Ohme was on-line and waiting.

Let him wait, the Warlord thought. He has time, I do not.

Carrying the scrip, Sagan walked through his quarters, coming to stand before what was presumed by everyone aboard, Admiral Aks included, to be a vault holding the wealth of several major systems. A security device, specially designed by the Warlord, prohibited entry. Five sharp needles protruded from a pad located to the right of the door. The five needles were arranged in a pattern that matched the scars of five puncture wounds on the palm of the Warlord's right hand. The wounds were fresh, their edges slightly inflamed; he'd used the bloodsword during his battle aboard the Corasian vessel. Sagan impaled his hand on the five needles.

A virus identical to the virus in his sword flowed into his veins. The virus was deadly to anyone lacking Sagan's genetic structure, which meant that the virus was deadly to anyone except the Warlord. The door slid open. He entered; the door slid shut and locked. Sagan stood, not in a vault, but in a chapel, whose existence, if it had been known, would have meant his death.

The darkness inside the vault was intense, no artificial light permitted. Sagan did not need light. He knew by touch and instinct the location of every object in the chapel. Kneeling on a black silk cushion before the black obsidian altar, the Warlord spread the battered scrip upon the cold stone. His movements were deft, no wasted motion. Yet he was unhurried, reverent, calm. He was almost tempted to stay, linger in the soothing, incense-scented darkness until death took him.

He heard, through the sealed door, the insistent beep of the computer. Snaga Ohme, the bomb. Sagan's weapon, the rulership of the galaxy. The temptation to eternal rest passed swiftly.

The Warlord's hands ran over the altar, knowing exactly what he sought and where to find it. He grasped a silver dagger whose hilt was an eight-pointed star and slid it into a plain leather sheath, placed the sheath into the scrip. Wrapping a silver chalice decorated with eight-pointed stars in black velvet, he thrust it into the scrip. He lifted a small, silver bowl, poured out the rare and costly oil it contained, letting it run down the sides of the obsidian altar, and added the bowl to the scrip.

Finally, a small rosewood box containing a starjewel, *his* starjewel, gone unregarded for years, but important now for what it would be, not for what it had been.

Last on the altar lay robes made of finest black velvet. Sagan lifted the fabric, brought the hem to his lips, kissed it as he'd been taught. He thrust the robes of a priest of the outlawed Order of Adamant into the leather scrip that once belonged to Hugues de Payens, founder of the Knights Templar, and cinched its drawstring tight.

Rising, the Warlord shoved the cushion aside with his

booted foot. The vault's door opened, and he walked out, making certain to seal it after him. Soon, he thought grimly, I won't have to put up with this secretive nonsense. Soon, I will do what I please, President Peter Robes and the Galactic Congress be damned. Sagan walked over, sat down before the vidscreen. Its digital clock reminded him of the waning minutes.

"Yes, Ohme, what is it? Be brief, I don't have much time."

The Adonian's handsome face appeared on screen. He was impeccably dressed in the latest and most costly evening wear—black jacket, white tie, a vest of shimmering rainbow thread. He made a graceful gesture, jewels flashed.

"Gad, darling! I've just heard. It's the reason I called, as a matter of fact. Sorry to hear you're about to be blown up, but then war is hell, isn't it, sweetheart?"

"What do you want, Ohme?" Sagan was fast losing patience.

"I find it rather embarrassing, speaking of such crass considerations at a time like this, but—since you asked—I'd like my money. I've laid out a considerable amount for this bauble of yours—"

"You know our deal. Cash on delivery."

One of the Adonian's plucked eyebrows rose. A smile crossed the curved lips. He leaned back in his chair, his hand fluttering, languid, jewels flashing. "Darling boy, what I'm about to say seems cruel, but business is business, after all. Let's be reasonable, Derek. How can I deliver the bomb to you when you're about to be annihilated? I want to be paid . . . now. Transfer the money into my account."

"When I have the bomb, you will have the cash."

"No, no. That won't do at all, I'm afraid." Snaga Ohme sighed delicately. "I had hoped approaching death would make you more tractable. I really can't afford to wait any longer. I am giving you fair warning, dear boy. If I'm not paid, I shall put the bomb on the open market. Highest bidder. First come, first served, so to speak."

"You are passing a death sentence on yourself, Snaga Ohme."

The Adonian smiled charmingly, flicked his hands. The light from the jewels danced and sparkled. "Boom, darling!" Laughing, he ended the transmission.

Derek Sagan rose to his feet. He slung the scrip over his shoulder, drew on his ceremonial red and gold cape, its

capacious folds neatly hiding the scrip from the eyes of the
curious.

I'll deal with Snaga Ohme later, he thought. Right now, I
have a battle to fight and to win.

··◁■ ■▷··

Maigrey divined Sagan's intent only when he aimed the
lasgun on her. She had just seconds to alter her electromag-
netic aura to absorb the impact of the stunning ray. Hastily
raised, her defenses were weak and, though the full force of
the blow was dissipated, it hit her like a giant fist, slamming
into her body.

Probably just as well, she thought, lying on the deck,
struggling to cling to consciousness. I could never have acted
convincingly enough to fool Sagan otherwise.

It was a temptation, once her eyes were closed, to leave
them closed, to sink into dark oblivion, let it ease the pain of
body and mind. She dared not move, lest they realize she was
shamming, and her fatigue nearly made the decision for her.
She was aware of Sagan's touch, heard his words as in a dream.
Voices became submerged in a steady stream of warmth and
quiet that was slowly stealing over her, stealing her away with
it. Someone, probably Admiral Aks, thoughtfully covered her
with a blanket. This simple kindly gesture nearly made
Maigrey cry again; she had to bite her lip hard to keep back the
tears.

Drowsy, she let her mind float free. Like iron drawn to the
magnet, it hovered near Sagan's. Preoccupied with the danger,
his mind was absorbed in his plans, his plots, his ideas, his
fears. The Warlord did not notice the lady's presence so near
him. She was light, airy, a hint of subtle perfume in his
nostrils, the flutter of a butterfly wing on his skin. She was
aware of everything he did, every thought he had.

The chapel didn't surprise her. She knew of its existence as
she knew of his existence. One would have been deficient
without the other. The leather scrip belonging to a forgotten
knight was an old friend; Maigrey'd been present during the
ceremony when Sagan had received it from the brothers of the
Order of Adamant. The other objects—the dagger, the dish,
the chalice—were as much a part of him as the Star of the
Guardians was a part of her. She was only mildly surprised at
the existence of the rosewood box. He had renounced the Star

of the Guardians, betrayed it, disgraced it, but he couldn't give it up.

His voice, coming to her muffled, seemed filtered through a thick, rose-tinted mist.

Yes, Ohme, what is it? Be brief, I don't have much time.

Ohme! Snaga Ohme! The name was like a sharp pinprick, a glass of cold water tossed on her face. She regained consciousness instantly, too instantly and not carefully, to judge by the jingle of armor, the guard turning to look at her. Maigrey concentrated on lying perfectly still, and the guard turned away. She had to make certain she didn't betray herself to Sagan, had to keep her thoughts from touching his with too heavy a hand. Unaware of her, discounting her, he'd let his guard down.

I am giving you fair warning, dear boy. If I'm not paid, I shall put the bomb on the open market. Highest bidder. First come, first served, so to speak.

And why shouldn't I be the one to buy it?

The thought was like a jolt of electricity through Maigrey's body. She began to shiver uncontrollably and huddled more closely beneath the blanket. Excitement was a magic elixir, burning away aches and fatigue and despair. She was gulping it down so fast she felt dizzy, drunk. Calm, she counseled. Calmly.

First, Sagan. She'd been careless, he might have read her thoughts, come storming through the ship to stop her.

No, he was furious at the alien; his mind was in a turmoil. He himself was endeavoring to proceed with calm. He couldn't waste time on her. What was she, anyway? Helpless? A prisoner?

Not for long. Not for long.

Could it be accomplished? Could she really deal for the bomb? It would be difficult, but the beginning of a plan, the vague shape and outline, was forming. Yes, it was feasible. All she had to do was get away. And that should be relatively easy, in a ship about to die.

The most dangerous part of her plan would be the next few seconds, escaping from her guards, slipping off the bridge. She could fight; she had the bloodsword. But that would call attention to her and, more important, she didn't have the time. Sagan was already on his way back.

Maigrey concentrated, marshaling her mental forces, summoning the power. The Blood Royal. Genetically bred over centuries, designed to rule, to lead. Theirs was a magic capable of logical definition, scientific mysticism.

What could you do, if you wanted, my lady? Dion had asked her once.

What could I do? I could split the bulkheads open. I could short out all the electrical systems. I could make each man in this bar rise up and slay himself.

So she had told the young man and she'd told him the truth. But none of that would be necessary right now, not that she had the energy to try bulkhead splitting or mass murder. Mass hypnosis was far less taxing and would accomplish the same objective.

Maigrey stirred beneath the blanket, sighed, and seemed to settle herself more comfortably. As she hoped, each man near her turned to stare at her. Fortunately, none touched her. One started toward her, but the centurion shook his head, gestured him back with weapon drawn. Admiral Aks glanced in her direction, said something indistinguishable and unimportant to a lieutenant standing near, who also looked in her direction.

No man noticed or realized that when he looked at her he was caught, that he stood frozen, immobile, hypnotized. The effect lasted only a split second. No one remembered it afterward. Each man turned away with an image in his mind of a woman lying unconscious beneath a blanket on the deck at their feet. So powerful was the image that, when the woman rose to her feet, the man's mind refused to believe what his eyes insisted upon. Faced with two distinct and contradictory images, the brain of each man on the bridge chose the strongest, rejected the seemingly impossible.

Walking softly, moving fluidly as a ghost, Maigrey glided away and no one on deck knew she had gone.

··◁▭ ▭▷··

The bridge was almost completely dark and nearly empty of its personnel. All lights except for running lights and those on the computers, instruments, and vid equipment had been shut down. The ferocity of the barrage the ship was currently sustaining indicated to the Warlord that *Phoenix* was drawing nearer the Corasian vessel with every passing second. A glance at the instruments confirmed his observation.

Murmured voices of crewmen relaying information and the pounding of the explosions that rattled the hull were the only sounds. Most of the crew had been ordered off. Sagan, glancing at the vidscreen, could see the evac ships beginning to pull away. He knew the Corasians could "see" them, as well. He allowed himself a moment of congratulation.

"All appears to be in order, Admiral. You have carried out your instructions well. We have less than an hour left in the safety window. Take the men remaining and proceed to your ship."

Aks was clearly unhappy. "Are you leaving now, as well, my lord?"

"No, Admiral. Someone must stay aboard to guide *Phoenix* as near the Corasian ship as possible. I will take that duty upon myself."

"I respectfully request permission to remain with your lordship."

"Permission denied. Do as you are ordered, Admiral. Captain Williams can use some assistance on *Defiant*. Meet me there. I shall be on board within the next forty minutes."

Aks started to argue, caught the Warlord's weary, shadowed gaze, and said softly, "Yes, my lord." He turned to leave, stopped, and motioned to a steel tray covered with a white cloth. "Dr. Giesk left that for you, my lord. A stimulation shot, I believe."

Sagan's lip curled in disdain. The Blood Royal needed no such artificial stimuli. He could retreat into his own being, find the strength he needed within.

Admiral Aks bowed without a word and prepared to leave the bridge, taking the remainder of the crew with him. All were reluctant to go. Many cast pleading glances at their Warlord, glances that were met with a gaze as cold and hard as adamant. Soon the bridge was deserted except for the two silent Honor Guard standing watch over Lady Maigrey—lying unconscious on the deck—and the Warlord.

Sagan turned the ship's outer cameras away from the Corasian ship and onto *Phoenix*, seeing his ship through the eyes of his enemy. It appeared dark, lifeless—a dead thing floating in space. Most of the evac boats were speeding away. He saw his own shuttle pulling out. He must remember to commend his captain, who had ordered the Warlord's crest on the side of the vessel lighted. Corasians have no "eyes" but their sensitive sighting devices would be certain to note Sagan's phoenix emblem. They must assume the Warlord was on board, beating a strategic retreat.

Sagan made a slight change in course, giving the ship the

appearance of an abandoned wreck, drifting at random. The Corasians had ceased their fire on the flagship and were beginning to turn their attention to the attendant smaller destroyers, intending to cripple them and salvage what was left. Sagan could picture the Corasians gloating over their prize. When the battle was ended, they would lock a tractor beam on to *Phoenix* and tow it back to their galaxy, take it apart, and use the technological advances to enhance their own out-of-date fleet.

This prize, however, had a surprise inside.

Sagan glanced at the time, though he had no need to do so. His inner, mental clock kept it for him to the millisecond. At a dead run, it would take him fifteen minutes to reach his spaceplane. His centurions and Lady Maigrey would need to leave ahead of him. He walked over to his men, who came to attention, saluting, fist over heart. Their faces were impassive, calm. One could never have told, from their expressions, that they were the only ones left on board a ticking time bomb.

"Escort the Lady Maigrey to my spaceplane. I—"

Sagan looked down. The deck was empty. Aghast, he raised his head, confronted his men. "Where is she?"

"Right there, my lord. She never moved, never stirred. We were worried—" The centurion followed Sagan's angry gaze, blinked, and gasped. "My lord! I swear—"

"Never mind! Report to my spaceplane!"

"My lord, we—"

"Go!" Sagan roared.

The centurions fled, booted feet pounding on metal, the echoes sounding unnaturally loud and eerie in the silence.

Maigrey was gone. Probably to *Defiant*, planning to rescue the boy, save John Dixter. Or was she? Something nagged at Sagan's mind. He couldn't touch hers; the barriers were up, the shadows thick and heavy. He sensed shapes in the shadows, however, and what he saw vaguely disquieted him.

He didn't dare risk a transmission to *Defiant*. He could only trust that the Creator was with him.

Sagan slumped into a chair. He was tired. It was frightening, how tired he was. His neck hurt, where Maigrey'd struck him down on board the Corasian vessel. The muscles were beginning to stiffen. The Warlord closed his eyes, leaned back. Calm. Peace. Serenity. Look within and find the strength you need.

Only it wasn't there. He'd lost his ship. Oh, he would win

the battle, *this* battle. But there would be another. He knew his foe now, knew the true foe—an old man in the magenta robes, an old man Sagan had accidentally glimpsed in a transmission to Peter Robes. The Warlord understood that the fight with this enemy would be a fight to the death. And Sagan wasn't at all certain he had the ability, the strength, the cunning to win.

The Warlord sighed, raised his head, opened his eyes. He reached out his hand, slowly removed the white cloth from the steel tray. Lifting the syringe, he stared at it a moment, then pressed it against the skin of his upper forearm.

Crouched in a doorway in the main part of the ship, listening to the drums beating the retreat, Maigrey watched men dash up and down the corridor. She wasn't out of danger yet. Dressed in the body armor that outlined every curve of her form, her long pale hair sliding out of its braid, she would be easily recognizable in a ship on which no women served. To say nothing of the fact that the men all knew her, knew her to be Sagan's prisoner.

Fortunately, it was dark, emergency lights only were in operation. Harsh white beams gleamed at intervals, forming pools of light in the corridors, leaving most of the area in shadow.

Now or never. Maigrey left her doorway, walking hunched over, her hand to her face. Keeping to the shadows, she flitted down the passageway, heading for the flight deck. What she would do once she got there was open to question.

She literally stumbled over her answer, tripped over a dead body.

Lying in a particularly dark portion of the ship, the man had gone unnoticed by those passing by who might have aided him. He'd been a pilot, Maigrey noted from the bulky flight suit, the helmet that he'd dropped when his strength gave out. She refrained from thanking the Creator—she could never be thankful for a man's death—but she did bless His guidance that led her down this particular passage.

She dragged the body into a dark corridor, keeping clear of the pools of light, and stripped the flight suit from the corpse.

The drumbeats continued, would continue until the drummers themselves left their posts. Maigrey heard them, felt them, the vibrations thrumming through her body. She had no doubt that she would hear them in her dreams. How much time? Thirty minutes, her mental clock told her. The corridor rocked, tilted. The ship was drifting, no longer under control.

The drumbeats ceased. The ship was almost deserted now. The silence echoed more loudly than the noise before it. Her fingers, slippery with blood, shook as she tried to release the clasps on the flight suit. Each second might be the last. Maigrey grit her teeth, forced herself to stop thinking about it.

A huge metal fragment embedded in the man's chest cavity had been his death. He hadn't sustained that injury flying. He must have been standing in the wrong place at the wrong time. It made her wonder what the flight deck was like, what damage it had taken. Still, the evac ships had to be going out. . . .

Maigrey struggled into the flight suit, pulled it over her body armor, fastened it up tightly. It was too big; she felt huge and bulky as an elephant. Picking up the man's helmet, she started to put it on, then paused. Reaching down, she closed the staring eyes.

"*'Requiem aeternam dona eis, Domine; et lux perpetua luceat eis,'*" she murmured softly. "'Rest eternal grant them, O Lord; and let light perpetual shine upon them.'"

My lady! came a voice.

It sounded so near! Maigrey leapt up in fright, whirled around. Sagan wasn't there. The voice was in her head, in her being. She drew a shivering breath, reprimanded herself. The Warlord couldn't be anywhere near. He couldn't leave the bridge. She should have remembered that.

Ignoring him, shutting her mind to his probing, she dipped her hand in the soot and blood and spilled oil that coated the deck and smeared the gunk over her face. Putting on the helmet, Maigrey hurried back out into the main corridor.

But she couldn't shut out his voice entirely.

We will meet again, my lady, you and I.

Chapter ❖❖❖ Five

Presume not that I am the thing I was . . .
William Shakespeare, *Henry IV*, Part II, Act V, Scene 4

Dion landed his spaceplane on *Defiant* without incident, helpfully guided by the destroyer's flight controllers.

"Remember," he told the computer, once they were aboard and the docking bay doors were shutting behind him, "make certain that fuel light is malfunctioning."

"I'm not programmed—"

"Think again. You made certain that the transmitter was malfunctioning for the Warlord, didn't you?"

The computer did not respond, but Dion noted that a red light appeared over the fuel gauge.

The young man was met by a harassed junior officer. Obviously annoyed at being forced to cope with a childish prank during a crisis, the officer was at the same time painfully aware that this child was in the Warlord's favor.

Apparently, thought Dion, the man hadn't received updated information.

"Come along, young man, don't dawdle." The officer was brusque. Catching hold of the sleeve of Dion's flight suit, he propelled the boy down a corridor. "I have informed Lord Sagan of your safe arrival. I was afraid he might have been concerned."

"I'm sure he was." Dion kept a straight face. "Did you speak directly to him?"

"Of course not," the officer snapped, shoving his way through a crowd of men who had just been evacuated from *Phoenix*. "I don't have the authorization. You've been assigned temporary quarters. They're in the brig, I'm afraid—"

"The brig!" Dion jerked his arm away from the man's grasp. "Did Lord Sagan order—"

"Sorry," the officer said, casting a sidelong glance at the young man, "but that's all the space we have available." He laid firm claim to Dion's arm. "First I'm to escort you to the— Now what the devil's the matter?"

"I feel . . . faint. . . ."

Dion's eyes rolled back in his head; his knees buckled. Tall and muscular, the seventeen-year-old was bigger than the officer, whose own knees began to give beneath the young man's weight. The officer hung on grimly, propping Dion up, shouting for help. Two marines came to his assistance. Between them, they dragged the stumbling young man out of the crowded passageway into what appeared to be a large storage closet and deposited him on a pile of rags. Dion closed his eyes, leaned his head against a mop.

"Medic!" The officer was shouting into his commlink.

"You won't get one, sir," said one of the marines. "They're all at the fighting."

"I don't need a doctor," Dion managed to gasp. "I . . . get these spells sometimes. I need rest, that's all."

The officer regarded him dubiously. "Can you walk?"

"No. It wouldn't be good for me. I'm . . . I'm afraid I'd . . . pass out." Dion's head lolled back against the mop handle. "Just let me lie here a moment."

"Look, you need us, sir?" The marine appeared edgy. "Our unit's been ordered to D deck."

The officer scowled, tugged at a scraggly mustache. "No, go on," he said finally, with ill grace.

The marines left, boots pounding on the deck, their equipment rattling.

"I've got my own duties to attend to." The officer glared at Dion accusingly. "I can't stay here and baby-sit you."

"There's no need, sir. I'll be all right. I need rest . . . if I could just rest . . ."

The officer examined the young man. Dion didn't have to put on much of an act. He didn't feel that good and he knew he must look terrible. The Corasians' torture, the shock of discovering Sagan had betrayed his friends, of discovering Sagan had betrayed him—all must have left marks on his face. They had on his soul.

"I'll send someone to fetch you," the officer said in a somewhat gentler tone, turning on his heel. "Stay right here.

Don't go anywhere. There's fighting on this ship. You don't
want to blunder into it."

"No, sir. Thank you, sir."

The officer disappeared. Dion jumped to his feet, cat-
padding to the door of the closet, looked out. He waited until
he saw the man vanish down a corridor, then headed in the
opposite direction. Rounding a corner, he caught sight of the
two marines who'd helped him. He plunged into the crowd,
and followed them.

Defiant was in a state of chaos. Evac ships, arriving from the
crippled *Phoenix*, disgorged loads of men. *Phoenix*'s marines
were sent immediately to reinforce the embattled troops
fighting the mercenaries, but the warship's pilots, clerks,
cooks, and everyone else were left stranded, not knowing what
to do or where to go. Officers roamed about trying to find
someone who knew something about anything. In the confusion, no one gave Dion a second glance.

The young man let the crowd carry him along. He lost sight
of the first two marines, but others were heading in the same
general direction and he figured he was going the right way.
Eventually he found a landmark—a mess hall—and placed it
on the mental blueprint of *Defiant* he was carrying in his head.
Yes, he was close . . . very close.

The crowd came to a sudden halt, everyone bunching up
together, peering over each other's heads, yelling and shouting, demanding to know what was going on. Those standing
near Dion began to look at him oddly, and he realized that he
was a fish out of water—a pilot in the midst of marines.

"There's real fighting going on up ahead, fly-boy," said one.
"You better spread your wings and flap out of here."

Others joined in, giving him additional advice on what he
could do and where he could do it. A sergeant's head was
swiveling his direction.

"Isn't th-this the way to the ready room?" Dion stammered,
backing up, bumping into men who shoved him good-
naturedly and gave him advice on where to find the ready
room—none of the locations suggested likely to be on this
plane of existence. Dion extricated himself from the mass and
tumbled down a corridor that merged with the one in which
he'd been standing. This passage was empty, probably because
it led nowhere directly. An elevator stood at the end.

Dion headed for that, not knowing what else to do, his
cheeks and ears burning from the various comments shouted

after him. It took forever for the elevator to arrive. When it did, he ducked into it hurriedly and let the doors shut on him, sighing in relief. Here, at least, it was quiet. He could think.

"What level?" the elevator inquired.

Dion ignored it, tried to think what to do now. After all, he hadn't really expected to just walk into a raging fight. He might have known, if he'd thought about it, that the battle zone would be cordoned off.

The elevator adopted a more insistent tone.

"What level?"

Dion called up the blueprint in his mind. Yes, that was a possibility. "One," he answered, and the elevator descended with a speed that left his stomach up on fourteen.

Arriving at the bottom, in the very bowels of the ship, Dion emerged from the elevator into an uncomfortably warm, steamy atmosphere, and was startled to realize he had landed in the laundry.

The pungent smell of chemical solvents made his nose twitch; he sneezed violently. Men bustled about their business—washing, drying, folding, pressing. It wasn't as trivial an operation as it looked to a shocked Dion. Clean, sterile sheets were needed for sick bay; the doctors and male nurses needed clean surgical gowns.

All Dion could think was that on the decks above, men saw their own life's blood soak their clothes.

"And will the wine stain come out of the captain's dress shirt?" he muttered to himself.

He glanced around, getting his bearings. He'd mistaken the corridor he'd been in, had taken the wrong elevator. Making the necessary corrections, he continued on his way, ignoring the looks of blank astonishment that met him. Apparently, the godlike pilots of the Galactic Democratic Republic Space Corps never descended into the laundry. No one spoke to him or detained him, however. These men had their own problems, their own responsibilities. An obviously lost, possibly deranged cadet wasn't one of them.

Dion found himself in a tangle of corridors—narrow, cramped, dark, and foul-smelling. Innumerable pipes wheezed and rattled; coils of electrical wiring dropped down from the overhead like snakes. He kept going, following the plan in his mind, and came eventually to his destination—a freight elevator.

His one fear: that the elevator'd been shut down in the emergency. His one hope: that in the confusion no one would have remembered it. Other freight elevators would be in use, hauling up heavy equipment used in the fighting. But not this one. Not one that led directly to Delta deck, not unless the mercenaries themselves decided to put it into operation.

He hit the elevator control, saw it light, and heard, with relief, a jolt and the hiss of hydraulics. The heavy-duty lift moved slowly, ponderously. Dion glanced up and down the corridor, fearful of being discovered. He hit the control again, knowing that it wouldn't hurry the elevator and that hitting it would do nothing but relieve his own frustrations. But if it didn't get here soon, if he thought too much about what he was doing, he might just turn and walk away. Finally the elevator hit bottom, doors opening with a screech Dion was certain Captain Williams must have heard on the bridge.

He jumped inside. "Delta deck, level one . . . no, two. Level two," he corrected.

Nothing happened. ·

"Delta deck, level two!" Dion repeated loudly.

The elevator remained unmoving. The boy swore, thinking it had malfunctioned, until he saw the control box near the double doors. It operated manually. Surging forward, he jammed his hand on the button, nearly lost his footing as the elevator lurched upward. Centimeter by centimeter it crept. Dion's heartbeat increased proportionate to the levels they passed. He had only the vaguest idea of what he would face when it stopped and the doors opened, and he realized then, rather late, that his only weapon was the bloodsword. Not a very effective weapon in a firefight, even if he had been properly trained in its use.

The elevator began to slow, not anywhere near the correct level. Dion panicked.

"They'll find me and this time I won't be able to fake a fit. That officer must have discovered my absence by now. The entire ship will be on alert, looking for me!" The young man pressed back against the wall, hidden in the shadows, the bloodsword in his hand. But the elevator continued moving. When it did come to a stop, the digital numbers read D.2. Dion sighed in relief.

The doors slid open. He remained where he was, flat against the wall, watching, waiting. He knew from the blueprint where he should be, knew what he should see before him—he should be directly above Delta deck. A maze of platforms, connecting catwalks, winches, and hoists, this area was used by maintenance personnel and engineers. Dion considered it unlikely that anyone on either side would think of posting a guard at the entrance to a freight elevator, but he waited warily to make sure.

He couldn't see anyone, but that wasn't saying much. He couldn't see anything very well. Smoke, rising from the deck below, burned his eyes, making them water. The noise level was appalling—explosions, rocket bursts, screams. . . .

Dion darted out of the elevator, heard the doors grind shut behind him. He was standing on a platform made of solid steel that extended out several meters in front of him, ending in a railing. A crisscrossing network of catwalks branched out from the platform, hurtling into a smoke-filled darkness lit by occasional flaring bursts. He could barely see the hulking shapes of the gigantic machinery used to raise and lower the spaceplanes into position.

Back on *Phoenix,* Dion had watched the service crews walk the narrow catwalks, and marveled at their agility, envied their jaunty confidence as they performed feats of acrobatic skill thirty meters or more above his head. Just looking at them gave him a sinking feeling in the pit of his stomach. He never imagined he'd be joining them.

The young man removed the bloodsword from his hand, winced slightly as the needles pulled out of his flesh, leaving spots of blood behind. He wiped his palm on his flight suit and edged his way forward, peering hesitantly over the railing. He needn't have worried about the drop making him giddy or someone down below spotting him. He couldn't see a thing except smoke and flame.

Pain shot up his arm. Dion looked at his hand, saw it clenched around the metal railing, the fingers white with the strain. He wondered if he was going to have to pry himself loose. He thought of Tusk, somewhere down there.

"Anything's better than being stuck up here alone!" Dion told himself. He released his hold on the railing and crept onto the catwalk, crawling forward on his hands and knees.

He'd been pounding himself on the back over his ingenuity in finding this means of sneaking into the battle zone. But now, with smoke choking him, groping blindly along a catwalk that was maybe a meter wide, with nothing beneath him but a long fall to an extremely hard deck, he wondered if he'd been so smart. His eyes were streaming, the smoke burned his lungs.

He coughed, blinked back tears, and almost fell from his perch. This wasn't working.

"Before long, I'm going to get too light-headed to continue. I have to get off of here."

Unable to see where he was going, he bumped headlong into a support beam and clutched at it thankfully. His hands closed over what felt like ladder rungs, leading up and down. He swung himself down. His feet came into fumbling contact with the ladder, and he began his slow descent.

Halfway there, it occurred to him that he was an ideal target. All it would take was one marine to look in his direction—

"No," he said suddenly, glancing at his outfit. "One of the mercenaries. Fuck it! I'm dressed in a goddam regulation Space Corps flight suit, complete with insignia. Chances are I'm going to be shot by my own friends! I could take it off," he added with a surge of hope that immediately died. He was wearing regulation body armor underneath.

Cursing himself for not having thought of this sooner, Dion slipped, lost his footing, and slid the rest of the way down the ladder. He landed heavily on the deck below.

Jolted by his fall, he huddled near the protective beam, peered through the smoke-filled shadows, and tried to figure out where he was and in what direction to move. No direction appeared particularly pleasant or healthful. The zip/flash of lasguns sizzled past, crisscrossing all around him. He couldn't tell who was firing at whom.

"It'd be just great if I went through all this and ended up walking right smack into Sagan's forces!"

But if he stayed here much longer, he'd put down roots. A dark, hulking shape loomed near him. Leaving the safety of the beam, Dion dove for it, recognizing it at the last moment as a fighter plane. A beam rifle opened fire. Sparks showered down around him, ricocheting off the wings. He slid beneath the plane's belly, lay flat on his own. He recognized the plane—it belonged to one of the mercenaries, an old rejuvenated RV. He recalled Williams's report. *The mercenaries have barricaded themselves with their spaceplanes* . . .

"This should mean I'm on Tusk's side of the battlefield."

Dion squirmed around, hoping to catch a glimpse of someone—anyone—through the smoke and flame. A lascannon opened fire behind him. Twisting, keeping his head down, he looked back, thought he recognized a scaly greenish gray hide.

"Jarun!" he shouted, and immediately went into a fit of coughing, the smoke filling his lungs.

The firing ceased.

"Did you hear something?" The voice sounded oddly mechanical, and it took Dion a moment to realize it was coming from a translator device.

"Yeah, I thought so." The other voice was human. "Who the hell'd be out there?"

"Jarun!" Dion yelled desperately.

"We hear ya! And you got just three seconds to convince us why we shouldn't fry your hide!"

"It's Dion! I'm looking for Tusk!"

A long green-gray tentacle snaked out, wrapped itself around Dion's boot, and pulled the young man across the deck. A human hand grabbed hold of his collar, dragged him behind a hastily built barricade consisting of several large metal barrels.

Lying on his back, breathless, Dion stared into the four eyes of the Jarun, the two eyes of a human, and the single barrel of a beam rifle.

"It *is* the kid," the Jarun said through his translator, his actual voice sounding like numerous screeching cats fighting inside a well.

"What kid?" the human demanded, holding the weapon aimed at Dion's head.

"Friend of Tusk's. He's okay."

"Yeah? What the hell's he doin' dressed up like one of the Warlord's pet monkeys?"

"It's a long story, Reefer, put down the gun. Hey, kid. Next time, don't crawl under the belly of a plane for cover. One laser hit in the fuel tank and—" The alien made a sound that approximated the screeching cats hitting bottom.

Dion glanced back, gulped, and nodded. "Where's Tusk?"

"Hell, kid"—Reefer aimed the gun back in what Dion supposed was the general direction of the enemy—"I don't even know where I am. You know, Xrmt?"

"No." The Jarun fired a searing beam into smoke-filled darkness.

"How about General Dixter?"

"Dead," Reefer said shortly.

"Dead!" Dion gasped, feeling as though someone had punched him hard in the stomach.

"Cut in two by a beam rifle."

"Naw, that was Colonel Mudahby," the Jarun protested.

"Heard it was Dixter," Reefer argued. A laser bolt slammed into a metal beam overhead, showering sparks all around them. Dion scrunched down as flat as possible on the deck, resenting the very pockets on his flight suit that wouldn't let him flatten down farther.

"Dixter got blown apart by a grenade."

The Jarun fired. Reefer fired.

Dion started breathing again. These two had no idea what was going on! Again he remembered what he'd overheard about the battle from Captain Williams's conversation with Admiral Aks. If Dixter was anywhere, he'd probably be on Charlie deck.

"Any idea how to reach the others?" Dion shouted over the firing.

"What others?"

"Our people fighting on Charlie deck!"

"What deck we on?"

"Delta," Dion began, then realized his questions were futile. Closing his eyes, he tried to envision the situation. The alien must have landed his RV facing the front of the hangar. That was standard procedure. Which meant Charlie deck had to be somewhere to his left.

"Thanks," he said, and crawled off under the protective cover of the Jarun's fire.

Moving to his left, he saw that he had guessed correctly. The huge hangar bay doors towered over him, sealed shut, trapping those inside. The smoke was thinner back here, the firing was not as concentrated, and Dion risked standing upright. Rubbing his bruised knees, he reacclimated himself and started forward.

A whistling sound sent him diving beneath the wreckage of something—he couldn't tell what in the smoke. A hand caught hold of him around the neck, flipped him over onto his back.

"Damn! It's a Galactic pilot! Say your prayers, ass-licker!"

The blade of a combat knife gleamed above him. Dion shouted, struggled wildly. A black arm shot out and stopped the knife's descent.

"Link, you bloodthirsty S.O.B.! It's Dion!"

"Tusk!" Dion could have burst into tears. He grabbed hold of the mercenary thankfully.

"I'll be damned!" Link tossed the knife in the air, caught it expertly, and tucked it back in his boot. "Sorry, kid. Thought I had a live one."

"Can't say I'm glad to see you here, kid." Tusk gripped Dion's arm tightly, smiled grimly. "But I'm glad to see you're alive."

Dion couldn't answer; smoke, leftover terror, and shock robbed him of his voice. He stared at his friends, stunned by what he saw. Tusk's face was drawn and haggard; he seemed to have aged a decade. The ebony skin glistened with sweat, his eyes were red-rimmed. Blood streaked his face, his lips were cracked and blistered. Link, crouched nearby, managed a grin, but it looked ghastly through a mask of blood and soot. The horrible reality of their desperate situation hit Dion in the pit of his stomach.

"Where's Nola?" the young man managed to ask, clearing his throat. "She flew with you, didn't she?"

"Best damn gunner I ever had." Tusk jerked a thumb behind him. Dion peered over his shoulder to see a woman huddled on a pile of flight jackets, her head swathed in bloody bandages.

"She'll be all right," Link said, noting Dion's sudden pallor.

"Yeah," Tusk grunted. "Nice quiet prison cell. Do wonders for her."

The two mercenaries exchanged glances. The boy wasn't fooled. He knew there'd be no prison cell. He'd heard Sagan's orders. The mercenaries were to be executed. He knew then that Tusk and Link knew it, too.

"Where's Dixter?" Dion shouted.

A lasgun beam slanted through the darkness.

Tusk and Link raised up, fired in the beam's direction. A brief but furious exchange ensued, then ceased. Link rolled over on his back, wriggled into a more comfortable position.

"Hell, kid, Dixter's d— Ouch! Damn it, Tusk. What'd you kick me for?"

"Dixter's on Charlie deck," Tusk said, not looking at Dion.

Tusk's heard the general's dead, Dion realized.

Link was carefully inspecting his gun. Smoke drifted overhead. Lethal beams streaked through the darkness. An explosion, then someone screamed—a high, piercing note that was suddenly cut off. Behind him, Dion heard Nola moan. The woman stirred fitfully. Tusk crawled back to her, gently pulled his flight jacket up over her shoulders. Dion followed him.

"Who's in charge around here?" he demanded.

"No one, kid. Each of us is on his own, just tryin' to stay alive. I don't even know how many of us are left."

"Listen, Tusk, I heard Captain Williams talking to Admiral Aks. This battle isn't going well for the Warlord's forces. And I've been thinking. They don't dare use any heavy artillery—mortars and rockets—inside the ship. They can't cram too many men into this confined space or they'll start shooting each other. You're not outgunned and you can't be that far outnumbered. If you made a concentrated push right now, tried to go for the hangar bay controls—"

Tusk snorted in derision. "Thanks for droppin' by, kid. You better get back to your friends, now. Tell the Warlord I said he can take a flying leap—" Where Tusk recommended the Warlord could leap was lost in a blast from Link's lasgun.

"Tusk, I—" Dion began desperately.

"Look, kid!" Tusk grabbed him by the collar of his flight suit. "It's hopeless. Dixter's dead. We're all going to die. I don't know what you're doin' here, but you got a Galactic uniform on. *You* can get out. You better do it!"

Dion shook himself free of Tusk's hold. "I'm going to find Dixter. Okay if I borrow this?" He took Nola's lasgun, started off through the smoke.

"Dion! Damn it, kid—"

He heard Tusk shout, but Dion didn't turn around. He'd spotted what looked to be a way out.

··◄■ ■►··

Dion opened a door, peered into a narrow corridor. According to the blueprint, this corridor connected Delta deck with Charlie. The young man advanced cautiously, weapon drawn, expecting a raging battle.

The corridor was strangely, eerily quiet. No smoke, no signs of life or death. A door at the end was labeled with a large C. Dion dashed toward it, his heart in his throat. He hit the controls with his hand so hard he bruised his palm.

The door slid open. He darted inside, prepared to take immediate cover, and blundered into a desk. The room was brightly lit; he couldn't see anything after coming in from the darkness of the corridor. He shoved the desk out of his way, but another step brought him up against another desk. Blinking, he saw the place was filled with them! Rolled-up star charts and a coffee maker humming to itself in a corner gave him an idea where he was—a pilot's ready room.

Shoving desks aside, he headed for a steelglass viewport that must face out onto Charlie deck. Dion pressed his nose against the steelglass, expecting to see the same chaos he'd left on Delta: smoke, laser bursts, tracer fire. He recognized the mercenaries' spaceplanes, but the only signs of combat were trailing wisps of smoke being sucked into *Defiant*'s ventilation system.

"Charlie deck!" he muttered. "It has to be! But what's happened?"

The fighting's ended! Which means—

Dion's knees felt weak. He sat down suddenly at a desk, stared out onto the deck, searching for people, seeing no one. That's it, then. They're all dead.

"What should I do?" he asked himself bleakly, feeling empty, drained. "Go back to Tusk. I can at least help him and Nola and Link escape, take them off in my spaceplane. Hell. That wouldn't work. They'd never leave. But *I* could. I could escape. Get out while I can, like Tusk said. No one would ever know. . . .

"Yes . . . he would," Dion said softly. "Sagan would know. He *always* knows! And, once again, he'd know that I ran. He'd figure I was scared."

Dion rose to his feet. "Let him find my body with the bodies of my friends. I'll—"

Out of the corner of his eye, he saw the man, saw the gun. . . .

Pain . . . and then nothing.

Chapter ·→⊷◦⊶→· Six

Have you built your ship of death, O have you?
  "The Ship of Death," D. H. Lawrence

Disguised as a pilot—a wounded pilot, her "borrowed" flight suit covered with blood—Maigrey hoped, in the confusion, to make her way onto one of the evac ships. She arrived on one of *Phoenix's* flight decks and hovered in the background, keeping to the shadows, watching, appraising the situation. Time was running out, maybe another fifteen minutes left in the safety window. But this, she discovered, had not been one of her better ideas.

First, there was no confusion. No panic. Each man, apparently, had his own assigned place on his own assigned ship. The men—those who were left, and there weren't many—were proceeding on board the evac ships in the well-drilled orderly fashion she might have expected of Sagan's crew. Second, disguised as a pilot, she had no idea what her assigned station was. Gnawing on her lip, swearing beneath her breath, she watched for several minutes, hoping to see some breakdown in discipline, wondering if she couldn't bluff her way on board by claiming she had been knocked out, missed her own evac ship.

No, that would draw attention to her. Sagan had undoubtedly alerted the guards to her disappearance. They'd be watching for her.

"The hospital ship," Maigrey muttered. She recalled Sagan saying something about using his own shuttle to transport wounded. The wounded wouldn't have any assigned stations! She glanced down at the bloody hole in the front of her flight suit and headed immediately, at a run, for the hangar where Sagan's shuttle was kept.

Arriving there, she remembered just in time that she was

supposed to be injured and stopped outside the entrance
to the hangar to get into her role. Of course, once she got onto
the shuttle, there'd be the problem of the medics wanting to
examine her.

"One worry at a time." Maigrey was just about to press her
hand over the bloodstained rip and stagger forward when the
door shot open.

In front of her stood Sagan's own personal sleek white
spaceplane. The plane he would use to leave the ship.

Maigrey recoiled back into the shadows. This is the last
place I need to be! she thought wildly. The Warlord could
arrive at any moment. But how the hell else can I get off?

A heavy hand grasped her by the shoulder.

Maigrey's breath stopped. It's not Sagan! her mind reassured her. She would have sensed his presence. But it took her
heart a moment to catch up with her brain's logic. She stared
through her helmet at the hand, its fingers scraping roughly
against her neck.

The hand was large, clean, too clean for a man on board a
fighting ship.

"Rogers!" came a voice from the general proximity of the
hand.

Maigrey turned to face the man, jerking free of the hand's
grip in the same movement. The hand's owner was like his
appendage—large and too neat, too clean. His uniform had a
small smudge of soot on one sleeve; otherwise it was spotless,
not even wrinkled. Whatever hole he'd found to hide in must
be a good one.

"Major," she said, remembering in time that—according to
the insignia on the uniform—she was a captain, and saluting.
The helmet's face shield, though clear, would distort her
features; the dirt and blood she'd smeared on her skin would
help make recognition difficult, especially in the semi-
darkness.

But the man's eyes narrowed, he leaned forward, stared at
her closely. "You're not Rogers!"

"So, what if I'm not?" she returned, facing him down. "You
don't really give a damn who I am, do you?"

The major grinned, glanced significantly at the blood on the
front of her flight suit. "Maybe I don't. Are you even a pilot?"

She could either kill him or go along with him. One jab to
the throat, it would be all over, and Maigrey had the distinct
impression that no one would miss this bastard. She was

wondering what his scheme was when she saw another person move out of the shadows. A young man, clad in a flight suit. Suddenly, Maigrey knew what was going on.

"Yes, I'm a pilot." Fortunately her voice was low for a woman's and further distorted through the helmet mike. "And I need to get off this ship."

The major grinned unpleasantly. "Yeah, I thought so. It'll cost you."

"I left my wallet in my other pants."

"Then you and your other pants can stay here and fry. I ain't runnin' a charity. Hey, what's this?"

He reached inside her flightsuit, caught hold of the starjewel, glittering brightly on its chain. The major's eyes widened. "What the hell is it? A diamond? I never saw one that big!"

Grinning at her, he grasped hold of the jewel's silver chain and twisted. The catch gave, the chain slid from around her neck, the starjewel gleamed in his hand. "You just bought your way off this bomb."

Maigrey said nothing, made no protest. She couldn't, her breath was gone—not through concern over the jewel's loss. She wasn't worried about it. A starjewel, taken by force, has a way of returning to its owner. It was her plan, now suddenly complete, flawless, perfect and brilliant as the jewel itself, that stole away her breath.

You just bought your way . . . bomb.

The major tossed the starjewel in the air, closed his fist over it, and stuffed it in his shirt pocket. "Let's get a move on, then. Follow me."

The ship was quiet, except for the muffled sound of an occasional explosion. Time was ticking by. The officer hastened onto the hangar deck, Maigrey and the young pilot running after him. They were headed for Sagan's private plane, and Maigrey feared she'd made a mistake. The officer never glanced at it, passed it right by. He strode rapidly to the far end of the hangar bay. Here stood several Scimitars—several wrecked Scimitars.

"I was right," she murmured. "You bastard!"

The major gestured. "Here's your ticket to freedom."

"You expect us to fly out in those?" Maigrey demanded.

"I don't expect nothing. *I'm* not wearing a dead man's flight suit. What are you? An escaped prisoner, figured you'd sneak away in the confusion? Or maybe a deserter? All you got to worry about is the kid here"—the major jerked a thumb at the young pilot—"but I don't think he'll turn you in. He's too anxious to get off himself."

Maigrey glanced at the young pilot, saw his face flush, then harden. He was only a trainee pilot; the Scimitar pin on his uniform was silver, not gold. She wondered what he'd been busted for; something pretty serious, to make him this desperate.

The major leaned near, clamped his heavy hand over Maigrey's shoulder. The man would probably never know just how close he came to having it snapped off at the wrist. "You fly that plane out." He pointed at one of the wrecks. "The kid'll take the other one."

"You're crazy! An experienced pilot couldn't fly that plane! You can't expect this . . . this cadet to—" Maigrey turned to the young pilot. "How many hours have you logged?"

"Enough." The young man's tone was defensive.

A calm voice over the loudspeakers announced that the last of the evac ships were leaving.

"You better hurry," Maigrey said to the major, "or you'll miss your flight. And take the kid here with you."

The major shrugged. "The prison evac already left. If the kid wants off this bomb, he can either fly that Scimitar or walk. Same with you."

He took off at a dead run. Maigrey was half-inclined to stop him, not certain what she'd do to him, but plenty certain she'd enjoy doing it.

"It's all right, Starlady!" the young pilot said. "Really. I'll fly the plane."

Startled at his recognition, trying not to show it, Maigrey glanced at him, shook her head. "Were you talking to me? I'm afraid you have the wrong—?"

"Oh, I know who you are." The young pilot smiled grimly. "The Warlord's Starlady. I saw you fight Lord Sagan. The major will figure out who you are, too, eventually. And when he does, he'll kick himself. He could have made a lot more money off you than he will off that jewel."

"Yeah." Maigrey was examining both spaceplanes, only half-listening. "Look, kid. We don't have much time. This first plane's not in too bad shape. I think I can get it as far as *Defiant*, at least. Come with me—" Reaching out, she laid her hand on his arm.

He moved away from her touch, shaking his head. "No! I need this flight. I'll prove I can handle myself this time! I'm off the jump-juice. And maybe this'll make up for—" The young pilot checked what he had been about to say. Turning, he headed for the Scimitar.

I could club him, knock him out, drag him aboard my plane, Maigrey thought. How many other young hotheads has that bastard major "helped" to escape or desert? How many have died? She could hear, some distance away, an evac ship warming its engines, preparing for takeoff. She and this kid were probably among the last few remaining on *Phoenix*. Her gaze went to Sagan's plane, which was ready, waiting.

After all, I've got my own problems, she reminded herself. I have responsibilities and—

"Oh, hell!" Maigrey ran after the pilot, caught him as he was scrambling up the ladder of the charred and battered plane.

"Don't try it!" She shouted to be heard over the roar of the engines, the gong warning everyone to clear the area, the shivering rattle of the hangar bay doors, preparing to open. "Come with me!"

The young man either didn't hear or he was pretending he didn't. He waved his hand to her jauntily, climbed down into the cockpit.

Well, I did what I could, Maigrey told herself gloomily. Maybe he has a chance.

Lowering herself into the cockpit of her own plane, she began to swear out loud. The outside hadn't looked bad. Inside was a mess. The pilot's chair was soaked with blood. The charred and blackened control panel gave Maigrey an idea how the blood got there. She wondered what instruments the on-board explosion had knocked out, hoped it was nothing absolutely essential. At least the fact that the pilot had been able to make it back with his crippled plane was a good sign.

The engines fired, and though Maigrey had no instruments to tell her if they were functioning properly, they *sounded* okay. The hangar bay doors were sliding open. No one was manning the controls, but the doors would open automatically when engines were fired. Her computer programming was malfunctioning, she discovered, and the starboard shields were jammed, wouldn't operate.

"Wrecker One, this is Wrecker Two. Can you copy? Over."

"This is nothing to joke about!" Maigrey snapped. Fool kid. He better start taking this seriously.

"Sorry, sir." He chuckled. "I mean, lady."

"You fly on out ahead of me." Maigrey tried to soften her

tone. What he needed to hear was confidence, not the echo of her own worries and fears. "And stay close in case you—in case either of us gets into trouble."

"You can count on me, lady."

The young man's spaceplane swooped out. Maigrey watched it climb, saw it begin to turn a lazy backward roll—

God, no!

"Level off!" She fought to keep her voice calm, to keep from screaming at him.

The plane continued to roll over, performing a slow, graceful, deadly loop.

"I can't!" The young pilot's voice cracked in terror. "The controls won't respond!"

"You have to override the—"

"I'm going to cras—"

The Scimitar smashed into *Phoenix*'s hull, exploded. To die in a ball of fire.

Maigrey pressed her lips tightly together. She had to keep her attention focused on her own flying. It would take all her skill and nerve to make it as far as *Defiant*. Leaving *Phoenix*, she didn't look behind her, kept her gaze purposefully averted from the charred and smoking blotch on the hull.

Veering away from the Corasian ship, she tried to get a fix on *Defiant*. The destroyer was out of visual range; Sagan must have warned it off. But Maigrey located it on her scanner and, after some difficulty with the computer, managed to set her course.

Now all she had to do was hang on and fly.

"Creator," she whispered, shivering in the cold that was creeping through the hole in her flight suit, "give me the major who sent that kid to die. That's all I ask. Give him to me."

Chapter ⊸•◦•⊷ Seven

We took him for a coward, but he's the very devil incarnate.
William Shakespeare,
Two Gentlemen of Verona, Act V, Scene 1

"He's coming around, sir."

"How is he?" John Dixter crouched down on his haunches, his hand ruffled Dion's mane of red-gold hair. The general moved aside, allowing room for Bennett, his aide, carrying a medical kit. Bennett's deft hands examined the young man, felt the lump behind Dion's left ear.

Dion groaned, blinked, and tried to sit up. Dixter gently but firmly pushed him back down.

"Well, young man, you very nearly gave your life for the Galactic Democratic Republic. If Bennett hadn't recognized you, Gobar would have broken your neck."

"General Dixter!" Dion stared at the man. "They told me you were dead!"

"Not yet," Dixter said dryly. "How are you feeling?"

"Like my head's going to split open!"

"You're lucky, son. You made an excellent target, wandering around that well-lighted room in full view of God and everyone."

"Just a bump, sir," Bennett said.

"No concussion?" Dixter asked in low tones.

"I don't believe so, sir. The skin isn't broken." Bennett dumped two pills in Dion's hand. "Take these."

"What's this?"

"Aspirin."

"Sorry, son," Dixter said, seeing that the boy looked disappointed. "But it's the only painkiller we've got. We ran out of anything stronger." He glanced at several blanket-covered forms lying on the deck nearby.

59

The young man followed his gaze, flushed, accepted the pills, and swallowed them. He sat up, trying to act as if nothing was the matter with him.

"Have you won, sir?" Dion asked, looking around the hangar bay. Everything was quiet, the mercenaries standing or sitting around in small groups, talking together in low tones.

"No, no. Far from it. The proverbial lull before the storm, I'm afraid." Dixter smiled tiredly, rubbed his stubbled jaw. "We managed to push the marines back, sealed off all the entrances by jamming the controls. But they'll be bringing in the heavy stuff soon, probably brain-gas—"

"And you're just sitting around, waiting for them?" Dion struggled to his feet.

"Not much else we can do, son," the general replied coolly. "Actually, however, our computer experts are working on overriding the locking systems on the hangar bay controls. The pilots have their planes ready to go. All we have to do is buy them a little more time. Now, tell me. How in the name of the Creator did you get here?"

"I . . . came from Delta deck. Over there." Dion waved a hand vaguely.

"I meant how'd you get away from the Corasians? Last I heard, Tusk said you'd been captured."

Dixter watched the young man's face intently, saw him grow pale. Dion was obviously debating whether to answer or not, perhaps decided that some explanation was due. "I was captured. It . . . it was pretty bad. Sagan and the Lady Maigrey came after me, rescued me. Then, I heard that Sagan had double-crossed you, that he'd gone back on his word and ordered you and Tusk and everyone captured. Maigrey sent me to warn you. I stole a plane and . . . here I am. Guess I'm late, huh?" He stole a glance at Dixter, apparently hoping the general wouldn't ask any more questions.

Fortunately, Dixter had something else on his mind. "Maigrey sent you? Where is she?"

Dion put a hand gingerly to the lump behind his ear, winced in pain. "I left her on *Phoenix*, sir. I asked her to come with me." The young man frowned. "But she said she had to stay . . . *with him.*"

The general heard the young man's bitter emphasis, understood the implication. "She stayed behind to protect you? To keep . . . um . . . *him* from following you?"

"So she said. It's just that—I saw the two of them together and . . . and, well, never mind."

Dixter watched the expressive face, knew—by experience—what the young man must be feeling. The general wished he could help Dion, but he had his own pain to deal with.

Funny, Dixter thought, I thought I'd come to terms with the pain years ago. I wish I could see her again, one last time. There are a lot of things I'd like to say. . . . But maybe it's better this way. She was always superstitious about good-byes.

Dixter reached out, took Dion's hand, shook it. "It's good to see you again, son, know you're alive. If you could take back a message to her from me—"

"What do you mean, sir? 'Take back a message.'" Dion ceased wrestling with his private hell, understood that he had entered another's. He looked up in alarm. "You can send it yourself. You said the planes were ready to go—"

"Not nearly enough, son," Dixter let the boy down gently. "We can't get everyone off. We managed to knock out the tractor beams, so once my people escape, they'll be in the clear. But someone has to stay behind, fight the rearguard action, keep the bay doors open. We—"

A violent explosion rocked the hangar deck. Men and women leapt to their feet, grabbing weapons, taking up positions. Dixter looked ahead toward the front of the hangar bay. Dion stared hard, but it was impossible to see around the numerous spaceplanes, some of them wrecked, others obviously ready and waiting to go.

"Bennett, the field radio."

Dixter's aide was there, equipment on hand.

Dixter spoke into the small, compact unit. "Moore, what's going on?"

"They've blown the main hatch, sir. We're all set for 'em up here. Lilly says give her fifteen minutes more and she'll have those bay doors wide open."

"Right. Good luck. Out." Calmly ignoring a series of small explosions and an answering burst of lascannon fire, the general turned to Dion. "What's it like on Delta? We lost contact with them a long time ago."

"Chaos, sir. No one's in command. Small groups, scattered around. They think you're dead. They've lost all hope. . . ."

"Hope." Dixter shook his head. The brown eyes, in their maze of wrinkles, looked suddenly faded, weary.

"'Only the dead are without hope, sir,'" Dion said.

Dixter smiled, remembered where he'd heard that saying before. "Yes, but as Maigrey would add, they have other benefits. Well, young man, what do you propose to do? I see you've got something in mind."

Dion flushed. "I'd like to go back there, sir. Take command."

"Take command . . ." Dixter was looking at Dion but the general was, in reality, seeing Dion's uncle, seeing a king who had never, a day in his life, truly taken command. Same blood, but in the old king it had moved sluggishly. In this boy it burned.

"I've got an idea, sir. I think it has a chance of succeeding and I really don't have time to explain it. I'll need a field-phone." Dion leaned down, picked one up.

"Here, now, young man!" A shocked Bennett reached out to snatch his equipment back.

Dixter laid a quieting hand on his aide's arm, turned away, motioned Bennett to attend.

"Let him have it," the general said softly.

His aide stared at him in disbelief. "You can't be serious, sir! He's . . . a child!"

"Alexander the Great was fifteen when he fought his first war. Take a good look at him, Bennett."

The aide glanced reluctantly around. The blue eyes were hard as glare ice. The youthful face was pale, composed and frozen as a snowbank. The shining red hair of the Starfires, disheveled, running rampant, shone like a pillar of flame.

"After all," Dixter murmured, talking more to himself than to Bennett, "Dion is a prince. And if God's with that young man, then maybe He'll be with my people. And if He's not"—the general shrugged—"what do we have to lose?"

"A fieldphone," Bennett observed crisply. "And that is an extremely expensive—"

Dixter grinned, clapped his aide on the back. "Put it on my tab. Very well, young man. You can take your radio. Here you go. Need anything else?" He was unable to conceal his ironic tone.

Fortunately Dion was too pent up and excited to notice. "No, sir. Thank you."

Another explosion, this one much closer, caused them all to duck, sent a shower of sparks over the general. Bennett hastily brushed them off the uniform, lamenting over numerous burn holes. Given the rumpled, slept-in, soot-, sweat-, and bloodstained state of his uniform, Dixter couldn't tell that a few holes made much difference.

"You better get going, son. No . . . no good-byes. It's bad luck."

"Yes, sir. Thank you, sir. I—" Dion held out his hand. The general shook it gravely. "I'll see you soon, sir."

Tucking the fieldphone into a pocket of his flight suit, Dion made his way through the tangle of wreckage and bodies, returning to the pilot ready room and the corridor linking Charlie deck with Delta.

"An interesting young man," said Dixter, watching him go. "A pity I won't be around to see what happens to him."

··◁■ ■▷··

"Your computer has not given the correct code response, Scimitar. Halt and identify yourself."

Correct code response. Maigrey swore beneath her breath, something she'd been doing a lot lately, she noted. What the devil was going on? Why had they changed the damn codes? Then she remembered. Some of the mercenaries, Dion's friend Tusk among them, flew stolen Scimitars. They'd been given the codes when they were on the side of the angels, when they were fighting *for* Sagan in his fight against the Corasians. It was only logical for him to order the codes changed now that they were fighting against the Warlord. It wouldn't do to let the wolf into *Defiant*'s fold.

"Well, I am the wolf," Maigrey said to herself grimly. "And I'm landing, code or no blasted code." She pondered, deciding on her strategy. Maintain the disguise, bluff her way through . . . The hell with it. She was too damn tired. Tired and, now that she thought of it, hungry.

"Listen to me, whoever you are and whatever rank you are and," she added, voice tight and cold, "you better take a good look at that rank because you're not going to be a lieutenant or a corporal or a sergeant much longer unless you obey my command. I am Lady Maigrey Morianna and I am flying a plane that's shot to hell. Even if I did know your friggin' code, which I don't, since I've been fighting the Corasians, the only thing my computer could do with it is exactly what I'd like to do with it and what we'll both be happy to do with it if and when we get the opportunity to meet you."

She drew a deep breath, let it out, almost purred. "Now, you will give me that landing clearance, won't you?"

Maigrey sat back.

A pause, then a voice came. "You have been cleared for landing, your ladyship. Emergency equipment standing by."

"Thank you. And I want an armed detail of MPs waiting to meet me."

"Repeat that last—"

"You heard me." Maigrey switched him off. Better to keep him unbalanced, not give him time to go trotting off to some superior officer, who might remember that though she was a privileged prisoner, Maigrey was a prisoner nonetheless and it wouldn't be proper form to put an armed detail under her command. Hopefully *Defiant* would be in such a state of confusion, they'd react automatically to her authority without thinking about it. If not—or if Sagan managed to get through to them first—she might very well find the armed detail waiting to take *her* into custody.

Maigrey touched the red mark on her skin, the mark left by the starjewel's chain. She called up a mental image of the jewel. The crystal shone clear, radiant, lit from within by its own inner white-blue light. Calming, soothing, it reminded her of a Will greater, more powerful than her own.

Maigrey pressed the points of the imaginary starjewel against her cheek, closed her eyes. She could almost feel tiny pinpricks tingle through her nerves. She followed them, going deep within herself to a place that was dark and empty, a place that harbored no emotion, a place of oblivion.

When she emerged, a few moments later, she was rested, calm. She had her plan; she knew exactly what she must do.

She was only sorry she hadn't thought to have the armed detail bring along a chicken sandwich.

Dion dashed back through the pilot ready room—this time shutting off the lights, keeping low. He hesitated entering the corridor. Letting the door slide open only a crack, he listened, peered out.

Nothing. It was still silent, still empty. He drew a breath and charged down the passageway. At the entrance to Delta deck, he pressed the controls, dove headlong inside when the door slid open. Landing on his stomach, he slammed up hard against a pile of rubble. Never again would he let himself get hit from behind.

The fighting on Delta appeared, by the sound of it, to be

heavy but sporadic. Bursts of laser fire came from all directions. The smoke was so thick it was impossible to see anything, and breathing was difficult. Dion ripped a piece of fabric from the shirt of a dead mercenary lying next to him. The young man tied it around his nose and mouth. Crude, but it would keep out the worst of the fumes.

His flight suit with its Galactic Air Corps markings was a danger. Yet, hopefully, it would also prove his salvation. He couldn't abandon it, though he'd been nearly killed twice because of it. The dead had another gift to offer him. Stripping the flak jacket from the body, Dion pulled it on over his flight suit. The jacket was heavy and hot over the already bulky flight suit, but it beat getting shot by his own people.

Lying prone, he considered the situation. Being pilots, the mercenaries were armed mainly with hand weapons—small lasguns, perhaps a beam rifle here and there. The marines had lascannons, grenades. The mercenaries were fighting in detached groups, each intent on its own survival. If they could be made to unite, if they had heavy weaponry . . .

Dion twisted around, stared through the murk, ignoring the stinging smoke in his eyes. Impatiently, he blinked back tears. Had he found what he'd been seeking? The young man risked leaving his cover, crawled forward a meter or so to make certain. Yes! He clenched his fist in excitement and slithered his way back to the rubble.

Dion waited, watched until he located the position of gunfire nearest him, coming from the front of the hangar bay, a position he hoped was still being held by the mercenaries. If not, well, he had the flight suit on under the jacket. He supposed he could always say the jacket was on because he felt cold.

A lull came in the fighting. Dion leapt up, ran hunched over, keeping low until he reached three humans and an alien crouched behind a trash masher. Their weapons swiveled, turned instantly on the figure emerging from the smoke. Dion kept his hands outstretched, lasgun in plain view. The men saw his jacket, checked their reflexive action, and relaxed.

Dion joined them, somewhat at a loss. It was easy to say he was going to take command. He had never really considered how to do it. He decided the direct approach was the best and yanked the cloth away from his mouth.

"I'm Dion Starfire, and I'm taking command."

Energy bolts burst overhead, showering them with sparks.

Everyone crouched down, then jumped up to fire back furiously. When this interlude ceased, the men settled back. None of them so much as glanced at Dion.

Injured pride banished fear, anger hardened his voice. "I said I'm taking command!"

"Shit," one said to another, "this is all we need."

His buddy glanced at Dion. "The adults are busy, kid. Go play soldier somewhere else."

Blood pounded in the boy's ears—the Blood Royal, he would realize if he had thought about it. Probably the hardest battle he would ever fight was right there, fighting for control of himself.

"What we need"—Dion kept his voice calm—"is heavier equipment. Lascannons, grenades."

"Yes, sir." The alien spoke through its translator, snapping off a mocking salute with a thick, squishy arm. "I'll run right over to supply, sir!"

The humans grinned at each other. A flare burst overhead. It was only a flare, but Dion didn't know that. Involuntarily, he ducked, cringed, waiting for the explosion. The mercenaries noticed, shook their heads in disgust, and continued peering through the smoke.

"Damn!" one said, with sudden irritability. "Why the hell don't they just come on and get this over with?"

Dion straightened up. "Listen to me! The equipment we need is right out there." He pointed straight ahead. "The enemy's abandoned a position not far from here—"

"Yeah, and if you ask 'em nice, kid," one of the humans said, "maybe they'll quit shooting at us long enough for us to go out and gather it up!"

Dion glared around in frustration, saw a burst of tracer fire coming from their right. "Who's over there? Some of our people?"

One of the men shrugged, nodded without interest. Another brief, furious round of ineffectual shooting silenced all conversation. When it ended, the men hunkered down, faces tense, carefully blank.

"I'll be back," Dion told them finally, frustrated. "Wait for me here."

"Sure thing, General," the alien said. The others didn't bother to reply.

Dion jumped to his feet, ran the short distance between one group and the next. A staccato of laser fire erupted behind him, sending him crashing unceremoniously into three women, who had taken refuge behind a girder and what looked to be part of a plane's broken wing.

They stared at him in astonishment as he barreled into their position.

He'd learned his lesson. Crouching down in front of them, he gasped, "The men from over there sent me. We're making a sortie . . . out there . . . lascannon, grenades. Need . . . covering fire."

"You got it," a woman said.

"Can you see . . . signal . . . from there."

She grinned at him. "I can see that red hair of yours a kilometer off, kid. Go on back. Tell your buddies we'll make sure the marines keep their heads down."

Dion nodded, his breath gone, then turned and ran back to the trash masher. He wondered that he wasn't feeling scared—certainly not the panicked, debilitating terror he'd experienced in his spaceplane. It was probably, he told himself, because he just plain didn't care anymore.

His squad appeared highly surprised and not particularly pleased to see him again.

"If it ain't the general," the alien growled.

Dion ignored him. "Our people over there are going to give us covering fire. That is, they're going to give *me* covering fire. I'll go out alone if I have to, but I can't carry many guns back here by myself. Are you with me?"

Laser fire sizzled past him. He didn't dodge for cover. He felt reckless, exhilarated, immortal. He had meant what he said. He would go it alone if he had to.

"Hell," one of the humans said to his companions. "We're all gonna die anyway. I say we go with him."

"Now!" Dion shouted, and he was off, running flat out across the deck, jumping over wreckage and bodies.

From somewhere to his right, he heard and saw flashes of flame; the women had spotted him, were giving him the covering fire they'd promised. He was halfway to his destination when he realized he had no idea if anyone was following him. Suddenly, the very air seemed to be exploding all around him. He crashed headlong into a crude barricade.

And there, hurling themselves after him—the alien landing right on top of him—was his motley squad. His first command.

Dion pushed the grunting, heavy body of the alien off him and peered over the edge of the barricade. He saw two

lascannons surrounded by three dead marines. Two of the
bodies had grenades attached to their belts.

"Hunh! Not bad, kid," one of the men commented.

Dion caught his breath, started to rise to his feet. The man
grabbed hold of him, dragged him down. "Begging the
general's pardon, but those cannons have to be carried just
right or they sorta blow up in your face. We'll get 'em. You
cover us, you and Ned here."

"Ned!" The alien wheezed with what Dion assumed was
laughter. "That's what they call me. Can you believe it? Ned!"
It shook its skinless, bony head.

"Hold the fort, General," the man advised, and before Dion
quite knew what was happening, his squad was off.

Dion jumped up from behind the barricade, firing his
lasgun wildly. The alien opened fire. Its strange weapon—
designed to fit its three-fingered hand—shot a burst of energy
bolts that nearly blinded the boy. Something exploded near
him; stinging pain shot through his left arm and was promptly
forgotten.

His men grabbed the lascannon and as many grenades as
each could carry, stuffing them down the fronts of their flak
jackets, and came running back, stumbling beneath the weight
of the heavy cannon. They headed for the trash masher. Dion
and the alien slowly retreated. The women covered them,
keeping up almost continuous, deadly fire.

"Run for it!" The women shouted at him.

Dion ran, the alien pounding along beside him. Someone
caught hold of Dion, pulled him down. The young man looked
around, dazed, and was amazed to find himself behind the
trash masher. His lungs burned; he gulped air.

One of the men had also managed to snag a canteen. He
drank sparingly, offered it to Dion.

"What next, General?"

Dion took hold of the canteen, started to take a drink, and
was afraid suddenly he might be sick. He handed it back.

"Get together as many of you as you can. Move
out . . . that direction." He waved his left hand vaguely, saw
a gaping hole in the flak jacket he was wearing, noticed blood
trickling down his fingers. He wondered whose it was. "The
controls . . . for hangar bay. We've got . . . capture them.
Open . . ." He was having trouble catching his breath.
"Escape."

"Gotcha. How'll we know where the controls are?"

Dion forced his mind to slow down, not gallop past details. "Flares," he said, remembering the burst overhead that had scared him. "Flares," he repeated.

He staggered to his feet.

"Hey, General. You've been hit. You better rest a minute—"

Dion shook his head. He didn't have much time.

"Thank you," he said politely to his first command, and went off to find Tusk.

··◀■ ■▶··

The men watched until the red hair was lost in the smoke. Then they hefted their equipment, prepared to obey orders.

"Wait a goddam minute! How old do you suppose that kid is?" one asked.

"Dunno. Maybe sixteen, seventeen," his buddy answered.

"You got any idea why we're doing this?"

"No." All of them, Ned included, shook their heads.

"Me neither. Except . . ." the man paused, pondered, "I think maybe it's the eyes. They sort of burn right through a guy. Any of you ever seen eyes like that?"

None of them, including Ned, who had six eyes of his own, ever had.

Dion's squad moved out.

Chapter ❖⊃◯⊂❖ Eight

> . . . *quod vindicta*
> *Nemo magis gaudet quam femina.*
>
> . . . no one
> delights more in vengeance than a woman.
>
> Juvenal, *Satires*

"I don't need any help, thank you. No, I'm not hurt!"

The MP couldn't hear the words but he understood the gesture. Watching through a viewscreen in the corridor outside the hangar bay, he saw the pilot wave off assistance and extricate herself from the smashed-up Scimitar. Emergency crews swarmed over it, checking for potential fires, radiation leaks.

"Why did you bother?" One of the crewmen appeared to be shouting. A hulking cyborg encased in a protective suit, he twiddled a robotic arm at what was left of the spaceplane.

The pilot removed her helmet, said something that would seem to be, from the movement of her lips, "It beat walking!"

The cyborg was highly amused at the response.

Exiting the hangar bay, the pilot entered the corridor. The MP drew his men up in ceremonial form, awaiting her arrival. The woman saw them. They saluted, she saluted, fist over her heart. Her face was smeared with grease and soot, her pale hair had drifted free of its confining braids, her flight suit was punctured and stained with blood. Though she appeared bone-weary, she stood straight, shoulders squared.

"I am Lady Maigrey Morianna. Where is Captain Williams? I want to speak with him."

The MP was completely taken aback by this request, and somewhat confused. Escaping prisoners, such as this woman was purported to be, didn't generally arrive on board a ship and demand to see the captain.

"Captain Williams is . . . uh . . . unavailable at the moment, your . . . ladyship. The current emergency situation . . . If I could be of assistance . . ."

Maigrey fixed the MP with a scrutinizing gaze. He was conscious of undergoing some sort of evaluation. Apparently he passed, for she nodded once, gravely.

"Yes, officer, thank you. Has the latest shuttle arrived from *Phoenix?*"

"I don't know, my lady." He hedged for time. "I can check—"

"Please do so. There is a felon on board, a murderer. I am responsible to my lord for his capture."

The MP spoke into the commlink in his helmet. The woman stood nearby, tapping her foot impatiently, a slight frown creasing her forehead over the delay.

"Captain Williams," the MP said quietly.

"Williams here."

"I have Lady Morianna, sir. She has asked to speak to you."

"To me? What the deuce for?"

"She says she's been sent here by Lord Sagan to capture a felon, a—a murderer, sir."

"But she's an escaped prisoner!" Williams sounded rattled. According to reports, the battle with the mercenaries wasn't going well.

"Yes, sir. Have you been able to contact Lord Sagan, sir?"

"No." Williams snapped the answer.

So the rumors must be true, the MP thought. They were trying to keep the lid on, but it was obvious all these men being transferred from *Phoenix* to *Defiant* weren't reinforcements. The Warlord must be in serious trouble.

Maigrey's foot-tapping grew louder. Tucking her helmet beneath her arm, she lightly touched the MP on the arm. "We should hurry, before my prisoner loses himself in the crowd."

"Yes, my lady. I'm attempting to get the information now. Begging the captain's pardon," the MP continued, talking to Williams in an undertone, "but if Lord Sagan *did* send the woman, then shouldn't we do what we can to assist—"

"And what if he didn't?" Williams returned, perplexed and frustrated. "We may well be assisting her to waltz right out of here."

"Yes, sir." The MP offered the captain a modicum of silent sympathy. Williams might be damned if he did what the woman wanted, could very well be damned if he didn't.

Distant voices sounded in the background, competing for

the captain's attention. "Carry on, Sergeant," he said finally in a harassed tone. "Arrest this prisoner, then take both him *and* the lady to the brig. If she protests, tell her that it's for her own safety."

"Yes, sir." The MP turned back to Maigrey. "The last shuttle has docked on Able deck, my lady. Down this corridor and to our left."

Maigrey smiled at him, a peculiar, crooked smile. He had the distinct and uncanny impression that she'd heard every word. He hesitated, feeling suddenly extremely uncomfortable, wondering if he shouldn't contact the captain again. But what would he say? No, he would do what he'd been ordered to do. That was always safe.

Gesturing to his men, who fell in behind him, the MP and the woman proceeded down the passage. They rounded a corner, ran into a large group of white-coated men, medicbots bearing litters, and other personnel from the hospital shuttle. Another group from *Phoenix* emerged into the corridor at the same time from a different direction, creating an immediate logjam of bodies and 'bots.

"That's him!" Maigrey pointed.

"Seize him!"

The MPs floundered through the crowd, pushing and shoving. Grabbing hold of the major, they clapped him in fuse-irons. Those who had been standing near the wretched man disappeared immediately, having no desire to be held guilty by association. The major protested loudly and volubly, too loudly. The MP had been around a long time. He'd seen the major's expression when the man first felt the fuse-iron close over his wrist. He wasn't surprised or shocked, as an innocent man would have been. The major's face had darkened, brows contracted in swift and sullen anger. The MPs hauled him to the lady and their own officer. Seeing them, the major rearranged his features, looking and sounding highly offended.

"By the gods, Sergeant, I'll have your stripes for dinner! What's the meaning of this?" His face was blotchy; his eyes protruded from beneath a thick forehead.

"The officer is acting on my orders, Major." Maigrey spoke quietly. She'd been standing quietly. The major hadn't even noticed her.

The major blustered and blew, then his gaze went to the woman's torn and bloodied uniform, then to the features. The

MP, watching closely, saw the bluster fizzle out, saw the blood drain from the major's cheeks, his jaw working.

"I—I don't know what's going on—"

"Surprised to see me alive? Or perhaps you think I'm a ghost? You must have a lot of ghosts haunting you, Major."

The man recovered his senses, said what he should have said in the first place, except now it merely made matters worse. "You're arresting the wrong person, officer. This woman was a prisoner aboard our ship. I tried to capture her, but she got away from me and flew off in a wrecked Scimitar before I could stop her!"

The MP was elbowed from behind. Whipping around, he glared over his shoulder.

"Sorry, sir!" stammered a red-faced marine, who'd been shoved into the MP. A steady stream of men and equipment continued to surge through the narrow passageway. The MP and his men were impeding the flow.

"Let's move along," the MP began. "We can discuss this in the—"

"The charge is murder," Maigrey interrupted. "One count, probably others will surface on investigation. Inform my lord that I will be in touch with him concerning this matter."

The MP considered. Whatever else is going on, this man is obviously guilty of something, he thought. I'll be safe in hauling him off, dumping him in the brig for a while. "Yes, my lady. Take him below," he ordered his guards.

"Bitch! I'll see you in hell!" Nearly escaping his captors, the major made a lunge at Maigrey.

Deftly, she slid her hand into his front shirt pocket. The MP saw something sparkle brightly before her fingers closed around it. The major's guards wrestled him back.

"And now, my lady"—the MP reached out to take hold of her—"if you will accompany me—"

"Officer!" A medic shoved his way between the two of them. "Officer, what the devil are you doing? Clear this area! My stretcher bearers can't get through! These men are critically wounded!"

The major, swearing at the top of his lungs, continued struggling. "You can't do this to me! I'll have you up on charges! Every last one of you! I'll see you terminated!" He was a big man; the MPs were having trouble holding on to him. The shouting was drawing a crowd of curious onlookers.

"I insist that you clear this area! Clear this area!" The medic danced around, waving his arms and yammering.

The flow in the corridor bottled up. Some men tried to shove past, others stopped and craned their heads, hoping to catch a glimpse of the latest crisis. In the distance, at the end of the corridor, a group of marines appeared, trundling a canister of brain-gas down the passage.

"Hey!" the sergeant of the marines shouted. "Clear this area! We gotta get through!"

"Sir—" one of the MPs began.

"Bloody outrage—" the major howled.

"I insist—" the medic shrieked.

"Clout him one if he doesn't shut up!" the MP bellowed, and, being rather vague as to his pronoun, he had the satisfaction of seeing everyone in the immediate vicinity relapse into sudden silence.

Deciding that the best thing to do was to get his prisoners out of here, the MP turned to Maigrey. "My lady, if you will accompany—" He stopped talking, mouth open, but no words came out.

The woman was gone.

··◆═ ═▶··

General Dixter's forces, trapped on Charlie deck, had surrounded the control room and were keeping the marines at bay by holding the entrances into the hangar bays against them. Dixter's main fear was that Williams would use brain-gas, a chemical which rendered an enemy immobile by either knocking him out or, in some extreme cases, killing him. The marines had masks to protect themselves against the gas; the mercenaries did not. If the marines used brain-gas, the battle would be over.

Williams had, in fact, received the supply of brain-gas he'd requested from *Phoenix*, but he had been prevented from using it. Brain-gas was generally used out in the open air. Computer analysis had revealed the possibility that, released inside a small area, the poisonous fumes might be sucked inside *Defiant*'s ventilating systems, plunging everyone aboard ship into an inadvertent siesta. The marines, unable to use the gas, were forced to rely on small-arms fire and grenades. Rockets and mortars were out, they might puncture the hull. And so the mercenaries had a chance. Inside a small control room, their computer expert—a heavyset woman named

Lilly—ignored the fighting swirling around her, worked diligently at wresting command of the hangar bay doors away from central control.

The mercenaries who still had planes to fly were gathered in the ready room.

"I need volunteers," Dixter told them, "to stay behind, hold the control room, keep the tractor beams out of commission."

Humans, aliens exchanged glances. Everyone knew that those who stayed behind were doomed—a quick death if they were lucky, a prisoner of the Warlord if they weren't. Everyone knew, too, that their general was staying behind, that he wouldn't abandon his people. There was a sudden surge of people forward, clamoring and shouting to volunteer. General Dixter was nearly trampled in the rush.

"Thank you all," he said when he could speak, his voice choked by his emotion. "But many of our comrades have already died, trying to gain for you the ability to leave. Every one of us captured or killed from now on is a victory mark for the Warlord. I want as many of you to leave as possible." Dixter waved down the protests. "Listen to me!" He had to shout to be heard. "I just received word"—he held up his fieldphone—"that our people on Delta deck are starting to push the marines back. As soon as you are safely gone, those of us staying behind will help our friends on Delta. There'll probably be enough planes to take us all off. We'll meet at the rendezvous."

"Hey, General," Gobar called out, "the Warlord promised to pay us! When do we get our money?"

The mercenaries laughed, Dixter joining in. "I'll send him a bill."

"We'll wring our pay out of him. Drop by drop. You can be sure of that, sir," a woman said quietly, and the laughter died to an ominous silence.

Dixter glanced around at his people, tried to think of something to add, but only shook his head. Bennett, monitoring the fieldphone, hurried over to confer. Those who had served with the general a long time took a certain grim delight in noting that the aide's usually immaculate uniform was somewhat rumpled and had a spot of grease on one knee.

"You know," one said solemnly, gazing at Bennett, "just to see that—it's almost been worth it."

Dixter turned from his aide and faced his people. "Lilly's

done it! The controls are ours! Move out. Hurry, we don't have much time."

No one stirred.

Dixter's expression grew stern; the graying brows came together. "That's an order."

Reluctantly, his people did as they were commanded, trooping out of the ready room, plunging into the smoke-filled hangar bay. But every one of them took a small bit of the precious time available to shake hands or at least touch—as if for luck—their general. He said something to each, wished them Godspeed, promised time and again to meet them at the rendezvous point—with their payroll.

"If you're not, sir, we'll be back for you," each promised.

Dixter only smiled. At the very end of the line stood a bloodied, disheveled, and weary-looking woman dressed in the uniform of a Galactic pilot. Reaching out, she clasped his hand, spoke wistfully.

"John, I'm starved. You wouldn't happen to have a chicken sandwich on you?"

Dixter glanced at her, looked hard at her, stared at her in disbelief.

"My God!" he murmured. Throwing his arms around the woman, he hugged her close. Neither said a word, each clinging to the other.

Maigrey let go of him, took a step back. "Go on with your work. I'll wait here for you."

When the last of the pilots was gone and all those leaving were safely aboard their planes, those who were staying behind took shelter in the ready room. Bennett made certain the entrance was locked and sealed. The hangar bay doors shivered, then began to open. The rumbling vibrations shook the deck. The planes' engines fired, many of the smaller ones blasting off before the doors were more than halfway up.

Those waiting in the ready room with Dixter called the planes off. "There goes Ratazar."

"Who's that behind her?"

"Spike-hand Pete. And K'um and his twin brother."

"They're shot up pretty bad. I hope they make it."

"They'll make it. They would, just to spite me. I got a forty-eagle bet with him says we never see each other again! . . ."

"Sir," Bennett's voice came level and quiet over the roar of the engines of the departing planes, "we've lost contact with the control room."

Dixter glanced through the steelglass viewport at the hangar bay doors. There were still numerous planes waiting to take off.

Bennett saw the concern, understood. "Lilly said—before the connection went—that she had managed to jam the controls open. It will take the enemy some time to fix them, sir, I should imagine."

"Yes. Thank you, Bennett." Dixter's lips pressed together tightly, grimly. He leaned his head on his hand, massaged his forehead.

"There's nothing more you can do now, sir. Why don't you sit down, let me bring you a cup of coffee? The machine over in the corner is still operational."

"He's right, John," Maigrey said, coming up from behind. She rested her cheek against Dixter's shoulder. "Come, sit down."

Most of the mercenaries in the room remained crowded at the viewport. A few sank down to rest, thankful for the respite, knowing it wouldn't last long.

Maigrey brought up two metal desks, placed them side by side. Wriggling out of the bulky flight suit, she dumped it on the deck and seated herself at the desk's attached chair. Dixter joined her.

"You look awful," she told him cheerfully.

"You look worse." Dixter smoothed back a strand of her pale hair. "You're covered with blood. Are you hurt?"

"It's not mine." Maigrey wiped her face with her hand and stared at her fingers ruefully.

"Anyone I know?"

She smiled, shook her head. "Wishful thinking. The Warlord is alive and as well as can be expected, considering his ship's been shot out from underneath him."

Dixter appeared grave. "So we've gone through all this just to be destroyed by the Corasians?"

"No. Sagan may have lost the battle but he's going to win the war. He's using the old fire ship maneuver—moving *Phoenix* in close to the Corasian vessel; when it blows, it'll take them with it."

Bennett returned with coffee. "All the planes are away safely, sir."

Dixter smiled; light touched the faded brown eyes. The mercenaries in the ready room cheered.

"And I heard you say you were hungry, my lady," the aide added, depositing several foil-wrapped bars in front of Maigrey. "These were all I could find, I'm afraid."

"Blessings on you!" Maigrey said fervently, tearing open the foil, revealing a congealed mass of something that appeared to be highly nutritious and completely inedible. She sniffed at it, grimaced. "Veg-bars. Oh, well. You want one?"

"No," Dixter said hastily, shaking his head. "I had to live on those things for a year, once. When I was on the run."

Maigrey bit into the bar, chewed it, swallowed. Her gaze wandered to the people in the room. She sighed, shook her head. "I—I feel responsible."

Dixter reached out his hand, took hold of hers, held it fast. "You're not, Maigrey. My people made their own decisions to come. We did what we set out to do; we defeated the Corasians. You warned us of Sagan's treachery and we were ready for him. That's the reason we were able to hold out this long. I don't suppose," he added with a half-smile, sipping at his coffee, "that you stopped by just for lunch? What is it you need? A plane? You're leaving me again."

A crimson flush stained Maigrey's pale face, the scar on her cheek was livid white against the flushed skin, the hand in his began to tremble. "I wish I could stay! If I had my choice I would be with you and fight him until . . . until—" Her fingers clenched; her nails dug into his flesh. "But I can't! I've found out something about—" She glanced around furtively. "About . . . what we talked about on Vangelis."

Dixter appeared alarmed. The lines in the weathered face deepened. Leaning near, he spoke in an undertone. "Ohme?"

"Hush! Yes." She nodded, drew him closer. "I think there's a way to . . . deal with it. But I must do it myself. Soon! And that's why I can't—I can't—"

"I understand, Maigrey. I do." John lifted her hand to his lips, kissed it gently.

Maigrey lowered her head, rested her scarred cheek on his hand. He felt her tears trickle down between his fingers. Stroking back the pale hair, he brushed aside wispy ends escaping from the loosened braid. An explosion shook the deck. Heads lifted, people half-rose to their feet.

"Coffee break's over, I'm afraid." Fishing a handkerchief out of his pocket, Dixter handed it to Maigrey.

She wiped the tears and blood from her face, her tone brusque and matter-of-fact. "I need a spaceplane. A sound one. One that will get me to . . . where I need to be."

"The only planes you'll find are on Delta deck. And a fierce battle is raging over there, from what I've heard."

Maigrey waved that aside. "And Dion? Have you seen him? I hoped to find him with you."

"Yes, I've seen him. He's leading the assault on Delta."

"What?" Maigrey stared. "Have you gone mad, John Dixter?"

The general raised his hands, defending himself against her accusing gray eyes. "It was his idea, lady, not mine." Slowly, tiredly, he stood up. "Although I admit I went along with him."

"He's only a child!" Maigrey bounced to her feet, confronted him.

"If you and Sagan are right about him, Maigrey, he's a child of the Blood Royal," the general said quietly.

Maigrey opened her mouth, paused, swallowed her angry words, shook her head in despair. "You're right, John. And Sagan's right, too, damn him! Testing God!" She met John Dixter's eyes, tired but shrewd in their maze of sun-tightened wrinkles. "You could come with me."

"Yes," he acknowledged.

"But you won't," she said softly.

He shook his head, smiling at her.

Carefully, Maigrey tucked the handkerchief back into the breast pocket of his rumpled uniform, then kissed the weathered cheek. Another explosion, this one nearer, set the desks rattling, spilled the coffee. Dixter tilted her chin up, put his finger over her lips.

"No good-byes. It brings us luck," he said. "Come on. It's time we moved out."

Drawing the bloodsword from its scabbard, Maigrey meticulously fit the metal prongs into the five red marks on the palm of her right hand. "Yes, it brings us luck," she said, but only to herself.

Chapter ·•◦◦◦•· Nine

In every parting there is an image of death.
George Eliot, *Scenes from Clerical Life*

"This scheme of yours is crazy. You know that, don't you?" Tusk asked.

"What have we got to lose?" Dion returned, scrambling down the side of Tusk's Scimitar. Lasgun in hand, the mercenary covered him from below.

"Nothin'. That's the only reason I'm going along with it. What did XJ have to say?" Tusk nodded at the Scimitar, referring to his irascible computer-partner, standing guard inside.

"That flares cost one and a half crowns apiece and I wasn't to waste them," Dion said, grinning.

Laser fire streaked around them. The two flattened themselves against the plane. Keeping low, they dashed back to rejoin Link and the other mercenaries Dion had recruited. An explosion sent them diving for cover.

"Shit," Reefer swore, peering through the smoke, "the bastards blew up my plane."

"You can fly out with me," Link offered. Standing up, he fired a volley, ducked back down again when it was returned.

"I've got the flares, General Dixter, sir." Dion was speaking into the fieldphone. "I've contacted everyone I could find, sent others out to spread the word. We're ready when you are."

"How's Nola?" Tusk demanded.

Link shrugged. "No better. No worse. Some woman's with her now."

Tusk glanced back through the tangle of wreckage that sheltered the wounded, saw a form that looked vaguely familiar to him. "Who is it?"

"Dunno. She came charging in here while you and the kid were out scrounging. What have you got there?"

"A beam rifle." Tusk tossed the heavy weapon to Link. "A couple of grenades. The kid's got the flares. I'm gonna go back and check on Nola."

"Sure. That woman was asking about you and the kid anyway."

Tusk stared through the smoke, eyes narrowed. "Son of a bitch!" he whispered. "Kid!" He reached out, caught hold of Dion—who was continuing to try to talk to the general.

"Ouch!" Dion winced. "That's my hurt arm, Tusk, for God's sake! Shush! What was that, sir?" Listening, the boy's face grew intent, frowning. "No, sir. We've discussed this before. I'm the only one who can make this plan work. Yes, sir. I'll do what I can. We'll wait for your signal. Out."

"Dion!" Tusk said urgently, tugging at the boy and pointing at the woman bent over the unconscious Nola. "Look who's here! That's—"

"I know who it is," Dion said, glancing at the woman, then looking away. "General Dixter's forces are moving into position. He'll send us word when they're ready. It'll take me ten minutes to cross the enemy lines and get around to the Delta's control room entrance. Give me that long, then you—"

"Dion," Tusk interrupted. "She's waving. She wants to talk to us."

Dion paused; the full lips tightened. "I know what she wants. General Dixter just told me." He thought a moment, seeming irritated at the interruption. "All right. C'mon."

The two crouched low, crawled over machine parts and ducked around several large metal crates. The wounded lay on piles of flak jackets, crude beds of polystyrene packing, or the bare deck. Some were feverish, others moaning or twisting in pain. The woman walked among them, resting her hand on foreheads, whispering soft words. Tusk saw several grow more quiet at her touch.

"Lady Maigrey," Tusk said.

She straightened from bending over a patient, turned, and smiled, extending her hand. "Tusca."

The fingers he touched were cool to his sweating hands, her grip firm. Her gaze shifted from him to Dion, standing slightly behind his friend. The smile faded; the woman's gray eyes darkened, bleak as the steel bulkhead surrounding them.

"Dion," she said, extending her hand to the young man.

He ignored it, his pallid face expressionless. "My lady," he said formally. "Congratulations on your . . . escape." His lip curled in a slight sneer.

"Dion! What the hell's gotten into you—" Tusk began angrily.

Maigrey silenced him with a glance. "Dion, I hoped you would understand—"

"I understand!" Dion's wild red-golden hair bristled like a lion's mane, shining and bright in the smoke-filled darkness. "He sent you to bring me back, didn't he? Didn't he?"

"You silly boy." Maigrey spoke with a deadly calm that flattened out the waves of the battle raging around them, making Dion and Tusk feel as if they were in the eye of a storm. "He could have brought you back without so much as lifting his hand."

Dion blinked, lips parted. A slow flush crept from his neck to his face. "Why . . . why—"

"Figure it out for yourself," Maigrey answered. "We don't have much time. I came to find you, take you with me."

"Where?" Dion was immediately suspicious.

"I can't tell you, not here." Maigrey glanced sidelong at Tusk. "Not because I don't trust you!" Her hand once again caught hold of the mercenary's, and he was startled to feel how cold her touch had grown. "God forbid! It's just . . . the less you know, the better."

"You're right there, lady," Tusk said to himself. "Except it's a little late. I already know too much."

Dion had regained his composure, continued to speak formally, as to a stranger. "I know where you're going, my lady. General Dixter told me. I'm sorry, but I can't accompany you. This is my plan, you see. I'm the only one who can pull it off. The general told me you needed a spaceplane," he added quickly, overriding her attempt to speak. "I was thinking, if it's all right with Tusk, you could use his."

Tusk's jaw dropped. "Kid—"

Dion hurried on. "You and Nola can fly out with me. It would be safer anyway. I have the codes and clearance. We'll use the 'captured prisoner' routine. The one you told me about, that you used when you got caught by those pirates on the outer fringes . . ."

"Yeah, yeah. I know." Tusk looked at the lady, waiting for her to take charge, end the argument, end Dion's wild scheme, put the boy firmly in his place and march off with him in tow.

The woman's gray-eyed gaze never left Dion's face. It grew shadowed, troubled, as if she were hearing voices from within. At length, the gray eyes turned to Tusk. The pain in them seared him.

"I know giving up your plane will be a great sacrifice for you, Mendaharin Tusca. But I would appreciate it greatly. My mission is . . . most urgent."

He saw something else in her eyes, something she was saying to him and him alone. Her hand went to her throat, tugged at a chain she wore around her neck. Tusk knew what was attached to that chain—the Star of the Guardians. His father had worn one like it. Tusk's hand went to the gem he wore in his left earlobe, a tiny replica. He knew then what the woman was asking of him.

The very thing he'd tried to avoid all his life had come running around full circle to slam right into him.

Dion nudged him, reminding him they were running out of time.

"Sure, you can take the plane, my . . . my lady." Tusk cleared his throat. "I'm glad to get rid of it. I got to warn you about that computer, though—"

"Thank you, Tusca!" Maigrey clasped his hand tightly.

Damn it, I didn't agree to the other! Tusk wanted to protest, but the words got garbled. He choked and coughed.

Dion was already preparing to leave, picking up a beam rifle, divesting himself of the leather flak jacket he'd been wearing over his Galactic uniform. "Ten minutes, Tusk," he reminded him.

"Yeah," Tusk grunted.

"Meet me at the control room. Can you get Nola there?"

"I'll manage," Tusk said briefly.

Dion glanced over at Maigrey, who stood regarding him quietly. The young man seemed at a loss to know what to say; the woman didn't offer him any help. Finally, flushing scarlet, Dion mumbled "Thank you" in a voice that was practically unintelligible. Turning abruptly, he left.

Tusk set the timer on his watch. "We better get going, my lady. I'll escort you to my plane—"

"There's no need." Maigrey shook her head. "You stay with your friend as long as you can."

"How is Nola?" Tusk asked, his gaze going to the young

woman lying beneath a bloodstained jacket. "She looks better.
Were you able to do anything for her?"

"Not much, I'm afraid." Maigrey sounded suddenly tired.
"I've sent her into a mild hypno-trance. It will ease her pain
and reduce the body's stress, but she needs medical attention."

"She's liable to get it real soon," Tusk said gloomily.

Maigrey laid her hand on his arm. "Have faith in Dion. God
is with him."

"Do you believe that?" Tusk demanded, looking directly
into the gray eyes.

The woman paused; the gray eyes darkened, wavered.
Then, with a small half-smile, she looked straight at him. "I
have to," she said simply. "You're his Guardian now, Tusca—"

"No—"

"You can't deny it, Tusca, any more than you can deny your
black skin, your brown eyes. Like those, this is your heritage.
It was yours the day you were born. You think I'm abandoning
him . . ."

Tusk felt his black skin grow uncomfortably warm. "No, of
course not. I'm—"

"What I'm doing is for him. If Sagan succeeds—" Maigrey
broke off, seemed confused. "I'm sorry, Tusca!" she said,
shaking her head. "I'm sorry. God be with you."

He watched her thread her way through the obstacles and
the enemy fire. He could still feel, though, the chill touch of
her hand on his arm.

"Sorry! Yeah, you're sorry!" he said to her bitterly. "Sorry
for what? The pain? The responsibility? The fact that I was
born to it, that I never had a choice? All right, so that isn't
quite true. I had choices. I could have ignored my father's
dying request, could have told the kid's Guardian to go take a
flying leap, could have ditched Dion any number of times, any
number of places. Like XJ says, it's a hell of a big galaxy. But
I didn't.

"I can't be his Guardian!" Tusk shouted after her, suddenly.
"It's like guarding a . . . a . . . damn comet!"

No matter. She didn't hear him. But at least he felt better
having said it. He heard someone call his name, saw Link
waving to him frantically. Tusk glanced down at his watch. It
was almost time. Sighing, he knelt beside Nola, made her as
comfortable as he could, envying her now tranquil, untroubled
sleep.

···◄■ ■►···

Derek Sagan walked the corridors of his dying ship. Safety's window had closed some time ago. He had only minutes to reach his plane if he was to put the necessary distance between himself and the ball of fire that would soon be *Phoenix*. Yet he walked, he did not run. His last act, before leaving the bridge, had been to bid farewell to the engineers staying behind.

The press would have a field day with this. He'd be a hero to some, a coward to many others. He'd won the battle, driven the Corasians from the system, sacrificed his own ship in a clever strategy to destroy the enemy. But unless he destroyed himself at the same time, threw himself on the burning pyre, his enemies would yell "Foul!" Strange how the public didn't consider a man a hero unless he'd given his life for a cause. Many times, it took twice as much courage to live as to die.

But he would live. And he intended to make a great many people regret it.

The stimulation drug caused the Warlord to feel as if he'd had a good night's rest and an excellent meal. He had shaken off the depression which had afflicted him earlier, put it down to fatigue. He could walk the corridors of his empty ship, know that he was walking them for the last time, and his mind was able to dwell on the future, not the past.

His plans were vague—he couldn't, didn't want to define them as yet. He was playing a game of living chess and too many pieces were running rampant on the board. His queen had disappeared. His pawn, the boy, had been sent out to the front ranks to do battle. It would be up to Sagan to keep his pawn and make use of him or sacrifice him to the end. His bishop, Snaga Ohme, was nursing thoughts of playing both sides against each other. The Adonian would have to be taught a lesson. What his opponent was plotting was unclear, but at least now Sagan could see the face of the enemy.

The Warlord arrived at his spaceplane. His Honor Guard was there, waiting for him. Instantly he glanced around the hangar bay, prey to a strange impression. Yes, Maigrey had been here. It was as if he could scent her perfume lingering in the area, hear the echo of her voice. Where had she gone? What was she planning? Would she complicate his game or make it easier for him to win? At least he knew she hated and feared their mutual enemy as much as he did. Unfortunately, however, she didn't—at the moment—know who that enemy was.

Sagan entered the spaceplane, the Honor Guard squeezing in behind him. It was a tight fit; all three were large-muscled, well-proportioned men, and the spaceplane's cockpit had been designed to hold only himself and perhaps one co-pilot comfortably. He activated all systems, checked to see all was functioning, taking his time. The Honor Guard kept quiet. Discipline forbade them speaking unless spoken to. Their faces were impassive, but, glancing behind him, Sagan could see sweat beading on their foreheads, tongues pass nervously over dry lips.

The Warlord permitted himself a wry smile and fired the plane's engines. He took off, leaving *Phoenix* with only one final, backward glance. His hand rested on the leather scrip he had placed at his side.

The Corasian mothership, looming near, didn't bother to fire on him. A single small spaceplane would be nothing but a speck of dust to them, intent as they were on capturing their larger prize.

Sagan punched in the coordinates for *Defiant*, sat back and relaxed, concentrated on his flying. The game was, for the moment, out of his hands. He had just one move to make, a move involving a knight, a move that would ensure the queen's good behavior.

"*Defiant*, this is the Warlord. Pass this message to Captain Williams. I am on my way. Take no further action against the mercenaries until I arrive."

··◁■ ■▷··

This is all far too easy, Maigrey told herself.

She had reached Tusk's Scimitar without difficulty and though she'd been cautious, keeping under cover, she had the impression she could have marched up to it beating drums and clanging cymbals. The marines continued their assault, but she recognized that most of the fireworks were being set off for effect. The marines were waiting. What for?

A new commander.

Sagan. Like the patient fisherman, who feels the tiniest nibble flow through the line, Maigrey felt the Warlord's coming in her blood. The line connecting them tensed, trembled.

I should warn John. Yes, that's it. Warn John!

She started to search for someone to take a message, stopped.

It won't make any difference.

She was tired, so very tired. But she had to keep going. To quit now was to make it all worthless.

Maigrey scaled the ladder leading up the side of the spaceplane, dropped down through the open hatch.

"Who's there? Who is that?" a mechanical voice demanded. "Halt or I'll shoot!"

Harsh lights switched on, blinding her. Cameras whirred; glass eyes placed in the overhead focused in on her.

"A female!" The computer sounded disgusted. "Another female! Trust Tusk! Someday I'm going to sew his fly shut! Look, you hussy, this isn't the ladies' powder room. You turn right at the end of the hall and—"

"Is that an XJ-27 model?" Maigrey cocked her head, listening.

"What if it is?" the computer snapped suspiciously.

"The model that was the most advanced ever developed? The model that was known for its independent thinking, its high degree of logic, its infallible judgment, its vast technological knowledge combined with an extremely sensitive nature and agreeable personality?"

"Could be." The computer sounded mollified. "Who's asking?"

"If so, then I am truly fortunate. My name is Maigrey Morianna. I am in desperate need and to find an XJ-27 model in my hour of extreme peril—"

"Maigrey Morianna!" The computer was awed. Its lights flickered. "*The* Maigrey Morianna? Member of the famed Golden Squadron?"

"I was, once, long ago."

"My lady! Come for'ard! Make yourself at home. Excuse the mess. Tusk *insists* on leaving his underwear lying around! Don't trip over those tools. Mind your step. Don't bump your head against those overhead pipes. Just kick those boots under the storage compartment. Excuse the blood, I haven't had time to mop up. . . ."

Maigrey walked through the living quarters of the long-range Scimitar, scaled the ladder with practiced ease, jumped down into the Scimitar's small two-man cockpit.

"Forgive my earlier rudeness, ma'am," XJ said in formal tones. "I've been forced to keep low company, of late, and I fear it has rubbed off on me. Flying with a pilot of your skill and expertise will no doubt serve to remind me that I was destined for a higher calling than constantly saving Tusk—that third-rate Galactic Republic Space Corps dropout—from his own mistakes."

Maigrey carefully kept her expression grave. If she began to laugh, she'd break down and cry. She slid into the pilot's chair.

"I've never flown one of these types of Scimitars before, XJ. I'll be relying on you to assist me."

"I will be honored, ma'am—I mean, your ladyship. Will there be anyone else accompanying us? Such as the previously mentioned dropout?"

Maigrey bit her lip, mumbled something.

"I beg your pardon, your ladyship?"

"I said no, XJ. No one else."

"No. . . ." The computer's lights dimmed. It whirred to itself, started to speak, made a blurping sound, and instantly cut itself off. The words FORGIVE ME, SLIGHT MALFUNCTION flashed across the screen.

"XJ?" Maigrey looked at it worriedly.

"No problem. I'm back." The computer's audio was extremely nonchalant, casual. "Not that I care in the slightest, your ladyship, but if anything's happened to that good-for-nothing former partner of mine—I'm referring, of course, to Mendaharin Tusca—I should record it in my files."

"Nothing's happened to Tusk, XJ," Maigrey said gently. "He's flying out with Dion. He was kind enough to loan you to me for just a short while. You two will soon be back together again—"

"Don't do me any favors, your ladyship!" XJ's lights winked cheerfully again. "Will we be blasting off shortly?"

"As soon as possible."

"Then I'll just take this opportunity to reprogram life-support to suit your needs. How many respirations do you take a minute?"

"Fourteen, under stress," Maigrey answered, studying the plane's controls.

"Ah," XJ purred, "a true professional! At last!"

··◆ ➡··

Maigrey was exhausted, that was the problem. Exhausted and hungry. She hadn't slept in God knew how long. She hadn't eaten anything except that horrid veg-bar that tasted like rock and was about as digestible. Her tears were a nervous response, triggered by lack of sleep and low blood sugar. She tried to stop them, but they kept coming.

Maigrey saw the flares through her tears—blurred flashes of red exploding in the smoke-filled gloom of the hangar bay. She barely saw, through her tears, the hangar bay doors open. She barely found, through the tears, the right switches to manipulate, the correct buttons to push.

Fortunately, the computer was able to handle most of the takeoff procedure. Maigrey sat back, crying silently, and let XJ manage.

The Scimitar glided out of the hangar, swooped into starlit blackness. Other mercenaries flew beside her; voices crackled over the commlink, trying to raise her.

"Shut it off," she told XJ.

"But there are enemy planes, your ladyship—"

"They won't bother us."

And they didn't. Hovering at a safe distance, Sagan's pilots watched the mercenaries escape and did nothing to stop them.

The line between them was unreeling, but no matter how far from him she traveled, it would never snap. Out in space, through her tears, from the corner of her eye, she saw what appeared to be—from that distance—a tiny spark. The spark flared, expanded, became a gigantic ball of flame.

A small sun. For an instant—another star. Another star in a myriad of stars.

And then it was gone, and the place where it had been was left that much darker by contrast.

No good-byes. It brings us luck. . . .

"There isn't any luck for us, John. There never was," she said, and tasted the bitter salt of her tears on her lips. "Good-bye."

Chapter ···❖➤◖◗❖··· Ten

In what distant deeps or skies,
Burnt the fire of thine eyes?
On what wings dare he aspire?
What the hand dare seize the fire?
William Blake, *"The Tyger"*

The ventilation system aboard *Defiant* was rapidly clearing the hangar bay area of smoke. Crews were dismantling and hauling off wrecked spaceplanes, mopping up blood. The injured had already been removed. The burial detail was at work, tagging corpses, removing the personal effects, recording names and numbers. The bodies of the marines lay in neat, ordered rows, waiting to be zipped into bags and consigned to the deep. The bodies of the mercenaries had been dragged off to one side and lay in a heap until someone received orders on what to do with them.

The Warlord placed the toe of his boot beneath the shoulder of one of the dead mercenaries, flipped it over, studied the face. The corpse was that of a black-skinned male, but not, apparently, anyone Sagan recognized, for he turned away from it without interest.

"They're all dead, then?"

"Yes, my lord, with few exceptions. We offered them a chance for surrender, but they refused."

"There was no need to surrender, Captain," the Warlord remarked coolly. "They were winning."

"Yes, my lord."

Captain Williams wasn't watching his footing, stepped in a puddle of blood, slipped, and nearly lost his balance. A lieutenant of the marines, marching stolidly along at the captain's side, reached out a hand and saved his superior officer from an embarrassing fall. Williams flushed, dug his finger into the collar of his dress uniform in an attempt to loosen it. He felt as though he were strangling.

"But there were some survivors?" Sagan asked.

"Yes, my lord. We received your orders concerning the parties in whom you were interested. I passed the word to the marines."

The Warlord looked at the lieutenant, invited him to speak. The marine officer was young, but hard and sharp as a bayonet. He had taken over command from his dying captain. His men had done their duty, fought well, and any blame for the failure of the "containment" could be laid squarely on the shoulders of the unfortunate captain of the *Defiant*. Very little awed or impressed the young marine officer, including, obviously, talking to his Warlord.

"I followed orders, sir, and issued descriptions of those wanted for questioning to my men. And I consider it damn lucky to have discovered even one of them alive."

"You're to be commended, Lieutenant," Sagan said.

"Thank you, sir, but I can't take the credit," the marine said stolidly. "One of his own people saved the man's life. He's over here, sir, if you would care to see him. We've been awaiting your orders concerning him."

The Warlord indicated that this would suit him. Glancing around, he said irritably, "Where's Giesk? Doctor, are you coming?"

The doctor, who had stopped to study one of the corpses with professional interest, lifted his head, looked around vaguely. "Did someone call me? Oh, yes, my lord! Right behind you, my lord."

The lieutenant led the way to what had once been a pilot's ready room. A gaping hole had been blasted through a wall; the viewport was shattered. Several metal desks had been melted and fused together. Others lay scattered about up-ended or had been blown apart completely. Numerous bodies, mostly of dead mercenaries, were being removed.

"They made their stand here, sir," the lieutenant said. "Their numbers were few by this time—"

"Yes, since most of them had already made good their escape," Sagan interrupted.

The wretched Williams could say nothing. The lieutenant remained cool. After all, it hadn't been his fault.

"Yes, sir. This way. Watch your step, my lord. Those wires are still hot."

Two marines stood guard over a man who lay unconscious on the deck. They had done what they could to make him comfortable and covered him with a blanket, but he had not been moved. Saluting, the marines stepped aside.

"Giesk." Sagan motioned.

The doctor hurried forward, bent down over his patient, prodding and poking and peering. Whipping open a case, he produced a semeitor, a diagnostic machine, attached several leads to the man's head, and spent some time studying whatever information they were transmitting.

"Well, Giesk?" the Warlord demanded, with an impatience uncharacteristic of him. The stimulation shot was wearing off. He could use another, but was damned if he'd ask for it.

"He'll live, my lord. A mild concussion, but otherwise uninjured." The doctor glanced around at the burned and mangled bodies lying nearby. "He was extremely lucky, I'd say."

"He won't consider himself lucky," Sagan murmured. Bending down, he examined the man closely. "What's this?" Lifting one of the flaccid arms, he attempted to pry something from between the fingers. Though unconscious, the man held the object fast and it took the Warlord some effort to remove it. He held it up. The others looked at it curiously, were disappointed when they saw what it was.

"A handkerchief, my lord," the lieutenant said, seeming to feel called upon to make an identification.

The Warlord appeared highly gratified by his discovery. He smoothed it out upon one knee, noted that it was damp and stained with blood.

"Whose tears did you dry with this, John Dixter?" Sagan asked in an undertone, audible only to Giesk, who wasn't paying the least attention.

Packing up his semeitor, the doctor began fussing over his patient, tucking the blanket around the shoulders and unnecessarily warning the litter-bearers—who had been standing by—to move slowly and not jostle him.

Folding the handkerchief carefully in half, then in half again, the Warlord tucked it in the palm of his left glove, treating the square of plain, serviceable cotton as a treasured and valued artifact.

The lieutenant shot the captain a questioning glance out of the corner of his eye, but Williams could offer no help. He was thankful only to see that his lordship's humor had measurably improved.

"When will he regain consciousness, Giesk?" Sagan asked, rising to his feet.

"Not for some time, I would guess, my lord. I must relieve the pressure on the brain and then—"

"I'm to be informed the moment he is able to speak. Keep him in isolation, bound hand and foot. You men"—Sagan gestured to two of his centurions, who never left his side—"accompany Giesk. I want a twenty-four-hour guard over this prisoner. Attend to it personally."

"Yes, my lord."

Corpsmen gently slid the litter beneath their patient and activated its controls. Its jets breathed out a cushion of air and it whirred forward.

"Not too fast, not too fast," Giesk ordered, eyeing it critically.

The corpsmen knew their jobs, however, and the litter glided ahead smoothly and evenly. A touch guided it in the correct direction, and it floated off, sailing serenely above the wreckage and the dead, moving with far more ease than those forced to follow it afoot.

"One other of the mercenaries was captured alive in this area, my lord. He's conscious, if you would like to speak with him." The lieutenant made a peremptory motion and two marines came forward.

Marching between them, stance correct, posture rigid as that of his guards, was a middle-aged man in a slightly soiled but neatly pressed, old-fashioned uniform of a style that had not been worn since before the revolution. He stood stiffly at attention, his gaze fixed at a point somewhere to the left of Sagan's left shoulder.

"Your name?" the Warlord said, a ghost of a smile on his tight lips.

"Bennett, sir, aide to General Dixter."

"Rank?"

"Sergeant major, sir."

"How did the 'general' receive his injury, Sergeant Major? It's rather peculiar, considering the fierce fighting, that he should be suffering from nothing more severe than a bump on the head."

"My name is Bennett, sir. Rank: sergeant major."

The ghost of the smile became more visible, though the

Warlord's voice remained grave. "I believe you could answer that question, Sergeant Major, without giving aid and comfort to the enemy."

Bennett appeared to consider the matter, his chin thrust forward. The man's eyes shifted for the first time to regard the Warlord directly. "I struck him, sir."

"You did?" Sagan appeared considerably startled.

"Yes, sir. I could see he was determined on dying, sir, and that couldn't be allowed."

The Warlord's gravity increased. "I am afraid he won't be particularly grateful to you for saving him, Sergeant Major. He will be 'questioned,' of course."

"Yes, my lord." A nerve twitched in Bennett's jaw; a trickle of sweat ran down his forehead.

"However, you could spare him a very unpleasant hour, Sergeant Major. You remember Lady Maigrey Morianna, don't you, Bennett?"

The aide's eyes shifted, left the Warlord's face, traveled again to the point beyond his shoulder.

"You met her on Vangelis," Sagan continued. "You would recognize her, of course, if you saw her again. And you did see her again, didn't you, Sergeant Major?" The Warlord drew nearer to the man. The aide's jaw clenched, but he remained standing stiff, unmoving. "She came here, didn't she? She spoke to John Dixter. What did they discuss, Bennett? Where was she going? What did she intend to do? Was the boy, Dion, with her?"

"My name is Bennett, sir. Rank: sergeant—"

The marine lieutenant struck the aide in the face. "The Warlord asked you a question, dog."

Bennett reeled beneath the blow, rocked back on his feet. His guards caught and held him. Shaking his head muzzily, licking a trickle of blood from a cut lip, he slowly resumed his correct posture, his eyes staring into nothing. "My name is Bennett. Rank: sergeant—"

"That will do, Lieutenant," Sagan said, seeing the marine's fist double. "We have more effective methods. Take him away."

"Interrogation chamber, my lord?"

"Certainly. There's no hurry, however." The Warlord fingered the hem of the handkerchief that protruded from his glove. "I believe I know most of the answers."

"'Scuse me, Cap'tn." A grizzled sergeant, head of the burial detail by his red sash, edged his way in front of Williams.

"Yes, Mackenna, what is it?"

"We was wonderin' what to do with them there bodies. The bodies of the enemy, sir."

"Toss them out the hatch," Williams said, not particularly liking the reminder.

Who was it, Sagan wondered, who advised commanders to accord the bodies of the enemy the respect you accord your own dead? Rommel?

"Belay that," he ordered. "They fought bravely and well. And, when all is said and done, they were victorious. They will be read into the deep, the same as our men."

"Aye, aye, me lord." The sergeant saluted, a crooked grin showing his approbation. Lumbering off, he shouted, "We're to do right by 'em. I told ye so, ye lubbers!"

Sagan remained standing in thoughtful silence, turned to Captain Williams.

Knowing the unfortunate moment had come, the captain blenched and struggled to retain his composure.

"And now, Captain, I believe we should discuss how most of the mercenaries you had trapped on Delta deck managed to escape."

··⇐ ⇒··

The noise in the hangar bay almost precluded talking. Cranes hoisted the skeletal remains of spaceplanes into waiting motorized bins. The remains would be sent to the lower decks to be scavenged for parts or melted down for their metal.

Captain Williams was forced to shout to make himself heard and, after twenty minutes of talking, his voice was hoarse, nearly gone.

"The control room for Delta deck has two entrances, my lord. One on the portside, leading to the hangar bay, the other on starboard, facing the main part of the ship. The entrance onto the hangar bay was sealed and heavily guarded."

They approached the area, the captain gesturing as he spoke. Now that he had come to the crisis point, Williams was calm. It had happened; nothing could change the outcome. He could accept his fate—court-martial, disgrace, perhaps death. He even found himself looking forward with anticipation to his Warlord's reaction to the bizarre tale the captain had to unfold.

"The mercenaries managed to take us by surprise on

Charlie, my lord. Immediately after they freed Dixter from the brig, they attacked the control room and held it, despite incurring heavy casualties. Those on Charlie were organized, acting under Dixter's leadership. Those on Delta were not, making no concerted attempt at the beginning to take the control room. They were fighting for their lives. Then, according to the officers I questioned, something happened to alter the situation. Someone was able to take command, bring them together."

"The Lady Maigrey," the Warlord said, in a chill tone that went through the captain like splintered glass, "whom you had managed to capture, then lost."

Williams paled, but maintained his composure. "At first I thought so, my lord, but not now. Not now."

Sagan snorted, unconvinced. They reached the control room, entered it from the hangar bay side. Numerous bodies, both marines and mercenaries, lay on the deck.

"We had our forces deployed in this area. The mercenaries came at us in what we assumed was a final, last-ditch, suicidal assault. We held them off easily, sir."

"You *held*!" Sagan gazed at the captain in cold, narrow-eyed disbelief.

"Yes, sir." William motioned to two guards, who were standing on either side of the sealed door. One activated it, and the door slid aside. "If you would go into the control room, my lord." The captain stood back, deferentially, to allow the Warlord to precede him.

Entering, Sagan stopped, stared. "My God!"

The hatch sealed behind him, shutting off the noise from the hangar deck, leaving them in deathly silence. The control room was small, almost all available space taken up by the instruments and equipment used to control the various functions of the machines on the hangar deck. And now, almost every centimeter—overhead, deck, desktops, computer screens, control panels—was spattered with blood. Chairs with gigantic holes shot in them lay overturned on the deck. Bodies—some shot in the back—sprawled over the equipment or leaned up against the bulkheads.

"I thought I should leave it the way we found it, sir," said Williams quietly. "I thought you should see it. These men were technicians, sir. None of them was armed."

"Yes," Sagan said. Brows contracted, his face gave no indication of his thoughts, but it seemed, from the shadowed eyes, that—battle-hardened as he was—the sight of the carnage affected him.

"I had posted guards in here, of course, my lord. One of them is alive, though I don't know for how long. I've heard his report, my lord. I respectfully submit that you hear it yourself."

In one corner, blood had gathered into a large pool that sloshed up gently against the bulkhead with the movement of *Defiant*. Sagan turned his gaze to Williams, who met the eyes stoically, unflinching.

"Yes," the Warlord said, "I would like to hear it."

··◆ ➡·

The wounded soldier struggled to rise when he saw his captain and the Warlord approach his bed. Sagan laid his hand upon a bandage-webbed shoulder, applying gentle pressure, easing the man back down. Despite the doctor's best efforts, the mattress beneath the man was soaked in blood. Crimson patches were beginning to stain the fresh bandage web that had been sprayed across the chest.

"Lie easy, Private"—Sagan glanced at the name above the bed—"Amahal. I understand you've made your report to Captain Williams already. I would like to hear it myself, if you feel up to it."

"Yes, my lord." The man's voice was weak. His eyes had the crystalline stare of sedation, but they were focused and clear, and though his words came slowly, they were coherent. The nerve block was strong; it had ended the pain but left the mind clear and in a relaxed state. Such drugs were not widely used; they tended to be highly addictive. That wouldn't be a problem for the young soldier.

"I was sent to guard the control room, my lord. There were three of us. We were watching the fighting on the deck. You could see it . . . from the viewport—" The soldier coughed, choked. A male nurse moved swiftly, turning the man's head, holding a pan underneath the mouth to catch the flow of blood. Williams averted his face, left to answer a call from the bridge. The Warlord waited patiently.

"Is that better so?" the nurse asked softly.

"Yes," the soldier whispered.

The nurse removed the pan, lifted a cloth soaked in cooling liquid, and started to cleanse the man's face. The Warlord took the cloth from the nurse's hands.

"Go on, soldier," he said, deftly wiping the pink-frothed lips. The wounded private shook his head feebly, embarrassed at his Warlord's performing such a menial task.

Wringing out the cloth, Sagan laved the man's feverish forehead and temples. The private shivered, flushed faintly with pleasure at the attention, his livid skin regaining a mockery of the life that was seeping from him.

"We heard . . . a banging on the hatch behind us. We thought it was . . . reinforcements. Baker opened it and . . . and there was a . . . a kid, my lord."

Sagan's hands jerked. Abruptly, he returned the cloth to the waiting nurse.

"A 'kid,' soldier?"

"A young man, my lord. He couldn't have been more than . . . sixteen or seventeen. He had red hair and he . . . was wearing a flight suit. Like he was dressed up for a costume party . . . maybe. He was holding this beam rifle . . ."

The private's voice faded. A spasm of pain contorted the face. The male nurse moved, bringing up a hypodermic. The Warlord closed his hand over the nurse's arm, stopping him.

"Continue, private."

"Baker told him . . . to go . . . play . . . somewhere else. The kid didn't say anything. He stepped inside, raised the rifle, and . . . fired."

Sagan removed his hand from the nurse's arm.

"The eyes . . ." the private whispered, his own widening in awe and horror. "I saw his eyes . . ."

The nurse started to administer the drug, saw it wouldn't be necessary. The froth on the ashen lips lay undisturbed. The Warlord murmured something beneath his breath.

"*Requiem aeternam dona eis, Domine—*"

"*—et lux perpetua luceat eis.*" The nurse's voice slid beneath Sagan's.

The Warlord glanced at the nurse in astonishment. The two of them were alone. A screen concealed the dying man from his fellows.

"I am one of the Order, my lord," the nurse said in a soft, low voice. "Many of us are, who serve in this capacity."

"The Order is dead, officially banned," Sagan said coldly.

"Yes, my lord," the male nurse replied. Slim, cool fingers rested for an instant on Sagan's left arm where, hidden beneath the body armor, self-inflicted scars cut deep into the flesh. "If you ever need us, my lord."

Drawing a sheet up over the body, the nurse moved on to his next patient.

His words were a whisper across the Warlord's confused thoughts. Sagan doubted, after a moment, if he'd even heard it or had, in his exhaustion, imagined it.

Williams returned, looked at the Warlord questioningly. Sagan knew he should make some response, but he felt stupefied from the news, his fatigue, the aftereffects of the stimulation shot that made him feel worse than he had before. Age was beginning to tell. He was, what . . . forty-eight? Not old at all for the Blood Royal, who generally lived far into their hundreds.

"I will burn up before then," he said to himself. Time was sliding through his fingers, like the liquid from that pink-stained cloth. Youth . . .

He could see Dion, standing in the entrance to the control room, the young man's eyes blue as flame.

··◄■ ■►··

"You understand now, my lord?" Williams asked in a quiet tone. They had arrived back on the bridge.

"Yes," Sagan said. "I understand. What happened to . . . the young man?"

"He apparently escaped in the confusion, my lord." Williams's mouth twisted, aware he was further damning himself.

"With the Lady Maigrey?"

"No, my lord. I don't believe so. The young man was spotted marching down the corridor, his gun trained on a black-skinned male. No one stopped him. After all, my lord, he was wearing our own uniform. We know he returned to his spaceplane. An officer reported seeing the young man and his prisoner helping a third, apparently wounded, person into the spaceplane. All three were wearing uniforms. The young man knew the correct codes and had the proper clearance."

Williams spread his hand deprecatingly. "By the time we received your instructions to take him prisoner, my lord, it was too late. His spaceplane had already been allowed to take off."

"You can relax, Captain." Sagan stretched, trying to ease the cramped muscles in the small of his back. "You won't receive a commendation for your actions, but you won't be penalized for them, either. You were up against forces beyond your ability to comprehend."

The statement was reassuring, though hardly complimentary. Williams's face reflected the knowledge that he had just seen all hopes of a swift and meteoric rise in his career plummet to the ground. He swallowed his protests, however; afraid, perhaps, of succumbing to a sudden "illness" as had the late Captain Nada.

"I wonder, my lord," Williams said instead, "why he did it."

"Did what, Captain?" Sagan's thoughts were far away, reaching out, probing.

"The senseless butchery, my lord! There was no need. He was armed. He'd caught them completely by surprise."

"Perhaps he tried. What would your men's response have been, Captain, if he'd asked them to open that hangar bay, allow the mercenaries to escape?"

Williams didn't hesitate. "They would have refused, my lord."

"There's your answer, Captain. First they insult him, then they won't take him seriously."

Williams remained unconvinced. "He could have insisted, coerced them. Most likely they would have done what he wanted. A man tends to, when he has a beam rifle pressed up against his skull. It was the act of a madman, my lord."

No, Sagan thought, it was the act of a young man who's mad as hell, frustrated as hell, and scared as hell. And he won! He pulled it off, by God! There might be more to that young man than I first suspected.

"You've activated the tracking device aboard the craft, of course."

"Yes, my lord. The plane has gone into hyperspace, but we will have a firm fix on it when it emerges and touches down."

"Excellent. And what of the Lady Maigrey?"

"Our belief is that she escaped with the other mercenaries, my lord. That call I received in sick bay was from the aide, Bennett's, interrogators. The sergeant major proved extremely stubborn, but my men were eventually able to learn that the lady was here and she was in contact with John Dixter. They spoke together in private at some length. Bennett was able to overhear them. The lady referred to a conversation she and the general had on Vangelis. She said, and I quote, my lord, 'I think I have found a way to deal with it.'"

"Anything else?"

"Dixter's response was a single word."

"And that was?"

Williams turned his back on the crew on the bridge. The Warlord did the same, both staring out the viewscreen at the remnants of *Phoenix* and the Corasian vessel, burning off the starboard bow.

"A word that he did not recognize. A rather unusual word. It sounded like 'ohme,' my lord."

Sagan glanced at the captain sharply, wondering if Williams truly did not know what he had just said. The Adonian weapons dealer was notorious, his name figuring prominently in the vidmags and among those interested in acquiring the capability of blowing their neighbors into small pieces. What was not supposed to be generally known was that the Warlord was dealing with him. Such knowledge had cost Nada his life.

This captain's face remained impassive, however. If Williams knew, he wasn't letting on—which had been Nada's mistake.

Not a bad officer, this captain, Sagan decided. I might forgive his stupidity . . . in time.

"Excuse me, my lord." One of the centurions advanced. "There is an urgent transmission for you—"

Probably from his dunderheaded commander-in-chief, President Peter Robes.

"Not now!" Sagan snapped.

"Begging your pardon, my lord," a communications officer struck in, looking extremely nervous, "but she says it is import—"

"*She!*" Sagan strode rapidly over to the console.

"No picture, my lord. Audio only."

"My lady. Track her!" Sagan added in an undertone.

"That won't be possible, my lord," Maigrey replied. "I am making the Jump in exactly one minute. I am communicating with you to tell you that I've left you a prisoner."

"A prisoner?" Sagan hadn't thought anything could astonish him further. Apparently he'd been wrong.

"Yes, my lord. The man is a prison guard, taking bribes from prisoners to help them escape, then sending them out in junk planes. I offer the following recording to be used as evidence in his court-martial."

What they heard was, Sagan eventually figured out, a recording of a transmission between Maigrey and a pilot in another plane. The recording was brief, as had been the young pilot's life.

"I trust you to see justice done, my lord."

"It will be, my lady," he said gravely.

She sounded very much like he felt. "Until we meet again . . . *Dominus tecum*—God be with you, my lord."

"Transmission ended, sir," the officer said.

The Warlord stood staring thoughtfully at the console, then turned on his heel. "I'll be in my quarters, Captain."

"Very good, my lord."

"I didn't really need to discover what she said to Dixter," Sagan said to himself, pondering. "I didn't have to drag her plans out of the unfortunate Bennett. I know what she intends to try to do. The Blood Royal surges in your veins, Maigrey, carrying its poison into your soul. You left Dion to his fate. You left John Dixter to die. Why? Because you can see and feel and sniff and taste the prize! Power! You want it as badly as I do. But what will you sell to gain it?

"Your soul, my lady? No matter. Your scheming will be all for nought. Because, in the end, you will bring the power to me. *Et cum spiritu tuo*—And His spirit be with you, my lady," Sagan added, beneath his breath, with the flicker of a smile.

Book II

Pearl of Great Price

Again, the kingdom of heaven is like unto a merchant man, seeking goodly pearls: who, when he found one pearl of great price, sold all that he had, and bought it.

St. Matthew, 13:45, 46

Chapter ·✦◗◖◗✦· One

Docebo iniquos vias tuas . . .
Then will I teach transgressors Thy ways . . .
Gregorio Allegri, *Miserere*

The Warlord sat in a chair in his temporary quarters aboard *Defiant*. He was relaxed, eyes closed, listening to music from his past. The chanting of male voices filled the air around him; he seemed to breathe them in. The simultaneous combination of the parts of the sacred text each formed an individual melody, harmonizing with the others, the deep bass of the men counterpointed by the sweet, searing tenor of youth. The *Miserere*, by Allegri. Late sixteenth century. Nine voices.

"*Miserere mei, Deus, secundum magnam misericordiam tuam.*" "Have mercy upon me, O God, according to Thy loving kindness."

The voices, like those of the Sirens, took hold of Sagan with melodic hands, drew him back to a time when he had been most deeply happy, most profoundly miserable—the first twelve years of his life. He had been raised in a monastery, raised by the monks as an atonement for the sins of a brother, raised in silence by a priest-father, who, from the day his little son was born, never spoke a word to him or to anyone.

"*Ecce enim in iniquitatibus conceptus sum; et in peccatis concepit me mater mea.*" "Behold, I was shapen in iniquity; and in sin did my mother conceive me."

That part was true enough. A High Priest of the Order of Adamant, enamored of a nobleman's daughter, finds his lust overwhelms him. Forswearing his vows of chastity, he slips out of the monastery walls, meets the object of his lust, embraces her. One night is enough to quench his ardor. Filled with remorse, he forsakes the girl and returns to hide within the monastery walls. But his seed has been planted. Nine months later, he discovers the bitter fruit, wrapped in linen, placed at the monastery door.

Confessing all, he removes himself from his high office, casts upon himself a vow of silence and of isolation. From that night forth, his brethren see him only at prayers or silently performing the meanest, most degrading tasks in the small community. The scandal is hushed up, the nobleman's daughter removed to a far-distant planet. The child is taken in, hidden from the world behind stone walls, raised in cool darkness and reverent prayer.

"*Ne projicias me a facie tua; et spiritum sanctum tuum ne auferas a me.*" "Cast me not away from Thy presence; and take not Thy Holy Spirit from me."

Sagan formed the words with his lips, the melody echoing in his heart. What had brought him to remember all this? Perhaps meeting the young monk serving as a male nurse aboard *Defiant*. The Warlord should have had faith; he should have known the Order could not die, though its members had been slaughtered during the revolution. It had gone underground, sunk into the darkness with which it was most familiar, and grew there as the child grows in the womb, waiting impatiently for the light.

Sagan had been twelve when the king, old Starfire himself, received word (rumor had it that Sagan's mother revealed the truth) that a child of the Blood Royal was being raised apart from the world, hidden in a monastery, without proper teaching. Not even the king's arm could have reached into the closed stone walls, for the church was a strong power. But the father had seen his son's extraordinary gifts. The priest made it known that he wanted the boy educated, trained to use the quicksilver mind, the "magic" of the Blood Royal. Sagan had been removed from the stone walls.

That night, his last night, was the one and only time in his life he wept, and that had been alone, shut in his monk's cell, in the candlelit darkness. For days after, he had burned with the shame of the memory.

"*Sacrificium Deo spiritus contribulatus* . . ." "The sacrifices of God are a broken spirit . . ."

At the Royal Academy for Men, created especially for the sons of the Blood Royal, Derek Sagan was the most brilliant student and the most disliked. He had seen from his first days how far above the rest he was, not only in intelligence but in mental and physical discipline. Tall, strong, powerful, he bested the others in every test. Aloof, brooding, proud-spirited, charismatic, he could have made them love him.

He preferred it that they hate him.

". . . *cor contritum et humiliatum Deus non despicies.*" "A broken and a contrite heart, O God, Thou wilt not despise."

And then had come the fair-haired child—a girl, wild as a catamount, daughter of a barbarian warrior father who flew to his enemies in spaceships, landed, and attacked them on horseback. Sent to the Royal Academy for Women, she had been expelled at the age of six for attempting to stab the headmistress.

As a last resort, she had been sent to the male branch of the Academy, to live with her elder brother—a gentle young man, who took after their dead mother, and who had been re-nounced by their father. Of course, the Creator's hand could be detected moving in all these events. It was here, at the Royal Academy, the masters had discovered that the pale-haired girl and the dark-souled boy were connected by the rare phenomenon occurring occasionally in the Blood Royal—the mind-link.

"My lord."

The voice broke in harshly and discordantly, disrupting his music and his thoughts. Sagan looked up. It was the captain of his guard, and the matter must be urgent, or the man would not have disturbed him.

"What is it?"

"The President asks to speak to you, my lord."

Sagan felt himself tense, as before a battle. He'd been expecting this summons. He could have, undoubtedly should have, reported directly to the President earlier. But he had decided to wait, preferred to make Robes come to him. That, at least, is what he told himself. But the adrenaline quickening his heartbeat, the tingling in his blood, forced him to admit that perhaps he'd been putting off this interview for another reason.

This meeting would confirm his fears. And if he found them to be true, it would set in motion the rock that might eventually bring down the entire side of the mountain. He would either end up standing on top or be buried beneath the rubble.

The psalm ended as he left his quarters.

"*Tunc imponent super altare tuum vitulos.*" "Then shall they offer bullocks upon Thine altar."

·◄■ ■►··

"Citizen General Sagan."

"Mr. President."

"I suppose congratulations are in order. The news media are hailing you a hero."

Sagan shrugged, indifferent, though in truth it had been his own publicity agents who had circulated the reports, emphasizing the fact that his forces had been badly outnumbered, enlarging upon his own daring in sailing his dying ship into the enemy cruiser. Negotiations were under way for the movie; someone was writing a book.

The people needed a hero—a fact Sagan was shrewd enough to realize. The revolution had been extremely popular, but it was seventeen years ago. The people of the galaxy had lost their king, were now stuck with a Congress whose myriad members seemed to do little but argue and bicker and run for reelection.

Their President—first viewed as a political reformer, an intellectual who was still "one of us"—had become too much like one of them. The people were bored with him. They were tired of the myth of democracy, frustrated at being told they could make a difference when they knew damn good and well that they couldn't, and they were irritated at being constantly reminded that whatever was currently wrong in the galaxy was their fault.

Sagan was a hero to a galaxy that desperately needed heroes, desperately wanted a strong father figure to pat them on the head, assure them that they needn't worry anymore. They could close their eyes and go to sleep; he was here to protect them. And once they were asleep . . .

"Of course," President Robes said, with a hint of rebuke and a martyred expression, "*I* am the one who has to go before the Congress and the news media and explain the loss of a star cruiser."

The matter was of little concern to the Warlord. The cost of a star cruiser was so astronomical that the concept sailed right over the head of the average citizen.

"Perhaps, Mr. President," the Warlord said, keeping a close watch on Robes's face, "you should go before the people and explain how it was the Corasians managed to have made such remarkable technological advances over the years, advances that obviously required assistance. You might explain how our spy network was completely—or should I say conveniently—blind to the Corasian military buildup."

Peter Robes was looking particularly dapper in a brown cashmere suit that had a whisper of blue stripe in the fabric, a dark blue silk tie, and a matching handkerchief. His hair was groomed, his makeup perfect. He performed a sad smile, indicative of a fond parent's tolerance for an ingenious, albeit misguided, child.

"I've read the reports of some of your allegations in the more lurid of the newsvids, Derek. I know what they're worth, of course. I won't give them credence by denying them. Yet, I must admit, you hurt me deeply. We have been friends a long time, Derek. A long time."

The Warlord thought back to the days when, as a young revolutionary, he had actually admired the idealistic professor, who had led the rebellion against an aging and ineffective king. Sagan experienced no pang of regret or remorse, however. The Robes who stood before him was a shell of that man, a husk sucked dry. A monkey, dancing to his master's song.

And, as he watched closely, Sagan saw the monkey's eyes slide away from the Warlord, focus on something in a corner of the room not visible to the vid lens. The glance was swift and it darted back to Sagan again. The Warlord would have missed it if he hadn't been watching for it, waiting for it. The glance confirmed what he had suspected. The monkey's master was present.

What was Robes doing—asking Abdiel for help? Or merely seeking approbation? Whichever it was, he apparently got what he needed, for he switched roles, readjusting his features from the sorrowful mien of betrayed friend to the firm, brusque, and strong commander-in-chief.

"Citizen General, you will at once relinquish command to Admiral Aks and prepare to return to the capital. The Congress has requested that you make your report in person. Citizeness Maigrey Morianna and the young man who calls himself Dion Starfire and is purportedly the son of the late criminal against the people will accompany you. The citizeness will stand trial for her royalist activities. The young man will, we hope, embrace our democratic principles and make a statement to the effect that he denounces his parents and all for which they stood. When may we expect you, the young man, and the citizeness?"

When hell freezes over.

"I deeply regret," Sagan said aloud, "that circumstances do not permit me to comply with your request, Mr. President."

Robes's coral-touched lips tightened; his eyes did a fine job of icily glinting. "That wasn't a request, Citizen General. It was a command."

"All the more reason for me to regret that I won't be able to obey."

And though Robes was putting on a wonderful performance of outraged indignation, Sagan was interested to observe that his refusal had come as no surprise.

"What possible excuse—"

"If I may, Mr. President. The situation in this part of the galaxy is far too volatile for me to absent myself from my duties. The Corasians have been beaten and beaten badly, but their attack might have been a feint. And second, it is impossible for me to transport the Lady Maigrey to the capital. Both she and the young man, Dion Starfire, escaped during the battle."

This news did come as a surprise. Sagan saw Robes's eyes shift once more to the corner of the room. He received some sort of answer, for his attention almost immediately returned to Sagan.

"Indeed, Citizen General. *This* news was not released to the press. I foresee a drop for you in the popularity polls once the word gets out."

"I purposefully withheld it, Mr. President, not to aggrandize myself, but because . . ." Sagan hesitated. So much depended on this. Win or lose on a single throw.

"Yes? Because what, Citizen General?"

The Warlord cast the lure. "I know where the Lady Maigrey has fled, Mr. President. We will be able to capture her again only if she is lulled into a false sense of security."

Again the eyes fled to the corner and back again.

"Where has she gone, Citizen General?"

The bait hit the water. "The planet Laskar, Mr. President."

Robes affected astonishment nicely. "Why would she go to that hellhole? She's not drug-addicted, is she, Derek?"

"Hardly, Mr. President. I have no idea why she has gone there." That was a lie.

Robes knew it was a lie. "Is the boy with her?"

"I don't believe so. I have no idea where the boy is, Mr. President." Another lie.

Again he wasn't believed, but then he hadn't expected to be

believed. Let them chase after Maigrey. Sagan would keep his eye on Dion, keep the boy safe. The Warlord had his spies; he knew where the boy was, who was with him. All he had to do anytime was to reach out his hand, grab the young man's collar, and drag him back. Right now, however, he had far more urgent matters.

"We are extremely disappointed in you, Citizen General," President Robes said with a nicely timed sigh. "I regret to have to do this, but you leave me no choice. A military tribunal will be convened. You will either appear before it voluntarily to answer for your conduct or, if you do not appear, I will be forced to place you under arrest."

The Warlord almost smiled at this fanfaronade—the idea was ludicrous—but he recalled that Abdiel was sitting in the corner . . . watching . . . listening . . . and the cold fear in Sagan's bowels froze his amusement. He bowed silently.

"You are dismissed, Citizen General." Robes's voice and demeanor were mantled with offended dignity. The image faded from the vidscreen, leaving it dark.

The Warlord, standing before it, would have given five years of his life to be able to eavesdrop on the conversation he was aware must follow. Then, on reflection, he decided he wouldn't. He knew what Abdiel would do now.

Or thought he did.

Chapter ·•❄◯❄•· Two

Questo e luogo di lacrime!
Giacomo Puccini, *Tosca*

With consciousness came the crushing realization that he was not dead.

John Dixter opened eyes whose lids were heavy and gritty, as if they'd had sand piled on top of them. He lay in a hospital bed located in a tiny, harshly lit, steel-sided room, chilling to the spirit and the flesh. A dull pain throbbed in his head. He was naked; his clothes were nowhere in sight. His wrists hurt. He tried to move them, discovered his hands were clamped firmly to the sides of the bed. Same with his ankles. Shivering, he hunched down beneath the white, antiseptic blankets, shut his eyes, and swore silently, bitterly.

How long had he been here? He had no idea. Every time he came to, they injected him with something. Drifting in and out of a drug-induced semiconsciousness, he seemed to have spent most of his waking hours trying to catch hold of reality, only to watch it flutter away on bright butterfly wings into a hazy sky.

He recalled vaguely that someone kept asking him questions. The questions must have been extremely funny, or perhaps it was the thought that he would answer them that had been funny. He remembered nothing about them except laughing uproariously, laughing until tears came to his eyes.

The vibrations from a voice, speaking with unnecessary loudness, resounded on one of the damaged nerves in his head, sent a sharp flash of pain through his skull. He grimaced, bit back a groan, and waited, tense and rigid, for the male nurse to come at him with the hypo. He saw the nurse start toward the bed, but this time the doctor intercepted him.

"No, no. Not today. We're expecting company. Inform his

112

lordship that the prisoner, Dixter, has regained his full faculties and is able to speak with him now."

"Yes, Doctor," another voice responded. Boots rang on steel; there was the clink of armor. Someone was talking into a commlink.

Dixter squirmed around as best he could, opened his eyes a slit, and focused on the guard, on the lasgun he wore at his side. There'll come a time when they have to release me from my bindings—escort me to the bathroom, for example, he thought. A lunge . . . the guard taken by surprise . . . firing at me at point-blank range . . .

It would all be over in a flash.

Brisk hands took hold of him, turned him deftly from his side onto his back. Dixter made a reflexive attempt to jerk his arms free, but the metal cut into his flesh, bruised his wrists.

"Now, now," the doctor said, "we'll injure ourselves if we keep that up. Rest. Relax."

Dixter glared up into a weasel-nosed face, a high forehead topped by slicked-back, thinning hair, and a smile that was right out of the medical books—either under the chapter labeled "Bedside Manner" or the one titled "The Outward, Visible Signs of Rigor Mortis."

"I'm Doctor Giesk," the man continued. "You sustained a rather nasty bump on the head, with subsequent concussion, but you're going to be fine . . . er"—the doctor glanced at a name overhead—"John. Now, let's have a look at you."

"Is that why you drugged me?" At least that's what he wanted to say. His tongue stuck to the roof of his mouth. The words came out an unintelligible mumble.

"Water? Is that what we want, John? The drugs do leave a rather foul taste in our mouth, don't they? Just a moment, though, until I've examined you."

Bound hand and foot, Dixter had to submit to being poked and prodded, having bright lights flashed painfully in his eyes, and hearing this weasel call him by his given name.

"Here, now, let's see if we can keep some water down—"

Dixter averted his face. "Giesk," he said thickly, talking slowly, forcing his swollen tongue and stiff lips to form the words. "I remember that name. Weren't you sentenced to be executed on Mescopolis?"

The doctor raised a deprecating eyebrow. "That trial was a travesty of justice. Now, open wide—"

Dixter gagged, coughed, and continued talking. The words

came easier all the time. "Experimenting on the bodies of patients who weren't exactly dead yet. I believe that was the charge, wasn't it?"

Giesk sniffed. "Laymen take such a narrow-minded view of research. The advances I made in medical technology have yet to be matched—"

A steel panel slid aside. The centurion posted in the room came to attention, saluting, fist over heart.

"That will do, Giesk." The Warlord entered, followed by his Honor Guard. "How is the patient?"

"As well as can be expected, my lord. He has a small crack in the occipital—"

"Thank you, Giesk." Sagan made a gesture with his hand. "You have leave to step outside for a moment, Doctor."

"Yes, my lord. Certainly, my lord."

"Captain, take your men, wait for me in the corridor. I am not to be disturbed."

"Yes, my lord." The centurion wheeled, marched his men out. The steel panel slid shut behind them. The Warlord advanced to the controls, sealed it.

Dixter's body tensed; one of the muscles in his legs shook with an involuntary tremor. He forced himself to lie still, feeling the sweat chill on his body.

Sagan came back to stand by the bed, moving slowly, taking his time. To divert his thoughts from what he guessed would be an unpleasant few moments, Dixter studied the Warlord curiously. The face was stern and grim as ever, but the general noted that the lines were deeper, darker, the eyes more shadowed. The tight skin sagged around the jaw, denoting fatigue, the high-planed cheekbones seemed to have sunken. He was clad, not in his customary armor, but in soft, red robes that fell in long folds from a golden pin done in the shape of a phoenix, clasped at the shoulder.

"Water?" The Warlord lifted a plastic bottle that had been fitted with a tube for drinking.

"No." Dixter swallowed painfully, shook his head.

"It may be a long interview," Sagan said wryly.

The general reconsidered, nodded. The Warlord held the bottle to Dixter's lips. Dixter took a long pull, swallowed, took another to moisten his mouth and lips. "Thank you," he muttered gruffly.

The Warlord replaced the bottle on the bedstand, stood silent, staring down thoughtfully at the general. Sagan's right arm bent at the elbow, rested against his abdomen. The left arm was extended, held in relaxed posture at his side.

"They tell me you have a high resistance to the interrogation drug, John Dixter."

"Was that what it was?" he inquired politely. "I thought you'd sent in comedians to entertain me."

"Yes, I understand you found it all quite amusing. *'Questo e luogo di lacrime!'* Do you recognize the quote?"

Dixter shook his head.

"I thought you might. It's from the Lady Maigrey's favorite opera—*Tosca*, by Puccini. *'Questo e luogo di lacrime!'* 'This is a place for tears!' Cavarodossi, the hero, has been arrested by a powerful baron and brought to his torture chambers. The hero—like you—considers his arrest a laughing matter. The baron warns him with that line of what is to come. Quite a fascinating opera, *Tosca*. Puccini's audiences didn't know what to make of it. There were no suffering kings and queens, to which they were accustomed. No. Only a singer and her lover and the libertine baron, who tortures her lover while Tosca is forced to watch."

Dixter had the impression Sagan was saying something important here, something dangerous, but the general's brain seemed to be still chasing butterflies, for he could make nothing of it. He shifted restlessly beneath the blankets.

Sagan noted the movement, eyed the man speculatively. "We are both soldiers, Dixter. We've known each other a long time. There may be animosity between us, but there is also—I believe—respect?"

"It was an old dictum of yours, Sagan. Respect your enemy," Dixter said heavily, making a feeble gesture with his bound hand. "That . . . trap. It was all for my benefit, wasn't it?"

"Yes, it was all for your benefit, but don't flatter yourself, General. You didn't do anything clever. You simply asked too many questions. After all, what did it really matter to you who supplied that torpedo boat to the Vangelis government?"

Dixter sighed. "You could have dealt with me anytime. Captured me—"

"When? Prior to the battle? No, I needed your people to help me win it. After, if you remember, I had you arrested. Your people freed you. You might say they brought their doom upon themselves."

"You would never have let them go."

Sagan shrugged. "Perhaps not. At any rate, I succeeded in my objectives. All of them."

Questions burned on Dixter's lips, but he didn't dare ask them. Patience, he counseled himself, fidgeting beneath the blankets, trying to ease the cramp in his leg. Looking up, he saw the Warlord watching him intently, a slight smile on the thin lips. The general had the uncomfortable impression that every thought passing through his head had been duly noted by those dark, shadowed eyes.

"You discovered information on Vangelis concerning the alien, Snaga Ohme. You passed that information along to the Lady Maigrey, didn't you?"

Dixter blinked, kept his expression bland. "I don't recall that the subject ever came up between us."

"Come, come, John Dixter. You don't expect me to believe that you two spent all that time together alone on Vangelis discussing old times." The Warlord's left hand lowered to the bed; the fingers began to idly run back and forth over the sheets near the general's bound arm.

"That's it, I'm afraid, Derek." Dixter smiled pleasantly. "We had a lot to talk about. It had been a long time since we'd seen . . . each other. . . ." His voice died. He was silent, remembering.

"We've interrogated your aide," the Warlord continued, as if he hadn't heard. "What's the sergeant major's name? Bennett?"

Dixter's head snapped up. "Bennett doesn't know anything! Let him go. It's me you want!"

"Oh, you'll have your turn, John Dixter." Sagan's hand moved from the sheet to the general's bound arm. His fingers brushed against the skin, their touch hot against the man's cold flesh.

Dixter flinched involuntarily, gritted his teeth.

"But not just now. Not just yet." The Warlord opened his right hand. A crumpled, bloodstained handkerchief slowly unfolded in the harsh light like the petals of a flower. Dixter, caught off guard, stared at it, realized too late his recognition must be obvious on his face.

"Maigrey seems to have left this behind," Sagan said. "I will return it to her . . . at my earliest opportunity."

"No need." Dixter kept his voice even. "It's not hers. It's mine."

"All the more reason for her to cherish it." The Warlord's fist closed over the handkerchief, crushing it.

This is a place for tears. . . . The libertine baron, who tortures her lover while Tosca is forced to watch. Suddenly Dixter understood what was to be his fate, how he would be used. Slowly, he shook his head.

"Maigrey's a soldier. She's seen men die before."

"But not one she loves." The Warlord leaned near. "And it will take you a long time to die, John Dixter. A long time."

Dixter was master of himself now. Calmly, he looked up. "Watching a man she loves die with honor may be easier for her than watching one she loves live in dishonor."

The thrust hit home, though Dixter knew it only by the flicker of fire in Sagan's dark eyes, not by any change in the man's stance or facial expression.

"You refuse to cooperate, John Dixter?"

"What else did you expect, Derek?" Dixter was tired. His head ached, he wanted this conversation to end.

"I leave you with one final thought. I know where Lady Maigrey has gone, what she plans. But an enemy awaits her on Laskar, one of which she knows nothing. The foe she will face on that planet is one far beyond her strength. I wonder if she realizes . . ."

The Warlord fell silent, his thoughts and his attention turned inward, as if listening for some faraway voice. Apparently he didn't hear it, for his attention snapped back to Dixter. "Any information you could give me about what she knows, what she plans to do, might enable me to save her—"

"*Save* her! You're almost as funny as your other clowns, Sagan. Thanks for the attempt to raise my level of musical knowledge." Dixter leaned his head back against the pillow, closed his eyes. "Shut the door on your way out, will you?"

The Warlord remained standing near him. Dixter could almost feel the dark eyes on him, could almost feel them try to peel the skin from him, to see inside. The mental flaying was nearly as painful as a physical one. It took an effort to keep his eyes shut.

And then Sagan was gone. Dixter heard the whisper of the robes against the deck, the slap of an open palm against the controls, the soft whoosh of the panel sliding open.

Robes rustled; Sagan had turned. "I'll leave you with a name. I'm sure it's one you'll recognize: Abdiel."

He walked away. The booted feet of the centurion resuming his duties entered. The panel slid shut.

John Dixter opened his eyes, stared at the ceiling.

He's lying! he told himself desperately. It's nothing but a trick, a trick to make me talk. Abdiel is dead. . . .

Dixter's hands clenched. The metal bonds cut into his flesh, leaving red spots of blood on the sterile sheets.

··◁■ ■▷··

Outside the general's cell, Dr. Giesk and the Warlord observed the man's agony through one-way steelglass.

"Shall I order another injection, my lord? We might have much better success this time."

"No, there's no need," Sagan said, turning away, borrowing another quote from the Baron von Scarpia. "'*Morde il veleno.*'"

"My lord?"

"'My poison is working.'"

Chapter ··◦◦◦◦◦·· Three

. . . there was a way to Hell, even from the gates of heaven.

John Bunyan, *The Pilgrim's Progress*

"Like I was saying, Tusk, Dixter's alive! The Warlord's holding him hostage aboard *Defiant*."

"Hostage for what?" Tusk demanded irritably, not liking Link's superior attitude.

Link tilted back in his chair, planted his boots on the table, and spread his hands. "You got me!" he said, looking over at Dion and winking.

Dion had leapt to his feet. "What if—"

"Forget it, kid. Just forget it!" Tusk leaned over, muttered savagely to Link, "Why the hell did you bring that up in front of him?"

"He's got a right to know." Link folded his hands over his chest, fingers intertwined. "Well, well! Look who's here!" he added, grinning. Nola stood framed in the doorway. "Aren't we looking lovely today."

"Shove it, Link," the woman said.

"How's your shoulder?" Tusk asked.

"It hurts. Dion, there's some character down below says he's got a message for you."

"For me?" Dion frowned.

"The Warlord," Tusk said, rising to his feet. "C'mon, Link. We'll deal with the—"

"Have them bring him up," Dion ordered.

"Kid, I—"

"Have them bring him up, please."

Nola shrugged, disappeared. Tusk scowled, but said nothing, and marched over to stare out the slit in the wall that represented a window.

The mercenaries had returned to the stone fortress on Vangelis. Some had argued against going back there. Sagan himself had been to the fortress. He knew exactly where it was, what its defenses were like. But it was precisely these defenses that argued for it. Built on top of a cliff jutting up from the flat desert floor, the fortress allowed those within an unobstructed view of the land for kilometers around it. A mouse would have been visible, making its small way across the barren rock beneath the cloudless cobalt blue sky.

It had been seventy-two hours since the mercenaries had managed to escape the Warlord's trap. Their spaceplanes dotted the landscape around the fortress proper. They took up positions inside and waited grimly for Sagan to come and finish them off.

He hadn't shown up, however, and Tusk had been spending a lot of his time wondering why. Now, with Link's news, he had a good idea. Sagan didn't need to bother. He had captured their general and the Warlord knew that Dixter's people would never allow him to remain a prisoner.

Perhaps this "character's" arrival was the opening of negotiations.

Fidgeting, Tusk left the window, paced the stone floor. Located on the upper level of the fortress, the room was large and open to the air, since rainfall was so scarce as to be practically nonexistent. A battered wooden table stood in the center, surrounded by chairs in various stages of dilapidation. Link took his lasgun from its holster, casually placed it on the table in front of him.

"Tusk?" Nola's voice.

"Yeah, we're ready. Bring him in."

The door was shoved open. Nola and two of the mercenaries entered, escorting a hooded and robed figure between them.

"We spotted him coming in a 'copter. We'd have shot him down, only he broadcast he was a messenger. We scanned him and the chopper before we let him land. Both clean, no explosives. Once he was on the ground, he said he had a message for the kid here."

The mercenaries held the man by the arms, not gently. The man stood quietly, calmly, unmoving. His face, except for the eyes, was hidden behind the folds of a kaffiyeh; not unusual, the headgear was worn by many in the deserts of Vangelis.

There was something odd about the eyes, Tusk thought. He'd never seen eyes so completely devoid of expression.

He leaned over to Dion. "The guy's blind!"

Dion regarded the messenger intently.

"I'm Dion Starfire. What message have you brought me?"

The man reacted to the sound of the voice much like a person who is blind. But, turning to face Dion, the messenger's eyes focused on the young man and it was obvious that he could see. He didn't, however, appear to be much interested.

A 'droid? Tusk wondered. No. 'Droids had more life programmed into them than this.

"My message is for Dion Starfire," the man said in a voice that was even, calm, and flat. "Alone."

"We're his friends," Tusk growled, sitting down, making it clear he intended to stay seated.

Dion's frown deepened, the blue eyes gleamed in the brilliant sunshine pouring into the room, the red hair seemed ablaze. "Nola isn't feeling well. Link, will you and the others take her downstairs?"

"Dion," Tusk leaned over to whisper, "admittedly this creep doesn't look like much, but we might need some backup." He added aloud, "Link, you stay—"

"Link, please take Nola back to the sick bay."

Nola seemed about to protest. Link was on his feet, apparently prepared to humor the kid, but looking at Tusk for command. Tusk saw Dion's jaw clench, saw the expression of imperious, almost petulant decision harden the youthful face.

"The kid's the boss," Tusk said, feeling uncomfortable, not certain how to handle this new side of the young man. "The message is for him, after all."

Link, shrugging in his easy, nonchalant manner, took his gun from the table, thrust it into its holster. He detoured around the messenger, who did not move and who might have been mistaken for one of the room's wooden support posts.

"Come, my dear. I'll put you to bed." Link grinned, slid his arm around Nola's waist.

Nola cast a troubled glance over her shoulder at Tusk but allowed herself to be led away. The other mercenaries followed.

"Tusk, check the door."

"What the— Kid, they're your friends!"

"Please check the door."

Tusk, grumbling, rose to his feet to do as he was told and was startled to find Link lounging just outside.

"I thought you went with Nola," Tusk said.

"She gave me the brush. She's been bitchy ever since she got hit. I figured I might hang around out here, make sure you two didn't get into any trouble."

"Uh, thanks, but I . . . uh . . . I'd really appreciate it if you looked after Nola."

"Sure. I'm easy." Link sauntered off.

Tusk, frowning, puzzled, returned to the room. "What do you make of that?"

"Simple." As Dion spoke to him, his eyes remained fixed on the messenger. "How do you think he knew the Warlord was holding Dixter?"

Tusk stared at him, gawking. "Link? A spy! No! C'mon, kid!"

Dion didn't respond. He signaled Tusk to be silent, spoke to the messenger.

"We're alone. What do you have to say to me?"

"I was ordered to give my message to you alone—"

"Tusk stays or you leave. Which is it?" The young man's tone was pleasant, but there was no doubting his resolve.

The messenger acquiesced with a slight inclination of his head. "The message is from the Lady Maigrey Morianna. It is by word of mouth and given to me only. She asked me to speak thus: 'Dion Starfire, I am in danger and in need of your help. Meet me on the planet Laskar. This man knows where I can be found.' That is the end.".

Tusk snorted. "A trap!" But Dion closed his hand tightly over the mercenary's arm, counseling silence.

"By 'this man' I presume she means you?"

The messenger again inclined his head.

His actions, his voice, everything about this guy gave Tusk the creeps. Tusk stared at him, trying to figure it out, when he suddenly realized what it was. The guy's eyes didn't have the sightless stare of the blind, they had the sightless stare of the dead! No life in them, behind them. No thought, no feeling.

A shiver rippled up Tusk's spine. His mother would have said someone was standing on his grave. He appreciated Dion's touch, suddenly, glad to feel someone warm and alive. He noted that the young man kept his hand on his arm, as if he'd experienced the same uncanny sensations.

"Where did you see Lady Morianna?" Tusk demanded.

The man slowly pivoted his head, turned the dead eyes to Tusk, and the mercenary was immediately sorry he'd drawn attention to himself.

"I may say nothing more than that which I have been bidden to say."

"Are we to come with you?"

"I travel before you, Dion Starfire. I am to return immediately. You will come when you may, though it should be soon. Apprise no one of your plans or your destination."

"Thank you," Dion said, removing his hand from Tusk's arm, making a gesture of dismissal.

The man did not stir. "May I inform the Lady Maigrey Morianna of your decision?"

"I will come, of course."

"Dion!" Tusk protested, scandalized. "It's phony! This guy's phony!"

"Maigrey could be in trouble—"

"Yeah! So an experienced warrior, who's fought more battles than you have zits, calls for help from a seventeen-year-old kid! Sure, I'll buy that all day long!"

Dion's face burned. "Tell Lady Maigrey I will be there."

The messenger seemed neither pleased nor the reverse at the decision. Whether the young man stayed or went or shot him where he stood appeared to be a matter of complete indifference to the robed and hooded figure. He waited a moment to ascertain if more information was forthcoming. Finding it was not, he walked out of the room without a word.

"Shit!" Tusk swore, banging his fist on the table.

"You don't have to go."

"I do so!"

"Don't give me that crap about being my Guardian!" Dion turned, suddenly furious.

"I don't like it any better than you do, but I got no goddam choice! Even if I'm not your Guardian, I'm your friend and, kid, don't you see? It's a trap!"

"Then who set it?" Dion shouted back. He glanced outside, lowered his voice. "The Warlord?" he asked in an undertone.

Tusk opened his mouth, snapped it shut again. "Not likely!" he muttered, after a moment's thought. "Sagan wouldn't believe you'd be stupid enough to fall for that line."

Dion paled in anger, spoke with controlled effort. "No, it

couldn't have been Sagan. The messenger's arrival obviously
caught Link by surprise—"

"You don't know for certain that Link's a spy for the
Warlord. The guy's a blowhard, sure, but he's not a traitor—"

"He'd do anything for money. And he probably doesn't see
any harm in getting paid just to keep an eye on me or to repeat
'rumors.' All the more reason"—Dion moved to stand close to
Tusk—"for us to get out of here."

Tusk mumbled something, scowled.

"Besides," Dion continued, "there's a chance the message
could be legitimate. She might really need me." The voice
grew grim. "After all, she saw me in action."

Not by half, she didn't, thought Tusk, remembering with
the same sense of shock he'd felt on board *Defiant* seeing Dion
coming toward him, flight suit spattered with blood and that
strange, exultant madness in the blue eyes.

The boy waited—not for Tusk to say yes, they would go or
no, they wouldn't. He was waiting merely to see if Tusk agreed
to come along. If not, Dion would go alone and there would be
nothing, short of knocking the kid out and tying him to a tree,
that would stop him.

That or tipping off the Warlord.

Damn! My brain's fried! Tusk thought. How could I think of
such a thing? It was that walking corpse of a messenger. . . .

"Well?" Dion said. "Are you coming with me or are you
going to stay here with . . . Link?"

Tusk heard the subtle pause. The kid knows what I'm
thinking! Jeez, what next?

"I should stay!" Tusk retorted. "This is the worst thing you
could do, kid. The very worst. You're right! I'd sooner send
you to Sagan!"

"But you won't." Dion shook his red mane of hair.

"You know damn good and well I won't! I've never yet done
what I shoulda done. I guess there's no reason to start now."

"That's not why."

"No? Then I'd appreciate hearing what is!"

The boy's sensual lips curved to a slow smile. "Whether you
like it or not, you're my Guardian."

"Which makes you my goddam king? Fuck it! The real
reason is that I wouldn't hand a devil dartworm over to the
Warlord! I wouldn't hand"—Tusk gestured wildly—"Link over
to the Warlord! Especially now that he's got Dixter. What do
we do about the general, anyway?"

"Taking Dixter hostage is not for our benefit," Dion said softly. His face was grave. The blue eyes looked far away. "We can't do anything about that now, Tusk. All the more need to reach Lady Maigrey on Laskar."

"Yeah, well, if she's anywhere within ten thousand light-years of Laskar, I'll eat my socks."

Dion ignored him. "Good, let's get going. We'll slip out after dark, when Link's likely to be good and drunk. Would Nola come with us, do you think? We could use a gunner."

"Sure, she'll come."

Dion walked over to the door, realized Tusk wasn't following, and turned around. "What is it now?" the young man demanded impatiently.

"Oh, nothing much," Tusk said airily. "Just a small matter of money. How do you plan to fund this expedition, kid? That fancy prototype plane of yours sucks down fuel faster'n Link sucks down jump-juice. We're gonna need food, gear, cash to spend finding a place to park on Laskar—a city *not* known for its low standard of living!"

Dion opened his mouth, shut it again. Crimson flushed his cheeks. "I hadn't thought of that."

"Yeah, well. Most heroes don't. XJ keeps my credit line tied up with a security code lock. No way I can touch it, even if I had any credit left, which I don't. What about you?"

Dion was obviously embarrassed, frustrated. "I'm no help, I'm afraid—"

Tusk stood scratching his head, figuring. "You might be, kid, at that. You might be, after all. That fancy plane of yours's got a lot of little extras on board. We'll strip it to the bare bones, make a trip to the nearest pawnshop—"

"Strip my plane!" Dion caught Tusk's baleful eye, subsided. "That's . . . that's a good idea. Will the money we get be enough?"

"No. But I know how to make more." Strolling forward, Tusk slipped his arm through the boy's, talked confidentially as they walked out the door. "That system of yours for calculating odds on ante-up hands . . . it work every time?"

"It's mathematically sound, but—"

"Mathematically sound. Good, kid." Tusk patted the young man on the arm. "I like the ring of that. Mathematically sound. We'll find Link. Let's hope Sagan paid him in advance. The Warlord doesn't know it, but he's about to fund a trip to Laskar."

·-◄■ ■►-·

"Your ladyship."

"Yes, XJ?"

"We are coming out of the Jump, approaching the planet Laskar."

"Eighteen. Nineteen. Twenty! Thank you, XJ." Maigrey ceased her exercising, fell back on the deck with a groan, and lay still, breathing deeply. Exerting herself, she removed the weights from around her wrists and ankles, performed several stretching exercises to relieve the tightness in her muscles. Finally, mopping her face with a towel, she slid down the ladder to the bridge, strapped herself into the pilot's chair in readiness for the maneuver known as the "Jump back."

"Heart rate, one eighty," observed the computer. "That's high for a . . . um . . . woman." XJ appeared slightly confused.

"A woman *my age*?" Maigrey grinned and tossed the towel down onto the deck. "Don't worry," she added, seeing the computer's glassy eye swiveling toward the towel disapprovingly. "I'll tidy up the place after the Jump."

"You *have* been overexerting yourself, your ladyship—"

"It beats thinking." And she wouldn't think, not about anything but the situation at hand.

"I beg your pardon—"

"Nothing, XJ. Talking to myself." Maigrey sat silent, tapping her fingers on the arm of the chair.

"Your ladyship?"

"XJ."

"While we're waiting, the rebellion is something of a hobby of mine. I've never met an eyewitness before, a person who was actually there. I'd appreciate hearing your account—"

"My account would be rather boring, I'm afraid," Maigrey said, smiling faintly, her fingers absently stroking the scar on her cheek.

"Oh, but I'm certain that it wouldn't—"

"Yes, it would. You see, XJ, I can't remember a thing."

The computer appeared dubious but obviously didn't want to contradict. "I can understand how painful it must be for you," it suggested delicately.

"Not painful at all." Maigrey shrugged. "I simply can't remember. I was injured severely. The doctors believe my memory loss had something to do with that."

"Yes, your ladyship, but John Dixter said—"

"How much time has passed since we left *Defiant*? Standard military time, please."

"Seventy-six hours, thirty-seven minutes, and—"

"Thank you."

"—forty-two seconds. I'm familiar with several methods used to cure memory loss, your ladyship. All you have to do is think back to what you were doing the day before—"

"How soon will we be able to contact planet Laskar? Approximately."

"Five hours, your ladyship. Where was I? Ah, yes, the day before the revolution, you were—"

"I think you had better concentrate on the Jump."

"But, your ladyship—"

"That will be all."

The computer relapsed into whirring silence.

Maigrey rubbed her forehead, sighed.

The day before the revolt. I was in the Palace, wondering where Sagan was, worrying about Semele. The baby was due to arrive anytime. And John Dixter—

No! She blocked off that avenue of thought instantly.

The grand ceremony, the banquet honoring their squadron, was the next day. Sagan should have been there, but he'd taken an unexplained leave of absence a month before. An emergency, he'd said. His mind was completely closed to mine. I had no idea what he was plotting.

Or did I? How could I have failed to know, to understand? What if I knew and betrayed —

Angrily, Maigrey shook her head, backed away from that thought as well. Whenever she began to try to remember that time, a feeling of dread and terror crept over her. She longed to run, to hide. It was fortunate she was strapped into the chair or she would have leapt up, made some attempt to escape.

Five hours to Laskar, she reminded herself. The present is what counts. The past is dead and buried. Well, at least it's dead. Dion. Dion is the one who matters.

Maigrey banished the ghosts, leaned back in the chair, and concentrated on the present.

What is Sagan doing now? I have to be careful, the line between us is stretched so taut that the slightest touch will set it quivering like a live thing. I know he knows where I'm going, possibly even what I'm plotting. And he must know that I would know that he would know.

Maigrey sighed again, rested her head on her hand. All this knowledge was giving her a headache.

Still, I have the advantage: time and distance and the freedom to use both. I am, after all, nothing more than an escaping prisoner. He is a starfleet commander, a citizen general. A Warlord who has just lost his flagship, a political power in deep trouble with a political rival. Sagan will have work to do. He can't simply drop everything and chase across the galaxy, no matter how valuable the prize. He will try to stop me, of course. I have to figure out how, and then block his move before he can make it.

Maigrey smiled. On a chessboard, the queen has free range of motion. The king is able to move only a square at a time.

"Now," she pondered aloud, "I could land on Laskar and try to gain access to Snaga Ohme on my own, representing myself as what? A private citizen who just happened to have heard about this bomb? No, that's obviously out. Besides, it would take days, months perhaps, to gain an interview with the Adonian. I don't have that kind of time.

"I need official backing. I need someone the alien trusts. Scratch that. I need someone the alien knows, someone he would expect. I need to *be* someone he would expect."

"Coming up on the Jump, your ladyship."

"Thank you," Maigrey murmured absently. "Yes. That's the only possible way it will work. There's a risk, but hopefully, in the confusion . . ." Briskly, she sat up straight, brushed her hair out of her face. "XJ, when we get within range of Laskar, I want you to put a call through to the commander of the galactic army base located there."

"You do?" XJ's lights flickered in shock.

"Yes, I do. And I want you to transmit this message. To the commandant, Fort Laskar—" Maigrey clasped her hands, put her fingers to her lips, and began to dictate.

The computer took down her words, its circuits nearly overloading at the temerity of the plan.

"At least . . ." Maigrey reflected, picking up the towel after the Jump was completed and stuffing it into a storage bin where XJ couldn't see it. "At least Dion is safe and well out of this."

The knowledge didn't do much to ease her conscience, but it helped.

Chapter ⊷⊶ Four

But the men of Sodom were wicked and sinners before the Lord exceedingly.

Genesis 13:13

Laskar was a planet with only one continent. That continent had on it only one state and that state only one city. Located on the fringes of the galaxy, the planet had little else to recommend it. It was, depending on where you were, either hot and too humid, or hot and too dry. Most appalling, some type of chemical present in the atmosphere caused Laskar's sun to appear to be green in color—not a brilliant, emerald green, but more of a chartreuse. The green sun bathed the planet in a pale green light that gave every object the appearance of slow decay. Humans, in particular, found the sight nauseating. But then most humans who visited the planet rarely saw the sun.

Laskar had one thing in its favor—its distance from everything else in the galaxy. It had been originally a military outpost; a town of sorts had grown up around the base. Far from civilization, the town was far from civilization's laws, but it was extremely close to soldiers who had lots of money and no place to spend it. Enterprising business people, of the type who prefer that no one investigate their dealings too closely, moved in to Laskar, set up house, opened up shop, and began operations.

Pleasure—or the quest for it—became the planet's foremost source of revenue. Anyone or anything could be had at almost any price. Prostitution, gambling, drugs—no one on Laskar ran a "legitimate" business. Grocery stores sold more paraphernalia and prophylactics than they did food and what you could buy in the frozen meat department was a tribute to human and alien ingenuity. Assassins for hire advertised openly. The Thieves Guild was a thriving concern, operating an eye bank as a charitable sideline. Needless to say, chamber of commerce meetings on Laskar tended to be lively affairs.

The planet was a mecca for those who had nothing and therefore nothing to lose, those who had everything and were bored, and those—like Snaga Ohme—who simply wanted to pursue private pursuits in private. Once, shortly after the revolution, certain zealous members of Congress had launched a campaign to clean up Laskar. An alarming drop in government revenue followed. The matter was promptly referred to committee and that was the end of it. Laskar paid well to be left alone.

Brigadier General Vilhelm Haupt, commander of the Galactic Republic Democratic Armed Forces stationed at Fort Laskar, gazed out the window of his office, morosely contemplating the green sunset. He detested this planet. A stern, moral man, Haupt hated the assignment that had brought him here, though he knew very well (and prided himself on the fact) that it was his own virtues which had won him the position.

The commander of this post must be incorruptible, must have no vices, be subject to no temptation. Haupt's military record was above reproach and, morally speaking, he was the most boring man in the entire universe. When the last commander on Laskar had gone AWOL to open her own brothel, Haupt had been the unanimous choice of his superiors to replace her.

The sun spread its nauseating glow across the sky—chartreuse deepening to puce, giving the clouds the colorful effect of a gangrenous wound. Haupt grimaced, wondering if any human ever truly grew accustomed to the sight. Irritably, he snapped the window blinds shut, went back to his desk. Fortunately night was coming soon. Although night brought its own problems.

He sat down to file his report. Another soldier was missing, had not reported back to base.

Fort Laskar had one of the highest desertion rates in the army. Most of the city was off-limits to military personnel, but that only had the effect of making it more glamorous. Bars that weren't restricted actually put up signs announcing that they were in hopes of increasing business.

The brigadier recited the facts of the case of the AWOL soldier to the computer in a tone of complete and utter contempt. Undoubtedly the cops would find the man's body in an alley, throat slashed, money stolen. And for what? Haupt snorted and made a mental note to have the man's description given to the Laskar police, along with the requisite bribe money to encourage them to look for him.

"Brigadier—" His aide entered.

"Ah, yes, glad you came in, Corporal. Make a note to show that vid to all personnel again, will you? The one about the dangers of entering restricted zones."

The corporal made a face. "Yes, sir. Brigadier, we've received a report that a long-range Scimitar has been sighted entering our orbit and has requested permission to land."

Haupt raised his eyebrows so far that they appeared ready to slide up and over the crown of his bald head. "A single long-range Scimitar? Alone?"

"It appears to be, sir."

"Not part of a fleet?"

"The fleet is not reported to be in the area, sir."

"How very strange." Haupt's eyebrows dropped down into a frown above the pinched nose. The brigadier didn't like anything strange. He glanced up, a glimmer of hope. "Perhaps it's in trouble?"

"I don't believe so, sir. It has put out no distress call."

"Who's aboard?"

"A Major Penthesilea, sir."

"Penthcsilea. Never heard of him."

The corporal spoke reluctantly, unable to withhold the bad news any longer. "*She* says she is a special courier from Citizen General Sagan, sir."

"Good God!" Haupt stared.

"Yes, sir," the aide agreed.

"I suppose I should be on hand to meet her," Haupt said, rising and casting a nervous glance in a mirror. Reassuring himself on the immaculate state of his uniform, he twitched his coat down, adjusted the stiff, high collar.

"Yes, sir. Should I turn out the band, sir?"

Haupt considered. "No, let's keep this low profile." The citizen general might be the darling of the media; however— from the scuttlebutt Haupt had picked up from HQ—Sagan was out of favor in higher places. Haupt didn't dare do anything to offend this powerful Warlord, but he didn't have to welcome Sagan's courier with fifes and drums, either.

The brigadier paused on his way out of his office. "You have,

I presume, verified this with Citizen General Sagan, haven't you, Corporal?"

"We're trying, sir, but we're having difficulty reaching anyone who knows anything about the situation. We keep getting passed to someone higher up—"

Haupt snorted. He disliked excuses. The corporal, aware of this, fell silent.

"Keep trying," the brigadier ordered and stalked off.

On the way to the landing area, Haupt tried to figure out why he was being honored with this visit. It boded nothing good, he decided. He knew perfectly well—everyone in the galaxy knew—that Citizen General Sagan never employed women on any business whatsoever, never permitted them to serve aboard his ship. To have broken that rule, to have made a woman a major and a special courier— Well! She must be some woman, the brigadier thought gloomily, and wondered what her speciality was—knives, poisons, perhaps explosives . . .

Arriving at the landing site, the brigadier discovered that the Scimitar had already touched down and that half the base had turned out to view the female who represented the Warlord. Most had probably heard word of her coming long before their commander, Haupt realized bitterly. Rumors spread like head lice on this base. Everyone from cooks to clerks to captains was standing around, gawking at the plane, commenting on the fact that it looked to have been in recent combat: gun turret wrecked, shields damaged, hull scorched.

So much for low profile.

"'Tention!" called out someone, spying the brigadier.

Everyone snapped to, trying to look as if they belonged here.

"You people, go about your business! Sergeant, disperse this crowd!"

A figure was climbing out of the battered Scimitar. Haupt hurried forward, placed himself at the bottom of the ladder. He had been attempting to picture the type of woman Derek Sagan might employ and was prepared for anything from a female gorilla to an Amazon with one breast missing. The slender female clad in a neat Galactic Air Corps flight suit came as somewhat of a surprise and a relief to him. Perhaps there'd been a mistake, his commlink operators had misunderstood. The woman appeared perfectly ordinary, he thought, watching her descend the ladder with practiced ease and skill. Arriving on the ground, she turned to face him.

Brigadier Haupt looked into her eyes, took the shock in the pit of his stomach. He'd served on an arctic planet once, a vast, frozen wasteland. The eyes reminded him strongly of that bleak planet—empty, cold. So chilled was he by the eyes that it was some moments before he noticed the dreadful scar that slashed the right side of her face.

His heart sank. Apparently no mistake had been made.

"Brigadier General— What was the name?" the woman asked.

"Haupt," he said, and involuntarily started to salute, then realized that generals did not salute majors. Generals especially did not salute majors who had not saluted them first. This major had not saluted him and obviously had no intention of so doing.

Haupt was extremely angry. Warlord or no Warlord behind her, this officer was bound by the same rules of military conduct as all the rest of them. Rules that had been cherished through centuries, rules that propagated respect for a superior. The brigadier would have upbraided the woman on this, would have issued a verbal reprimand, but he found himself faltering and strangely tongue-tied in the grave, intense gaze of the woman's gray eyes.

"I am Major Penthesilea," the woman said suddenly, and held out her right hand. "How do you do?"

Haupt was completely nonplussed. He stared at the slender, taper-fingered hand whose nails were trimmed short like a man's. He had the oddest sensation that he was expected to kiss the smooth, white skin, as he would have been expected to in the old, prerevolution days. And then the woman turned the hand over. Haupt saw the five marks on the palm and every ounce of fluid in his body seemed to drain from it.

Only three more years to retirement, a pension! Good God, had it been too much to ask? Haupt lifted his bulging-eyed gaze from the palm and stared forlornly at the woman.

"My—my lady—" he began, but she shook her head swiftly, slightly. Apparently, this was to be their little secret. Haupt felt sick. "M-major," he said loudly, and was rewarded with a smile that was pale as a winter sun. "Welcome . . . welcome to Laskar." He had no idea what he was saying.

"Thank you, sir." She took his limp and unresisting hand and shook it firmly.

Haupt had touched warmer corpses and disengaged himself from her grip as quickly as possible. "I—I have quarters prepared for you. If you would come this way—"

"Thank you again, sir, but I intend to remain aboard my spaceplane during my stay here. Security reasons. I'm certain you understand."

He didn't, but that was of no consequence. Whoever this ghost was who had risen out of the past where the Blood Royal (with the exception of Derek Sagan) were supposed to be dead and buried, she could live in a coffin if she chose to do so. At least until Haupt figured out what was going on.

"Yes, my . . . Major."

"Is there somewhere we can speak in private?" she asked.

"My office," Haupt said faintly.

The woman nodded; and the two walked back across the compound toward the base. En route, Haupt was pleased to note his people going about their duties, although there certainly seemed to be an unusually high number of personnel involved in duties around the landing zone this evening. He saw that the major returned the salutes accorded the two officers, but he also noted that she used the Warlord's salute—fist over heart—rather than the regulation hand to hat brim.

It was an extraordinarily hot night on Laskar, Haupt thought, feeling sweat trickle down the back of his uniform. He could envision the large, unsightly spot it must be making. A glance showed him that the woman, clad in the bulky flight suit, appeared cool, completely unaffected.

"Would you care for a drink first, Major? The officers' club—"

The woman shook her head. "The matter is one of extreme urgency, sir."

"I am at your comman—" Haupt paused. A brigadier was never at a major's command. He saw the half-smile on the curved lips increase slightly, saw it touch and twist the scar on the right side of the face.

Who in the name of God . . . or the devil . . . was she?

The major said nothing more to him. Haupt noted her eyes taking in every detail of the base as they walked, much—it occurred to him—like one who is on reconnaissance in enemy territory. The brigadier kept silent, thinking back to the days before the revolution, trying to figure out who this woman was.

Penthesilea—an alias, of course. The brigadier had a smattering of literary background. He was fond of reading. It was—outside of a glass of sherry before bed—his only form of relaxation. He realized why the name Penthesilea had conjured up visions of Amazons in his mind. Penthesilea had been an Amazon queen who had fought at the battle of Troy and who, according to legend, was loved by Achilles.

It was not a tale calculated to comfort Haupt, who was wondering if the woman had chosen the name at random or if it had other, deeper connotations. The brigadier wished to heaven he'd paid more attention to gossip in the old days. He knew nothing about Derek Sagan's background, other than that he had betrayed his king and comrades for the sake of the revolution.

Haupt ushered the woman into the outer office. The corporal leapt to his feet, saluting. The major returned it with grave dignity.

"Sir," the corporal reported, "we have still been unable to contact Citizen General Sagan—"

"Sagan? Does this have to do with my arrival?" The major turned her gray eyes on Haupt.

Hot blood crept up the brigadier's neck, reddening his already warm face. He wondered angrily why he was being made to feel like a traitor over what was a perfectly routine procedure.

"Major, I—that is, I hope it doesn't seem like—"

"Nonsense, sir," the woman said crisply. "Of course an intelligent officer such as yourself would have taken care to verify my story. Have you reached my lord?"

"No, Major," the corporal answered. "I'm getting the runaround—"

The woman came near Haupt. Resting her slender, chill fingers gently on his arm—he could feel the cold touch through the cloth of his uniform—she leaned near him.

"My mission is dangerous and highly secret. There are those who would prevent me from completing it and who would stop at nothing in order to accomplish their objective. I cannot order you to break off attempting to contact Lord Sagan, sir. I can only advise you, General, that it would be extremely unwise to broadcast my presence on this base throughout the universe." The gray eyes were the hue and hardness of the barrel of a beam rifle. "My lord would not be pleased."

Haupt shivered. "Blast it, Corporal, I've told you repeatedly that you keep the air-conditioning too cold in here. Turn up the thermostat! The major and I will be in conference. Hold my calls."

"Yes, sir. Right away, sir."

"And I see no reason to disturb the citizen general over this matter." Haupt gestured to his office with one hand. Placing the other stiffly behind his back, elbow bent, he made a fluttering motion with his fingers to his aide.

The corporal saw, understood, and, as soon as the door had closed behind the two, left the room and headed directly for the communications center.

··◐■ ■◑›··

"Now, Major," Haupt said, settling himself behind his desk. The woman was seated in a chair in front of him. "What can I do for you . . . and the citizen general?"

"I am here to make contact with an alien named Snaga Ohme. Do you know him?"

"Ohme?" Haupt's jaw sagged.

"Yes. Snaga Ohme. An Adonian, dealing in weapons."

"I know him. Everyone in the galaxy knows him. May I ask what—"

"No, you may not." The major smiled; her voice softened. "The less you know about this, the better, sir."

Haupt rose nervously to his feet, walked to the window, and stood staring out at the garishly lit sky. The green sun had set, and Laskar had come to life, its neon lights blazing, turning night in the city streets to kaleidoscopic day. The brigadier clasped his hands behind his back, clenched his fingers tightly. He'd thought he'd had it figured out. The woman was an imposter, of course. A spy. Her trick to try to persuade him not to contact Sagan had been unbelievably transparent. She was probably one of those damn royalists Haupt had heard about. He'd intended to stall her until the citizen general could be notified.

What was she after? Military secrets, computer access codes, perhaps. Any number of things . . . except Snaga Ohme. That made no sense. . . .

"Brigadier," the woman said. "Time is pressing."

Haupt glanced around. "What is it you want me to do, Major?"

"It's very simple. Contact Ohme. Tell him that I am here and who has sent me. Arrange a meeting with him for me. The alien knows you. I presume he likes to maintain good relations with the army. He will do what you request."

Haupt returned to his desk, sat down, and picked up a computer stylus. He ran his fingers up and down it, an unconscious, nervous habit. "Why," he asked in a low voice, "doesn't the citizen general arrange a meeting for you with the alien himself?"

The pupils of the gray eyes dilated; the gray was like a cloud of debris around a black hole. Haupt felt himself caught, sucked into the empty vortex.

"Do you really want to know my lord's secrets?" she asked in a soft voice.

Haupt shuddered. He'd heard rumors about Derek Sagan. The rebel angel, who had once shone as brightly in the heavens as the morning star, was plotting to rise up and challenge the gods. That, at least, was the current talk around HQ.

Three years to retirement. Haupt ran his hand over his bald head. He had a house picked out on a planet far away from this one, located in the heart of the galaxy. He'd planned to buy a dog, one of those artificial kind that was programmed to behave. . . .

"Brigadier, sir." The aide's voice over his desklink broke in on his thoughts.

"I ordered you to hold my calls!" Haupt snapped.

"Begging your pardon, but I thought you should hear this, sir. We have received a message from Citizen General Sagan."

Haupt cast a swift glance at the woman, saw the gray eyes narrow in irritation.

The brigadier glared at the unfortunate corporal on the desklink screen. "You were ordered not to disturb the citizen general—"

"I didn't, sir," the man said, and there was a ring of truth in the voice. "The message came in just this moment."

Haupt looked at the major, saw her sitting at her ease, composed, calm. She might have been carved of ice.

"Well, what is the message, Corporal?"

If it was to have her arrested, he hoped his aide had been intelligent enough to have sent an armed guard.

"Citizen General Sagan to Brigadier General Haupt: 'By my command, you are hereby ordered to render all aid and assistance to Major Penthesilea as requested by her.' End of communiqué, sir."

"Is this verified?" Haupt demanded.

"Yes, sir. The citizen general's own private code."

Haupt breathed a sigh, turned to the woman. "Well, Major, of course I will—" He stopped, his words forgotten.

The woman's face had gone livid. The only blood visible in the ashen skin pulsed in the scar. Haupt rose swiftly.

"Major, you're not well! Can I get you—"

"Nothing, thank you," she said through lips that didn't move. "Please, just do as I have requested. Contact Ohme. Time grows short. Very short indeed." The last was a whisper. She didn't look at him but stared straight ahead, her eyes unfocused, seeing nothing.

Mystified, yet secure in the knowledge that he was acting on orders and could not be held accountable by anyone, including himself, Haupt motioned to his aide.

"Corporal, put through a call to the Adonian, Snaga Ohme."

Chapter ❧ *Five*

Sparafucil mi nomino.

Sparafucile is my name.

Giuseppe Verdi, *Rigoletto*

"My lord." The voice of the captain of the shuttlecraft came over the commlink.

"Yes, Captain?"

"A small spaceplane has requested clearance to dock. Shall we proceed?"

"Has it given the correct code response?"

"Yes, my lord."

"Allow it to come in. Have a guard meet the pilot in the docking bay. Bring the pilot to my quarters immediately."

"Yes, my lord."

"Oh, and Captain. Leave the pilot his weapons. He would not give them up without a struggle, and I don't have time to try to reason with him."

"Yes, my lord." The officer did not sound happy.

"He will not harm *me*, Captain, and—so long as he is not crossed—he will harm none of the crew. No one is to harm *him* on pain of death. Is that understood?"

"Very good, my lord." The captain's voice clicked off.

The Warlord paced the quarters of his shuttlecraft, the cramped space. The crew of the shuttle had listened to him walk the night away, his booted footsteps sounding regular and steady until they became like the beating of their own hearts and they heard them no longer.

Eighty-four hours had passed since this game had begun. Sagan once again envisioned his pieces on the chessboard, studied every play his opponent could possibly make, and, after long hours, was satisfied that he had each covered, his own strategy mapped out. He relapsed into a chair, sipped at a glass of cool water, and composed himself to meet his visitor.

Sagan felt the slight jolt of the docking, the other ship attaching itself barnaclelike to the shuttlecraft. A whoosh of air locks, the clanging bang of hatches opening and shutting.

"My lord," came a voice.

Sagan touched a pad on a console on the arm of his chair. A panel slid aside. Two of his Honor Guard stood framed in the entryway. Between them was what appeared to be a large bundle of rags. At a hand gesture from the Warlord, the bundle became animated and slouched into the room. The centurions saluted and, pivoting, took up position outside the chamber. Sagan touched the pad and the panel slid shut. Another touch sealed it.

The bundle shook itself, much like a dog, and a head emerged from the midst of the rags, somewhere near the top. A pair of the bright black gleaming eyes, one eye positioned considerably higher on the face than the other, glanced swiftly about the room. Hands, strong and quick-fingered, groped their way through the rags like talons protruding from a bird's feathers. The man had, on entering, moved with a shuffling slouch that gave evidence of a crooked, humped back. Seeing from his survey of the room that he and the Warlord were alone, the man straightened, adding a good five inches to his height, and shuffled forward.

"Sagan Lord," the man said.

"Sparafucile," acknowledged the Warlord. He waved a commanding hand. "Sit down. We have much to discuss."

Years past, in what was now known as the second Dark Ages, scientists working underground in hidden laboratories had conducted genetic experiments designed to produce members of both human and alien species who were physically and mentally superior to the rest of their kind. Out of these experiments had come successes—such as the Blood Royal. Out of these had come failures. Most of the failures had been mercifully destroyed. A few had escaped or been allowed to live for continuing research purposes. It was these failures who were undoubtedly this man's ancestors.

At least so Sagan surmised. No one knew for certain, but he deemed it likely. The misshapen face, the unusual strength, the exceptional intelligence, the amoral nature came from ancestors who themselves had come from test tubes. Dr. Giesk had brought the "half-breed," as the man was known, to the Warlord's attention and Sagan had been quick to recognize the breed's talents. Well aware that money can buy such a man but will not buy his loyalty, the Warlord had not bought the breed, but had, in a way, adopted him. Sagan fed the breed, clothed him, protected him from his numerous enemies, listened to the category of his wrongs. The Warlord had even given the breed a name—a thing the breed's own wretched mother had not bothered to do.

Sparafucile belonged to his lord, body and soul . . . if the breed owned a soul.

"It is very dark in here, Sagan Lord," the breed observed, still standing. He spoke in a hoarse, sibilant whisper that had the odd characteristic of being as loud and distinguishable as normal conversational tones, if slightly more disconcerting.

"I cannot imagine the dark offends you," the Warlord answered.

"No, no." Sparafucile smiled, an expression that was not pleasant. The smile did ghastly things to his face, one cheekbone being considerably higher and more protruding than the other. The upturning of the thick wide lips caused the left eye—the lower of the two—to shut nearly all the way, giving the smile the appearance of a leer. "I like the darkness. It aids and abets me. But I don't like this darkness. I think this darkness reflects your mood, Sagan Lord."

"Perhaps." The Warlord was lenient, indulgent with his favorite. He motioned again. "Will you be seated?"

"Thank you, Sagan Lord." The words spoken were not servile, but given with respect. The half-breed turned slowly and shuffled slowly to a chair opposite that of the Warlord. Seating himself, he stretched out long legs encased in soft leather boots, folded his hands comfortably over his rags, and appeared to fall asleep. This appearance of lethargy had fooled many in the breed's time, most to their later regret. A striking snake was not swifter or deadlier than Sparafucile.

"Refreshment?"

The half-breed shook his head.

"Your report, then."

"In what order, Sagan Lord?"

"Chronological."

The breed shrugged, paused a moment to gather his thoughts. "Twenty-four hours ago, Abdiel land on Laskar."

The Warlord's face did not change expression, but the fingers of the right hand clenched over the arm of the chair on which it rested. Sparafucile noticed, while seeming not to notice. Only the glitter of the eyes could be seen from within the rags.

"He build a quick-build"—Sagan understood this to mean a prefab structure—"in small desert ravine twenty kilometers from house of the Adonian, Snaga Ohme."

"How near is Abdiel to Fort Laskar?"

"Twenty kilometers. He is in middle."

"Are any of the mind-dead with him?"

"Thirty, Sagan Lord."

The darkness was not as dark as the Warlord's expression. The breed slid his spinal column another few centimeters down into the chair, almost disappearing within the rags.

"What has he done since his arrival?"

"He make contact with the Adonian."

"Damn!" The Warlord swore softly. "Did Abdiel go to Snaga Ohme himself, in person?"

"No, Sagan Lord. He send one of the dead men."

"Do you know what they discussed?"

"The man does not live who can walk unobserved into the house of the Adonian, Sagan Lord. My listening devices do not function there, either. The Adonian is very clever in the art of jamming signals."

Sparafucile was not making excuses, merely stating facts, and the Warlord, knowing his creature's talents, accepted his reasoning without question.

"But we can assume Abdiel is merely opening negotiations," Sagan said, speaking low, as if to himself.

The breed, uncertain if this remark was addressed to him or not, kept quiet.

The Warlord returned to the business at hand. "Anything else on the mind-seizer?"

"No, Sagan Lord."

"Proceed then to the lady."

"Twelve hours after Abdiel arrive on Laskar, the lady arrive."

"Yes, I received your report concerning *her*."

Sparafucile appeared to think he detected a note of rebuke. "You are not mad, Sagan Lord? Perhaps you think I should have sent report on Abdiel—"

"No!" Sagan shook his head in emphasis. "Transmit nothing pertaining to him! Bring all information directly to me, as per your original orders."

The breed was reassured. "The base commander, he make contact with the Adonian."

"You were able to hear their conversation?"

Sparafucile grinned. "The ear I put in his office can hear the sound of the dust blowing across the floor, Sagan Lord. I could tell you how fast the lady's heart beats, eh?"

"I'm not interested in her heartbeat . . . and neither are you," the Warlord added pointedly, knowing his creature's one weakness.

Sparafucile laughed—a short, croaking bark that ceased with a gurgle, sounding much as if he'd choked himself. "I hear all the talk, Sagan Lord. Haupt and Ohme do not speak long. The commandant tells the Adonian that the lady is here, that she is sent by you. The Adonian is pleased. The lady has appointment with Ohme tomorrow. Noon, Laskar time."

"You can be back by then?"

"You know my skill. You know my craft." The black eyes above the mound of rags were shrewd, attentive. "What are orders, Sagan Lord?"

"Follow the woman to Ohme's estate. When she comes out—" Sagan paused, broke off, then asked abruptly, "Is Abdiel aware of the Lady Maigrey's presence on Laskar?"

Sparafucile gave the question due consideration, shook his head with finality. "No, Sagan Lord."

"But that will change soon. He will sense her, much as I would. Much as I *do*," he rephrased his sentence softly, beneath his breath. "And, undoubtedly, knowing Ohme, he will inform each of the other's presence, use the two against each other in order to drive up the price. The news will come as a shock to my lady, I fear, but I trust she will stand up beneath the blow." The Warlord was quiet, considering his plans.

Sparafucile waited in respectful silence.

Sagan drew a breath, made up his mind. "When she comes out of Snaga Ohme's house, my friend, you will follow her at a discreet distance. Keep her in sight, but do not reveal yourself to her."

"A question, Sagan Lord. The lady will succeed in her mission to the Adonian?"

"Yes, she will succeed. When she comes out of his house, she will have an object—"

"What is object?"

"A secret, my friend. A secret you will be paid well to let remain a secret."

"Very good, Sagan Lord. Then it is all very simple. Let me take secret from lady."

"Could you take it from me, Sparafucile," Sagan inquired gravely, "if I didn't want you to have it?"

The breed appeared awed, shook his head. "No, Sagan Lord."

"Then you would not be able to take it from her."

Sparafucile's eyes narrowed; he was dubious. The Warlord opened his right palm, revealing the five marks barely visible in the dim light. He said nothing, but the breed understood the meaning, uncrossed his legs in acknowledgment.

"Keep watch over the woman, Sparafucile. The moment she acquires the object, she will be in extreme peril. Make certain that both she and the object arrive safely back at the fort."

"I understand, Sagan Lord. And then?"

"And then I will deal with the lady. You will return and maintain your observation of Abdiel."

"Yes, Sagan Lord."

"Continue bringing reports to me in person. I will be at Fort Laskar."

The rags moved, indicating that the breed had given his acquiescence.

"Are you in need of anything? Weapons? Money?"

Knowing this was his dismissal, Sparafucile gathered himself together and rose, by degrees, to a standing position. In answer to the Warlord's questions, the breed thrust forth the strong hands and flexed them, indicating that these were his best weapons. He then held one palm out and up, admitting a need for money.

Sagan complied, lifting a leather pouch he had waiting, and tossing it to the breed, who caught it deftly. The half-breed did not glance inside. The chink of platinum—the preferred medium of exchange on Laskar—had been obvious to his sharp ears. The pouch and the hands disappeared inside the rags. His body hunched and shrank together until he was nothing more than a twisted beggar removing his unsavory person from the Warlord's presence.

The panel slid open at the lord's command. The Honor Guard presented themselves, escorted the breed back to his ship.

"My lord," came the captain's voice over the commlink.

"Yes."

"I have someone on line, waiting to speak to you."

Sagan frowned in irritation. He needed time to think. "Who is it?"

"He said to tell you the name was Captain Link, my lord." The officer spoke with faint disgust. He had not been impressed with Captain Link.

Dread brushed its claws across the Warlord's soul.

"Put him through to me."

"Yes, my lord."

"Sagan? That you?"

"Yes, Captain," the Warlord said.

"Uh, I got some bad news, I'm afraid, your Warlordship."

"What is it, Captain?"

"Just one thing first. Do I still get the rest of my money? I was in this ante-up game, see, and I had a run of bad luck—"

"You will still receive your payment. Depending on your information, you *may* be allowed to live long enough to spend it."

A long pause. Then, "Uh, yeah. Well. The fact is . . . er . . . the kid's gone."

"Gone? Where? To *Defiant*?" Sagan had been expecting Dion to launch some wild scheme to rescue John Dixter.

"I don't think so. You see, your lordship, I don't exactly know *where* they've gone. I think the kid caught on to me."

"Very good, Dion," Sagan murmured. "I'm impressed."

"He got this message—"

"Message? From whom?"

"Near as I could understand from something the kid said when he thought I was . . . er . . . passed out, the message came from that woman named Maigrave or something like that."

"And now the boy is gone. Off-planet?"

"Plane's nowhere to be found. Controller said the pilot requested off-world clearance."

"Is anyone with him?"

"Nola . . . and Tusk, your lordship. Both of them are missing, too, and it makes sense that they would have gone with the kid."

Of course. The Guardian. It was logical. Maigrey had contacted the boy, warned him to leave Vangelis, sent him into hiding. It was logical, but then why didn't it seem right?

"You are a fool, Captain Link. Fortunately for your continued good health, you are a useful fool. If the boy returns or you hear anything from either him or Mendaharin Tusca, inform me at once."

"Yes, lord." Link sounded subdued.

"That will be all. Oh, by the way, how did the message come? Subspace?"

"Subhuman is more like it, your lordship. Some weird-looking character brought it. I didn't get a close look at the guy. His face was hidden in those desert-sheikh-type robes they wear on Vangelis but what I saw of it sent me to the jump-juice bottle, if you know what I mean."

Dread dug its nails in deeper. Sagan broke off the transmission, sat lost in thought.

Something was not right. Something was going wrong, very wrong. He longed to reach out his hand, grab whatever it was, shake it, slap it, force it to obey his will. He reached out his hand . . . only to feel the darkness slide through his fingers.

Chapter ·◆⊃◯⊂◆· Six

Business is business. Pleasure is pleasure.
George Alec Effinger, *When Gravity Fails*

"I repeat. Your master has been most woefully misinformed." Snaga Ohme reached out a jewel-bedecked hand, tilted a small mirror that stood on his desk, and paused to study the effect of the sunlight upon his fair skin. He kept his gaze on the mirror, preferring the sight of his own handsome features to the empty eyes of the mind-dead, seated across the desk from him. "'T'isn't my fault, so don't go ranting and raving about it."

Somewhat of an exaggeration. The empty eyes had not so much as blinked, the level voice of the mind-dead had merely expressed its master's considered opinion that Snaga Ohme was lying.

The Adonian carefully touched up several strands of black hair that curled around a shell-like ear, pinched the lobe to make it pink, massaged his hands to keep them white.

"Very well, I'm lying." Ohme shrugged negligently. "The Warlord's representative— a woman, I might add—is *not* coming to see me at noon today. I am putting off your master simply to tease him, to irritate him, to annoy him." Each phrase accompanied by a graceful wave of an elegant hand. "If your master becomes too highly annoyed, he may take his business elsewhere."

The empty eyes closed a moment, as if listening to a voice within. Snaga Ohme took advantage of the opportunity to exchange amused glances with a handsome man standing in a corner of the Adonian's office, a man who served Ohme in the capacity of confidential secretary, cook, valet, bodyguard, rumor had it lover, and—since the man held numerous

147

degrees in nuclear physics and mathematics—scientific adviser.

The empty eyes opened. Their disconcerting, slightly out-of-focus gaze approached the general vicinity of the Adonian. "Who is this agent, then?" the mind-dead asked. "A woman, you say? Again, you are lying. Lord Sagan would never trust a mission of such a delicate nature to anyone but himself."

"Then it's the Warlord himself, coming in drag," Snaga Ohme cried, highly elated. "Gad, Bosk, Sagan in drag! What a marvelous image! I am much indebted to this walking cadaver here for having provided it!" The Adonian, his amusement soon spent, turned his gaze back to the man seated across from him. A slight touch of impatience tinged Ohme's voice. He was easily bored and was beginning to find this conversation—and his lifeless visitor—tiring. "All I know about the agent is that, according to Brigadier General Haupt, she is a she, not a he. Admittedly, Haupt is not the most intelligent of humans, but he does, I assume, have the capacity to distinguish the female of the species from the male."

The Adonian held out his hands, studied his cuticles with a critical eye. "Though, of course, Derek Sagan in taffeta petticoats and a feather boa might be able to fool him completely. With enough lipstick."

Bosk stepped forward, placed his well-muscled body behind the visitor's chair. When Snaga Ohme began contemplating his manicure, it was a sign that the interview was nearing an end.

"You will stall this agent, then. Allow us to match the offer." The mind-dead sitting in the chair did not move, did not shift his unblinking, lifeless gaze.

"I can't see how my business dealings could possibly be any concern of yours or your master's." Snaga Ohme propped his elbow up on the arm of his chair, holding his left hand in the air to keep the veins from swelling in an unsightly manner, and sent a languid glance to Bosk. The bodyguard placed a hand on the visitor's shoulder. The hand could have wrapped twice around the mind-dead's slender neck.

The visitor rose to his feet, leaned over the desk. "Do not forget who and what my master is, Snaga Ohme." The voice was level, even.

The Adonian slid his right hand beneath his desk. A beam of light flashed, almost faster than the eye could follow. The chair in which the visitor had been seated vanished in a sizzle, a pop, and a puff of smoke, leaving behind the acrid odor of melted plastic.

"Never," Snaga Ohme replied with a charming smile.

His show was rather wasted on the mind-dead, however, who was not in the least impressed. The expressionless face remained blank; the eyes blinked, but only as an involuntary reaction to the sudden flash of laser light. The deadly beam had passed bare centimeters from the man's arm, but he had not flinched. Turning, he walked away from the desk, heading for the door. Bosk hastened to open it. Another handsome and superbly built footman escorted the man to the front entrance of the Adonian's palatial dwelling.

"You should have fried him," Bosk said, wheeling another chair, identical to the one destroyed, into the lavishly decorated office.

Snaga Ohme yawned. "Abdiel would have only sent another in his place or perhaps come himself." The Adonian sniffed at a flower in the lapel of his morning jacket. "*That* I simply couldn't abide! The man is sinfully ugly! All those horrid nodes and knobs and welts, patches of skin falling off. Ugh!" He shuddered.

Bosk placed the chair in its proper position, marked by a small metal plate embedded in the luxurious carpet. Glancing up, he made certain it was in line with the laser hidden in the painting that hung over Ohme's desk—a portrait of the Adonian, done in classical tradition, dressed in velvet doublet with a feather-adorned, gold-braided cocked hat, hose and garters around his shapely legs. The lethal beam, when activated, shot out of the portrait's left eye and was one of many such devices located not only in the Adonian's office but throughout the house and the gardens surrounding it. Snaga Ohme could, at the touch of a button, wipe out an invading army.

The Adonian stood up, smoothed his coattails, glanced admiringly at the smooth line of his vest across his tight-muscled stomach, and carefully adjusted the cuffs at his wrists.

"Abdiel does have a point," he conceded. "'Tisn't like Sagan to send *anyone* to do his business, much less a female. The man has liquid oxygen in his veins instead of blood. What do we know about this agent of his?"

"She calls herself Penthesilea and purports to hold the rank of major. She's not, however, listed in any of our files of Sagan's officers, spies, or hired assassins. Our sources on the base report she arrived in a spaceplane that had obviously been through recent combat. Haupt was dubious about her himself, but the Warlord gave orders—his own personal code—to render the woman all possible assistance."

"Odd. Very odd. Is she beautiful?"

"That was, of course, my first thought, although it would be extremely unlike Sagan to try to either bribe you or seduce you. His mind doesn't work that way. My source tells me that the woman is in her forties, human years, and while she has an adequate figure and quite lovely hair, her face is marred by a hideous scar."

"Gad!" Snaga Ohme grimaced. "I trust she has the civility to cover it up while she's here. But you reassure me, Bosk. She sounds just Sagan's type. Well, well. It will be interesting to see what she has to offer. When is she due?"

"An hour or so. Speaking of offers, will you really sell the bomb to her?"

"My dear Bosk"—Snaga Ohme poured himself a glass of champagne from a bottle chilling in a silver ice bucket; raising it, he admired the bubbles floating to the surface, then sipped at it delicately—"if I handle this right, I can sell it to everyone!"

··◁■ ■▷··

The Lady Maigrey, beyond all doubt, is Sagan's representative.

"Indeed," Abdiel murmured. "And Snaga Ohme has no idea?"

None, my master. The mind-dead did not speak aloud; he had no need to. Abdiel heard every word quite clearly. He could also speak to his disciples mentally, and from great distances, and frequently did, when they were out performing some task for him. But, when they were alone, he did not. He always spoke aloud for no particular reason except that he occasionally enjoyed hearing the sound of a voice.

The mind-dead. The servants of the mind-seizers are known by that appellation among those (and there are few) who still remember the Order of Dark Lightning. The name is actually a misnomer. Those humans who served Abdiel were not mind-dead. They merely looked it. *Mind-controlled* would be more precisely the correct term.

The viral infection injected by the mind-seizer into a body of one of the Blood Royal allows the seizer empathetic closeness with the person and, if the seizer is quite strong-willed and his victim weak, the "bonding" grants the mind-seizer a certain amount of ascendancy. The benefits of empathetic connection between themselves had been enough for most members of the Order of Dark Lightning. But sharing thoughts and ideas with each other had not been enough for certain others, including their intelligent and cunning leader, who called himself Abdiel. He wanted power, wanted lesser beings to do his bidding, to obey his every command without question.

Abdiel wanted 'droids—living 'droids. Real androids had too many limitations, the most serious being the lack of imagination, the inability to adapt to new situations. The Blood Royal were not suited to his purpose; even the weakest maintained a certain amount of resistance to him. But ordinary mortals were eminently satisfactory. Unfortunately, injecting ordinary mortals with the virus had a rather serious side effect: death.

The mind-seizer worked diligently to overcome this draw-back, altering the structure of the virus, watering it down, so to speak, so that it would operate effectively on ordinary nervous systems without mutating into the virulent cancer that killed within days. He achieved success, though how many paid the cost of his experimentation was unknown.

To his credit, Abdiel never took unwilling victims. He had no need. For some, to be alive is to be in hell. For some, life is fear, insecurity, sorrow, longing, frustration. And for these, Abdiel could make life a heaven.

Once connected with Abdiel, a person would never know fear, for fear is an instinct of self-preservation and the mind-dead have no such instinct. Abdiel controlled all aspects of his people's lives, waking and sleeping. He even ruled their dreams.

He could provide exquisite pleasure. He could also, of course, provide excruciating pain, but Abdiel refrained from mentioning that in his sales pitch to the unhappy beings who came to him. His disciples never knew fear, never knew hunger, never knew pain (unless they somehow managed to displease him), or frustration. He gave them everything, including the belief that they were free.

"When does the Lady Maigrey meet with the Adonian?"

Noon, my master.

"And what of Lord Sagan?"

His shuttle is reported to have left Defiant, *destination and whereabouts unknown.*

"But they are obvious. Where else would he come? But why— Mmmm. Is it possible? Could he and I have the same plan? Of course. It makes perfect sense. You say there is no possible way to break into the dwelling of the Adonian?"

I have given the matter careful consideration, my master. It is my judgment, based on my observations and thorough study, that it was easier storming the Glitter Palace the night of the revolution than it would be attacking the fortress of Snaga Ohme. An army could not do it and succeed.

"Lord Sagan could not do it, for example?"

If he could, my master, would he not have done so before now?

"Excellent point, Mikael. Yes, he and I have both devised the same strategy. Both our hands reaching for the same pawn." Abdiel rubbed his hands, dislodged a chunk of scabbed-over flesh. Absently, he scratched at it, brushed it to the floor. "Mine will be the quicker. And the boy?"

He is on his way.

"Alone?"

With friends—a human male and a human female.

"Excellent! Excellent! This, then, is what you will order done."

Abdiel took hold of the hand of the mind-dead known as Mikael—all those who held this position of command were known as Mikael. There had been twelve Mikaels through the years. The others were now dead. (The cancer no longer killed within three days, but it killed, nonetheless.)

The mind-seizer placed his palm over the palm of his disciple, jabbing the needles into the man's flesh. Mikael did not flinch; he felt no pain that his master did not want him to feel.

Abdiel gave the mind-dead his orders.

The bonding was not really necessary. Abdiel could have given his commands by word of mouth or passed them from his brain to the brain of his disciple. But the mind-seizer had discovered his minions performed their tasks more efficiently if he renewed physical contact with them from time to time.

To say nothing of the fact that the bonding was the one and only physical pleasure he enjoyed.

Chapter ❖◗◖❖ Seven

Queen to King's Knight 4.

Chess move

Leaving Haupt's office after hearing Sagan's startling message, Maigrey spent an unsatisfactory hour trying to figure out the Warlord's game. She was hampered in her efforts by the fact of his nearness—not his physical presence, but his mental. If she devoted too much thought to him, she had the unnerving impression that she would hear his voice providing her with the answers. At length, she abandoned the attempt as being too unnerving.

A mind-clearing rummage through XJ's musical files produced numerous selections of whatever screeching harmonics the younger generation was currently using to rebel against their elders. She did discover several files long buried in the computer's memory.

"What's this? Palestrina? XJ, how did you get Palestrina?"

"What is it?" the computer demanded nervously. "A virus?"

"No, no, not a virus. Palestrina was a composer. He wrote music for the ancient church. He was . . . one of Sagan's favorites."

"You're sure it's not a virus? It sounds like a virus," XJ insisted in gloomy tones.

"Yes, I'm sure." Maigrey smiled. "Where did you copy it? I don't believe Mendaharin Tusca would enjoy this type of music."

"Tusk? He tried playing *his* type of music in here once. Came near melting my circuits. That Pally stuff must have been copied from the Warlord's files. I . . . um . . . once spent some time with his computer. Not a bad sort, personally, but I could never get used to the military mind-set. . . ."

"Play the music," Maigrey ordered softly.

XJ did as commanded. The chorus of monks' voices echoed in the small spaceplane.

"I like that," XJ said after a moment. "What're they saying?"

Et tibi dabo claves regni caelorum.

"'I will give unto thee the keys to the kingdom of heaven,'" Maigrey translated. She went to bed and slept soundly. Her discipline would allow her to do nothing else.

··✧▆ ▆✧··

Morning on Laskar dawned. The sky was hazy and overcast, its green color tinged with brown, sullen and oppressive.

"There'll be a storm before the day's out," XJ predicted.

Maigrey thought it highly likely.

"Brigadier General Haupt reports the hoverjeep you requested is outside, your ladyship," the computer continued. "The estate's entrance is about forty kilometers from here."

"Yes, thank you, XJ," Maigrey said, preoccupied, trying to decide what to wear, having completely confounded Brigadier General Haupt by requesting that various articles of female clothing be sent to her spaceplane.

The base housed numerous women of various races and species. The corporal assigned to the task had been able to supply Maigrey with everything she requested. She spread the various garments out over every flat surface she could find on the small spaceplane, much to XJ's disgust.

"I thought this was a hazardous mission, your ladyship," the computer complained, indignant over a pair of spike-heeled shoes resting atop its console.

"It is." Maigrey held up a purple brocade evening dress by its puffy, beaded sleeves. "What do you think of this?"

"Blondes can't wear that shade of purple. Makes your skin tone look gray. And you couldn't move fast in that tight skirt. Why don't you just wear your uniform . . . like any sensible *man* would do?"

"Oh, I could slit the side seams of the skirt open. I've done that before. But you're right. This dress won't do. And neither would a uniform. Adonians have rigid standards of propriety. Dressed as a man, I probably wouldn't even be allowed in Ohme's presence. And if I were, I'd lose ground in the bargaining. I'd be considered a freak, a spectacle. I wouldn't be taken seriously. And, above all, he *will* take me seriously." She laid the dress aside, picked up a long, shapeless black bundle, and studied it. "Yes, this. This will do."

"A bathrobe?" The computer was highly scandalized.

"A *chador*."

Maigrey shook out the shapeless garment, then drew the enveloping robes over her lightweight body armor. She struggled beneath the meters of smothering cloth in her efforts to find openings for her head and arms and finally emerged, face flushed, hair disheveled, shaking the gown down around her. Black cloth enveloped her slender form, shrouding her from shoulders to toes. Very little flesh was left exposed. A high collar wrapped around her neck. Long flowing sleeves, ending in tight-fitting cuffs, extended over her wrists and the backs of her hands.

"Charming," the computer sneered.

Maigrey studied herself in Tusk's shaving mirror, her fingers moving to touch the scar on her cheek.

Adonians love that which is beautiful, abhor that which is ugly, flawed, marred. I could conceal the scar, I know. Plastiskin would provide me with a complexion smooth and white as milk.

She lifted the chador's black veil and wound it slowly and deliberately around her face, her head, her neck, and her shoulders.

It was useless attempting to cover the scar. She had never tried it, but she knew it wouldn't work. Though others couldn't see it, she could. And because she could see it, the scar would be visible even to the blind. Yet it wouldn't do to offend the sensibilities of the Adonian. Maigrey pulled the veil over her nose and mouth, hiding everything except the gray eyes.

"I have to admit that . . . er . . . that shroud's not a bad idea, your ladyship," XJ remarked grudgingly. "You could hide a missile launcher inside that body bag! By the way, you'll find a missile launcher in the storage compartment there underneath the trash compactor. Also a nice assortment of blades, grenades, and a needle-gun that fits in a shoulder holster—"

Maigrey moved to the storage compartment, knelt, and opened it up. But her hands went past the assortment of weapons, collected by Tusk over the years, to a small rosewood box the mercenary would not have recognized as belonging to him. She caressed the polished wood. When her fingers began to tremble, she hurriedly thrust it beneath the folds of the chador, secreting it in a zippered pocket of the body armor.

Rising to her feet, she started toward the ladder leading up

and out of the spaceplane. She frowned slightly, having
forgotten that she would have to negotiate the climb encumbered by the robe's flowing skirts. "Keep the hatch sealed,"
she ordered XJ. "No one is to come aboard in my absence."

"Sure, sure. Wait, your ladyship! You've forgotten to take
any weapons! Women!" the computer muttered, but was
sufficiently impressed with the lady to keep its volume low.

"Thank you, XJ." Maigrey, skirts in one hand, was climbing
the ladder with difficulty. "But from what I understand of the
Adonian's security, I couldn't smuggle a butter knife into his
house."

"You said yourself this character couldn't be trusted. Listen,
your ladyship," XJ said eagerly, "I've got plastic explosive,
looks and tastes just like chewing gum! Put a wad in your
mouth and no one'd ever suspect. You've only got to be careful
about one thing—don't blow bubbles. . . ."

"No, thank you, XJ. It won't be necessary."

Maigrey stopped at the top of the ladder, thrust open the
hatch, and looked out over the large, walled complex that was
Fort Laskar. A squad was drilling on the parade ground, men
and women baking in the hot sun, being driven by a bulldog of
a sergeant snapping at their heels. In another area, the fort's
band practiced, its music brisk and metallic, punctuated by
the rattle of drums. Five suborbital fighters flew high overhead, dark spots against the nauseous green sun. Sonic waves
broke over the base, rattling windowpanes, jarring taut
nerves.

Standing on the ladder, preparatory to climbing up and out,
Maigrey rested her hands on the hull, rested her chin on her
hands, and gazed out over the people, the buildings, the walls
to the bleak and barren horizon and beyond.

Sagan was far away, yet he was near, so near to her that it
seemed if she stretched forth her hand, she would touch him.
He walked at her side, hovering over her like some dark angel.
She had only to speak, and he would answer.

The mental link between them was strong; it had never
been stronger, not even in the days of their youth, when they
had been far closer than they were now.

"Or perhaps not," she said to herself. "Then we were bound
by light, by intellect, by victory, by beauty. We were strong,
immortal, invincible. We were young. But now he and I are
bound by chains much stronger: by darkness, by age and
experience, by sorrow and pain, by fear . . . and by death."

"Your ladyship, please reconsider!" XJ, in its remote unit, popped up out of the hatch, lights flashing in consternation, small arms wiggling. "The Adonian's dangerous! You can't go alone, unarmed!"

Maigrey's hand lightly touched the black fabric of the chador covering the rosewood box hidden at her breast. "I won't be going unarmed." Her gaze, intent, somber, shifted to the heavens, to the storm clouds gathering on the horizon. "And I won't be going alone."

···◁■ ■▷···

Maigrey brought the hoverjeep to a halt, allowing it to settle down into the dust of the road. She had traveled through vast open desert, diving down into a steep, narrow ravine, rocketing up a rock-strewn defile, and finally arriving at Snaga Ohme's estate. A tall bronze gate, set into a high-standing wall made of the garish, multicolored crystalline brick that was popular on (and no doubt imported from) the man's home planet of Adonia, formed the entrance to the fortresslike dwelling.

Maigrey, craning her neck, could barely see the tops of giant trees lifting their green limbs above the wall. Bold abstract patterns, formed out of the myriad colored bricks, dazzled the eye. The bronze gate was highly polished, the gleam from the metal nearly blinding, even in the hazy sunlight. And it was all strictly for show. Maigrey could hear the faint hum of the force field that was the true guardian of the Adonian's vast wealth.

Leaning back in the seat of the hoverjeep, she watched and waited for her presence to be acknowledged.

Several bricks suddenly slid aside. Numerous computer remotes, of the type known as "killer remotes" because of their armaments, floated out of the wall and took up positions around her vehicle. One, the leader, bobbed over to Maigrey, keeping level with her head.

"Please remove yourself from your vehicle," the remote instructed, speaking general military.

Maigrey did as she was told. Several of the remotes surrounded the hoverjeep, inspecting it with their scanners.

"A beam rifle," one reported.

"Deactivate it," the lead remote ordered.

"It's dangerous country out there," Maigrey protested, gesturing with a black-robed hand. "I have to drive back. . . ." She had switched languages, using *muslamic*, the language of the women of the chador.

The remote was nonplussed. It answered her in the same language, speaking fluently and idiomatically.

"We will reactivate the weapon upon your return," the remote informed her. "Name?"

"Major Penthesilea. I am expected."

"Snaga Ohme expects everything and nothing," the remote intoned. "You have clearance to pass. Your vehicle will remain under our care. When I open the gate, walk through immediately; do not dawdle. Proceed directly to the tram. Do not step off the path. I repeat. Do not step off the path. Once inside the tram, do not make any attempt to remove yourself from the tram while it is in motion. This is for your own safety and protection. Do you understand?"

"Yes."

"Accompany me, please." The remote led her forward to the gate, the other remotes backing off but keeping her under close surveillance.

The bronze gate swung open at Maigrey's approach; she heard the hum of the force field change in tone. Passing through the gate, accompanied by the remote, she noticed the walls decorated with what she might have expected from an Adonian—Snaga Ohme's portrait.

"I am fluent in all major languages of the galaxy," the remote said offhandedly, leading Maigrey along a narrow path made of crushed marble.

Beautiful plants grew on either side of the path—flowers beautiful and deadly. No such crude devices as land mines for Snaga Ohme. Maigrey, counting quickly, recognized at a glance over twenty species of vegetation lethal to humans alone, plus at least six that would kill any living organism they could wrap their tendrils around. A slithering sound and a low snarling whine coming from the shadows of the manmade jungle informed her that the plants weren't the only killers roaming at large over the estate.

"I also speak Corasian," the remote added, as an afterthought.

"Snaga Ohme doesn't miss a bet, does he?" Maigrey glanced up, overhead. Sun and cloudy sky were still visible, but seemed to shimmer slightly. The sun had acquired a halo. "The force field extends up and over the estate?"

"Of course. It protects us from conventional bombers,

nuclear strikes, laser attacks from space, and locusts," the remote said. A tram on a monorail glided forward; doors swung open.

"Locusts?" Maigrey repeated in some surprise.

"Damn nuisance—locusts. Please remain inside the tram until it comes to a full and complete stop. This is for your own safety. The average life expectancy in the jungle is forty seconds. Have a nice day."

The tram doors slid shut and sealed. The vehicle cruised away with Maigrey inside, moving slowly at first.

"Please be seated," the tram said, speaking *muslamic*. "Snaga Ohme welcomes you to his house and hopes that your stay will be a pleasant one. Make no attempt to open the door. It is wired to explode. Magazine?"

The tram picked up speed, rocketing along the monorail. Trees and plants and flowers passed in a dizzying blur. Maigrey thumbed through a year-old copy of *Laskarian Hot Spots*, found listed the name of the bar where she had first met John Dixter.

Closing the magazine, she tossed it aside and sat back against the leather seats, stared unseeing into the deadly jungle.

Chapter ❖ Eight

> . . . one pearl of great price . . .
>> St. Matthew, 13:45

"Do you recognize her?" Snaga Ohme asked.

"No. And we have most of Sagan's known agents on file. We've sent her description through the computer. There's no match."

"What about the breed? You don't have *him* on file?" Snaga Ohme said languidly.

Bosk appeared nettled. "*If* the breed really exists! No one's lived to tell of meeting him. You know my theory. I think he's a rumor Sagan started just to frighten his more gullible opponents. At any rate, she's not a half-breed, nor a 'droid. She's the genuine article."

Snaga Ohme and his cohort lounged in the Adonian's security room, observing their visitor on numerous screens. Hidden cameras, and some not so hidden, provided the Adonian a look at everyone living, working, or entering his dwelling. So thorough was his scrutiny that he could see a close-up of the woman's hands on one screen and at the same time observe a view of her skeletal make-up and the functioning of her vital organs on another.

"What is she—blood type, DNA, that sort of thing?"

Bosk was slightly embarrassed. "We can't tell. The testing equipment's not working properly."

"Not working!" Snaga Ohme stared at him in unparalleled amazement. "Since when?"

"Since . . . I don't know!" Bosk looked harassed. "Since she walked in the house, I suppose! It was operating well enough yesterday. I've got the repair crews on it."

"Odd." Snaga Ohme mused, sipping at champagne. "Still, I don't suppose it matters. She's not armed."

"A beam rifle in the jeep, but that's standard military procedure. She may not have known it was in there. She's wearing standard military light body armor. Other than that, the only object she has on her person is a small box made of rosewood."

"What's in the box?"

"Energy."

"Energy? What sort of energy? A rechargeable battery? What?"

"Just . . . energy." Bosh shrugged, kept his gaze averted.

"Dear boy, have you gone mad? Perhaps it's a bomb."

"No, it's not a bomb. It's benign, harmless. And it's just what I say it is—energy. Like she was carrying a small sun, for example."

"Take it away from her. Bring it to me."

"We tried." Bosk flushed. "She said if we touch it, the deal is off. According to our voice analyzer, she means it, too. She's not bluffing."

"And you're certain it's not an explosive?"

"We sent it through the neutralizer. Nothing."

"She didn't object to that?"

"No. Look, boss, you said yourself Sagan wouldn't try to kill you over a little thing like double-crossing him."

"I *am* extremely valuable to the Warlord," Ohme reflected. "And, for all his other faults, Derek isn't one to cut his nose off because his helmet rubs it wrong. But this woman of his is most puzzling. A mystery." The Adonian frowned.

"Don't make such a face, my dear!" Bosk reprimanded him, reaching out a hand to smooth his superior's flawless marble brow. "You can't think how it wrinkles you."

"Confound it, if I develop wrinkles, it won't be my fault! It will be hers! I detest mysteries! Take the woman to my office."

Bosk left on his errand. Snaga Ohme rose to his feet, turned his head to look in one of the ever-present mirrors. The frown line was no longer visible, had done no permanent damage. He was still beautiful.

··◁■· ■▷··

The Adonian's estate was larger in area than many civilized nations in the Galactic Democratic Republic. His house and the buildings attendant to it were taller and more numerous than those in some cities. None of the actual weapons manufacturing was carried out on Laskar. Raw materials were more

readily available and labor was cheaper on other planets.
Then, too, factories and laboratories tend to be ugly things and
the Adonian could not bear to be around anything ugly. His
one concession to the business side of his life were mazes of
target ranges, located in catacombs below his vast estate, and
a gigantic auditorium specially designed to show off his latest
inventions.

Once a year, the Adonian gave a party in that auditorium,
a party that was known the galaxy over. Invitations were sent
only to the rich and powerful or, in some instances, to those
Snaga Ohme's research teams determined had the potential for
becoming rich and powerful. Invitations to the Adonian's party
were, therefore, highly coveted. The reputation of several
hitherto "unknowns" had been made by being asked to the
party. One person, at least, was rumored to have killed himself
when his invitation—always hand-delivered in person by an
Adonian of extraordinary beauty and charm—didn't arrive.

Snaga Ohme's mansion was extraordinarily beautiful. It
was, Maigrey decided, *too* beautiful. The effect, on walking
through rooms and halls whose design and style and furnishings had been copied from the most beautiful rooms and halls
in the universe, was tantamount to sitting down to dinner and
discovering the table loaded with nothing but chocolate
éclairs, meringues, and whipped cream cakes.

One of the features of the tour through the stately mansion—a
tour obviously intended to flaunt Ohme's wealth—were the
rooms the Adonian fancifully called the Jewel Box. Known
throughout the galaxy for his collection of rare and priceless
gems, Snaga Ohme had devoted one entire wing to their display.
Enclosed in their steelglass cases, the jewels gleamed and
glittered, flamed and sparkled. The very latest techniques in
lighting were used to set off each to its best advantage. Here,
Maigrey had to admit, was true wealth, true splendor.

"Our most prized pieces," Bosk said. "The crown jewels—
sold by the government following the revolution in order to
raise money to aid those impoverished by the decadent
life-style of the king and his family."

Decadent life-style. Maigrey sighed softly. Poor king. Poor,
misguided king.

"Interested in the crown, are you? Yes, it is the most
valuable object in the collection, worth the wealth of several
planets, I'm told. And such an entertaining history goes along
with it. See the dark blotch there, beneath the fire diamond?

It's blood. His late Majesty was wearing this very crown the night of the revolution, the night of his—"

A roaring in her ears drowned the voice. Maigrey breathed in smoke, her skin was scorched by flame. She was running, running desperately. . . .

A barrier in her mind crashed down, shutting off the memories, leaving her in darkness. For a terrifying instant, she was blind, disoriented, had no idea where she was. And then the blank wall that had blocked her vision dissolved. She saw Bosk and the jewels—the man prattling on, oblivious to his guest's inattention. Maigrey blessed the foresight that had led her to hide her face beneath the veil.

She walked away, cutting off Bosk in mid-speech.

Every room in the house was the same—sumptuously beautiful. The servants were beautiful, the pets were beautiful, the people in the oil paintings were beautiful. Maigrey was exhausted with beauty by the time she and her escort reached the private office of the Adonian. Located in its own separate wing, the office was connected to the main house by a tunnel whose colored lights, dancing to recorded music, were incredibly beautiful.

"Major Penthesilea? I trust I am pronouncing that correctly?" Snaga Ohme rose to greet her, actually crossed the large, thick-carpeted room to take her hand in his and press it warmly.

From his welcome, she might have been bringing him his heart's desire—which she was, but he couldn't know that yet. Adonians were invariably charming; they couldn't help it, it was an inborn trait. Ohme would have greeted his most detested enemy in the same fashion.

Maigrey glanced around the office and was relieved to note that, though the room was beautiful in design and furnished quite beautifully, Snaga Ohme had been forced of necessity to permit a certain amount of ugliness. His arsenal of weapons, hidden among the paintings, the statuary, and other objets d'art, had been cleverly concealed, but an expert eye could find them. Maigrey located what she hoped were most of them, felt at home for the first time since she'd entered the estate.

"I am Snaga Ohme." The Adonian introduced himself with a charming humility, as if his face wasn't one of the most reproduced and recognizable in the galaxy.

Ohme led his guest to a chair at his desk, held it for her

himself, hovered over her as if she were made of the most
fragile, exquisite porcelain and might shatter at a harsh touch.
He made numerous anxious inquiries: Was the chair comfortable for her? Was the room temperature too warm? Too cool?
Would she accept a glass of champagne? A plate of imported
strawberries? A cushion for her head? A cushion for her feet?

Maigrey, accustomed to dealing with Adonians, assured
Snaga Ohme several times that she had never in her entire life
been happier or more contented than she was at this particular
moment. It amused her, on looking up, to see focused on her
the tiny glass eye of the lethal laser that could obliterate her in
seconds.

Finally, after assuring himself that he could do nothing to
increase her happiness, Snaga Ohme seated himself behind a
massive desk carved of ebony. Like his gardens, like his office,
he was beautiful on the surface, deadly beneath.

Soft, luxuriant, wavy black hair framed a face virile and
strong and masculine. His white teeth were perfect, his lips
curved sensually. His eyes were liquid gold, like olive oil. He
spoke in a rich baritone voice. Settled into his chair, Ohme
fixed his golden-eyed gaze on his guest. His hand, moving
unobtrusively, glided beneath his desk. Harsh light illuminated Maigrey, half-blinding her, leaving the Adonian in
shadow.

Standing behind Maigrey was Bosk. Hands folded respectfully, he seemed by his demeanor to have been born for no
other purpose than to serve Ohme's honored guests. Maigrey
knew better, knew a trained killer when she saw one.

Rising to her feet, she moved to another chair, a chair that
stood in darkness. The Adonian was all sudden concern. Had
she been sitting in a draft?

"The light," she said, "it hurts my eyes. I hope you don't
mind." Maigrey noted the laser beam, tracking her.

"Oh, but I do mind . . . Major." Another light switched
on, illuminated her in a pool of radiance.

Snaga Ohme glanced at himself in the mirror on his desk,
then condescended to pay the woman the compliment of
looking at her. "You have such a low and musical voice, you
move so gracefully, your eyes are quite fine. Why do you hide
yourself from the sight of those who must adore you, if they
were privileged enough to see what can only be a lovely face?
Remove your veil."

"I have taken a vow that no man will see my face," Maigrey replied.

"Is Derek Sagan included in this 'vow' . . . Major?" Snaga Ohme leaned back in his chair, delicately placed the tips of his fingers together. The gold eyes were oily slits. Sparkling jewels from numerous rings glinted in the light.

Maigrey decided enough was enough. Lifting her right hand, she made a slight gesture. The light above her winked out. Every light in the room went out, plunging them all in darkness. A faint hum, that had been barely audible, ceased. She heard Snaga Ohme sit abruptly forward.

"Bosk!"

"I've got her covered!"

Maigrey felt a gun press against her head, beneath the right earlobe. She relaxed back into the creaking leather of the chair.

"Control room?" The Adonian was, by the sound of it, pressing buttons and flipping switches.

"Checking!" a voice shouted from the ceiling. "No malfunction. Everything just blew! Some type of tremendous electrical overload. Most of the circuits are . . . fried!"

"The wiring in these older homes is dreadfully substandard," Maigrey observed.

"The devil with the wiring!" Snaga Ohme rose to his feet, turned, and pawed his way through several layers of heavy velvet and silk curtains until he came to large steelglass windows. He shoved the curtains open. The room was flooded with green sunlight that had an odd cast to it—the approaching storm. Gazing at Maigrey, the Adonian's olive-oil eyes seemed to have turned suddenly rancid.

"Who are you?" he demanded.

"You know my name," she answered. "Perhaps your associate could remove his weapon—which, by the way, is no longer functioning—and we could continue with our business. I am not an assassin. I assure you, Snaga Ohme, had I been sent to kill you, you would be dead right now."

Bosk looked for the red light indicating that the lasgun was operational. Not finding it, he threw the weapon to the floor, grabbed Maigrey roughly by the shoulder. "I'll take her to the dungeon—"

"No, no." Snaga Ohme was regarding Maigrey thoughtfully. His voice regained its former politic politeness. "Don't be discourteous to our guest, Bosk. Forgive him, Major, he worries about me more than my own mother. As you say, let us get back to business."

The Adonian smoothed the wrinkles in his suit, adjusted his tie, and relapsed back into his chair. An oblique motion of his hand sent Bosk, grumbling beneath his breath, to take his place at the side of the desk.

"I have something to sell, Major. You want to buy it. It is extremely costly." Ohme spread his hands, sighing. "The age-old law of supply and demand. The demand is great and the supply limited. There is, in fact, only one and there are several customers interested in obtaining it. You, if I understand correctly, represent Lord Sagan—"

"—who," Maigrey interposed, "if I understand correctly, fronted the money for the research and development of the . . . object . . ."

"Yes, that is true, and therefore I am willing to keep the price down for his lordship, adding only a small fee for the trouble and inconvenience due to his failure to pay on time. Unfortunately, Major," said Ohme with a sigh, "I have the impression that here is where our deal begins and . . . here it ends. A TRUC-load of golden eagles would hardly be sufficient payment, and you have brought nothing. I do not accept credit."

Snaga Ohme rose to his feet. Glancing at himself in the mirror, he smoothed nonexistent creases from his jacket. "Meeting you has been an interesting experience, Major. Extend my regards to Lord Sagan."

Maigrey slid her hand beneath the folds of the black robes, reached into the pocket of her body armor, and withdrew the rosewood box. She saw, out of the corner of her eye, Bosk tense and take a step toward her. She saw Snaga Ohme make a quick gesture, warding the man away. They had known of the box's existence, obviously, but they could not know what was inside. The inherent properties of the jewel itself would mask it from any type of detection equipment.

Maigrey ignored Ohme, ignored Bosk. She concentrated on the box, on keeping her hand from shaking, though a tremor ran through her body. Never before, in all the long and noble history of the Guardians, had anyone done such a thing as she was about to do. She had not realized it would be so difficult and, for a moment, was afraid she couldn't go through with it.

If she didn't, she would lose, Sagan would win.

Maigrey set her hand upon the box, lifted the lid.

Bosk sucked in an awed breath. Snaga Ohme made no sound; he had ceased to breathe.

It was as if Maigrey had stretched out her hand and caught and held the sunbeams shining through the window. And yet the light was more brilliant. It was as if she had plucked a moon from the night sky. And yet it was more radiant. It was as if she held forth a star. . . .

Faced with a choice of breathing or passing out, Snaga Ohme caught his breath. "A starjewel," he said in his own language.

"Does the jewel cover the price of the bomb?" Maigrey inquired coolly.

"Lady, whoever you are, I must be honest!" Desire cracked Snaga Ohme's voice. He reached out a trembling hand. "What you offer is worth far more . . . far more! I've never seen . . . I didn't know any still existed. . . . All were destroyed. . . ."

Maigrey snapped the lid shut, nearly catching the Adonian's fingers, and sat back, calm and composed, her hand covering the box.

"And now I want to see what it is I am buying."

Snaga Ohme's eyes were on the box. His fingers twitched. The handsome face had flushed a shade of red that, had he observed himself in the mirror, he would have seen was profoundly ugly. He wasn't looking in the mirror, however. For the first and perhaps only time in his life, he had forgotten his appearance. He pointed at the box.

"Bosk . . ." Ohme ordered.

Maigrey raised her right hand, opened it palm out, for the Adonian to see. "I wouldn't," she said softly.

The green-tinted sunlight, now darkened to a sullen browngray by the storm clouds, shone on five scars, five puncture marks in the palm. The Adonian sank back into his chair, knees giving way, his body gone nerveless.

"Bring the bomb," he ordered Bosk.

The associate cast a sharp, questioning look at the Adonian. Receiving no oblique sign, Bosk did as he was told. He crossed the room, stood before what appeared to be a blank wall of black marble, placed his hand on an unseen panel, and spoke several words softly, beneath his breath. The panel slid aside. Maigrey couldn't see clearly from her angle, but the first panel apparently opened on a second, because Bosk was forced to perform a similar ritual. There came the sound of metal scraping against rock. He thrust his arm into the opening in the wall and spoke again, then withdrew it slowly. In his hands, he held gingerly, reverently—as the knights of old might have held the Holy Grail—a crystal cube.

Bringing it over, he set the cube on the desk in front of Snaga Ohme.

Maigrey studied it, feeling relief, mingled with disappointment. She was relieved she didn't have to transport something the size of a neutron bomb, yet what kind of bomb could this be?

The crystal cube was solid, stood about ten centimeters high, and was ten wide. Inside the cube, embedded in the crystal, was a pyramid made of pure gold. A small, flat computer keyboard containing numerous small keys—twenty-six, by Maigrey's hasty count—adorned the cube's top. The point of the pyramid was connected to the underside of the keyboard. Maigrey studied the keys; each bore a symbol, unrecognizable.

She retrieved the rosewood box, tucked it beneath the folds of the chador. "Most impressive—for a paperweight."

Hardly, my lady. Pick it up, a voice invited.

It wasn't the Adonian who spoke. It was Sagan.

Maigrey shivered. The words were a spear driven through her body. Fearfully, she looked behind her, expecting to see him step out of the walls.

No one else was in the room. She was alone. Slowly, she stretched out her hands, touched and lifted the crystal cube.

She wasn't quite alone, however. Bosk and Snaga Ohme were still there, apparently, though they seemed as distant from her as if they'd been standing on Laskar's sun. She was vaguely aware that, when she lifted the bomb, both leapt to their feet. Bosk was yammering about something, threatening somebody. Snaga Ohme was remonstrating with the man, seemingly. Maigrey couldn't hear him distinctly, didn't care what he said. She heard only the voice inside her head, inside her being.

Do you know what you hold, my lady?

"No."

Think back, Maigrey, remember a time long ago. Color, quark, beauty . . . death.

Color, quark, beauty, death—a strange litany.

And then she knew. All feeling left her fingers. Numb, chilled, she held on to the cube only out of desperation.

A color bomb. Space-rotation bomb.

It had long been theorized that if the quarks of an atom could be pulled apart and the color bond which held them together stretched to its limit, the space between them could be rotated in such a way that, upon release, the quarks rushing back together would collide, totally annihilating matter, producing pure energy.

This was similar to the principle by which objects were able to travel faster than the speed of light. But this theory was the dark side, the unholy side. For once begun, the explosion would set off a chain reaction, affecting atom after atom. Annihilation would spread, instantaneously. Theoretically the explosion would stop . . . eventually . . . far out in space where matter was reduced to a single atom drifting in a vast void. But not before entire solar systems had died a flaming death. And there were certain scientists—mostly liberals of a bleeding heart variety—who had speculated that the horrific forces unleashed might tear a hole in the universe, destroying everything in the galaxy and beyond instantly, utterly. A rent in creation's fragile fabric.

No one, until now, had been blessed—or cursed—with the temerity, the audacity, the means and ability to construct a space-rotation bomb. King Starfire had never permitted it, refused even to discuss it. President Robes had purportedly made overtures to Congress, seeking funds to begin research and development, but the aforementioned liberals created such a public furor in the press that Congress always overwhelmingly voted against it.

Robes might have proceeded with the project under the sheltering cloak of galactic security but the scientific community and the press—eagerly watching for just such a slip—would have pounced on him, gone for the throat.

Sagan was another matter. The Warlord had grown so powerful, possessed such wealth and military might, that he could tell Congress to go to hell.

And now he had the means of sending them there.

Or rather, Maigrey thought, I have it.

Ultimate power. The rulership of the galactic empire. The lives . . . the deaths . . . of trillions upon trillions. *Et tibi dabo claves regni caelorum.* She held, in her hands, the keys to the kingdom of heaven.

Yes, my lady, you hold ultimate power. And how you long

for it! The scar may be upon your face, but it cuts deeper. It cuts to the soul!

The scar. The flaw. The fatal flaw. The taint in the Blood Royal. Born and bred to rule—the ability to utilize power became the need to utilize it, then need became desire, desire degenerated to lust.

"And why shouldn't I rule?" Maigrey asked, hands clutching the crystal cube, fingers caressing the smooth, cold sides, the sharp, biting corners pricking her skin. "I would restore the monarchy. My rule would be fair, just, wise. I would teach Dion, raise him up to become a king!"

A sparkle of light, bright and pure and cold, caught her eye, chilled the fever burning in her blood. The starjewel, the Star of the Guardians, the symbol of her pledge to serve a king, not become one.

"I suppose I should be like Galadriel in the old storybook," she said bitterly. "'Diminish, and go into the west.' I won't, my lord! The hobbit has given me the ring and, by God, I'm going to use it!"

You forget, lady, that I alone possess the energy source needed to activate it, I only know the code that will start the sequence.

That was logical. Sagan had provided Ohme with the theory, the design, had allowed the Adonian to build the bomb, but the Warlord would have been a fool to place the means to explode it in Ohme's grasp. An energy source, something only Sagan could use, something to which only he had access. That shouldn't be too difficult to figure out, once she had the opportunity to examine the weapon.

As for the code, for anyone but her, coming up with that would be practically impossible. The symbols on the top of the box probably represented other symbols—what? It could be anything: numbers, an alphabet, musical notations. A computer could be programmed to randomly generate all the possibilities and discover the right one, but—using all the known languages in the galaxy, all the numerical systems—it would take lifetimes.

And then Maigrey knew. She knew at least the key to the code, and once she knew that . . .

"You are clever, my lord. A forgotten poet, writing in a forgotten language. But there is one person who remembers. *I* remember, my lord. I remember and I've been aware of the poet, for he's been in your mind of late. And, knowing the poet, it should not be difficult to come up with the poem—"

Sagan didn't answer, but she sensed his doubt, his confusion, and she knew she was right.

And then he was gone. He wasn't defeated. He had another move to make, she was certain. But, for now, she controlled the board, she was winning the game. It was an exhilarating and highly unusual feeling.

Bosk was still carrying on about something. Maigrey gradually became aware of his existence, returned to the reality around her. The man was red-faced, shouting, but he hadn't laid a hand on her. He didn't dare.

The might and the majesty of the Blood Royal surrounded her, guarded her like a force field. She could feel it crackle and spark. She could draw on it, bring this mansion down around Ohme's shell-shaped ears if she wanted. Melt the wiring! She would melt stone, melt flesh!

Snaga Ohme, on the other hand, was calm, in control, though he watched her narrowly.

And then it occurred to Maigrey that she was in possession of the starjewel *and* the bomb.

"I could walk out with both of them," she said to the Adonian. "Leave you with nothing. It would be nothing more than what you deserved, after all, for trying to double-cross my lord."

"Yes, my lady—whoever you are—you could." Snaga Ohme smiled; the liquid eyes were limpid pools of oil. "You can murder me where I stand, slay me with a touch, a look. But you won't. You're a Guardian. And with your great strength comes a great weakness: honor. Even Sagan, whose heart is said to be made of adamant, suffers from this curse. Honor is the crack in the armor. It destroyed most of you, years ago. It will destroy you who are left."

Maigrey was only half-listening. She felt a sense of urgency, suddenly, could hear the ticking of a clock. Sagan was on his way, coming to claim his "pearl of great price," his keys to the kingdom of heaven.

I have preparations to make, Maigrey realized. I can't waste time discussing honor with a man who probably doesn't know how to spell it.

She tucked the bomb awkwardly beneath her arm—the thing was heavy and difficult to hold properly, but she'd be damned if she'd set it down—and fumbled in the folds of the chador. Producing the rosewood box, she held it out to the Adonian.

Snaga Ohme's fingers closed on the box. Maigrey's, suddenly, couldn't let it go.

She saw the jewel again as she had seen it moments before, sparkling with its blue-white flame. But she couldn't really see it. The jewel was hidden in the box, shrouded in her black robes.

The scar on her face began to throb painfully. Her power was starting to crumble. She saw Snaga Ohme cast a quick, meaningful glance at his cohort, saw Bosk's lips part in an answering smile.

Swiftly, Maigrey released the box, almost threw it into the Adonian's grasping hand. He snatched it away, pressed it close to his breast.

"One of the footmen will show you out, Major."

Maigrey inclined her head, heard the rustle of the dark fabric of the veil. She was incapable of speech, wanted only to be away from this place. Concealing the bomb in the black winding cloth of the chador, she left without a backward glance.

··◁■ ■▷··

"The woman's on her way," Bosk reported.

Snaga Ohme didn't hear his cohort. The Adonian stood near the window, gazing at the radiant, shimmering starjewel with a rapturous expression, his fingers running over it, delighting in every carved facet of the rare gemstone.

Realizing that Ohme would be absorbed in the covetous contemplation of his prize for at least the next several hours, if not the next several days, Bosk was heading for the door, about to remove his unwanted self, when a hoarse, strangled cry arrested him.

"Boss? What?" Bosk whirled around in alarm, hand on his lasgun, with some wild thought that the fey woman had returned and was crawling in through the window.

Snaga Ohme remained alone and unharmed, however, staring at the starjewel, but his rapt gaze had been replaced by one of cunning and triumphant understanding.

"This is it!" Ohme breathed, holding the jewel in his hands, thrusting it forward for Bosk to see.

Bosk didn't see, however, and remained staring at his friend with a puzzled expression.

Ohme's head snapped up. "The woman! I want her!"

"But she's out the gate, boss. The remote just reported—"

"Damn!" The Adonian scowled, impervious to the fact that he was inflicting masses of wrinkles on himself. "Go after her, Bosk! Bring her back!"

"But what if she won't come?"

"Then shoot her!"

"But you just said you wanted her—"

"Dolt! Idiot!" The Adonian gazed greedily once more at the starjewel, then thrust it into a pocket. Suddenly, he darted forward, grabbed Bosk by the cheeks and kissed him resoundingly on his forehead. "Beloved Bosk! It's not her I want! It's the bomb! Don't you understand? The bomb!"

"But you made a deal—"

"Ah, you know my motto, Bosk. *Caveat emptor!* Yes, beloved Bosk, *caveat emptor* indeed!"

Chapter ·◈⊃◯⊂◈· Nine

Caveat emptor.

Let the buyer beware.

Ancient Roman dictum

Entering the tram car, Maigrey sank back into the cushy seat. She kept hold of the bomb; her hands burned against its cold, smooth crystal surface, as if she were touching a block of ice with wet fingers. Her thoughts were in tatters, streaming away from her before she could catch hold of them, blown by the twisting winds of exultation, confusion, and a vague horror of herself. The tram car trusted that she'd had a joyous and prosperous meeting with its master and asked if she'd like anything to read.

The journey to the gate was uneventful. The remote at the gate eyed the bomb with its glassy optics, and Maigrey tensed, but apparently the remote had orders to let her out with it safely. The gate opened, the force field's hum altered in tone, and she was safely off of Snaga Ohme's estate. Maigrey breathed a sigh of relief, caught herself doing so, and realized then that somewhere in the jumble of her confused mental state had been the warning that Ohme would try to recover his property.

"Honest as an Adonian," so the saying went, and it wasn't intended as a plaudit.

The remotes had brought the hoverjeep around. Maigrey inspected it thoroughly before entering. The beam rifle had been reactivated, as previously agreed. The vehicle had not been sabotaged, though she did find a tracking device, cleverly concealed.

She considered removing it, decided to leave it. Why make things difficult? Maigrey climbed in the jeep, placed the bomb carefully on the seat beside her, adjusted the beam rifle within easy reach. Activating the jeep, she sped down the steep, rocky path that led away from the Adonian's estate. She noticed that it had rained heavily while she'd been inside the Adonian's. Large puddles dotted the driveway and in the distance was the rumble of thunder. Apparently Ohme's force field kept out rain as well as locusts.

Steering the hoverjeep, concentrating on her driving gave her mind a focal point, enabled her to gather the remnants of her thoughts, weave them together, and cover the inner turmoil with a soothing blanket. She considered the warning her instincts had provided. Yes, undoubtedly Ohme would try to regain the bomb. It was logical, made perfect business sense. He had other buyers, he had the starjewel. What was stopping him?

Maigrey could almost hear his report to the Warlord.

"A pity about the poor woman, but, my dear Lord Sagan, I can't be held responsible! Laskar's been plagued by roving bands of drug addicts. The wretches will steal anything to support their foul habit. I warned Haupt not to allow the woman to travel alone. I did indeed. The thieves stole everything, or so I read in the police report. Hoverjeep, beam rifle, the jewel, the bomb. . . . I haven't the vaguest idea where it is now, my lord. You might try the local pawn shops. . . ."

Sagan would know differently, of course. He would know who really had the bomb—or who had undoubtedly already sold it to someone else by that time. But the Adonian's crime would be difficult to prove. Any retaliatory attack against Ohme would be costly and futile. The bomb would be gone. The other warlords and powerful people in the galaxy who depended on Snaga Ohme's genius would be extremely upset with Sagan for damaging their pet weapons manufacturer. And, like it or not, when the time came for Sagan to make his move, he would need those people as allies. He would also, much as he hated to admit it, need Snaga Ohme.

"I'll have to be ready for them." Maigrey had fallen into the habit of talking to herself during her long years of exile. "*That* shouldn't be too difficult. Ohme may be a genius when it comes to designing weapons, but the only strategic maneuvers Adonians practice are in bed!"

It would be an ambush, Maigrey decided. She'd be attacked before she arrived back at the base.

That settled, she was able to give other matters consideration. And she came to the conclusion that her true danger wasn't Snaga Ohme. Her true danger was the clock. The Warlord was moving nearer to Laskar with each passing second, and she wasn't ready for him. Now this stupid ambush would delay her further. It was all very irritating!

Maigrey reached the end of the drive, steered the hover-jeep onto a highway, known locally as Snaga's Road. The highway was a magnificent stretch of concrete, eight lanes, and had been designed to accommodate nearly every type of vehicle, from the old-fashioned, wheeled motor cars preferred by the romantic to the modern, air-cushioned jet and hover craft.

The highway led from the Adonian's estate into Laskar city proper. It had been built at great expense with galactic citizens' tax dollars and it was used once a year—the night of Ohme's famous party. On that evening, the highway would be jammed with vehicles, all traveling one direction.

Maigrey paused at the intersection of Ohme's drive and Ohme's road, considering. She could take this highway, the route she'd come, or she could cut across country.

"I can't throw off pursuit," she mused aloud, drumming her fingers on the steering mechanism, "nor do I necessarily want to. I don't want to make Ohme work too hard. The bastard might accidentally come up with something clever. Then there are those damned mountains, between here and the fort. They're not particularly tall, but crossing them will be time-consuming. I'm not that familiar with the countryside; I certainly can't afford to wander around lost! Blast the Adonian anyhow!" Maigrey pulled down the veil covering her mouth and nose; it seemed to be suffocating her. "I'll keep to the main road . . . and hope we get this over with soon!" The hover-jeep shot forward, roaring along the almost empty stretch of pavement.

Maigrey's hand toyed with the commlink controls. "I could call Haupt, tell him I'm in trouble. . . . No. The poor man's nervous enough, imagining he's responsible for me to the Warlord. Haupt'd probably send an entire armored division complete with air support to my rescue!" Maigrey's hand moved to the cool crystal of the bomb. "And the fewer who know about this, the better."

The jeep cruised down the deserted highway. Maigrey, tense, alert, was also constantly aware of the Warlord's approach. She continually glanced in the rearview mirror or turned her head, looking over her shoulder. She wasn't searching for the Adonian. Though she knew in her mind that the Warlord was light-years away, in her heart she had the eerie and unnerving impression that Sagan was creeping up right behind her.

Angrily, she shook it off. One worry at a time. She couldn't allow herself to become distracted. This wasn't going to be easy.

About five kilometers from the Adonian's mansion, the highway wound through a narrow pass cut into the mountains. Her jeep topped a rise and Maigrey saw, in the distance, an ancient model tanker truck rolling ponderously down the highway, heading straight toward her.

"My, my! What a remarkable coincidence," Maigrey said, slowing the jeep. She glanced swiftly at the rock-strewn cliffs rising up on either side of her. An army could hide undetected amid the boulders, pines, and thick undergrowth.

A sudden booming sound echoed through the pass. A wheel rim and bits of rubber flew from the truck; one of its tires had blown. The truck jackknifed, swerved across the highway onto Maigrey's lane, overturned, and burst into flames. The truck lay on its side, completely blocking the highway. The fire roared and crackled. Oily smoke roiled into the air. No one climbed out of the cab.

"Really, Ohme, how dumb do you think I am?" Maigrey grumbled, driving the jeep straight off the road into a ditch.

They would be watching for her, probably had her in their sights right now. Hopefully, they would think she'd swerved out of shock or panic. Hidden behind several large boulders and a sign that read LASKAR 20 KILOMETERS EAT AT TRACY'S, Maigrey worked quickly, knowing she couldn't remain down here long or they'd come looking for her. Stripping off her black veil, she attached it by two corners to the jeep's front control panel on the driver's side. The black robes came off next. She bundled the fabric into a shapeless lump and propped it up in the driver's seat. Removing the bomb, she placed it carefully on the ground near the sign's metal legs, covered the crystal with a mass of sweet-smelling sage.

Maigrey grabbed the beam rifle, lowered the jeep's bubble top, set the drive on automatic, and sent the vehicle back out onto the highway. Fortunately, the desert air was calm; the smoke from the wreckage spiraled straight up into the sky. Those watching would have a clear view.

The wreck was about an eighth of a kilometer ahead. Crouching behind a boulder, Maigrey watched the jeep cruise along the highway toward the wreck, the black veil fluttering in the wind. Sensing devices would stop the vehicle automatically when it came to an obstacle, and they did so. It was powering down, air cushions keeping it afloat a safe distance from the jackknifed truck.

Bright flashes of laser light sizzled. The black veil went up in a rush of white flame that consumed it in an instant. The black robes burned a few seconds longer, a thin column of smoke rising from the charred bundle.

Six heads popped up, three on either side of the highway. Six forms detached themselves from the rocks and warily approached the jeep. One inspected the "body," poked at it with his rifle butt.

"There's not much left," he said dubiously, voice carrying clearly in the thin air.

"Ah, she was a skinny thing. Forget it. Where's the bomb?"

The six men, two of whom Maigrey recognized from the Adonian's mansion, peered into the jeep.

"It's not here. Must be in the back storage compartment."

Four began to walk toward the rear of the jeep. One remained in front, still poking at the "body."

"I don't like this! I never saw a lasgun completely disintegrate—"

Maigrey rose, raised the beam rifle, opened fire. Two died before they knew what hit them. Number three had time to swear and fumble for his weapon before he was hit, the body blown backward over the jeep's trunk. Maigrey caught number four making a vain attempt to shield himself behind the body of the third. It didn't work.

By this time, however, numbers five and six had realized they'd been duped and were returning her fire. Maigrey kept low. Their aim could only be guesswork. They hadn't had time to locate her, or so she supposed.

But she misjudged them. A boulder near her exploded, shooting splinters of rock, sharp as arrowheads, through the air. Most bounced harmlessly off the body armor, but one cut the back of her left hand and another bit painfully into her neck, just below the jaw.

"Congratulations. You drew blood," she told the other two, and, taking careful aim, finished both of them off.

Maigrey remained concealed a few moments, eyeing the corpses and the surrounding territory. She thought it unlikely that the Adonians would have been clever enough to send one group forward, keep another in hiding, but there was always that possibility.

"I can't stay here all day," she muttered, seeing no one and nothing. "Sagan's coming, and Ohme's wasted enough of my time."

Cautiously, she raised herself up, beam rifle charged and ready.

Nothing. All was quiet. The only sounds were the wind howling among the rocks, the roar and crackle of flames from the burning truck. Maigrey retrieved the bomb and made a dash for the jeep.

Where they came from, she never knew. She could have sworn she had carefully inspected the area but was forced to admit that, in her haste and worry over the Warlord, she might have been careless. It seemed to her dazed mind, though, that they rose up out of the ground . . . or out of their own graves.

Maigrey had reached the hoverjeep, placed the bomb back carefully in the passenger seat beside her, when movement caught her eye. Fearfully she wheeled, raised the rifle. . . .

Four humans, three men and a woman, walked toward her, small stunguns in their hands. Each differed in appearance, yet all gave the impression of being exactly alike, perhaps because the faces wore exactly the same blank expression—the eyes focused on her were totally and utterly devoid of life.

"Drop your weapon, Lady Maigrey Morianna," the woman said. She appeared to be the leader of the four.

Maigrey didn't obey, not out of courage but because her mind had locked up, refused to function. She held the weapon in her hands, but her hands had no idea what to do with it, and therefore did nothing. She couldn't move, couldn't speak, couldn't think. The figures approaching her came not from the rocks and brush on the side of the highway, but from her past.

I am in a banquet hall, confusion rages around me. I hear the sound of explosions echo from another part of the palace. I can smell the smoke, the flame of death. Platus, on my left, clasps my hand, mouths words I can't hear. Danha Tusca on my right. His ebony skin gleams with sweat. Sagan has betrayed us, betrayed me. He holds aloft a flaming sword and out of the flame and smoke comes . . .

"My master bids you greeting, Lady Maigrey." The woman reached out and plucked the beam rifle from Maigrey's nerveless grasp. "You will accompany us to the 'copter. Your accommodations are prepared. We have only a prefab dwelling, rather crude. Still, my master hopes your stay with us will be comfortable—"

One of the men, standing behind the woman, dropped to the ground without a sound. Maigrey heard nothing, saw nothing. She stared at the corpse—a steel bolt had pierced the man's head. The second and third fell at Maigrey's feet. They died silently, as had their comrade.

But the female leader apparently heard the sound of the bodies slumping to the ground. She grabbed hold of Maigrey, used Maigrey's living body as a shield.

A man clad in rags with tattered hair and a face out of a drug hallucination glided toward them, moving like a panther.

Maigrey saw sunlight flash off a knife blade in his hand. Instinct, years of training, impelled her to act and she lunged sideways. The knife flashed past her, thudded into her captor's body with ease and practiced skill. Death was swift; the hand holding on to Maigrey jerked in a spasm of pain, relaxed.

Maigrey lost her balance. Both she and the corpse rolled to the ground, the body falling on top of her. The man dragged it off, hurled it to one side of the road, near its dead comrades. Confused and dazed, Maigrey crouched, waiting for the attacker to come after her, hand groping over the ground for a sharp rock, a stick—anything to use as a weapon. Her hand closed over the beam rifle.

The man came near her. Maigrey picked up the gun, watching him warily. The man halted, stood poised, hands in plain sight where she could see them. With one finger, he pointed.

"You hurt." The whispering voice was thick and rough. His fingers were dirty and covered with blood.

"Nothing serious. A flesh wound." Maigrey scrambled to her feet, keeping her eyes on the ragged man and the hoverjeep between him and her.

He moved with her, his motion fluid and graceful, reminding Maigrey again of a cat. Maigrey kept the rifle aimed at him.

"It's not quite proper form to hold a gun on someone who's just saved your life," she told him, "but I made one mistake today and I'll be damned if I'll make another. You'll just have to forgive me."

The man did not appear offended, but rather almost amused. Cocking his head to one side, he peered at her out of misaligned eyes. The unwashed, tangled hair fell forward, covered half his brutal face. "You okay to go on alone?"

"Yes," said Maigrey. "Yes, I'm all right."

The man gave a curt nod, walked to the corpse, and yanked out his knife. Wiping the blood on leather trousers that were barely visible through the rags of what might once have been a blanket or a poncho, the man thrust the blade back into the top of his boot. Without another word, he strolled off.

"Wait. Who are you?" Maigrey called out. "Where did you—? Why—?"

But the man vanished, disappearing among the rocks so swiftly and suddenly it seemed that he'd become invisible.

"Thank you," Maigrey said, rather belatedly.

She began to shake. The beam rifle seemed to weigh megagrams; she nearly dropped it.

"Stop it, you fool! You don't have time to fall apart." But she found it difficult to move, difficult to drag her fascinated gaze from the corpses of the four who'd attacked her. The female lay on her back, her eyes staring sightlessly at the smoke coiling into the sky, not a great deal of difference in expression between the eyes that had been living and the eyes now dead. Something stirred in Maigrey's mind, a hand trying to draw back a thick and heavy curtain shrouding her memory.

"Somewhere, I've seen eyes like that. . . ."

The memory was gone, however, not to be discovered hiding in the shadows, leaving behind only a smell of smoke and flame and the vague feeling of dread that always kept her from working harder to find it.

And Sagan was coming.

Maigrey circled around the hoverjeep, rifle ready, keeping an almost paranoid watch. No one, nothing bothered her. She brushed aside the ashes of what had once been her black robes, climbed into the jeep, and checked on the bomb. It rested on the seat, its crystal serenely sparkling in the nauseous green glow of the Laskarian twilight.

Carefully, Maigrey removed the tracking device, tossed it down on top of the body of one of the Adonian's henchmen. Ohme would at first figure his plan had succeeded; the jeep was incapacitated. Eventually, however, he'd begin to wonder why his men hadn't returned. As for whoever would wonder about the other four . . . or the other one . . .

Maigrey shook her head.

Sagan was coming.

She reprogrammed the jeep's controls, steered the vehicle around the flaming truck, sped off down the highway. She could see Fort Laskar in the distance.

"Please, God, just a little more time. Just give me a little more. . . ."

Chapter ··◄━●━►·· Ten

O God! I could be bounded in a nut-shell, and count myself a
king of infinite space, were it not that I have bad dreams.
William Shakespeare, *Hamlet*, Act II, Scene 2

"My God, Tusk! What's that?" Nola rolled over inside the
sleeping bag, clutched at the mercenary lying curled up beside
her.

Tusk groaned, pulled the upper part of the down-filled bag
over his head. "The kid. Nightmare. He had a couple on
Vangelis, after the battle."

Another scream echoed through the spaceplane. Dion
shouted incoherent words and they could hear him panting for
breath, as if he were running a long distance.

"Go to him," Nola ordered, shaking Tusk's bare shoulder.

"You go to him," the mercenary mumbled into the pillow.
"Women are . . . better . . . comforting, nurturing."

"I can't, Tusk," Nola whispered, drawing back, staring into
the darkness. "I—I'm afraid of him."

Another scream. "Shut the eyes! Why are they staring at me
like that? Shut the eyes!" Dion gasped for breath.

"And I'm not?" Tusk demanded. "All right! All right! I'm
going. I guess I'll have to if I'm gonna get any sleep! How the
devil do you get out of this damn thing?"

In his struggle to escape the sleeping bag, Tusk sat up too
quickly and struck his head on the console under which he and
Nola slept. Swearing volubly, he crawled out, hands groping
for a nuke lamp. He found it, turned it on, and swore again,
the harsh white light stabbing painfully into his sleep-gummed
eyes.

"Kid, hey, kid! Take it easy!" Tusk called, lurching bare-
footed through the small plane and into the cramped compartment where the pilot bunked. He played the light around until

he located the bed, nothing more than a shelf that could be stowed when the plane was cleared for action.

Dion, bathed in sweat, was sitting up. His eyes were wide open; he stared straight ahead into the darkness, made frantic motions with his hands.

"Shut the eyes!" he cried feverishly, grasping at air. "Shut them shut them shut them . . ."

Tusk sat down on the edge of the bunk. "Kid—"

Dion gave a yell that stood Tusk's hair on end and grabbed the mercenary by his shoulders with bruising strength.

"Dion! Ouch! Damn it! Leggo of me. C'mon! Snap out of it." Tusk clamped his hand firmly on the young man's jaw and shook his head back and forth.

Dion jerked free. Eyes wide in terror, he went for Tusk's throat. The mercenary dropped the nuke lamp. It bounced to the deck and rolled around on the uneven surface, setting the dark shadows dancing like witches at a revel. Suddenly Dion blinked, stared at Tusk in the flitting light, sobbed, and went limp in the mercenary's arms.

Tusk sighed and held the boy close, hands ruffling the sweat-damp hair. "It's okay," he said, patting the heaving shoulders awkwardly. "It was just a dream."

"I'm sorry." Dion pulled back stiffly. His face was white as the flaring light, the hair color distorted from flaming red to bronze. Purple shadows circled the blue eyes, his lips bled— he'd bitten through them. "I'm sorry. Go back to sleep. It won't happen again." He lay back on the bare bed, the pillow having slipped to the floor.

Tusk picked up the nuke lamp, glanced at a digital clock which displayed several times—space time, ground time for a particular planet . . . "Hell, it's too late to go back to bed now. It's mid-afternoon, Laskar ST."

"Laskar?" Dion propped himself up on his elbows. "You mean we landed?"

"Yeah, I brought us down last night, while you were asleep."

"Why didn't you wake me?"

"What for? Wake you up to tell you it's time to go to bed? Get serious, kid."

"But—" Dion's face flushed. He sat straight, swung his legs over the side of the bunk. "We could have gone out, started searching for—"

"No," Tusk said firmly. "No one goes roaming around

Laskar in the tail end of the night unless he's good and tired of living."

"Then we'll go now—"

"Just cool down your engine, kid. We got plenty of time. Nothin' opens till after dark." Tusk, fiddling nervously with the light, shining it up and down and everywhere except on the boy, joined him, sitting on the side of the bunk. "We got some time. Why don't you . . . tell me what happened to you in that control room on *Defiant*. Yeah, I know. Nothin'. Hell, kid, I saw your face when you came outta there! Blood on you from head to toe! You left bloody footprints when you walked!"

Tusk felt the tremor of the boy's shudder, put his hand on Dion's forearm. "They say it helps, you know, if you talk about it—"

Dion sat trembling, silent. Slowly, he shook his head, drew a deep breath, and turned to look at Tusk, the blue eyes calm. "No. It wouldn't. I know what's the matter. I'm weak. A coward. It's in the blood. Sagan told me."

"That traitor! That bastard! That . . . that . . ." Tusk seethed, hot words crowding into his mouth so fast he couldn't spit them out.

Dion rose to his feet. "I'm going to take a shower. I'll fix breakfast when I'm out. It's my turn."

"Breakfast? I— You— I'll tell you where—"

The young man ignored his ranting friend, squeezed his body into the tiny shower stall, and slid the panel shut. Tusk's words were drowned out by the sound of running water. The mercenary turned, kicked viciously at a storage chest with his bare foot, and howled in pain.

"That was bright," Nola commented, coming into the room, a bathrobe wrapped around her short, stocky body. She screwed up her eyes against the bright glare, crinkling the freckles spattered across her cheeks.

"Forgot I didn't have fuckin' boots on!" Tusk hobbled across the deck. "A coward! That's what Sagan told the kid, huh? That son of a— If he was here now I'd . . . I'd—"

"Kick him," Nola said softly, slipping her arm around Tusk.

He shook his head, looked exasperated, then, sighing, clasped his arms around the woman and hugged her tight. Holding her, he rested his chin lightly on her head, breathing the fragrance of her curly, sleep-tousled hair. "Why are we here, Nola? Why did we come? I tell you, I'm scared. More scared than I've ever been in my life, even when I thought we were all gonna die on *Defiant*."

Nola tilted her head back, looked up into the dark brown eyes. "Then why don't we leave, Tusk? You know the Starlady didn't send that message! Dion'll be furious, but at least he'll be ali—"

A pounding came on the outside of the plane's hull.

Nola hushed. Tusk released her slowly. "Too late." Moving to the controls, he activated the exterior commlink. "Yeah? Who is it?"

"Anselmo!" came a gruff boom. "Someone's been here, asking 'bout you."

"What'd you tell 'im?"

"What you said. But I don't think he believed me."

"He didn't," interjected a voice, another voice, a different voice.

"I think you better come out here, Tusk," Anselmo added. "Now! He's got a gun on me."

····◆■　■◆►····

"I apologize for the use of force, Dion Starfire," the messenger said in an expressionless tone, gazing at them with empty eyes. He slid the lasgun neatly back into a holster worn in the small of his back. "But the owner persisted in lying to me."

"How did you find us?" Tusk growled.

Dion, glancing around, wondered how anyone in the civilized universe could have found them. Towering above their heads, a bright purple neon sign, reading ANSELMO'S WRECKING & SA VAGE CO, blinked on and off against the noxious green sky. Beneath the neon, a billboard read: 10 SQUARE HECTOMETERS OF CLEAN TESTED RELIABLE USED PARTS. WE PAY TOP $$$ FOR LATE MODEL WRECKED SPACEPLANES, RVS, SHUTTLES, DROIDS AND BOTS. YOU SMASH 'EM, WE CASH 'EM.

"Why are we parked in a junkyard?" Dion asked Tusk quietly.

"Hell, kid, it's a great cover. *Used* to be," Tusk said, eyeing the messenger suspiciously. "I asked how you found us."

"That is not relevant. I am to take you to the Lady Maigrey immediately. Will you come?"

"Like hell it's not relevant! What's the deal, Anselmo?" Tusk sidled close to the junkyard owner, a large human of indeterminate race, almost as big around as he was tall.

"Lady Maigrey! Is she all right? Is she in danger?" Dion approached the messenger.

"She is, for the moment, safe and well," the messenger replied, his eyes fixed on Dion, perhaps seeing him, perhaps not. "The situation changes as we speak. You should waste no more time."

Anselmo was talking in low tones to Tusk. "I caught the creep pokin' 'round the yard this morning. How he got over the fence, I don't know. It's hot and the juice is on. Anyhow, I told 'im we wasn't open, and fer him t'come back this afternoon. He asks me if I seen a plane matchin' that description." Anselmo waved an enormous hand in the direction of Dion's spaceplane. "I told him we didn't have no wrecked plane like that in stock, and without so much as a how-do-you-do he pulls out that friggin' blaster, starts threatenin' to blow holes in people's stomachs."

"Well, you were safe enough there," Tusk said. "The laser beam isn't made that could penetrate your gut! So you led him right to us, eh, Anselmo?"

The messenger, overhearing, turned his blank face toward the mercenary. "What he does not tell you, Mendaharin Tusca, is that he offered to find a plane matching the description I gave him if I paid for it in advance."

"Look, it doesn't matter how he found us," Dion began impatiently. "We have to go—"

Tusk flashed Anselmo a vicious glance. The big man grunted and shrugged flabby shoulders. "Business is business, Tusk. Speaking of which, you owe me ten kilners."

"Ten!" Tusk gaped.

"A night."

"You thief! I'll be damned if I'll pay—"

"Tusk!" Dion glowered at his friend. "Go ahead and—"

"You'll pay," Anselmo said calmly. "I'm still the cheapest set-down around. In fact, I'm the *only* set-down around. You can't go nowhere else. Everyone's full up. Big party this weekend. Snaga Ohme's. People comin' in from all over the galaxy."

Nola caught her breath. "Snaga Ohme!"

The messenger shifted his vacant gaze to her. "You know of Snaga Ohme?"

"Uh, sure." Nola giggled nervously. "*Every* girl knows about Snaga Ohme. He's in *all* the mags. I'd forgotten that this planet is where he lives! I'd *love* to see his house!" She stepped near Tusk, entwined her hand in his, squeezed it tightly. "Who's that holo star he's been going around with lately? You know, the one I showed *General Dixter*."

"Dixter?" Tusk stared at her, puzzled. "Dixter never went to a holo in his life—"

"Yes, dear," Nola purred, digging her nails into his flesh, "*you* know the one I mean! The one he just went wild over . . . with the *long blond* hair. . . ."

Dion heaved an irritated sigh, turned to face the messenger. "Let's go."

The messenger nodded slowly. "Your friends are coming?"

"They'd obviously rather stay here and discuss holo stars—"

"We're coming, kid." Tusk glared at the messenger. "I guess you don't mind if we take our weapons, since you say there's likely to be danger."

The mercenary indicated his own blaster. Nola was armed with a needle-gun. Dion wore the bloodsword awkwardly, still unused to it. The handle, suspended from his belt, bounced on his thigh and he continually put his hand over it to stop the movement. The messenger flicked a glance over the conventional weapons. His gaze lingered longer on the bloodsword, but it evoked no spark of life or interest, nothing beyond another slow nod.

"Weapons would be advisable."

"Oh, glad you think so. Now, Anselmo, if you'll excuse us—"

"Cash." Anselmo planted his large body—a substantial obstacle—in Tusk's path. "A week in advance. And something extra for the inconvenience."

"What inconvenience?"

"Of having a gun stuck in my belly!"

Tusk, scowling, fished a purse out of one of the numerous pockets of his desert fatigues, slapped several bills into the junk dealer's grime-encrusted palm. Tusk started to walk off, but the hand closed over his shoulder with a grip like one of Anselmo's own wrecking machines.

"Not that I don't trust you," the dealer said, and began slowly counting the money.

Dion and the messenger walked on ahead toward a small 'copter, parked on the flat, green-tinted Laskarian terrain.

"Very well." Anselmo tucked the bills into a greasy wallet, thrust it into a cavernous pocket. "Be sure and don't make a mess, will ya?"

"Yeah, I'll keep my particular spot of the junkyard neat and tidy. Say, Anselmo," Tusk said conversationally, leaning near the junk dealer, all the time keeping one eye on the messenger, "you know everyone in, on, or around this planet. You ever seen that guy before?"

Anselmo grunted, shook his head. "And if I never see him again, it'll be too soon. When you come back, Tusk—*if* you come back—don't bring the stiff with you." Waddling off, the junk dealer rolled through the junkyard's fence gate, slammed it shut behind him.

Tusk started to follow Dion, but Nola yanked him back.

"Now what?" he asked irritably. "C'mon, will ya?"

He tried to drag her forward, but Nola was a strong woman, her short, compact body difficult to dislodge once she planted her feet.

"Look, sweetheart," Tusk said in wheedling tones, "we can't let Dion and the corpse just waltz off—"

"Will you listen to me a minute?" Nola hissed. "Go on. Start walking, if you must, but move slow. That Snaga Ohme he was talking about! *He's* the one I was investigating for General Dixter!"

"Huh?" Tusk still had holo stars on his mind.

"The weapons genius, on Vangelis! The one who was in touch with Lord Sagan! I found out that this Ohme character had been on Vangelis, working on some sort of top-secret project. I told Dixter what I found out. He never said any more to me about Ohme and when I asked the general, he got that kind of funny, tight-lipped look on his face and told me to forget I'd ever heard the name. That was right before the battle with the Corasians."

"So that's it!" Tusk said bitterly. "It's all beginning to make sense. That's why Sagan turned on us. He didn't want us, he wanted Dixter, and he had to make it look good so no one would suspect. And Dixter knew it. That's why he warned us to be ready. And now Sagan's got him! Damn! I knew we shouldn't have left!"

Tusk halted, looked irresolute, as if contemplating turning around, going back.

"Tusk," Nola whispered, "it *might* be coincidence that brought Dion here, to the planet where Snaga Ohme lives. It *might* be coincidence caused that messenger to actually exhibit some type of life-form response when the name Ohme was mentioned—"

"Yeah," Tusk cut in, "and I *might* be chairman of the Derek Sagan for Dictator fund-raising committee! But why the kid?"

"I don't know. But if Dixter is still alive, like Link said, we might be able to do him more good here than anywhere else. Not to mention keeping an eye on Dion. I think we should be careful, though. Real careful," Nola added. The two had started walking again and were nearing the 'copter. Dion was waiting for them, impatience visible in every straight-edged line of his body.

"Yeah, I think you're right," Tusk said, and closed his hand reassuringly over his lasgun. "Wait a minute, though," he added with a low whistle. "How the hell did that creep know my real name?"

··◁■ ■▷··

The 'copter, driven by the messenger, chopped through the hot and arid Laskarian air. Seated in front, Dion caught a glimpse of a large spacebase off in the distance to the right. Tusk, behind him, informed him that the base was Fort Laskar. Glistening tall buildings on their left marked the location of the city of Laskar. They glided over its outskirts. The streets were empty, dead as the messenger's eyes.

"It looks abandoned," Dion remarked.

"What?" Tusk bawled over the noise of the rotor.

"It looks abandoned!"

"Hell, kid, it's mid-afternoon!" Tusk shouted.

Dion tried to look as if this made sense. The 'copter swerved away from the city and flew over open country. The only sign of civilization was a long ribbon of highway, stretched out along the desert sand. The highway appeared as abandoned as the slumbering city, except for a billowing curl of black, oily smoke rising up into the cloudless sky.

"Something's on fire!" Dion pointed.

"Tanker truck," Tusk said, leaning out at a perilous angle in an attempt to see.

Their pilot flew the 'copter over the highway, avoiding the smoke. He pointed at a vast expanse of lush green, springing up suddenly out of the sand. "The estate of Snaga Ohme."

Dion barely glanced at it. Tusk and Nola appeared to take a great deal of interest in it, however, and the young man wondered idly what it must be like to be a famous celebrity, have your face splashed on mags and vids, people dying to know what you ate for breakfast, whom you slept with after lunch.

If I were king— Dion stopped, almost laughed out loud. King! What right do I have to be thinking about regaining the throne, the throne my uncle lost through weakness and indecisiveness, the throne my own father never lived to see.

Kings are made, not born. So Sagan told me. And all I've made thus far is a mess of everything. I disobeyed orders, led a squadron of brave men into trouble, and then didn't have the guts to lead them out. They died, because of me. I was captured by the Corasians, forced Sagan and Maigrey to come to my rescue, nearly got all three of us killed.

Oh, sure, I was responsible for pulling the trapped mercenaries together on *Defiant,* I thought up the plan for helping them escape. I guess you could say I risked my life, single-handedly attacking the control room.

Attack. Most of the men weren't even armed. The ones who were didn't even bother to aim them. Kid. Go run along and play, kid. They didn't take me seriously. Well, at the end, they took me seriously. Dead serious . . . all of them. Dead.

"Kid!" Tusk's hand was on his shoulder. He was shaking him, yelling in his ear. "You okay? You look kinda green. Never rode in a chopper before, huh? If you're gonna be sick, lean your head out over the side—"

Dion did as he was told, deposited most of his breakfast on the Laskarian landscape below. Tusk hung on to the back of his shirt collar to keep him from falling out.

His Majesty the King.

··◁■ ■▷··

The 'copter set down on a flat, barren, rock-floored canyon in an area referred to either as the middle of nowhere or the middle of Laskar and amounting to about the same thing. The messenger had seemed to take a circuitous route, perhaps to show them the sights, or perhaps to make it difficult to ever find this place again. Dion had quickly lost his bearings and he gathered, from what he could overhear of a muttered conversation between Tusk and Nola on landing, that the mercenary hadn't done much better.

A building erected on the sun-baked rock looked extremely incongruous and out of place. It was built out of a strange concoction of flat rectangular panels—each panel the same exact width and length.

"It looks like it's made out of playing cards!" Nola said with a giggle.

"Prefab." Tusk grunted, staring at it.

"What's that?" Dion asked.

"A home away from home. Made for those who don't like to leave their comforts behind. Those panels can be hauled aboard just about any middling-sized transport—a shuttlecraft, for example. The panels're super-fused cardboard. Lightweight, tougher than wood, almost as hard as steel. They snap together and, when they're up, they'll stay up for years. Kind of an odd place, though," Tusk suggested quietly, "for the Lady Maigrey to be. Don't you think so, kid?"

Dion studied the house stacked up in the desert. It was windowless, doorless, quiet. Several other 'copters stood on the landing site near where he and his companions had touched down. A large shuttlecraft was parked nearby. The green sun, slipping toward the horizon, cast long shadows that moved across the house of cardboard, making it appear to change in shape—growing longer, then shortening, then taller, then sinking. The house seemed more alive than anything around it.

"This way, if you please." The messenger waved a polite hand toward the house.

"Is the Lady Maigrey in there?" Dion stopped him.

The messenger presented a face barren as the rock on which he stood. "Not precisely," he said.

"What do you mean?" Dion felt a pang of fear and was immediately furious at himself. He saw, out of the corner of his eye, the blaster in Tusk's hand, Nola coolly leveling the needle-gun. Dion groped for the bloodsword, closed his hand around the hilt. "We're not taking another step until you tell us what's going on!"

"*I* will tell you what you want to know, Dion Starfire," shouted a voice.

A man stood in the doorway of the cardboard dwelling. He was clad in magenta robes and gave the impression, by being bent and stooped, of great age. But his movements were swift, his voice strong. He started toward them, covered the distance between Dion and the house with surprising speed. Reaching the young man, coming to stand in front of him, the man drew the magenta-colored hood from his head.

Dion had seen many strange life-forms in the galaxy, seen aliens considered disgusting to the human eye—people with eyeballs where their feet should be, people with heads in the general vicinity of their stomachs, people who looked somewhat like broccoli that's taken a turn for the worse. But Dion had never seen anything more loathsome than the sight of this man. Involuntarily, he took a step backward.

The old man's bald head perched on a scrawny neck that seemed as if it might snap beneath the weight. Patches of peeling skin, cracked and dry, dotted his domed forehead. Two large nodes swelled outward from the base of the head at the back and a series of welts ran along the major nerve paths up the neck, the face, around the skull. Despite the fact that the temperature where they stood must be well over one hundred degrees Fahrenheit, Dion noted that the old man, though clad in extremely heavy woolen robes, shivered as with a chill.

The old man stretched out a bony left arm in a gesture of welcome. Welts twined up the arm like snakes. When he moved it, bits of decaying skin flaked off, fell unheeded to the ground.

The old man spoke humbly, reverently. "Welcome to my house . . . Your Majesty."

Chapter ··◆●◑◒◗·· *Eleven*

Journeys end in lovers meeting.
William Shakespeare, *Twelfth Night*, Act II, Scene 3

"I have the schematic, your ladyship."

"You do? Bring it up!" Maigrey had been pacing the small cockpit of the spaceplane, four steps one way, four another. She nearly leapt at the computer when XJ spoke, then clutched the back of the pilot's chair and leaned over to look intently into the screen.

A three-dimensional view of the crystal space-rotation bomb appeared, showing in detail its complex circuitry and construction.

"Rotate it a hundred and eighty," Maigrey instructed.

The computer obeyed.

"Back again ninety."

The bomb on the screen obligingly turned. Maigrey viewed it from all possible angles, top and bottom. Suddenly, with an indrawn breath, she sank down into the pilot's chair.

"My God!" she whispered. "What have I done?"

"What *have* you done?" XJ demanded nervously, not liking her tone, not at all liking the fact that this powerful bomb was in the computer's spaceplane.

"That's why Snaga Ohme wanted it back. Not to sell it to someone else, but to use it himself! And I gave him the means! Dear God. Dear God!"

"You gave him the means to arm the bomb?" XJ asked, shocked, completing Maigrey's somewhat fragmented statements. "Are you certain, your ladyship? Begging your pardon, ma'am, but I've analyzed the bomb and run through every conceivable armament device known to man and alien, plus several that I just came up with myself, and nothing.

Absolutely nothing. Therefore I don't see how it's possible—"

"Try this, XJ." Maigrey lifted the stylus, drew a shape on the screen, inserted the shape into the schematic drawing. It fit perfectly. "And this chemical composition." She read it off.

"By gum!" XJ said, stunned. "That's it! You have one of those eight-pointed whoozles and you put it into the bomb and blam! But what are these things? Just a moment, I'm running it. They're . . . they're . . . Oh. Oh, my." The computer lapsed into an uncomfortable silence.

"Yes," Maigrey said wearily. "A starjewel. The Star of the Guardians. It's absolutely perfect, the one substance Sagan could be almost completely certain no one but he himself possesses. Except me, of course. And where was I when he was designing this bomb? Far away, no possible threat. Until I return and then I *am* a threat, if I find out about the bomb, and then John Dixter, my poor John, stumbles on the information, and then . . . and then . . . and then what do I do? I give my starjewel to the Adonian! Of course Snaga Ohme would recognize the jewel as the arming device. He built the damn bomb!"

"Your ladyship, please," XJ began awkwardly, distressed by her obvious despair. "I'm certain things aren't as bad as they seem—"

"Oh, no. Not yet. But just wait," Maigrey predicted. She let her head slump into her folded arms. God, she was tired! She longed to go to bed, go to sleep, never wake. . . .

She wrenched her head up. What was the matter with her? That awful experience on the highway. The sight of those creatures had rattled her more than it should have, drained her of energy, of the will to go on fighting. She had the bomb, after all. She would keep it, find a way to get the starjewel back. A Star of the Guardian taken by force has a way of returning to its owner. But one given away freely? . . .

Dragging her hair out of her face, she forced herself to concentrate. Time was running out. Sagan's shuttle had landed at Fort Laskar. He had not sent his men immediately to seize her. Fortunately, she guessed, protocol must be maintained at all costs. He would be expected to pay a courtesy call on the brigadier general.

Besides, there's no hurry, Maigrey told herself bitterly. Sagan knows I'm not going anywhere!

"Have you completed the rest of your analysis?" she asked the computer.

"Yes, your ladyship. A remarkable piece of work. I congratulate the maker."

"I'm sure he'd be pleased," Maigrey said dryly.

"It is, as you surmised, your ladyship, a space-rotation bomb, also known as a color bomb—"

"I *know* what it is! Is it functional?"

"Eminently, your ladyship." XJ sounded ominous.

"Can it be destroyed by any means?"

"Armed? Not without the possibility of setting it off."

"I understand. Run through the following simulation: With the starjewel in place, could you detonate the bomb if you were given the correct code sequence?"

"Working."

The computer returned, no longer glib but quiet, subdued. "Yes, ma'am."

"And if the bomb is not armed, could any outside force detonate it?"

"No, ma'am."

"I must be absolutely certain. If, say, this spaceplane were to explode right now, what would happen to the bomb?"

"Nothing, except it'd have a lot of melted, twisted metal wrapped around it. Not to mention pieces of us," XJ added, but it had turned down its audio.

"Good. I— Hush!"

Was that the sound of booted footsteps outside, on the concrete? Maigrey resisted firmly the temptation to open the panel covering the viewscreen. "Now, computer, I am locking in the next commands." She suited her actions to her words, performing the complicated sequence that removed all element of choice from the computer's mind. "You will obey without question."

"Yes, your ladyship." It seemed to Maigrey as if the computer's audio had developed a slight tremor.

"If anyone other than myself makes any attempt to take the bomb from this plane, you will self-destruct, blow up this plane and anyone inside."

"Yes, ma'am."

"You will give the bomb only to myself, with proper voice pattern identification and also—". Maigrey hesitated only slightly, "and also visual sighting of the starjewel, the jewel known as the Star of the Guardians. You have the jewel's picture and chemical structure and analysis on file. I recorded it this morning. It has to be *my* jewel, no other."

Sagan had his, of course, but each starjewel, carved from a separate gemstone, was the tiniest bit different. The differences were almost imperceptible, nothing that would affect the jewel's physical properties, more ethereal, nebulous, difficult to define. Legend had it that the starjewel absorbed a part of the soul of its owner, which accounted for the romantic myth (never proven to anyone's satisfaction) that the jewel's inner light faded, the gemstone went dark, when the owner died.

"Yes, my lady." XJ paused, then added, "Two men are standing outside the plane, my lady."

"Are they attempting to board it?"

"No, my lady. They're just standing there, waiting."

"Identification?"

"Honor Guard, my lady. Lord Sagan's crest."

"Thank you, XJ." It was all to be very dignified: no armed guards, beating on the hatch with their rifle butts, no threats to blow up the plane. Two men, waiting.

Maigrey rose to her feet. She would return the favor. She could afford to be magnanimous. She was, after all, the victor.

··◁■ ■▷··

Maigrey climbed down the ladder from the spaceplane, came face to face with the centurions, who stood rigidly at attention. Numerous onlookers had gathered around the plane to gape and stare and exchange the latest gossip. The spacebase, honored by the presence of a Warlord, was lit brightly as day. The harsh white light reflected off the ceremonial helms of the Honor Guard, glinted on ornate breastplates, which were decorated with a phoenix rising from flame.

Complete Roman panoply—ancient, archaic, impractical in a world whose people could move through space faster than the speed of light, yet somehow stolid and reassuring. Caesar's troops had worn it when they marched to what they had supposed was the end of their tiny world. Sagan's troops wore it marching into what was now a tiny universe. Mankind had survived all these thousands of centuries, survived its own follies, its own stupidities, its own greed and prejudices.

Survived because among the evil had been the noble, the honorable.

Or perhaps the noble and honorable had survived in spite of themselves.

Maigrey squinted in the harsh light, looked carefully at one of the rigid faces. "Marcus, isn't it?"

The face relaxed its stern mien ever so slightly, pleased at being recognized, remembered. "Yes, my lady."

"How are you, Marcus?"

"Well, thank you, my lady." Marcus flushed. His eyes avoided hers. "The Warlord's compliments, my lady, and he respectfully requests your presence in Brigadier General Haupt's office."

"In other words, come to him immediately or I'll be shot?" Maigrey murmured.

Marcus's flush deepened. "Yes, my lady," he said quietly, flicking a glance at her. His expression changed to one of concern. "You're injured, my lady?"

Maigrey put her hand to the jagged cut on her neck. In her haste, her excitement, she'd forgotten about it. The blood had clotted, sealed the wound shut, but it must look awful.

I must look awful, she realized, glancing down at the body armor stained with dirt and spattered with blood—some of it her own. She hadn't brushed her hair or washed her face. But she had hung the bloodsword around her waist. The starjewel should be around her neck. . . .

Maigrey clenched her hand over the empty place on her breast, drew herself up straight, shook the pale hair back over her shoulders.

"We must not keep my lord waiting." She walked forward swiftly.

The centurions, caught by surprise by her sudden move, almost had to run to catch up, to the vast amusement of the watchers.

··◁■ ■▷··

HQ was quiet, a contrast to the crowds gathered outside, hoping to catch a glimpse of the legendary Derek Sagan. MPs were allowing only those on official business to pass, and they gave Maigrey a close and scrutinizing examination as if wondering what possible official business this bloody and bedraggled female could have with his lordship. Her Honor

Guard was guarantee of passage, however. No one halted them.

Inside the headquarters building, the MPs had been replaced by Sagan's own personal guard. No one was allowed to enter these halls, official business or otherwise. Marcus was halted, made to give a password, though Maigrey knew that these men must know each other as well as or better than brothers, having lived together for years. Sagan was taking unusual precautions, and surely not on her account! What was wrong?

Danger's knife edge pricked Maigrey's skin, sent a tingle through her body.

The centurions passed them on through Haupt's outer office—even his aide had been replaced by the stern, grim-faced, uncommunicative centurions. Another, different password met them at each doorway. Marcus knew each one, never hesitated or fumbled. Each guard, with a respectful salute—fist to heart—allowed them to pass.

Outside the door to the brigadier's office stood the captain of the Honor Guard. He took personal charge of Maigrey, begging her pardon respectfully for the inconvenience and asking her to wait a moment while he announced her. Opening the door, he stepped inside.

"The Lady Maigrey Morianna."

"Show her ladyship in." Sagan's voice, cool, calm, masterful.

Maigrey'd been hearing it in her head for hours now. Why should the blood burn in her veins to hear it aloud?

The captain returned, held the door open for her, bowed as she passed. Conscious of an unnatural flush in her pale cheeks, of the dried blood on her neck and on her armor, of her unbrushed, uncombed hair, Maigrey strode past the captain without a glance and entered the office of Brigadier General Haupt.

The brigadier, resplendent in his dress uniform, jerked to his feet as if someone had yanked him up by a string attached to his back. Maigrey barely spared the man a glance. Sagan, too, rose to greet her, graceful for his height, the red cape, trimmed in gold, falling in elegant lines around him.

He wore his parade armor, Roman in fashion, like that of his men. The helm held in the crook of the left arm, cape floating behind him, he took several steps forward, reached out his right hand, and, clasping Maigrey's right hand, carried it to his lips.

Palm to palm. The five scars made by the bloodsword in her hand pressed against the five scars made by the bloodsword on his hand. A secret signal, devised between them long ago, which warned of immediate, desperate, imminent peril.

Shocked, wondering, suspicious, Maigrey flinched at the touch of the lips, the hand that felt unnaturally hot to her chilled flesh.

"My lady, forgive me for revealing your true identity without your permission, but I felt that we no longer need to use the alias of Major Penthesilea."

"As you will, my lord," she replied aloud, then, silently, the thoughts flashing between them swiftly as the glancing of their eyes. *What is this? What's going on? Some kind of trick? If so, it won't work!* She watched intently for a gleam of triumph, a smile of derision.

She saw, instead, fear.

No trick, my lady.

He released her hand, made her a grave bow, half-turned, and moved back to stand before Haupt's desk. The Warlord lifted an object from the desk, displayed it to Maigrey. "Remarkable piece, isn't this, my lady? When did you get it, Haupt? It's quite new, I believe."

The brigadier appeared highly startled. "Why, y-yes, Citizen General," he stammered. "It was presented me as a gift from the—the President himself. M-marking my retirement."

"I didn't know you were retiring, Brigadier," Sagan said pleasantly.

"I . . . d-didn't either," Haupt stammered. Drops of sweat on his bald head shone at every pore. He started to sit down, caught himself, and, flushing, jerked back to his feet.

"Do you have any idea what this is, Haupt?" Sagan inquired, holding the object on his palm.

"A paperweight?" said the wretched brigadier.

"Made of bloodstone." Sagan held the object directly beneath the overhead fluorescent light. "Bloodstone carved in a perfect ball, mounted on an obsidian base. Bloodstone, my lady."

Maigrey couldn't say a word. Her throat had constricted painfully, it ached and burned, her tongue was swollen, her mouth dry. Sagan shot her a sharp warning glance and she knew she had to say something. If what he was intimating was true, they were being watched, every word they spoke was being overheard. But it took an effort to make her numb lips form words.

"How . . . how interesting, my lord," she said faintly. *This is a trick!* she told him silently, accusing. *He can't possibly be alive! He died following the revolution. You had him assassinated! His death was in your records!*

Your death was also in my records. Sagan turned to face her, the bloodstone in his hand between them, demanded without words, *Look at me, my lady, and tell me that this is a trick.*

Maigrey had no need to look at him. She'd already seen. Much, too much, was explained. Memory was forcing aside the dark curtain, a hand rising from the grave, trying to drag her back to that terrible time.

"My lady is not well." A strong arm was around her, holding her, supporting her. The floor had unaccountably wandered out from beneath her feet. "Captain, a glass of water!" Sagan eased her into a chair.

"Brandy," Maigrey corrected. "Neat. No ice."

The Warlord eyed her intently, managed a grudging smile. "Brandy, then," he said.

The captain entered with a glass—a small one, Maigrey noted—of green liquid, placed it on a table at her right hand, and left the room, shutting the door behind him.

Sagan bent over, picked up the bloodstone paperweight that he'd dropped to catch Maigrey, returned it gravely to the brigadier's desk. Haupt, who knew something was going on but had no idea what, seemed much inclined to fall into his chair but was forced to remain standing as long as his commander stood. Sagan, however, put him out of his misery.

"Please be seated, Brigadier."

Haupt sank thankfully down into his chair, rested his hands limply on his desk, and stared at the paperweight.

Maigrey drank the green brandy slowly, in small sips, the welcome warmth of the fiery liquid restoring life to her body. None of them spoke, not even the two who could do so mentally. Maigrey knew their listener could hear words, but she was trying to remember—it had been almost seventeen years ago—if he could eavesdrop on their thoughts.

"Are you feeling better, my lady?" Sagan asked with grave politeness.

"Yes, my lord, thank you. I apologize for my weakness. This wound is minor, but . . . it pains me sometimes." Her hand trembled; she set the glass down quickly.

"Your meeting with Snaga Ohme went successfully?"

She glanced at him swiftly, replied coolly, "I am generally successful in anything I undertake, my lord."

"I trust the blood on your armor is not the blood of my dear friend the Adonian?"

"No." Maigrey started to add something else, found she couldn't, and took another sip of brandy. "I was attacked on my way back to base. Drug addicts, most likely. Out for anything they could get—"

Haupt went deathly white. "M-my lady! I didn't know! I offered her an escort, my lord!"

"You are in no way to blame, Brigadier," Maigrey said, smiling wanly. "I knew the risks when I went. No harm was done. I returned safely."

"With that which you were sent to acquire?" Sagan asked.

"If you want to put it that way, my lord."

The Warlord's gaze went to her breast, to the empty place upon it. Maigrey put her hand to her throat, an almost physical pain choking her. She shifted her gaze from him, fixed it, unseeing, on the bloodstone paperweight.

Sagan drew in a deep breath through his nose, turned suddenly, his cape rustling, booted feet scraping the floor. "Despite my lady's protestations, Brigadier, I do not believe she is well."

"I can send for the medic—"

"Thank you, sir, but that will not be necessary. My lady needs rest, somewhere quiet. I will take her back to my shuttle. Lady Maigrey?" Sagan extended his arm.

There's no business like show business.

Maigrey rose, placed her fingers lightly on the Warlord's arm. Haupt was on his feet again, looking as if he barely had strength enough to get there. Courtly bows, formal good nights, and Maigrey and Sagan were at the door.

The Warlord glanced behind him. "Brigadier, you have served the Lady Maigrey well. I hate to lose a good officer. I may be able to do something for you about that retirement. . . ."

Maigrey looked back at the man. Haupt's bald head gleamed, sweat trickled down his neck into the tight, braid-trimmed collar. He was being asked to choose sides and he knew it. He found his backbone, straightened.

"Yes, my lord. Thank you, my lord."

My lord. *Not* Citizen General. Sagan smiled, glanced significantly at the bloodstone that sat upon the desk. "I'd get rid of that, then, if I were you, sir," he said, and escorted Maigrey out the door.

Chapter ··◆─○○◆─·· Twelve

Have you not sometimes seen a handkerchief? . . .
    William Shakespeare, *Othello*, Act III, Scene 3

The route leading to the Warlord's shuttlecraft wound down hallways and through a tunnel underground, beneath the fort's landing and launching pads, runways, and 'copter ports. Maigrey and Sagan walked the carpeted corridors alone, the Honor Guard having cleared the area of all indigenous military personnel and others not so indigenous—such as the press, who had descended upon Fort Laskar like the locusts which so plagued Snaga Ohme.

Every twenty or so paces, the two passed one of the centurions, standing at rigid, mute attention. The captain and four of his men followed at a discreet distance. The hallways were empty, quiet. Lord and lady walked in a silence that seemed to amplify small sounds—a clink of armor, a muffled boot step, the rustle of the Warlord's cape, a sigh.

Maigrey removed her hand from Sagan's arm. "I suppose we may ring down the curtain on your little show now, my lord?"

"'All the world's a stage,' lady; however, I gather you are referring to something more specific."

"Your charade was, I admit, quite clever and well staged. The bloodstone was a marvelous prop. Haupt played his role admirably. The two of you should take it on the road!" Maigrey bit the words, her anger threatening to overwhelm her. He had fooled her completely. For several moments back there, she had been badly frightened. She quickened her steps, moving to walk slightly ahead of him.

Sagan said nothing, continued down the corridor at his measured, steady pace. His thoughts were closed off to Maigrey, sealed up, shut down. Her own mind was in such chaos, her own thoughts scattered, confused, running hither and yon, uncontrollable, like frightened mice: the strange, dead eyes of her attackers, the bloodstone, Sagan's fear. Maigrey knew, deep inside, that if she grabbed hold of all these and lined them up and considered them calmly, she would know the truth. But it would mean drawing aside the dark curtain.

"Where is the boy, Lady Maigrey?" Sagan asked.

"I haven't any idea. Why? Have you lost him again?" Maigrey walked on, not looking back, her head held stiffly.

"I thought perhaps you might know. You are, after all, his Guardian."

The shot told. Maigrey's hand went to the empty place on her breast, clasped the starjewel that wasn't there. The pain seared, burned. Tears stung her eyes, blinding her. Turning on her heel, she retraced her steps, headed back to her plane. Sagan made no move to stop her. He didn't have to. The Honor Guard closed ranks, ranged around her, blocking her path. Maigrey came to a halt, hair falling over her face, cursing him, cursing herself. His hand closed on her upper arm.

"Come, my lady," he said softly. "You are not well."

···◄■ ■►···

The Warlord's shuttlecraft was parked on the outskirts of the base, far from any buildings, surrounded by a vast expanse of concrete. The area was restricted. The fort's military police had it cordoned off, the Honor Guard stood watch, a ring of steel banded around the craft. Inside, the ship was dark; the only lights permitted were those necessary to the systems that were operational on the ground. The shuttle's crew moved about their duties efficiently and in silence.

Sagan and Maigrey proceeded through the craft to the Warlord's private chambers. Courteously, he stood aside, admitted her to his quarters with a bow which Maigrey acknowledged with an inclination of her head. Gliding past him, she stepped inside a room lit by only a pinpoint of bright white streaming down from a spotlight in the overhead.

"I am not to be disturbed, Captain," the Warlord said, the white light shining full on him, causing his shadow to expand up over the bulkheads, fill the room, close around her. "Except for the half-breed."

"Yes, my lord."

The door slid shut. Sagan sealed it.

Maigrey moved away from him, to the center of the small room that did its duty efficiently and without nonsense, serving in the capacity of office, communications room, and sitting room. Through another door, she could see a bedroom furnished without regard to comfort: cold, Spartan. Or perhaps not Spartan. More like a monk's cell.

The door to the bedroom slid shut. There was no escape, no way out. The two of them were isolated, alone, cut off from the rest of the world, the rest of the universe.

Nothing new. It seemed to her they had been like that from the very beginning, when the mind-link had first been forged, when he was thirteen and she was six and they were trying to rescue Stavros from that ridiculous statue. . . .

"And now, my lady," Sagan said gently, coming to stand very near her, "let us talk about the bomb."

"I won't give it to you. You must know that." Maigrey slumped down wearily in a chair beneath the bright light, her hand shielding her eyes from the glare. "Why didn't you try to stop me from taking it?"

"Try to stop you?" Sagan removed his helm, ran his hand through the thick black hair that was thinning at the top of the forehead, tinged with gray at the temples. Damp with sweat, it glistened purple in the light. He laid the helm to one side on a stand, unfastened his cloak, and draped it across the helm. Seating himself in a chair opposite Maigrey, he stretched out his long body, settled himself comfortably. "I couldn't have hired anyone to serve me better!"

The light shone between them, not on either directly. Their faces were masks—black shadows for mouth and nose and eyes, white cheekbones, white lips, a white scar.

"Abdiel—" Sagan began.

Maigrey stirred restlessly. "Must we continue this nonsense?"

The Warlord continued, unperturbed. "Abdiel would not have permitted me to acquire the bomb, my lady. He couldn't. He would have done everything in his power to destroy me."

"If we admit his existence, which I don't—why?"

"Because he knew I would use it."

"And therefore Abdiel let me acquire it—?"

"—because he assumes you won't."

Maigrey was silent. Her hand went to play with the chain around her neck, the chain that wasn't there. She glanced at him, fearful that he'd seen, moved her fingers to touch the wound. She drew them back, saw them dark with blood. It had broken open again. She looked across at the Warlord. "I think perhaps he underestimates me."

"I think perhaps he does, too." Sagan rose to his feet, came toward her. "Let me look at that cut."

Maigrey shifted in her chair, turned away from him, from the light, her pale hair falling forward over her shoulders. "It's nothing, I tell you—"

"Let me see it. Tilt your head back. Move into the light."

Maigrey sighed, bit her lip, and obeyed, sitting forward on the chair, holding her head back and at a slight angle. The Warlord bent over her, brushed the pale hair aside, his fingers deftly and dispassionately probing the wound on her neck. She flinched, gritted her teeth.

"Did that hurt?" he asked coolly.

"No." She lied, though it wasn't the wound that pained her.

Sagan smiled, the shadows around his mouth deepening. "The cut is superficial. I doubt if it will even leave a scar." He lingered on the word, his gaze flicking swiftly to her right cheek.

Maigrey sensed battle, tensed.

"It needs cleaning, however, antiseptic to prevent infection." The Warlord straightened, crossed the room, disappearing into the shadows. A panel slid aside, revealing a compartment. He removed and opened a metal box marked by a red cross.

"What's this? No dressings! Dr. Giesk has been neglectful in his duty, it seems. We shall have to make do"—Sagan reached into the broad belt of his Romanesque armor, drew forth a scrap of cloth that caught the light, seemed to burn in Maigrey's sight with a white flame—"with this handkerchief."

Light reflected off a plastiglass bottle; the Warlord dashed a pungent-smelling liquid onto the cloth. He turned, moved back toward her, the cloth held in his outstretched hand. Kneeling down, his body cut off the light, threw a shadow over her. He started to lift the cloth to the wound.

Maigrey's hand closed over his wrist, fingers digging into his flesh.

"Where did you get that?" She spoke without a voice.

"What? This handkerchief?" He opened his hand, revealed it to her. His smile deepened, darkening his eyes. "I took it from a prisoner, aboard *Defiant*."

Maigrey clasped hold of his arm more tightly, not in an attempt to hurt him—that would have been impossible—but because she suddenly needed the support. He gently disengaged her clutching hand.

"Sit back, lady. This is going to hurt."

Furious, she snatched the handkerchief away from him, tried to rise. He blocked her with his body. Clamping his hands over her wrists, pinning them to the armrests of the chair, he held her fast.

"John Dixter is alive . . . for the moment."

Maigrey froze at his touch, made no further move except to close her fingers more tightly over the handkerchief. She stared at him in silence, dark and impenetrable.

"I knew you'd be pleased to hear word of him," the Warlord continued implacably. His mental hold on her was strong; he eased the physical, his hands resting lightly on her forearms. "I was able to give him news of you . . . when the drug wore off long enough to permit him to distinguish reality from hallucination."

She couldn't breathe. His presence enveloped her, sucked the air from around her.

"I respect John Dixter, my lady. He is a strong-willed man, a man of honor and of principle, and he has the misfortune to love you dearly. . . ."

Maigrey struggled to draw breath; her lungs burned. A single tear slid down the scarred cheek, stopped halfway as if turned to ice, glistened in the harsh light.

"I think you might be interested, my lady, to know how John Dixter is spending his time aboard *Defiant*. At the moment, perhaps, he is lying on a steel table, stripped naked. Dr. Giesk is attaching the electrodes to various sensitive places on his body—the head, the chest, the groin, the fingertips, the soles of the feet . . ."

Maigrey's eyes lost their focus, stared not at him but through him, beyond him into a darkness only she could see. "So this is how it is to be," she murmured, fingers twisting the handkerchief.

"Yes, my lady," he answered softly. "Unless you return my property."

Maigrey thought a moment, then slowly shook her head. "No, my lord. I will not give it to you. Not until he is set free."

"And I will not free him unless I have the bomb." Sagan rose to his feet, moved away from her, seeming to leave a vacuum where he'd been. The air surged in to fill it. Maigrey inhaled deeply. The rush of oxygen made her dizzy.

Sagan took a turn about the small room, paused, and glanced back at her over his shoulder. "I don't suppose I could simply kill you and take the bomb."

Maigrey smiled faintly, shook her head. "No, my lord."

"Of course. Visual identification, voice pattern—that sort of precaution."

"Among others, my lord." Maigrey started to rise from the chair. Sagan politely extended his hand. She accepted his assistance, her chill fingers closing over his. He saw the livid marks his hands had made earlier on her wrists, darkening to bruises.

"It seems we are at an impasse, my lady." He kept hold of her hand, drew her near. "I have time. You have time. So, unfortunately, does John Dixter. Stavros lasted only three days, but then I was in a hurry. I can make Dixter's suffering last as long as it takes. Perhaps"—the Warlord released her hand, turned toward a communications center—"you would like to speak with him—"

"No!" She had gone deathly pale. Her restraining hand on his arm was rigid as a corpse's.

"The game is over, lady. Check and checkmate. You played well." The Warlord came to stand beside her. Reaching out his hand, he brushed it lightly, almost caressingly, over her scarred cheek. "But I played better. Shall we take a walk, over to your plane? Once I have the bomb in my possession I will give the order—"

"It won't do you any good," Maigrey interrupted.

Sagan's face darkened. "I warn you, my lady, John Dixter will suffer—"

"Then he must suffer," she said softly. The tear's twin slid down her face. Angrily, she dashed it away with the back of her hand. "What hope do the people of this galaxy have, what hope does Dion have, if you hold this flaming sword in your hand?"

"I would make the boy a king—"

"A king of straw! The prince of iron rules behind his back!"

Sagan advanced on her so suddenly and so swiftly that she was trapped in a corner before she could escape. "You didn't do this for the boy, Maigrey! You didn't risk your life to gain this 'flaming sword' for Dion!" The Warlord caught hold of her arms, held her fast, his body pressing hers against a wall of steel. "You forget, lady, I see through you like flawed crystal! You want the weapon for yourself. You sold everything you had, including your honor, to obtain it. And you're willing to let a man who loves and trusts you die a terrible death so that you can keep it—"

The metal was cold against her back. She began shivering. Crossing her arms, she huddled in upon herself, lowering her head, hiding behind a curtain of pale hair. "No," she whispered, and shrank away from him as far as possible. "No." If she said no over and over, repeated it like a chant, a litany, it might gain power, it might come to be true.

His hands suddenly eased their hurting grasp and were gentle, persuasive, drawing her near. He was warmth and strength and sanctuary. She could hide in his darkness and be completely forgotten and she herself could forget. . . .

"Lord Sagan." The voice boomed over the commlink.

Sagan smoothed his hand over the pale, fair hair. He brushed his fingers over the scar on her face, felt the trace of the tear, wet and chill on her skin.

"I left orders not to be disturbed."

"Yes, my lord. But you also told us to inform you if the half-breed contacted—"

"The half-breed?" Sagan glanced toward the commlink, as if the voice speaking had suddenly taken shape and form and become visible.

"He's here, my lord, and demands to speak to you at once."

The Warlord fell silent, stood looking down at Maigrey, not seeing her. His hands released her, he turned away from her, but not before she'd felt his body stiffen, tense.

"Send him in," Sagan commanded,.

"So," Maigrey said, following him as he crossed the room, advancing as he retreated, "the game isn't over yet, is it, my lord?"

"For you it is, my lady," he said coolly, with a sidelong glance.

You may hold my king in check, my lord, Maigrey told him silently, but not checkmate. The queen has one more move left. . . .

Sagan switched on more lights. The room was brilliantly illuminated, and Maigrey blinked, blinded by the glare. The panel glided aside. A figure emerged from the darkness, shuffling with cringing shoulders into the light as if possessed of an aversion to the radiance. It shambled and hunched its way into the room, a pile of slovenly rags.

Maigrey caught a quick glimpse of Marcus, standing guard

outside, his stern face twisted in aversion, fingers on his weapon obviously itching to rid his Warlord of a pest.

The door slid shut; Sagan sealed it. The figure straightened in a graceful, fluid motion, alarmingly like the uncoiling of a snake.

"My lady," the Warlord said, "may I present Sparafucile."

A malformed head lifted from the hunched shoulders; a misshapen face turned to Maigrey, misaligned eyes glinted, leering.

She caught her breath, took an involuntary step backward. "You!"

"Ah, yes," the Warlord remarked. "I had forgotten that you two have already met."

"Not formally, Sagan Lord." The half-breed, grinning, rested strong hands on the weapons belt at his waist.

He brought back to Maigrey the horror of the creatures who had attacked her, brought back her inability to think, to react. The dark curtain in her mind trembled, stirred by a disquieting breeze. She reached out her hand, groped for something solid, reassuring, and leaned against the arm of an unyielding couch. The other two in the room talked, but for long moments she couldn't hear them.

"Visitors? From Snaga Ohme?" Sagan was saying to the half-breed when Maigrey was once again able to attend to the conversation. "Surely the Adonian must know by now that the double-crosser has become the double-crossed."

"No, Sagan Lord, these people come not from Snaga Ohme. I know his men by sight and these are not them, though one is pretty enough to be, I think."

A shadow darkened Sagan's face. The same shadow fell over Maigrey's heart, though she couldn't give a name to her fear or see it clearly.

"Describe him," was all the Warlord said.

"A human boy, Sagan Lord, well made with fair skin and hair the color of blood and fire. Abdiel himself come to meet him. He take him by the hand, call the boy Dion."

"The hand," the Warlord murmured, opened his own right hand, stared down at the five scars on the palm, his face grim.

Remembered pain jolted through Maigrey's arm. She clasped one palm over the other. "Give it up, Sagan! I won't fall for it. Abdiel is dead! All the mind-seizers are dead! I read it in your files—"

"It is no trick, lady," the Warlord cried, losing his patience.

"Look inside me! See the truth! Abdiel is alive. He is here on Laskar and somehow he has managed to get hold of Dion . . . just as he got hold of us so many years ago!"

Maigrey had no need to look inside him. She had only to look inside herself to know the truth . . . or to admit it. Terrible memories of their captivity came to her, of the torture, more horrible because it was of the mind, as well as the body.

We were strong, we were prepared. We knew what to expect. We fought him, we escaped. But not Dion. He doesn't know. . . . He doesn't know.

The game board had been upended, the pieces scattered all to hell. Maigrey rubbed the scars on her palm, but the pain did not abate.

Chapter ··✦··· Thirteen

> So spake the Seraph Abdiel, faithful found,
> Among the faithless, faithful only he . . .
>
> John Milton, *Paradise Lost*

The old man took Dion's right hand in his own right hand. Abdiel's flesh was chill and clammy to the touch, the skin of the fingers and palm astonishingly smooth, as if it had been sanded. Dion returned the pressure of the strong grip, though he found it difficult, looking at the patches of rotting skin on the back of the hand, to repress a shudder of revulsion. The old man kept his left hand concealed in the long, flowing robes he wore wound around his thin body.

Dion didn't like the man's touch, tried to withdraw his hand, though he forced himself, out of courtesy, not to make the gesture seem hurried. Abdiel kept hold of him, however, and turned the boy's right hand palm up. Shrewd eyes noted the five scars, darted to the bloodsword Dion wore at his side.

"I see that you have been blooded. Quite right. Quite proper, my king. Though sometimes very dangerous. My name is Abdiel, did I mention that? The old. We forget things so easily. I don't suppose my Lady Maigrey spoke of me to you? Or your mentor, Platus, perhaps?" The voice was smooth and sanded as the flesh, warm and arid as the desert around them. "I heard of his death. I am sorry, deeply sorry."

Dion managed, finally, to free himself of the old man's grasp. "Where is the Lady Maigrey?" he asked coldly, and heard, behind him, Tusk's grunt of approval.

Abdiel heard it as well. The eyes shifted from the boy to the mercenary and to the young woman, both standing protectively just behind and to either side of Dion.

213

"Mendaharin Tusca," said Abdiel, with a bobbing motion of his body.

"Sorry." Tusca shook his head. "You must have me confused with someone else."

"Oh, your secret is safe with me, my dear Tusca. Quite safe. I knew your father. A pity. A pity. I did what I could to prevent his terrible death, but I was too late. It seems that I am always late."

Abdiel's gaze switched back to Dion, who noticed that the old man's eyes had no lashes, seemed to have no lids. The eyes themselves appeared never to close. If they blinked, the movement was so rapid that it escaped observation. When he looked at you, he seemed to be always looking at you.

The old man sighed. Shivering, he slid his hand back inside his robe, huddled deep within the heavy fabric.

Sweat trickled down Dion's forehead. He kept his expression stern. "I received a message from the Lady Maigrey. We either see her now or we're leaving."

"You will see her, my king." Abdiel reached out his hand again, plucked the sleeve of Dion's cotton, short-sleeved shirt (purchased with their poker winnings on Vangelis). "Perhaps not as you expect, but you will see her." The old man bobbed again. "Will you honor my humble dwelling with your presence, Your Majesty?"

Dion hesitated, undecided. But Tusk had already made up his mind.

"Kid! What the hell do you think you're doing?" He caught hold of Dion by the shoulder, drew him to one side. "Uh, 'scuse us a minute, old man, will you? Got to have a little chat with my friend. Private."

"I quite understand." Abdiel made a gesture with his hand; a patch of skin fell off and was blown away on the wind. "If you will permit me, I will return to my dwelling. I am subject to chills and cannot stay long in the out-of-doors. Whenever you are ready to enter my house, Your Majesty, I will be honored to receive you. My disciples and I await your coming with pleasure."

Wrapping his robes around him, the old man made a deep bow, glided across the barren, rocky ground, and disappeared into the house. Several of the dead-eyed disciples standing around the dwelling went in after him. Others remained outside and it seemed to Tusk, who was watching them warily, that he was being outcircled, outflanked. He turned back to Dion, saw the boy's jaw set, the blue eyes harden.

"Look, kid, be smart! We should get in that 'copter and get the hell out of here now."

"I don't think they're going to let us leave, Tusk," Nola said quietly. Two of the blankly staring humans had moved nearer the chopper.

"All the more reason to try it. There are three of us, we've got lasguns. We knock 'em out before they know what hit 'em— Why the devil am I wasting my breath?" Tusk raised his arms to heaven. "You're going in there, aren't you, kid? 'My king.' You really eat that stuff up."

Dion flushed in anger, opened his mouth, snapped it shut. Turning on his heel, he began to walk toward the house.

Tusk, glaring after the boy, felt a painful poke in his back. Nola was glaring at him.

"All right, all right! Hey, kid!" the mercenary shouted at Dion's departing figure. He hurried to catch up, Nola running along behind. "We're coming with you."

"You don't have to," Dion said coldly. "I'll have Abdiel's people take you back to your . . . your junkyard."

"Yeah, and I bet they would, too," Tusk muttered, but kept it beneath his breath. "Probably drop us off at five thousand without benefit of a 'chute." Aloud he said, "I'm not doing it for you, kid. I'm . . . kinda curious to know how he knew who I was. I've kept my real name quiet—"

"That's right, he *did* know!" Dion said. Eagerness and excitement made the blue eyes flame like sapphire. "He knew Platus, he knew your father. He probably knew all the Guardians years back, before the revolution. I wonder why Maigrey never mentioned him. They must have been friends."

"Not necessarily, kid. Not necessarily," Tusk said, but he said it to the sand blowing through the air and to Nola, who took hold of his hand and clasped it tightly.

Two of the lifeless beings, noting the trio's destination, came up and escorted them into the house of cards.

··◄■ ■►··

The heat, inside, was intense.

"It's a goddamn sauna!" Tusk breathed, mopping his face.

The dwelling was divided into innumerable small, square rooms piled up on top of each other, connected by stairs. The walls and floors were constructed of cedar. On entering, each was asked to please remove his or her shoes.

One of the zombies, as Tusk not-so-jokingly referred to them in an undertone to Nola, led them up a flight of stairs and down another and through a maze of empty boxlike rooms, and finally brought them into Abdiel's presence. The old man sat huddled near a small solar furnace. Heat radiated from red-glowing stones. Every so often, one of the zombies stepped forward and poured a cup of water on the rocks. Steam hissed into the air, its wisps reaching out to the old man.

The hot, moist air burned Dion's lungs. Tusk's black skin glistened like polished ebony. Nola's hair curled around her face in drop-covered ringlets.

Abdiel, shrouded in his thick robes, rose to his feet, bowing. "Enter and welcome, my king. I know that the temperature is uncomfortably warm for you. The bones of the aged are thin and brittle, our skin shriveled. The cold penetrates to the heart. Years from now"—the old man's eyes glinted—"you, too, will suffer the indignities of old age."

Something in the old man's tone made Tusk's blood run cold, the sweat chill on his body. "Not if he has his way, we won't," he whispered to Nola, who crept nearer to him.

The three entered the windowless room and took seats where Abdiel indicated, reclining on oblong-shaped, cushion-covered cedar couches that looked, to Tusk, too much like coffins for him to be exactly comfortable. He was startled and pleased, however, to feel cool air blowing on his face. Glancing up, the mercenary saw that it came from vents, located in the ceiling, directed only on himself, Dion, and Nola. The zombies, standing like statues around the room, were sweating profusely but did not appear to be otherwise uncomfortably affected by the heat.

Abdiel resumed his spot by the furnace, huddling near to it greedily. A hookah stood beside him. The water bubbling in the porcelain vase contrast soothingly with the hiss of the steam on the rocks. The old man put a pipe to his lips, sucked on it, then removed it and offered it politely to Tusk. A thin curl of smoke wafted from the bowl.

"No, thanks," the mercenary said. "I don't like having my mind bent out of shape."

"I find the drug eases the pain. I do not complain; my affliction was self-inflicted and I have derived great benefit from it." Abdiel removed his left hand from the winding coils of fabric, extended it, palm up. The red glow from the rocks shone on five needles, embedded in the palm.

Dion sucked in a startled breath. Tusk stood up without realizing he'd done so. Nola tugged sharply on his pants leg, and the mercenary slowly and numbly resumed his seat. His father's voice was talking to him, coming from somewhere out of the past. He wished desperately he'd listened to his old man, but what teenager, whose eyes look only ahead, wants to hear about days behind, days dead and gone?

"I am one of the Order of Dark Lightning," Abdiel said. "Ah, I see recognition dawn, my king."

"The Lady Maigrey said . . . something. You were all killed during the revolution. 'Good came out of evil,' she said."

"That's what she said?" Abdiel appeared saddened, grieved. "Ah, poor woman. Poor woman. She was right, almost. Sagan attempted to destroy us. He feared us, as well he should. But I survived. He could not destroy *me*! I am afraid, however, that I have arrived too late. Too late to help my Lady Maigrey."

"Why do you keep saying that?" Dion demanded impatiently. "Where is she? I want to see her! She sent me a message—"

"The message." The old man's skin attained a crimson hue; the sleepless eyes glittered. "I must make a confession, my king. *I* sent the message."

"I knew it!" Tusk was on his feet again. "C'mon, kid—"

"If you please. You are so hasty, Mendaharin Tusca. It was a fault of your father's and because I enjoy being reminded of him, I will overlook it. But I beg of you, do not interrupt again. This is between myself and your king."

"Tusk, sit down!" Dion snapped.

"Yes, Your Majesty!" Tusk made an elaborate bow. "Anything you say, Your Majesty!"

"Stop it!" Nola whispered. "You're acting like children. Both of you!"

Dion overheard her, flushed, looked momentarily ashamed. He cast Tusk an apologetic glance. Tusk subsided back onto the couch, muttering to himself. Nola gave him a vicious jab in the ribs, and he fell silent.

Dion turned back to the old man. "Is the Lady Maigrey in danger?"

"She is." Abdiel sighed. "She was. But, as I said, I arrived too late. Lord Sagan has landed on this planet. . . . You didn't know that?"

"No, I didn't," Dion said slowly. "Tusk—"

"I'm with you, kid."

Abdiel raised his hand. "There is no need for alarm. Do not be afraid, my king. You are now under my protection. I tried to save the lady, as well, but I could not. She is with him now. He possesses her, body and soul."

"I don't believe you! She fought him—"

"Yes, she fights him. Poor, brave woman. She has fought him for years, ever since they were children. The Creator was not kind to her, linking her to that dark-souled, evil man. Sagan's will is strong and, mind you, I don't know, but I fear something has happened that has finally beaten her down, drawn them close together. . . ." Abdiel put the pipe to his lips. Smoke curled up around the bald, sweat-covered head. The eyes, sharp as needles themselves, jabbed into Dion.

Tusk almost laughed aloud. Nola nudged him, nodded her head toward Dion. The boy's expressive face had darkened.

"Dion, you don't believe this crap!" Tusk began, "You know the lady—"

"You didn't see them together, Tusk," Dion said in a low voice. "I did. The two of them . . . on that Corasian ship. They were . . ." He fell silent, his cheeks burning.

"Were what? Ouch!" Tusk glared at Nola, nursed his arm that had imprints of her nails in his skin.

"They used to be lovers, you know," Abdiel said, puffing on the pipe, the water gurgling in the vase. "When they were young. They were to have been married. The revolution divided them. She remained loyal to her king—"

"She saved me," Dion said softly.

"Yes, and Sagan struck her down. Savagely, without mercy. Then he left her to die. He didn't even have the nerve to finish her off. He was always a coward, was Derek Sagan."

Dion said nothing, looked troubled, confused. Tusk knew how the boy felt. The mercenary certainly had no love for the Warlord. He'd used them, betrayed them. He was holding Dixter prisoner, putting him through God knew what torment. Still, Tusk would never have called Sagan a coward.

"You know, of course, why the Lady Maigrey came to Laskar?" Abdiel said.

"No." Dion shook his head.

The old man appeared concerned. "She didn't tell you?"

Dion's flush deepened. "There wasn't time! We were in the middle of a firefight—"

"Yes, *perhaps* that was the reason." Abdiel sighed delicately.

Tusk, seeing Dion's pain increasing, repressed an urge to wring the old man's neck.

"Or perhaps . . . But who can read a woman's heart? I will tell you what little I know. She came to Laskar at *his* bidding. She came to perform a task for him. Have you ever heard of a man named Snaga Ohme?"

Abdiel's gaze shifted suddenly to Nola. "I believe you said you'd heard of him, my dear?"

"Sure, I've heard of him." Nola shrugged. "Who hasn't?"

"Quite true. Though some, I think, have heard more of him than others. Be that as it may"—the eyes sent their needle gaze to Dion—"the Adonian is a genius when it comes to building weapons. In the last few years, Derek Sagan has devoted his life to inventing the most horrific killing device yet known to man. He sent his plans to Snaga Ohme, and the Adonian—who would sell his soul to the highest bidder— created it. The weapon is known as a space-rotation bomb and it has the power to destroy solar systems, perhaps even to destroy a universe. With such a weapon of terror in his control, the Warlord could place his bootheel upon the necks of every citizen in the galaxy.

"Snaga Ohme completed his work. The bomb is finished. Derek Sagan was about to accept delivery and commence his reign of darkness when the Corasians attacked him and he was forced to fight or lose his miserable life."

"He fought bravely!" Dion said, white to the lips.

"Rats generally do, when they are backed into a corner. His ship, through his own negligence, was blown out from underneath him. He escaped, naturally, but he was discommoded by the pressing duties of command and found that he could not pick up the bomb himself. He sent the Lady Maigrey in his stead."

"C'mon, kid. Let's get out of here," Tusk said, but he said it halfheartedly and he wasn't at all surprised to note that Dion didn't move.

"I don't believe you," Dion told the old man.

"I am proud of you, Your Majesty." Abdiel regarded him with a sad, admiring expression. "You remain faithful to her. That pleases me." He put his pipe to his lips, smoked, frowned, seemed to wrestle with himself. At length, he laid the pipe down, coiled up the tube carefully, and motioned for one of the zombies to remove the hookah from his side.

"I hate to destroy such loyalty, my king, but it is only right that you should know the truth. How else are you to help this poor woman, if, indeed, she can be helped? Mikael"—this to one of the zombies—"prepare the viewing chamber."

Mikael leaned over, whispered something in his master's ear, gesturing at the guests. Abdiel nodded, smiled, and with Mikael's assistance rose to his feet.

"My assistant has informed me that outside the sun is setting. Your journey has been long and tiring. Undoubtedly you are hungry. I would be greatly honored if you would be my guests for dinner."

"Thanks, but we really should be g—" Tusk began.

"I won't hear of it." Abdiel cut him off with a wave of his decrepit hand. "The viewing chamber won't be ready for some time. We so rarely set up the equipment. Mikael will show you to rooms where you may refresh yourselves. Lie down, if you like, and take a brief nap. Dinner will not be ready for an hour or so. I will see you afterward."

"You won't be dining with us?" Dion asked.

"No, my king. You would find my 'meal' singularly unappetizing. I could not exist on mere food." Abdiel held out his left hand, palm up, to the light, and tilted it slightly. The needles cast long, thin, dark shadows against his skin. "Your bloodsword, my king, holds the virus and neuro micromachines within it, injecting them into your body when you establish contact with the weapon. I have taken the virus and micromachines into my body, and my diet must be regulated accordingly. Twenty-one capsules three times daily constitute my repast. No, I will not be joining you for dinner."

This was the first good news Tusk had heard in a week and he was sorry to see that Dion looked disappointed. The young man was staring at Abdiel's palm with a kind of puzzled fascination.

"Ah, my king." Abdiel smiled benignly, placed his hand—the one without the needles—on the boy's arm and squeezed it affectionately. "I see your question in your eyes. You wonder why I have deliberately ruined my health, my life? You need not be embarrassed. I know many consider my appearance repulsive. This outward deformity occurred to all of us of the Order. The neuro micromachines tend to collect at the nerve endings, forming these nodes and nodules you see on my skin and at the back of my head. The virus eats up a great deal of energy, lowers my body temperature, forces me to live in what would be, to normal humans, sweltering heat. I suffer agonizing pain, sometimes. But the compensations, Dion! The compensations outweigh all physical discomfort . . . reduce my sufferings to nothing more than minor inconveniences."

Dion didn't appear convinced. Abdiel's smile broadened.

"I will offer you one example, my king, which may help you to understand. I presume that you are trained in the use of the bloodsword? You know, then, that the sword can create a bond between you and another member of the Blood Royal who also wields a sword. The mental bond is fragile, however, easily broken, and is completely reliant on the swords being in use.

"We of the Order discovered that we could, by bonding directly with each other instead of bonding through the sword, achieve a symbiosis of a most remarkable nature. We could actually become one with each other, share our dreams, our knowledge, combine our powers, two becoming stronger than one could possibly imagine. And this symbiosis did not diminish, my king! Once we tap into a member of the Blood Royal, once we inject our . . . shall we say . . . being into that person, we form a bond that can never be entirely broken. A brotherhood of the soul and body that lasts a lifetime!"

Dion opened his right hand, stared down at the five scars on his palm with rapt attention. Tusk's bowels clenched at the sight—the boy's hand near the old man's, the five needles protruding from the too-smooth flesh

"Dion, c'mon," Tusk said. He stepped forward, intending to break up this cozy twosome and drag Dion away.

Abdiel glanced at him, a tiny frown line forming on the domed forehead. The old man shot a look from the lidless eyes to his disciple.

The zombie named Mikael glided over.

"It is impolite to interrupt the master," Mikael said.

Tusk whipped out his lasgun, pressed it against the zombie's gut. "Yeah? It's impolite to burn a hole through your belly, but I'll do it if you don't get out of my way!"

Abdiel scratched at his decaying flesh, the old man appearing pained and faintly embarrassed by the inappropriate behavior of a guest.

"Tusk!" Dion was shocked. "Have you gone crazy? Put that gun away!"

"I mean it, kid! We're gettin' out of here. Nola—" Tusk paused, looked around. "Where's Nola?"

"The female was tired." Mikael's lifeless eyes stared at him, through him, never seeming to see him. "I ordered her escorted to her room. Perhaps you would care to join her?"

Tusk slowly lowered the weapon. "You're right. I'd 'care to join her.'" He shoved the lasgun in its holster with a deliberate, angry thrust, hoping Dion would notice and understand.

The young man regarded him coldly, the petulant mouth drawn tight. "I'll see you later, Tusk."

"Yeah, sure, kid."

Turning to leave, escorted by Mikael, Tusk saw Abdiel put a thin arm around the boy's waist, draw him near. The mercenary strained his ears, listening.

"Many years ago, when they were both young—about your age," Abdiel was saying, "the Lady Maigrey and Derek Sagan—that was before he had gone entirely evil—were initiated by me into the Order's secrets. It was a wonderful time. Our spirits communed, and I might have been able to help them, particularly Derek. But he grew impatient, because I would not teach him all that he wanted to know. He turned Maigrey against me, and I was forced to send the two away. . . ."

The old man's voice faded in the distance, taking Dion with it.

Mikael led Tusk through the maze of the house, upstairs and down and around innumerable sharp corners. No windows offered a view outside, but the mercenary had the impression from the number of stairs they climbed as opposed to those they descended that he was being led to an upper portion of the multileveled house.

Arriving at a door that looked like countless other doors they'd passed in a hall that looked like every other hall, Mikael halted, withdrew an old-fashioned metal key, and inserted it into an antiquated metal bolt lock. The key clicked, the zombie turned the swivel on the bolt, slid it aside. Tusk watched, puzzled, then understanding clicked with the lock.

"You guys aren't big on electricity around here, huh? Solar heat, no force fields, no lasguns or phaser weapons . . ."

Mikael pushed open the door, revealing a small, square, windowless room made of cedar that looked like every other room in the house.

The zombie gestured politely for Tusk to enter.

"Just a little test, if you don't mind." Tusk drew the lasgun, pointed it at the lock on the door, and fired.

Nothing. The weapon was dead.

"The master's body has a natural tendency to disrupt electric fields," the disciple explained. "He can control it, of course, but it tires him, being constantly forced to exert so much energy. We find it easier, when we are at home, to do without. Please step inside."

"Where's Nola?" Tusk demanded, looking around the room.

"Resting in her own room. Please step inside."

Tusk glowered. "What if I said Nola and I wanted to leave?"

"The woman is, I'm afraid, far too tired to travel. Please step inside."

My gun may not work but I could punch this bastard out, Tusk thought. Shit, though, I'd never find Nola in this rat's nest. And then there's the kid. . . .

Tusk, scowling, stepped inside. As he passed the door, he noted that the cedar was a veneer; the door itself was made of solid steel.

"Your dinner will be brought to your room," Mikael said, and shut the door. The bolt slid home.

Swearing beneath his breath, Tusk hurled the useless lasgun to the floor. It bounced, skittered across the hardwood, slammed up against the opposite wall.

"To my cell, you mean."

···✦ ➡··

"I apologize for Tusk," Dion said later, when he had finished dining—alone—in his room, and had been brought by Mikael into Abdiel's presence once again. "I don't know what gets into him sometimes."

"There is no need for apology, my king." The old man reached out his hand, rubbed the fingers gently along Dion's arm. "He is not of the pure Blood Royal, is he? His mother was, I believe, quite an ordinary human."

"Yes." Dion's first impulse was to withdraw from Abdiel's touch, but he was strangely attracted by it. It promised him things—just what, he didn't know, couldn't specify. Things he wanted, was hungry to obtain.

He submitted to Abdiel's caress, allowed the old man to lead him like a child to another cedar room, identical to the first and to all the others, except that this one was almost devoid of furnishings. A short-legged table stood in the center of the room, surrounded by cushions on the floor.

"Please, sit down, my king." Abdiel motioned, seated himself cross-legged on the cushions, his elbows resting on the table. The room was stiflingly hot. Dion, seating himself awkwardly across the table from Abdiel, saw that the old man was shivering.

"You can't expect those who are not of the Blood Royal to understand us, my king," Abdiel was saying. "You might as well ask the worm to empathize with the eagle. That is why I have not invited him to join us. Are you comfortable? We may be here a long while, once we began the viewing."

"The viewing?" Dion glanced around, puzzled. He had expected some sort of vidscreen but saw nothing like that.

Abdiel smiled, pointed to three objects that stood on the table: a thick, round, white candle, burning with a clear, bright flame, and two rocks that had each been honed into the shapes of perfect globes. "No, you will find no vidscreens here, my king. I have no need of them. And neither will you."

Abdiel placed the lighted candle in the center of the table, equidistant between himself and Dion. Taking one of the rocks in his hands, he handed it to the young man, kept the other rock himself.

Dion turned the rock over, studying it by the candlelight. The stone was a dark green, highly polished, and veined with streaks of warm red. He rolled it in his palm. The sensation produced by the smooth, polished rock moving against his skin was sensual and soothing.

"Heliotrope," he said, identifying it.

"Also known as the bloodstone. Very good, Your Majesty. Your education has not been neglected. Platus, your mentor, was a wise man, an intelligent man. A gentle man, too gentle for his own good, I fear."

Dion didn't answer; the memory of his dead Guardian, who had given his life for him, jabbed him painfully. He set the rock down on the table, kept his hand on it to prevent it from rolling. "You said we were going to view something that has to do with the Lady Maigrey." His voice harshened. He was, he reminded himself, here on serious business.

"I forget the impatience of youth. Very well, we will begin. Grasp the stone tightly with your hand—your left hand, my king. Give me the right."

Abdiel held his own bloodstone in his right hand. He

stretched across the table, reaching to Dion with the left. Candlelight danced and sparkled on the shining needles.

Dion didn't move. A shudder convulsed his body. He stared at the needles, his right hand opening and closing spasmodically.

"You will feel a sharp pain at first, my king, just as you do with the bloodsword. But the pain will soon pass." Abdiel's voice was soft, seductive, sensual as the feel of the smooth rock against the young man's skin. "Or rather, you won't notice it. The sensation of our minds, our souls, flowing together will completely obliterate any physical discomfort."

"Why must I do . . . this?" Dion asked through lips so numb he could barely move them. "What will happen?"

"You will see, young man. Your eyes will be opened. Not only your physical eyes, but the eyes of your soul. Once, long ago, Maigrey and Derek Sagan bonded with me. We retain that bond. I have the power to see them, to know what they are doing, saying, sometimes even thinking! I can share that power with you, Dion, if you will share your being with me."

Confused thoughts, words of Maigrey's came back to Dion about the stronger being able to gain ascendancy over the minds of the weaker. But what did that have to do with him? He'd been warned against Sagan, and he had not succumbed.

I am, after all, destined to be king.

"The power," Dion said, his eyes on the glistening needles. "Maigrey told me I possessed it, but I could never use it."

"A lie!" Abdiel breathed. "She is afraid. She fears the power in you. Of course you can use the power of the Blood Royal. You have only to reach out your hand, my king, and take it!"

Dion pressed his lips tightly together, stretched out his hand. Not trembling, not wavering, his palm with its five new, fresh scars closed over the palm of the old man.

Abdiel clasped it tight. The needles penetrated the boy's flesh.

Dion gasped in pain, shivered at the sensation of the virus flowing into his body, burning, pulsing, far stronger than with the bloodsword. His arm jerked. Abdiel held the boy's hand fast, stroked it, pressed the needles harder into the flesh.

"Look into the candle flame!" he ordered.

Dion, shuddering, moaned and tried to free himself.

"Look into the candle flame and see!"

The voice came from within, from his heart, from his mind. It was his, it was Abdiel's. Wonders unheard of, knowledge unguessed at stirred in Dion's brain. He couldn't use it yet, couldn't catch it, but he would. He would learn to. The ache of invasion subsided. Sublime pleasure suffused him. He would be old and wise when he was young and strong. He would be, with this power, forever and truly a king!

Dion lifted his head, looked into the flame, and saw.

Chapter ·→❊◯❊←· Fourteen

I've a grand memory for forgetting . . .
Robert Louis Stevenson, *Kidnapped*

Maigrey looked tired, tired and defeated. Her head drooped; her shoulders slumped. She put her hand to the wound on her neck. It must sting and burn, but the Warlord guessed that its pain was minor compared to old wounds that throbbed and bled, draining the exultation of victory from her. She thought she had won the war. She had now discovered she hadn't even been on the right battlefield. He knew how she felt. He'd been on the field, unfortunately facing the wrong direction.

"How long have you known?" Maigrey's voice broke the silence, but not by much. Sagan couldn't be certain if he had heard her. But he knew her question from her thoughts, and answered.

"Not long, my lady. Abdiel kept himself well hidden. I was aware of him a short time back, on *Phoenix*. Even then I wasn't certain. I made inquiries, studied the records of his supposed death. No one, of course, had seen or heard of him for many years. Not surprising. He could stand in front of you and, if he didn't want you to see him, you wouldn't see him. I sent Sparafucile to investigate, warned him how the mind-seizer operates." Sagan laid his hand on the half-breed's shoulder. "My friend was not blinded like the others. He saw him. Abdiel is a frequent, albeit unknown, guest at the presidential mansion."

Sparafucile grinned, pleased at the commendation. Maigrey cast the breed a disgusted glance from the corner of her eye. "Why didn't you just have Abdiel assassinated? Your 'friend' appears quite adept at that line of work."

"Why didn't *we* kill him once, that long time ago, lady? We

had the chance, yet we were thankful to escape with our lives.
You know his defenses, Maigrey! You're not thinking—"

"Damn it, I *know* I'm not thinking!" She rounded on him,
fists clenched in her anger. "I don't *want* to think! I'm tired and
I hurt and . . . my God, Sagan, he's got Dion! Do something! We've got to do something!"

He stared at her in astonishment, saw that she was frantic,
on the verge of hysteria. He grabbed hold of her wrists and
gave her a swift, firm shake. "What the devil is the matter with
you?"

Maigrey gulped, caught her breath. She stared at him
blankly, without recognition, bloodless lips gaping open. A
shudder convulsed her body; she drew back from him, shrinking in upon herself. He let her go. Shivering, she turned away
from him, rubbing her arms.

Your lady not fight the dead ones, Sagan Lord. Sparafucile's
report on the ambush returned to the Warlord. *She fight the
others and fight well. Boom! Boom! Boom! All of them gone.
But the dead ones . . . the lady froze. If Sparafucile had not
been there, the lady would, I think, be a dead one herself now.*

Sagan had disregarded the statement. Sparafucile had his
faults and one was that he invariably made himself the hero of
any situation. The Warlord had fought with Maigrey in
numerous battles and had never known her to freeze in the
face of danger. But then, he'd never known her to be
hysterical, either.

"Surely this news of Abdiel can come as no surprise to you,
my lady." Sagan probed, not delicately or gently. He didn't
have time. "You were attacked this afternoon by his mind-
dead. Surely you recognized them. The night of the revolution—"

Maigrey's head jerked involuntarily. She fixed him with a
look expressive of such horror and fear that the Warlord was
taken aback. She hid herself in an instant, averting her face,
retreating behind strong defenses. But she could not build her
walls fast enough, or thick enough. Sagan remembered that
look. He had the feeling he would remember it until the day
he died.

She was shivering so much she could barely stand. Lifting
his cape from the table, he wrapped it gently around her.
"You're exhausted. There's nothing we can do tonight. Get
some sleep—"

"Don't condescend to me!" Maigrey snapped, flinching

away from him, though she kept the cape and huddled into its warmth. "I apologize for my weakness, my lord. It won't happen again."

But it will, Sagan said to himself, dark eyes and thoughts on the pale woman shivering in his cloak. It will happen again, and the next time it could well prove fatal—to you, to me, to my plans, to the boy. I need you strong, Maigrey. I need you well.

"You're not the only one who has had a trying day, my lady. I, too, need to rest. We will continue our discussion in the morning. I hope you will do me the honor of being my guest. I have ordered quarters readied for you in my shuttle, just down the corridor."

"Thank you, my lord, for your hospitality." Maigrey bowed gravely, started to move past him. "But I will return to my spaceplane."

He blocked the way. "I cannot allow that, my lady—"

"Why? What are you afraid of?" she flashed bitterly. "That I'll 'escape' my prison? *You're* not my jailer, my lord. *I'm* the one who's locked myself into my cell!"

"It is your safety about which I am concerned, my lady," the Warlord said coolly. "Snaga Ohme knows you have the bomb and undoubtedly his spies in Haupt's command know where to find it. And then there is Abdiel, though perhaps he doesn't know yet—"

"He knows, Sagan Lord," Sparafucile struck in. The half-breed fished among the tattered rags, withdrew an object, displayed it in the palm of his hand—a green rock, veined with red, once carved in a perfect globe, now split into innumerable pieces.

"Where did you find this?" Sagan took the bloodstone's pieces gingerly, tossed them on the deck, ground them to dust beneath his heel.

"The lady's plane. I search like you tell me, and find it in the underfittings—"

Maigrey closed her eyes, sank down onto a chair, her strength gone.

"You have the bomb in the spaceplane, am I correct, my lady?" Sagan questioned. "If anyone attempts to take it by force, the computer will blow up the plane and anyone inside."

"That is, I believe, standard procedure, my lord." Her voice was low, hardly audible.

"You gave the computer instructions, however, that would

release the bomb . . . *verbal* instructions? Instructions that could have been . . . most likely *were* overheard. . . ."

Maigrey remained motionless. She might have been a marble statue, set to guard a tomb.

"Careless, my lady. Very careless. And after you had encountered the mind-dead as you did once this day—"

Gray eyes, glistening with fever, opened, stared at him. Bloodless lips parted, speaking silently. *You could have told me! You could have warned me!*

"Would you have believed me, my lady?" Sagan asked.

Maigrey looked away, rose unsteadily to her feet. "If you will excuse me, my lord—"

"Wait one moment, Maigrey." Sagan put his hand on her arm. "There is a very simple solution to all this. Give *me* the bomb. I can then concentrate my efforts on freeing Dion."

"Perhaps you would, my lord. Perhaps you wouldn't. Once you had this weapon, you might not think it necessary to save the boy. No, I will keep what I have. I paid dearly for it."

"You may pay dearly to keep it."

"A threat, my lord?"

"A statement of fact, my lady. Two of the most powerful and unscrupulous men in the galaxy will stop at nothing to obtain the bomb."

"Only two? You omit yourself—out of modesty, I presume."

"No, I omit myself for a reason. Like it or not, lady, in this I am your ally."

Maigrey smiled suddenly, sadly. "Yes, you are, though not precisely in the way you imagine. You see, Derek, in order to release the bomb, XJ-27 must both see me and hear me and be able to identify me."

"As you say, standard procedure." Sagan shrugged. "Go on. I take it that isn't all."

"The computer must also identify an object that I show to it, verifying this object by its physical properties and its—"

"Yes, yes," Sagan interrupted impatiently. "The object is?"

Maigrey's smile twisted the scar on her face. "The Star of the Guardians, my lord. *My* Star of the Guardians."

The Warlord regarded her for long moments in silence. Then he bowed gravely, from the waist. "I am impressed, my lady."

Maigrey inclined her head. "I thought you would be, my lord."

"You did strike a fair bargain for it—"

"I would have kept my part fairly if the Adonian had kept his."

"So now if I want to recover my property—"

"—you must help me recover mine."

"But with no guarantees."

"No guarantees. I am glad we understand each other, my lord."

Sagan nodded. "I think that, whatever else may have happened between us, we have always understood each other."

"Have we?" she asked him suddenly, abruptly. Again, in the gray eyes, he saw the shadow of unnamed horror. "Have we?" she repeated, with desperate earnestness.

The question was unexpected. He probed her thoughts but her mind was dark; he groped through an unfamiliar, unlit room. He chose not to answer.

She turned away. He escorted her to the door of his chambers. She walked next to him in silence, wrapped for warmth in his red cloak.

"Captain, take the Lady Maigrey to her quarters and post a guard outside her door."

"Yes, my lord."

She left him. Sagan watched the small procession walk down the corridor. Behind him, the half-breed made a shuffling movement, indicating he was prepared to leave if not wanted. Sagan made a sign with his hand, however, and Sparafucile waited quietly for his lord's attention to return to him.

The Warlord watched the light in the corridor shine on long, pale hair. "A pretty problem. Four of us want this 'pearl of great price.' Maigrey has it, but she must keep it. Snaga Ohme has the starjewel, but not the lady. I have the lady, but not the jewel. Abdiel has neither, he wants both. But he has Dion. I wonder how he figures to use Dion. . . ."

The lady disappeared into a room not far from his. He heard the door sigh shut, the scrape of the boots of the Honor Guard, taking up their positions outside. Sagan shook his head.

"I must have you strong," he repeated to her. "I must have you well."

Chapter ⚬–⚬◯⚬–⚬ Fifteen

A night of memories and sighs . . .
Walter Savage Landor, *"Rose Aylmer"*

It was midnight, the darkness at its deepest, approaching the flood. Laskar was a ship sailing upon night's rough sea. Its bright lights and noise and gaiety pitched and heaved on waves of money and liquor, drugs and sex. Occasionally it tossed an unwary passenger overboard, left him to drown in the murky depths.

Dion stumbled outside Abdiel's house, hoping the fresh air would help him regain his senses. But though the air had cooled rapidly with the setting of Laskar's green sun, the sand still retained the day's heat. Warmth radiated upward, like the solar furnace in the rooms inside.

The young man mopped his sweating face, reveled in the breeze that lifted the thick red hair, cooled his scalp, did little to cool the fever within him. His right arm burned and ached; the pain seemed to travel up into his brain. He sought vainly to try to organize and sort his thoughts, but they shimmered in the heat like mirages on the desert floor. He looked upward, into the black sky, dusted by sparkling stars.

Deep space: frigid, aloof, peaceful, vast. He could lose himself up there quickly, vanish into obscurity, become ordinary. For a moment, he longed for it as a parched man longs for cool water while his brain bubbled and seethed, a witch's caldron.

King! You shall be king. . . .

Clutching his pounding head, almost sick from the heat, Dion stumbled back into the house and ran bodily into one of the mind-dead.

"Tusk. I want to see Tusk," Dion demanded, grabbing hold

232

of the image of the mercenary, clinging to him in the upheaval of his senses. "He hasn't . . . left, has he?"

"No," Mikael said. "He has been waiting for you."

"Good. Take me to him."

Dion staggered upstairs and down, feeling his way with his hand on the walls more than walking, following Mikael's lead. The young man was completely lost. The house, with its numerous sharp corners and angles that each looked exactly like the one before and exactly like the one after, made no sense.

Mikael halted before a door. Dion, not watching, tumbled into him. The mind-dead steadied him with a strong, impersonal grip. Unlocking the door with a key, he pushed it open.

Tusk sprang out instantly, the mercenary's face contorted with fury and determination. Whether by accident or design, Mikael had maneuvered the unstable Dion to a position in front. The boy's body blocked the door. Tusk would have had to go through him to get out.

"Tusk?" Dion was startled out of his confused state by the mercenary's sudden and frightening appearance. "What's wrong? Is—"

Dion swayed on his feet. Tusk, swearing beneath his breath, caught hold of him, dragged him inside the room. Mikael slammed shut the door; the lock turned.

Tusk led Dion to the bed, eased the boy onto it. "I'll get you some water, kid. . . ."

"No." Dion shook his head, made a feeble gesture with his hand. "I . . . don't think I could keep it down."

"Name of the Creator, kid, what'd that bastard do to you?"

Dion glanced up, frowned. "Don't talk like that. If you mean Abdiel, he didn't do anything *to* me. He showed me the truth, that's all."

"Put your head between your knees. Take a deep breath. There. Feel better?"

Dion did as he was told, and in a moment, when the room quit turning topsy-turvily, he raised his head. Tusk, no longer floating balloonlike on the ceiling, was standing stolidly in front of him.

"What happened to your shoulder?" Dion noticed the mercenary rubbing his left arm.

"Hurt it, bashing it against the door."

"Why?" Dion stared at him.

"To get the hell outta here! This may come as a shock to

you, kid, but I don't much like being locked up in prison cells!"

"This isn't a prison. We can leave anytime we want."

"Yeah? Then why did Rigor Mortis there turn the lock and take away the key?"

"You were acting like such a bastard, I'd have locked you up, too."

"All right, kid." Tusk waved at the door. "Let's get going. We'll find Nola on the way out—"

"You go ahead. I'm not leaving." Dion massaged his right arm. The pain seemed to be growing in intensity.

Tusk grabbed Dion's wrist, turned the boy's palm to the light. Five welts oozed blood.

"What—?" Tusk understood, caught his breath with a clicking sound in his throat. He dropped the hand, stared at Dion in revulsion, edged away from him. "My God!"

Dion closed his hand swiftly.

"My God, kid!" Tusk repeated hoarsely. "You let him do that to you!"

"You can't understand! You're not of the Blood Royal," Dion said coldly, trying to ignore the pain.

"Damn right! And before I let that old man do something like that to me, I'd—" Tusk stopped.

Dion wasn't listening. The boy had curled in upon himself, shaking, shoulders hunched. "I saw her, Tusk!" he whispered. "I saw her! He was kissing her, Tusk!"

"Saw who?" Tusk gazed at the boy, perplexed. "Nola? Who was kissing Nola?"

"I'm not talking about Nola!" Dion bounded to his feet, paced the room. "Maigrey! Lady Maigrey!" He rounded suddenly on Tusk. The blue eyes burned, flames dancing on ice-cold water. "I saw her, Tusk! Through this!" Dion raised the bleeding right hand. "I saw her. She went to the house of that Snaga Ohme. She told him she was sent by Sagan. She sold him her starjewel, Tusk! The Star of the Guardians! For what? For a bomb that could blow up . . . blow up . . . everything." Dion waved his hands. "All of us. And you know what she did with it, Tusk?"

The mercenary tried to stem the incoherent flow. "Kid—"

Dion caught hold of Tusk, fingers squeezing the mercenary's flesh. "She met Sagan. In the office of the commander at Fort Laskar. The Warlord kissed her hand, Tusk! I saw him. I saw her. I saw her face. They left together, arm in arm. Friendly. Oh, yes, very friendly."

Dion started pacing again. Tusk followed him.

"How did you see this, kid? Vids? Did he have a spy camera—"

"The candle flame," Dion muttered. "I saw her in the candle flame. . . ."

"A candle—? Kid! It's a trick! He's put some sort of drug into your system! You hallucinated—"

"No, Tusk." Dion stopped his restless movement, turned and faced his friend. He was suddenly calm, terrifyingly calm. "It wasn't a hallucination. I know. Everything I saw, every word I heard, really happened. She's with him, Tusk. She's betrayed me."

"Kid, all right. Let's say . . . somehow you saw her and him. There's got to be some explanation. You know the lady! She wouldn't do anything to hurt you. She risked her life for you!"

Dion sighed, softened. "That's what Abdiel said."

"What?" Tusk scowled, not particularly liking this sudden new ally. "What'd the old man say?"

"He said that there must be . . . extenuating circumstances. He defended her, Tusk. I want to believe him. I want to believe in her. But I saw—"

"Dixter!" Tusk said, snapping his fingers. "That's it! Sagan's got Dixter. He'd use the general to force her to side with him, kid."

"Of course!" Hope's flame illuminated the blue eyes, burned bright and clear with strengthening resolve. "And now I know what I must do."

"Yeah, get outta here! Somehow or other we'll reach the lady—"

"No." Dion shook his head firmly. "The Warlord would never let us. He'd use me as he's used her. Or merely eliminate me altogether. He doesn't need me now. He doesn't need the true heir to the throne. He has the bomb. He can blackmail the galaxy. In fact, I'm a threat, a liability to him. I see my way, Tusk. I know what I must do. Abdiel will help me."

"Fine, kid, but he can help from a distance—"

"You can leave, Tusk." Dion's head was clear, his thoughts and plans and ideas shining like crystal. "Take Nola and go back to Vangelis. And thanks for everything. I truly appreciate it."

"And leave you? I can't. I'm—" Tusk's tongue stuck to the roof of his mouth.

"My Guardian? Not any longer. I don't need you now, Tusk. Abdiel is with me. He'll help me. He'll give me the strength, the power I need. Look." Dion went to the door, turned the handle. A click, and the door swung open. "Look. You're free. You can go."

"Not without Nola . . ."

"Tusk, I'm here! I was so frightened!" Nola stood dazedly in the hallway, Mikael right behind her. "What's going on?"

"We can leave," Tusk said evenly, without expression. "The kid doesn't need us. Abdiel's going to let us walk out of here, isn't he, Rigor?"

Mikael's face was imperturbable, no expression, eyes looking at nothing. "I am acting according to the master's wishes. Your Majesty"—the eyes swiveled in the boy's general direction—"my master wishes to confer with you, if you are free."

"Yes. I need to talk to him. We have plans to make, and not much time to make them."

Mikael glided unobtrusively into the room, came to stand behind Tusk. The mercenary reached out his hand, motioned Nola near him.

"Good-bye, Tusk. Good-bye, Nola," Dion said from the doorway. "Say hello to everyone on Vangelis for me. If everything works out, the lady and I will be with you soon."

"Yeah, sure. So long, kid." Tusk spoke through clenched teeth.

Cold beneath his sweat-soaked shirt, the sharp blade of a knife pressed against his skin.

··◁■ ■▷··

Laskar's night, so glaringly radiant in the city, gathered darker around the Warlord's shuttle by contrast. Near midnight, a ragged figure could be seen slinking out from it, padding swiftly, a shadow of a shadow that disturbed one of the centurions, who thought he saw something from the corner of his eye. A sharp-spoken order prevented him from taking action.

Sagan, having given Sparafucile his orders, stood thoughtful and alone in his own chambers. He pondered, weighing alternatives, and finally made up his mind. Stepping out into the dark and silent corridor, he walked down it, came to a stop before Maigrey's quarters.

The Honor Guard snapped to rigid attention.

"Centurion."

"My lord." The guard's eyes stared straight ahead.

"Carry my compliments to the captain and ask him to double the watch tonight."

The soldier's eyelids flickered nervously. "I am not permitted to leave my post, my lord."

"I will stand your guard, centurion."

The guard's brows came together. He shifted his gaze, eyes meeting his Warlord's. "My lady is asleep, my lord."

Sagan almost smiled. Another of Maigrey's champions. He recognized the man, now that he looked at him closely. "Marcus, isn't it?"

"Yes, my lord."

"I gave you an order, Marcus."

The centurion's lips tightened. He put his fist to his heart in salute, marched off to perform his duty. The Warlord waited until the man was gone, the corridor empty. Opening the door, he glided silently inside.

Security lights, small pinpricks in the darkness to guide those who must move by night, cast a dim, lambent glow over the woman asleep on the bed. She lay on her side on top of the bedclothes, fully dressed, as if she had flung herself down and not been able to rise again. The Warlord's cape, lying on the deck, resembled a pool of blood. He lifted it, settled it gently over her for a blanket.

Her left cheek was against the pillow. Her hair covered her face. Reaching down, his movement carefully quiet, the Warlord lifted the strands of pale hair and moved them aside.

She did not stir; her breathing remained deep and even. The scar was a livid streak on her smooth skin. Sagan started to touch it, run his finger along it. He changed his mind, held his hand poised above her.

"Lance the wound . . . drain off the poison. Painful, but necessary surgery, my lady."

Sagan laid his fingertips on her temple, spoke. "My memories, your memories: one."

Book III

The Betrayal

. . . made me dream of thunder and the gods.

Charles Dickens, *David Copperfield*

Chapter ◆━○●━◆ One

Thou art a traitor and a miscreant,
Too good to be so, and too bad to live . . .
William Shakespeare, *King Richard II*, Act I, Scene 1

Lord Derek Sagan, commander of the famed Golden Squadron, sat fuming with impatience in the backseat of the staff car. Discipline, he reminded himself. Discipline. But his hands itched to grab hold of the young driver by his uniform collar, hurl him out of the car and take over the wheel himself.

Sagan leaned forward. "Can't you make this thing go any faster?"

"This is a restricted zone, Commander," the corporal apologized nervously. "We're pushing it as is. But if it's an emergency—"

"No! Belay that." Sagan flung himself back into the luxurious leather seat, glowered at the magnificent scenery with a look that might have withered the graceful poplars.

Certainly it seemed to have withered the corporal, who kept his gaze stolidly in front of him, much to the risk of his vehicle. But he'd obviously far rather let some other craft zoom up on his tail than glance into the rearview cams and inadvertently meet the glare of those dark and burning eyes.

The tree-lined boulevard leading through the Glitter Palace park offered Sagan no distraction from his thoughts. He turned his brooding gaze forward, hoping for the hundredth time to see the gleaming towers of the castle, repeating to himself—for the hundredth time—that they couldn't possibly be near it yet. His gaze shifted to his driver, noted the man's discomfiture: neck rigid, jaw clenched to the point where his teeth must ache, hands white-knuckled on the wheel.

Sagan forced himself to relax, mentally taking himself to task. He'd been careless, allowing his tension to show. He could almost hear the corporal, on returning to his barracks, remark to a commanding officer, "Lord Sagan was as jumpy as a guy comin' down off the juice. The rumors must be true. Something's happening."

By way of making amends, Sagan leaned forward again, placed his hand in a friendly manner on the driver's shoulder. "Relax, Corporal. I didn't mean to criticize. No land vehicle can ever go fast enough to suit a space pilot."

Sagan saw immediately that he'd only made matters worse. The corporal was staring at the commander through the rearview cams in unparalleled astonishment. It occurred to Sagan that not once had he—a mighty lord, commander of the Golden Squadron, member of the Blood Royal, cousin to His Majesty the King—ever previously acknowledged the corporal as a fellow human being.

Sagan gave his acting up as a bad job. Relapsing into the seat, he permitted himself the luxury of indulging in his tension and drummed his fingers on the armrest. Let the corporal relay his suspicions back to base. There'd be no time to do anything about them anyway. It was too late. Already too late.

Poplars and oaks gave way to stands of firs, then aspen and linden and countless other varieties of tree life rescued from the ecologically ruined planet of old Earth, cradle of civilization. The staff car sped through the air about level with the uppermost branches, rustling the leaves in its wake. Below them stretched grassy lawns, decorated with carefully designed and carefully tended gardens, colors gleaming jewellike in the sun. Swans floated majestically on mirror-surfaced ponds, graceful gazelle leapt across swards of green grass. It was late afternoon, all peaceful and serene, shining in the sunlight.

"The palace, my lord," the corporal said, a note of profound relief in his voice.

Sagan's hand slowly ceased its restless drumming, came to a halt.

The vast lake stretched before him, its cobalt blue water still and dark; no wind blew this day on Minas Tares. In the lake's center, far distant but visible by the glare of sunlight off the glass, gleamed the towers of the Glitter Palace. A bridge of null-grav fused silversteel spanned the lake, soaring upward in a shining curve before sweeping down toward the palace. A marvel of engineering, this bridge, as the three others like it, was almost fifty kilometers long and stood without supports.

The bridges were, ostensibly and by law, the only routes one could travel to reach the palace. Of course, jet-propelled cars, such as the one in which Sagan rode, rendered the law not only ridiculous but dangerous. Just how ridiculous . . . and how dangerous . . . would be proven this night.

Derek Sagan had not been alone in attempting to convince His Majesty of the need for stricter security measures: force fields shielding the palace from attack from sky and ground, armed guards patrolling the perimeters, land mines in the gardens. King Starfire refused to consider the matter. Land mines would kill the gazelle, armed guards upset the swans. God was His Majesty's guard. God had placed him on his throne. God's hand held him safe and secure.

"This night," Derek Sagan said to himself, "God's hand will clench into a fist."

Armed guards, wearing the royal crest, stood at the silver-steel gates guarding the bridge. The corporal brought the staff car down to ground level. The guards glanced inside, saluted when they recognized the commander by his armor and the eight-pointed Star of the Guardians that flashed on his breast. Sagan returned the salute with more than his usual care. In hours, these men would be dead.

The staff car shot onto the silver span, flying low, as dictated by royal decree, traveling decorously at the posted speed. It was slow going, but Sagan, suddenly, was not in a hurry. It would be the last time he saw the royal mansion like this . . . ever.

The palace did not come into the viewer's full sight until he reached the top of the arch. Standing in the center of the midnight-dark, perfectly round lake, the Glitter Palace shone like myriad diamonds in a blue velvet crown. The four silver bridges formed a cross, with the palace and the lesser jewels—the buildings of the royal city—on an island in the center.

The entire palace was made of steelglass, the innumerable multitude of panes used in its construction each set at a minute angle to every other. By day, the panes of glittering glass caught the sun like the facets of a gemstone—refracted the light, reflected it, created shimmering, radiant sparkles of every color of the rainbow. The sight was dazzling to the eye and the mind. By night, the glass walls became the night, reflecting the icy white of the stars, holding captive the pale light of the moon. No lights shone from within the palace walls. The steelglass acted as a one-way mirror. Those inside were permitted to look out; those outside could not look in.

"You look out your windows, Your Majesty, but you do not see. You listen but you do not hear. You will listen tonight, Amodius Starfire. You will listen tonight."

"I beg your pardon, my lord? Did you say something?" The corporal was peering fearfully back at him, obviously afraid that his commander had taken it into his head to make another attempt at light conversation.

Sagan waved his hand irritably, brushing his words from the air, not aware—until then—that he'd spoken aloud. The corporal, relieved, urged the car forward with slightly more speed than propriety dictated.

The royal city's streets were empty, deserted. The art galleries and boutiques, restaurants and cafes were closed; the last tourist and employee buses had departed. The elite who could afford to live upon King's Island—many of them members of the Blood Royal—had returned to their townhouses or condos located on the island's perimeter to prepare for to-night's festive event. Traffic would be heavy, closer to the time of the ceremony when the Guardians, invited guests, and the news media began arriving. For now, the staff car had the cobbled streets nearly all to itself.

City streets flowed snakelike into a large park that melted unobtrusively into the royal military headquarters. The king grudgingly conceded the necessity for a military base upon his island, but would not permit any harsh reminders of war to obtrude upon the peaceful, serene beauty of Minas Tares. The base, therefore, looked more like a hunt club than a military HQ. Fancifully dressed sentries, whose main duty was to endure having their pictures taken with tourists, stood guard on an immaculately kept lawn surrounding several sparkling-facaded buildings.

A large crowd of humans and other life-forms was gathered around festival tents installed on the cricket ground. The promotions ceremony must be nearly concluded. Night would be falling soon. Five hundred senior staff officers gathered together in one place. Sagan smiled—a grim smile, not one of elation. The military had protested vociferously against such an insane proceeding, but His Majesty would not be deterred. It would look well on the vids, these high-ranking army officers swearing their fealty and loyalty, offering their lives for king and galaxy.

· Many would be called on to either make good that oath tonight . . . or forswear it.

The driver slowed to allow a caterer's truck to pass. Sagan, idly glancing at the crowd milling about the cricket ground, caught sight of the rumpled-uniformed figure of John Dixter, newly promoted general.

Dixter: a simple man, a good soldier, undoubtedly loyal to his king, and Maigrey's friend. Sagan rubbed his chin, considering. Maigrey's friend. That made things difficult. If she knew of the scheduled attack ahead of time, she would warn John Dixter. And while it was impossible that one man should have the power to stop the revolution, one man—especially a soldier of Dixter's caliber—could organize effective resistance. And it was essential that the military base, a symbol of the monarchy on Minas Tares, fall.

I had planned to tell her, Derek Sagan considered to himself silently. She agrees with me that Starfire is an inept, blind, bumbling old fool. And though she doesn't say so, because he's Semele's husband, she knows the crown prince isn't any better. Once I explain to her our places in the new revolutionary government, once I show her the power we can gain in the future of the new democracy, she will concede that the change is for the best.

Maigrey wouldn't betray me; I have no fear of that. But if she thought her friend was in danger, she'd find a way to alert him. Sagan's frown darkened. He tapped his hand on the armrest irritably. It's an unfortunate relationship, one that continually drags her down from the high pinnacle on which she should stand. Dixter was nothing but a nuisance to me before, but now I can see that, conceivably, he could be a threat. Tonight, however . . . tonight should end that. But it means that I can't tell her. No, I can't tell her.

The sun was setting when Derek Sagan arrived at the palace. The sky was streaked with bands of flame and gold, deepening to purple, and at its heart, a lurid splash of red. Night darkened the opposite horizon, darkened the palace except for the towers facing the west. The staff car landed, floating on cushions of air. A palace footman hastened forward to open the door.

Derek beat him to it, nearly knocking the man over in his haste. Climbing out of the car, he stared upward at the massive palace walls. Though thronged with life and light and gaiety within, they were dark and empty as the night without. One tower, spiraling taller than all the rest, one tower alone caught the last rays of the dying sun.

Sagan slowed his fevered pace to watch. The sun sank lower; the darkness rose up higher around the tower, a tide that could not be stopped. Still the light gleamed—a red-golden fire that burned brighter as the night grew blacker. He'd seen sunsets before, he'd viewed the palace's fabled glass walls at nearly every hour, day or night, yet he'd never seen anything like this. He had been raised to believe in portents, in signs from heaven. And right now, at this fated moment when victory or ignominious defeat stood balanced on a dagger's edge, he was extraordinarily sensitive to what God might be trying to tell him.

The sun sank lower and lower until only a fingernail's-breadth of fire shone above the already night-dark horizon. The flame reflected in the tower burned lower, like a guttering candle. The sun vanished. Night claimed the palace; the flickering fire on the tower flared and died. Darkness.

Sagan was satisfied and began to climb the crystal steps—row after endless row—sweeping upward to the palace's gigantic silver doors. A footman went before him, lighting his way with a star-torch, whose intense but small white beam would detract only minutely from the splendor of the night's dark magnificence reflected in the palace walls.

Reaching the top, Sagan dismissed the footman. The doors swung open to receive him. Warmth and light and noise spilled out, cascaded down the stairs. Derek paused, looked up one last time at the tower.

Dark still, but—shining above the battlements—a single star.

··◁■ ■▷··

Lady Maigrey Morianna attempted to fasten the silver chain around her neck. Her impatient fingers fumbled at the clasp. She thought she had it, turned from the mirror, and felt the starjewel slither down the front of her indigo blue velvet robes. Catching hold of it before it fell to the floor, swearing softly beneath her breath, she put the chain around her neck and began, again, to wrestle with the clasp. This time, it got caught in her hair.

A knock on the door interrupted her. Her lady-in-

waiting—an honorary position, granted to women of the minor
nobility—answered it. From the shocked look on the older
woman's face and the bright flush on the woman's cheeks,
Maigrey realized her swearing had increased in volume and
intensity. Sighing, she bit her lip and swallowed her words.
Her brother entered the room.

"Was that you? I thought I'd wandered into the barracks by
mistake," Platus said, mildly reproving.

"It's this damn necklace. It *won't* stay on! I think the clasp's
broken—"

Gentle hands took the starjewel away from her, fastened
the chain around her neck with ease. "Calm down," he
whispered, patting her on the shoulders

"Allow me to do your hair, my lady," the older woman said,
approaching.

"What's there to do? Run a brush through it? I—" Maigrey
caught her brother's eye, subsided rebelliously into a chair in
front of her mirror.

"'You're no longer on a troop ship. You're the daughter of a
planetary ruler, in the palace of her king,'" Maigrey muttered
to herself, mimicking Platus's voice.

The lady-in-waiting, lifting the brush, began to try to
untangle the pale, fine hair. Maigrey gritted her teeth, held
herself stiff and rigid under the torment.

"Why are you dressing so early?" Platus asked. "The
banquet isn't for hours yet."

"I'm going to see Semele before the reception begins. I
won't have time to change afterward."

"I didn't think she was allowed to have visitors."

"They'll make an exception for me."

The gray eyes reflected in the mirror were cool and
resolute. "Yes, I guess they probably will," her brother said
dryly. "How is she?"

"Confined to bed. They can't seem to stop the bleeding.
And she's gone into premature labor once already, two months
ago. She almost lost her baby then." Maigrey's hand clenched
to a fist. "No one told me, of course!"

The lady-in-waiting was making clucking noises, presumably in an effort to calm her charge.

"What could you have done, Maigrey?" Platus asked. "You
were in the middle of a war zone."

"I could have— Ouch! Damn it to hell and back! Give me
that!" Maigrey leapt to her feet, grabbed the brush from the

startled woman, and flung it into a corner of the room. "Get out!" she cried in a fury.

"Well, I never!" The lady-in-waiting sniffed, folded her hands across her broad middle.

"I think you had better leave," Platus said in mollifying tones. "My sister's a bit overexcited."

"Your sister, my lord, is a spoiled brat!" the lady-in-waiting pronounced with feeling, and flounced out of the room.

Platus shut the door on the woman, turned around to find his sister, in her best robes of state, on her knees on the floor, peering under the bed.

"Maigrey! You're covered with dust! What—"

"I've lost my shoes!"

"Here, get up. Go sit down. I'll look." Platus searched under the bed, found three shoes, two of which—he counted to his great good fortune—happened to match. He held them up. "Are these the ones? They're black. What happened to the shoes made to match your robes—"

"I tossed them. Those will do. No one's going to be looking at my feet anyway. Damn dress is so long, I'll be tripping over it half the night." She snatched the shoes from him, attempted to put one on.

"That's the wrong foot, dear," Platus said softly.

Maigrey hurled the shoe under a chair. Turning away, she rested her elbows on the vanity stand, let her head sink into her hands. "I think you should go, Platus."

Instead of leaving, he walked over, rested his hands on her shoulders. "He hasn't returned yet."

Maigrey raised her head, looked into the mirror at her brother's reflection. The two didn't resemble each other. Platus, in his early thirties, took after their mother. A gentle, sensitive woman who loved music and poetry, she was given in marriage—by royal command—to the ruler of a planet far distant from hers not only in light-years but in every way possible.

Such marriages were not uncommon among the Blood Royal, whose bloodlines the scientists were always attempting to strengthen. In this instance, the poor queen had the misfortune to be deemed a perfect mate for a barbarian king of a warrior people. She had the further misfortune to bear him a son as gentle and peace-loving as herself. The boy was a comfort to her, an extreme disappointment to his father. Platus was sent to the Royal Academy as soon as the king could decently rid himself of the fragile, intellectual child. The queen's life was unsupportable and, when her daughter Maigrey was born, the poor woman gave it up with little regret.

The warrior king had no use for a girl-child and ignored his daughter until one day, passing by the nursery, he saw the four-year-old neatly skewer one of her dolls with a small, handmade spear. From that day forward, his daughter never left her father's side until King Starfire, hearing rumors that a daughter of the Blood Royal was being raised in military camps, caused her to be forcibly removed.

Although Platus resembled their mother most closely, both children had inherited her light hair, slender build, and love for music and poetry. Platus was tall and lanky, his blond hair wispy and starting to thin on top. His hands were the hands of a musician, with tapering, delicate fingers. The blue eyes were mild and introspective. He was even-tempered, rarely angry, and was attempting to resign the Guardians due to his pacifist beliefs.

Maigrey's face was her mother's, the fearless gray eyes her father's. A skilled swordsman, a skilled pilot, she had made her warrior father proud of his little girl. She was fond of her brother, but didn't understand him. The two had never been particularly close and this decision of his to leave the Guardians had precipitated more than one bitter quarrel between them.

But there was a family resemblance, no matter how remote. Maigrey saw it now, looking into the mirror. The resemblance tended to be strongest when she was weary, sad . . . or afraid.

"No, he hasn't returned," she said.

"Perhaps he has, and you haven't seen him. His rooms are in the other wing—"

"I would know," Maigrey interrupted. "I would know if he were here. And he isn't."

The two didn't pursue the issue. Platus didn't like Derek Sagan, and Maigrey knew the feeling was mutual. She knew, too, that her brother was appalled at the thought of the mind-link. Brother and sister never discussed what Platus considered an unnatural bonding unless forced to by circumstance.

"A month's leave of absence isn't that remarkable. Where did he go, by the way? Did you find out?" he asked.

Maigrey, looking in the mirror, kept her expression impassive, her face immobile. "No," she said, shaking her hair over her shoulders and flinching away from her brother's solicitous and irritating touch. She stood up, hand toying nervously with the starjewel around her neck. "It's time I was going—"

"Maigrey"—Platus's mild voice hardened, was unusually stern—"the rumors of revolution fly thicker and grow darker by the hour. Do you know something about it? Sagan has made friends with that troublemaking professor, that Peter Robes. Derek has freely expressed admiration for the man, he's openly criticized the monarchy—"

"I've openly criticized the monarchy, brother. Does that make me a traitor?" Maigrey demanded, turning to face him. "Derek Sagan is our commanding officer. We owe him not only our loyalty but our lives. It's not for us to question his . . . his"—she faltered—"to question him," she concluded. She stood up, started to move past her brother. "If you will excuse me, I'm running late—"

Platus put his hands on her arms. "Maigrey—"

"Leave me alone!" she flashed.

"Maigrey!" He was earnest, intense. "Maigrey, if you know something, you have to tell it! Tell the king! Tell the captain of the guard! Tell me, Danha! Tell someone!"

She wasn't looking at him; she didn't struggle to break free of his grasp. She held perfectly still, staring at the glittering jewel around her neck.

Platus shook her—not harshly, he could never be harsh, not even when he was frightened. She raised her head, saw her face reflected in his eyes, and was startled to see how pale she was.

"I have faith in Derek," she said at last. "Whatever he's doing, it's for the best."

"How can you be so blind?" Platus lost his patience.

Maigrey struck his hands away from her. "I took an oath of loyalty to my commander—"

"You took an oath of allegiance to your king!"

"You can't understand, Platus. You're not a soldier!" She cast him a cool, disdainful glance. "Sometimes I wonder if you *are* my father's son! I know Father wondered it often enough!"

Platus paled. "Sometimes," he said, "I wish to God I wasn't."

Maigrey was immediately remorseful, tried to draw back her verbal blade, but it had already cut too deeply. Her brother forgave her readily, however, was calm and soothing to her, and left her almost immediately. His look, as he went, was grave and sorrowful. Almost pitying.

So superior, Maigrey thought when he was gone. Always so damn superior! Just like when we were kids in the Academy and he'd take it upon himself to try to run my life. Her fingers itched to seize the door and slam it after him, but she restrained herself. She was above that sort of behavior now.

Maigrey buckled the bloodsword around her waist. She would wear it until the banquet, then she'd be required to take it off. She supposed it wasn't necessary, going armed through the Glitter Palace, but she could no more walk out without the sword than she could walk out without her shoes. . . .

And where were they anyway?

Finding them, tripping over the long skirts as she irritably thrust the high heels onto her feet, she hurried out the door. She decided she wasn't the least bit sorry for what she'd said to her brother. It was the truth, after all. She'd heard the whispers all her life. And she hoped he *would* resign from the Guardians.

Derek was right. Platus didn't belong.

Chapter ❖ Two

> . . . you that do abet him . . .
> Cherish rebellion and are rebels all.
> William Shakespeare, *Richard II*, Act II, Scene 3

"I really shouldn't permit this," the doctor said. "Her Royal Highness's time is very close at hand. I would prefer she remain completely undisturbed."

Maigrey strongly considered grabbing the man by the lapels of his sterile white coat and hurling him through the steelglass window. She controlled herself, with an effort. "I should have been informed."

"Semele wouldn't allow it, Maigrey," said Augustus Starfire, Crown Prince. "Besides, what could you have done, off fighting the Corasians?"

"Her condition isn't that serious," the doctor snapped. "Bleeding like this isn't uncommon. Her Royal Highness has been restricted to her bed to prevent any major complications, and consequently there have been none. She has brought the pregnancy to full term. The baby is healthy, Her Royal Highness is well . . . or she will be, if she is allowed to rest."

"I won't stay long. I only want to visit with her for a few moments. She's my best friend. We haven't seen each other in months. I'll be leaving for my next tour of duty tomorrow."

"I've spoken to my wife." This from Augustus Starfire, looking to the doctor as one might look to a god. "She is feeling much better today and thinks that a visit from the Lady Maigrey would do her good. She promises not to tire herself. The delivery's going to be tonight." The prince reported the last in an undertone to Maigrey.

"I didn't say that for certain," the doctor rasped in acerbic tones, overhearing.

"But surely with all this modern technological equipment

you've got"—Maigrey gestured at numerous blinking screens keeping track of the patient's progress—"you could tell—"

"Lady Maigrey," the doctor interrupted. "We can travel faster than the speed of light. We can genetically alter life. We can destroy each other with remarkable skill and efficiency. But babies still come when they're damn good and ready. Mother Nature's been at her job for thousands of years and it's my belief that the less we interfere with her, the better off everyone will be."

"Semele should be in the hospital," Maigrey pronounced.

"My lady, when you have completed eight years of medical school and have served your internship and residency, I will then welcome your medical opinion. You may visit her," the doctor added magnanimously, perhaps by way of emphasizing his authority, "but remain only fifteen minutes."

"'Thus saith the Lord,'" Maigrey whispered to the crown prince, who responded with a nervous giggle.

Maigrey had forgotten Augustus's unfortunate tendency to giggle when he was keyed up and excited. Ordinarily, she thought it funny; she and Semele had teased him about it unmercifully when they were all in the Academy together. This evening, that high-pitched snigger grated on her nerves. She left him discussing breathing exercises with the doctor, and quietly entered the door to Semele's bedchamber.

Her first thought was that they hadn't needed to take Semele to the hospital because they'd brought the hospital to Semele. Fewer machines were needed to pilot a starship! Everything was so changed, she hardly knew where she was and paused, feeling suddenly ill at ease. The room smelled strongly of disinfectant, an odor so cold that not even the hothouse perfume of numberless bouquets of flowers could warm it. For a moment, Maigrey regretted that she'd come.

A head with dark tousled hair, lying on a pillow, turned from staring out a beautifully curtained window.

"Maigrey!" a well-remembered voice cried.

Suddenly her friend's bedroom returned to Maigrey as she had remembered it. She no longer saw the machines, she saw the damask-covered, hand-carved chairs and sofas, the end tables decorated by porcelain figurines frozen in time and lace-edged petticoats, dancing to silent minuets. Hand-embroidered tapestries, silken threads woven into tales of romance, shimmered on the walls, handwoven carpets adorned polished wooden floors.

Feeling at home, more at home than she'd felt in a long, long time, Maigrey crossed the spacious room to where her friend lay in a hospital bed, guarded by the machines and a machinelike nurse.

"You may leave us," Her Royal Highness said, dismissing the nurse as she might have dismissed her lady-in-waiting.

The nurse appeared dubious. Her Royal Highness was resolute, and the nurse compromised by removing her white-uniformed presence to a sofa on the other side of the room and turning on a vid.

"She's not a bad sort, really," Semele said, smiling up at Maigrey. "She's been telling me all the gossip from the hospital. You'd be amazed at the things a man and woman can do in a linen closet!"

Maigrey couldn't reply. Secretly shocked at the sight of her friend, she found it difficult to speak. Semele's vibrant beauty had made her one of the most sought-after women in the galaxy. Small and fragile, she lay in the mechanical monster of a bed that seemed to have swallowed her. Semele's flawless white skin, celebrated by the bad poets of the age, was now wan and translucent. Her lustrous black hair was limp and lifeless, the sheen gone.

"Ah, I can see by your face you're going to scold me, Maigy." Semele caught hold of her friend's hand in a mock pleading gesture. "Don't be mad because I didn't let them tell you. The fate of the galaxy depended on you, my dear. Who am I compared to that?" Semele's brown eyes were as warm and lively as ever, with a joy bubbling up from deep within.

Maigrey, somewhat reassured, made herself comfortable on the edge of the bed. "Who are you—only Her Royal Highness, princess of the aforesaid galaxy, and about to give birth to the heir to the throne. And I'll never forgive you for not letting me know you weren't well," she added, giving the hand, whose fingers sparkled with exquisite jewels, a playful smack.

"Don't be mean to me, Maigy," Semele said with a laughing pout. "Here you are, tall and slender, all dressed up, going to a banquet with the most scrumptious food, drinking champagne and dancing, while fat and dumpy old me is stuck in this godawful contraption of a bed, doing nothing—"

"—except having a baby. . . ." Maigrey tried not to notice how thin and white her friend's hand was.

"Just between ourselves, my dear, I'd rather be dancing."

"Liar!" Maigrey smiled at her.

"Maybe I am." Semele smiled back, her happiness bringing a glow of health to the pale complexion. "You look lovely tonight, Maigy. Blue is your color. It sets off your hair and reflects in your eyes. You should wear blue all the time."

"I shall personally instruct Commander Sagan to requisition blue battle armor to match my eyes," Maigrey teased.

"Laugh, wicked thing. You do look extremely pretty. Some special reason? A newly appointed young general wouldn't happen to be attending the banquet, would he?"

"John—that is, General Dixter—wasn't invited to the dinner. It's only for the Guardians, as you knew before you brought the subject up."

"That doesn't mean he can't come by afterward," Semele prodded.

"If you must know, he's going to meet me later. We're going out to celebrate his promotion."

"You look so stunning, it will be a shock to the poor man. He's probably never seen you out of uniform. Well, maybe he has"—her eyes glinted mischievously—"but I mean in a dress."

"Semele! How can you say such a thing?" Maigrey felt her cheeks burn.

"Prudery from a woman whose foul language gave Lady Rouncewell palpitations of the heart. I heard about that. She cornered poor Augustus in the hall and repeated every word at least twice. Why don't you say yes to him, Maigy?"

"To Augustus? I would, but I hear he has a hellcat for a wife. . . ."

"I mean John Dixter, and since when have I ever been anything but a perfect lady? He longs to marry you—"

"Longs to 'cherish and protect.'" Maigrey sighed.

"That can be very pleasant, dear friend," Semele said, with a smiling glance at a portrait of her husband on a little table near her bed.

"For you, Semele, not for me. He hates space flight. I can't live without it. One of us would have to sacrifice happiness for the other and consequently we'd both be miserable. Besides, I can't say yes to a question that's never been asked."

"I don't believe it! He's never asked you to marry him?"

"No. Like the ancient saying, my dear—what man truly wants to put his boots under a warrior-woman's bed?"

"From what I hear, Derek Sagan's boots aren't always on his feet," Semele said archly.

Maigrey, face flushed, stood up. "I think I better be going. . . ."

"Maigy, don't be mad! I've been trapped in this bed for four months! Gossip is my only form of recreation! Of course, I heard all about that time you two were stranded on that uncharted planet—"

"My plane had a computer malfunction. We spent the night fixing it," Maigrey mumbled, blushing furiously.

"I suppose that sounds more plausible than running out of gas. . . ." Semele's face grew suddenly serious. She clasped the hand she held tightly. "You don't love him, do you, Maigy?"

"Why is everyone so concerned about my relationship with Derek Sagan?" Maigrey demanded irritably, reminded of her uneasiness, her disquiet. But she let herself be pulled back down onto the bed. "What if I do love him? He's one of the most admired, respected men in the galaxy—"

"He's also one of the most feared, the most disliked," Semele said crisply, pushing herself to a sitting position. "Slide that pillow under my back. Thanks. Drat! There's the nurse, frowning at me, starting to come over here! I'm all right! Really! Go away! Shoo!"

The nurse, looking severe, returned to her vid program.

Semele crossed her hands over her swollen abdomen and fixed Maigrey with a pleading gaze. "I know you admire and respect him, Maigy, but don't mistake those feelings for love. You're close enough to him already with that horrid mind-link thing. Don't get any closer."

The flush had faded from Maigrey's cheeks. Her skin felt cold. She didn't look at her friend, but stared out the window at the setting sun.

"Maigy, he'll only bring you grief! He's incapable of love. He's cold, passionless—"

"Passionless?" Maigrey murmured, almost to herself.

"Well, maybe not passionless," Semele amended, "but he certainly controls his passions like no man I've ever known. I remember him at school, the first year I came to the Royal Academy for Men to study advanced mathematics. I was sixteen—"

"—and incredibly beautiful," Maigrey said, turning her fond gaze back to her friend, trying to entice her into changing the subject. "Everybody who looked at you fell in love with you."

"Except one," Semele said emphatically, refusing to be steered from her course. "Every time Derek Sagan looked at me I had the feeling he was mentally calculating my worth in terms of the breakdown of the chemical components of my body! And we are, as you know, about ninety percent water."

Reminded pleasantly of days not long gone by, Maigrey couldn't help but laugh. "He was raised in a monastery, after all—" she said in a low tone, feeling her cheeks flush again.

"That doesn't mean anything! He came to be born, didn't he? And while it may have been a religious experience for his father, from what I've heard his mother *wasn't* visited by a heavenly angel. . . ."

"Semele!" Maigrey was scandalized. "You're going to give *me* palpitations of the heart!"

"At least you can tell me how he was . . . at fixing your computer, of course," Semele said demurely.

Maigrey stood up. "I'm leaving."

"All right, all right, dear. The excitement of hearing about such a torrid affair probably wouldn't be good for me, anyway. No, please don't go! I'm finished. You've had your lecture for the evening. What can you expect from an old married woman, anyway?"

"But it really is time for me to leave, dear. Doctor God Almighty said fifteen minutes, and I'm afraid he'll strike me down with a lightning bolt if I disobey."

"But you haven't told me one dirty joke yet, and you know you're the only one who ever tells me—" Semele caught her breath; the hand holding Maigrey's tightened its grasp. She reached around to massage her back.

"Contraction?" Maigrey asked.

"Yes, dear. Just a twinge. It's early yet."

"I'm staying with you, then. The banquet can get on fine without me—"

"And you one of the guests of honor? Leaving a gap at the head table? Jeoffrey would hunt you down and stab you with a salad fork. Run along. This is just the beginning. First baby. I'll probably be at this for hours."

"They're giving you something for the pain, aren't they?"

"This from a woman who fought for three hours with a broken arm and never told anyone until the battle was over!" Semele sniffed. "Uh-oh. These damn machines have snitched on me. Here comes nurse *and* the doctor *and* Augustus. I hope my poor husband lives through this. He fainted during childbirth classes."

Maigrey leaned down, kissed her friend on the forehead.

"Frightened?" she whispered.

Semele lifted radiant eyes. "No, Maigy. Only happy. So very happy." She put her hand on her stomach. "My son will be born this night! My son!"

·◁■ ■▷·

Maigrey walked the corridors of the palace, worried, preoccupied, hardly knowing where she was going, moving by instinct more than design. Semele . . . Sagan. Whenever she left off worrying about one, it was only to wonder about the other.

She came to herself to discover that she was in the wrong part of the palace, near the chapel. The banquet hall was over in another wing of the gigantic building. The hallways were deserted; no one would be around here tonight. Then why had she come? It wasn't like her to wander about aimlessly, even when her mind was distracted. Maigrey was about to turn and retrace her steps, fearing she would be late for the banquet, when someone emerged from the incense-scented darkness.

"Sagan!"

"Maigrey." He didn't appear surprised to see her, and seemed somewhat astonished that she was surprised to see him.

"When did you return?"

"Just a few moments ago. I sent for you. Didn't you hear me?"

Maigrey put her hand confusedly to her temple. "Yes . . . I guess so." She glanced around. "I guess that's why I'm here. But . . . so much else was on my mind. So much else. . . ."

"Really?" Sagan's voice was smooth, carefully controlled. "What?"

Maigrey looked at him closely. Sagan detested functions of state. He attended only because it was a responsibility that went with his rank. He submitted to the proceedings with an ill grace, however, and was impatient, irascible, and in a foul temper for the entire evening. Yet not now. Not tonight. He was tense, taut, eager, and—as always before battle—cool and restrained. His thoughts were completely shielded from her.

She might as well try to penetrate null-grav fused steel. And he was wearing his battle armor, not the ceremonial robes of state.

"I—I'm not sure," she faltered. "Derek, what's happening?"

He took a step near her, caught hold of her hands in his. "What have you seen, Maigrey? The gift of vision. What has it shown you?"

Her eyes shifted from him to a point far beyond him, trying desperately to pierce the mists. "Danger, but I can't see it. Do you remember the time we boarded the vapor-breather's ship? I knew they were lying in wait for us . . . but I'm surrounded by dense fog. I can't see! I can't see!"

"Your hands are cold." Sagan brought her back from her vision. Holding both her hands in his, he massaged them gently. "Maigrey, do you trust me?"

She looked up at him. "You've been with Peter Robes. I know. I've seen you, I've felt you with him."

"Maigrey," Sagan repeated softly, drawing her hands to his lips. "Do you trust me?"

"Yes," she said without hesitation. "You are my commander."

"Good." He smiled, a smile that was dark and shadowed, kissed her hands, and released her from his grasp. "Then give me your sword."

Maigrey unbuckled the swordbelt, handed it to him. Deftly, he wrapped the belt around the hilt and thrust her sword into his belt, his flowing cape concealing it. "Is it charged?"

"Yes, of course. Why—"

Sagan stopped her, his hand on her mouth. "My lady, if the Creator wanted you to see, don't you think He would part the mists?"

Maigrey moved away from his touch, lowered her eyes, rubbed her chill hands together. "I'm frightened. Suddenly I'm so frightened. . . ."

Sagan took her in his arms, pressed her body close to his. His hand stroked the fine, pale hair sweeping over the blue velvet. She relaxed in his embrace, listened to his heartbeat quicken in his chest.

"I think of that night," she said to him. "I remember that night. . . ." Her arms were strong for a woman's; she tightened her embrace, felt his lips touch the crown of her head.

"There will be many nights for us, my lady," he said softly. "What is space travel, but one long endless night?"

What is death . . . ? The thought came to her unbidden, terrified her.

He removed his arms from around her, returned to the strict and stern commander.

"How is Her Royal Highness?" he asked briskly, pulling on a pair of soft, supple leather gloves.

"You mean Semele?" Maigrey had never before known him to refer to the princess by her formal title. They had, after all, gone to school together. "I'm worried about her. She's started into labor."

"Then the baby will be born tonight." Sagan paused in the act of putting on the right glove, a tiny frown line creasing his brow.

"The doctor's not sure. No one can predict . . . with babies. . . ." Maigrey shrugged, flushed, feeling suddenly uncomfortable discussing this subject with him.

Sagan seemed about to say something, seemed about to tell her, to part the mists himself. He regarded her earnestly, intently, as if measuring her.

Somehow, some way, she knew by his expression she came up short.

"Watch for my signal at the banquet tonight," he said. "When you see it, you and the others come to me. Be swift and be brave, my lady. The lives of those you love and have sworn to protect will depend upon it."

Maigrey was disappointed. "Yes, we'll be ready. But why can't you tell me—"

"I have my reasons." Sagan bent down, brushed her right cheek with his lips. "I'll be counting on you, Maigrey."

And he was gone, his long strides taking him rapidly into the deepening darkness.

Chapter ❖❖❖ Three

    . . . with the eyes of heavy mind
    I see thy glory like a shooting star
    Fall to the base earth from the firmament.
    William Shakespeare, *Richard II*, Act II, Scene 4

An android orchestra, classically programmed, was seated on a dais located at the far end of the banquet hall, playing a medley of royal anthems and marches gleaned from every part of the galaxy in honor of its rulers. The Guardians, clad in their blue velvet robes, starjewels their only adornment, filed into the vast chamber in order dictated by custom and protocol. Their names, as each was announced and presented to the assembled multitude, soared high above the music and echoed in the lofty vaults of the ceiling.

Thus they might echo in the lofty vaults of heaven, thought Maigrey, twisting her hands together nervously.

"Someday," Stavros observed, "you're going to pull your fingers off."

Maigrey didn't hear him, though she was standing right beside him. "'And as we are to have the best of guardians for our city, must they not be those who have most the character of guardians?'"

"No quoting of Plato until I've had at least one drink," Stavros protested. "The bar's packed. I'll never get near it. Still, we're the last people to enter. It might be worth a try—"

"No drinking." Maigrey grabbed hold of the sleeve of his robe, pulled him back. "Do you realize," she said, lowering her voice, "that if anything happened here tonight, almost every planetary government in the galaxy would lose one or more of its leaders?"

"Not even one lousy Scotch and water?" Stavros pleaded. "Oh, c'mon, Maigrey! Don't tell me you're taking these rumors seriously! What could happen? This is the Blood Royal we're talking about! Why, there's enough custom-designed, space-age-engineered, superior genetic talent in that hall to blow the towers off this palace and send them into orbit around the planet!"

"I don't like this either," Danha Tusca stated.

"You never like anything, so your opinion doesn't count!" Stavros snapped peevishly. He was thirsty.

"Platus and I have both heard strange rumblings from the military—"

"The military's similar to your stomach—always rumbling. Think about what you're saying, Danha! March an army in here and in five seconds, with a casual wave of their hands, the Blood Royal would have the soldiers turning their guns on themselves!"

"An ordinary army, perhaps," Maigrey said.

"What other kind is there?"

"I think someone should speak to the king," she persisted.

"We tried to tell His Majesty, Maigrey," growled the deep bass of Danha Tusca. "He wouldn't listen."

"That's not precisely true," Platus interjected, ignoring Danha's glower at being contradicted. "His Majesty listened to us quite courteously, thanked us for our concern quite courteously, then dismissed us."

"Quite courteously, I'll bet," Maigrey muttered.

"He didn't listen!" Danha repeated obstinately. "Starfire's a doddering old fool and I don't care who hears me say it! I'll say it to his face, if he wants!" The large and formidable ebony-skinned Guardian glared at a passing footman in such ire that the wretched fellow stammered an apology for something he hadn't done and disappeared in precipitous haste.

"Come now!" Stavros was easygoing, good-natured, and hated the arguments Danha relished. "Don't be hard on the old king. Look at it realistically. How could His Majesty have called the banquet off? This affair's the most publicized event of the past ten years! If he canceled it, the press'd be climbing all over him, demanding to know why. And if he told them, he'd be giving credence to the grumblings of a bunch of malcontents."

"The Lord is with him. The Lord will protect him. Hunh!" Danha grunted.

"The Lord helps those who help themselves." Maigrey sighed. Her gaze was fixed on the hall. She'd seen it countless times before, glittering with the light of crystal chandeliers. Tonight, she seemed to see it blazing with the light of devouring flames. "Trapped like rats. Weaponless. No bodyguards. . . ."

"Weaponless indeed!" Danha said grimly. "Did you give your sword to Sagan?"

"Yes, and I promised to wait for his signal, but he didn't say what was up," Stavros said, shrugging.

Platus looked grave. "Didn't you ask?"

"My dear man, I was fighting with this confounded robe! I had it on once, saw myself in the mirror, realized I was wearing the damn thing backside foremost. Instead of taking it off, I thought I'd save time by just wriggling out of it partway and then turning it around while it was still on me. So there I was, half in and half out of this blasted robe with my head caught in one of the sleeves when Sagan burst into my room and demanded my sword. I wasn't exactly in the mood for a chat."

"*I* asked him," Danha said, "and he wouldn't tell me. He said there wasn't time. He had an audience with His Majesty."

"He did?" Maigrey was astonished.

"No, he didn't," Platus said, a shadow passing over his thin face. "His Majesty refused to admit him."

"What was that?" Danha glanced around. "Did you hear that? It sounded like an explosion. . . ."

Stavros shook his head in exasperation. "Thunder. Must be a storm brewing. Look, Maigrey, if Danha's going to carry on like this all night, I insist on one drink, if for nothing else than to calm my shattered nerves."

"The sky was clear when I came in. That *was* an explosion and it came from the direction of the base. I don't like this," Danha repeated. "Perhaps one of us should go see—"

"Not a chance." Maigrey caught hold of the sleeve of the big man's blue robes and pulled him back. "Jeoffrey has his eye on us. You'd never make it to the door. Besides—"

"Don't try it, Danha," Stavros advised. "I attempted to escape one of His Majesty's soirees. That piercing scream of Jeoffrey's still echoes in my ears. Sometimes I wake at night and hear it and see him running after me, waving that silk hanky. I swear, it's hours before I can get back to sleep."

"Besides," Maigrey continued, irritated at the interruption, "we should wait here for Sagan . . . in case he needs us."

"And where is our commander, anyway?"

All three—Stavros, Platus, Danha—looked to Maigrey.

"He'll be here. And then everything·will be all right. Whatever is happening, Sagan knows about it, and he has everything under control."

"Sagan *knows* about it?" Platus repeated, the shadow on his face deepening. "What do you mean, Maigrey?"

She hadn't meant to say anything and shook her head.

"She means she knows where he's been this past month," Danha guessed, with the intuition of those who use the bloodsword. "And now so do I. He was with his friend, the revolutionary!"

"Was he, Maigrey? Was Sagan with Peter Robes?"

"Yes, he was! Don't look at me like that, Platus!" Maigrey demanded, growing angrier as she spoke. "And Danha— where would you be if Sagan hadn't taken out that troillian who had you pinned up against the bulkheads. And you, Stavros, you'd still be perched up on that stupid statue if it wasn't for him! And Platus, that booby trap you nearly walked into . . . All of us. We'd be dead right now, or in a Corasian meat locker if it wasn't for Derek! You owe your lives to him, every one of you! I refuse to stand here and listen to your insinuations—"

"Sister, calm down!" Platus smoothed Maigrey's pale hair with his hand, as he might have smoothed the ruffled fur of a cat. "No one's insinuating anything."

"Humpf!" Danha snorted, rumbling deep in his chest, like an enraged bull.

The doors to the hall slowly closed. The assembled dignitaries were taking their places at the long rows of white-clothed, crystal-, gold-, and silver-ornamented tables. The doors would open again for the guests of honor . . . and for His Majesty the King.

"It's almost time," Stavros said, in a more subdued tone than was customary for him. "There's His Majesty and the royal attendants."

"And there's Jeoffrey, searching for us." Danha, towering head and shoulders above most of the rest of the crowd, was able to see what was transpiring.

"No sign of Sagan?" Platus asked.

"None," Danha answered.

Jeoffrey, the velvet-breeched and beribboned Minister of Protocol, spotted them, frowned severely, and bustled over, waving a perfumed handkerchief at them as if it were a censer and he a priest, absolving them from their sins. He made a swift count of their group, came up one short, counted again, then hissed through the corner of his mouth, smiling congenially all the while for the benefit of any who might be watching.

"Where the devil's Derek Sagan?"

"He'll be here," Maigrey snapped. She was suddenly having trouble breathing. Her lungs burned; the flames she couldn't see were sucking away her breath.

"Damn the man! And the orchestra will be beginning the processional any moment. I'll simply *have* to make some excuse to His Majesty. Take your places. Just a moment, let me look at you. Good Lord! Lady Morianna! Your skirt is hiked up practically to your shins in back! And where *did* you get those perfectly dreadful shoes? Keep your feet under the table."

With a deft hand, Jeoffrey twitched Maigrey's robes into place, transferred his scathing glance to the men. "And *would* it be too much to ask, Danha Tusca, for you to obtain a robe whose hemline does *not* hit you three inches above the ankle?"

Danha merely growled. He didn't start a full-blown argument—a bad sign to those who knew him. Maigrey was almost sick; dread twisted inside her. Suddenly, unaccountably, she couldn't enter that hall.

"Perhaps I shouldn't join the procession," she said faintly. "Perhaps . . . I should wait for Lord Sagan. . . ."

It seemed likely, from his expression, that Jeoffrey was about to suffer an apoplectic fit on the spot.

"*One* of you missing is bad enough," he raved hysterically, his voice gaining an octave with each succeeding exclamation point, "and I shall undoubtedly spend several very unpleasant moments tomorrow *attempting* to explain it to His Majesty! *Two* of you missing would end my life! Simply *end* it!" He dabbed at his mouth with the scented handkerchief. "I shall hurl myself off the balcony this moment!"

"Let him," Danha said beneath his breath.

"That won't be necessary, Jeoffrey," Maigrey said, sighing. "It was merely a suggestion."

She took her place in the forming procession, Jeoffrey hovering near, keeping an eye on her in case she decided to bolt. The group started forward, moving toward the gigantic doors decorated with the royal coat of arms: a blazing star, a lion recumbent (to indicate His Majesty's peaceful rule), and the motto, *Tolle me*. Take me (as I am).

Everyone moved slowly, Jeoffrey timing the beat with a wave of the handkerchief. One, two. One, two. Maigrey felt like a prisoner in a chain gang, being marched to death row. She'd known less fear boarding an enemy warship. The head of the procession—a young boy carrying the Guardians' flag—approached the doors. Two powder-wigged, velvet-waistcoated footmen bowed and threw the doors open wide.

A blaze of light and heat and laughter gushed out. The opening drum rolls of the Golden Squadron's march stirred Maigrey's blood and propelled her forward. Laughter and talking ceased, replaced by rustles and murmurs, the scraping of chairs, and the general low rumble indicative of several hundred people rising to their feet or—in the case of species who lacked feet—performing whatever mark of respect was deemed proper.

Maigrey entered the room, moving in time to the march that was beating in her, her own heart's pace jumpy and erratic. It seemed to her that she was walking into a burning house. The hall was curtained with flame, the air superheated and filled with poisonous fumes. She struggled to breathe and kept marching, her squadron behind her, past the rows of crystal-bedecked tables, the smiling and whispering and applauding Guardians, many of whom were gaily lifting glasses of champagne in an impromptu toast.

Derek should have been walking in front of her. As commander, he had that right. No one seemed particularly amazed or disappointed at Sagan's absence. He wasn't liked; his dour and stern presence tended to cast a pall over any celebration. Maigrey supposed that Jeoffrey didn't need to resort to the balcony quite yet.

As second in command, she led her small squadron up the center aisle, past the rows and rows of cheering people, to the head table, His Majesty's table. It was fortunate for Maigrey that she'd done this many times before. When she arrived at the head table and turned to face the crowd, awaiting the arrival of the king, she couldn't have told a soul how she had managed to reach that point.

Her brother leaned near her; his thin fingers brushed her hand. "Maigrey, you look terrible! Are you all right?"

She caught hold of her brother's hand and clung to it. The words of the hobbit Frodo, spoken to the faithful Samwise on Mount Doom, came to her suddenly, unbidden, unwelcome.

"'I am glad you are here with me, here at the end of all things. . . .'"

Chapter ❖❖❖ Four

> . . . thy fierce hand
> Hath with the king's blood stain'd the king's own land.
> William Shakespeare, *Richard II*, Act IV, Scene 4

With a trumpet fanfare, His Majesty and the royal party entered last, the king bowing his head benignly to the left and right in acknowledgment of the cheers.

Amodius Starfire, in his late sixties, looked a great deal as he had in his early forties. The red hair that was the family hallmark had whitened at an early age; he touched it up, to keep it from an unfortunate tendency to turn orangish yellow. The lines of his face were gentle, tending to sag downward, giving him a constantly weary expression. The blue eyes had long ago lost their fire, if it had ever burned within him.

It was rumored that His Majesty was in ill health. His complexion had a gray tinge, he was often short of breath. The doctors had proposed giving him an artificial heart but His Majesty, with his firm reliance on God, had refused.

Amodius Starfire had never married, never produced an heir to the throne. The romantic said it was because he'd lost his only love in his youth, a victim of a Corasian attack on her planet. The spiteful said it was because he would have gone in mortal dread of the ambitions of his own children.

Whatever the reason, Augustus Starfire, the king's younger brother—almost forty years younger, born to their father in his old age—was next in line for the throne. It seemed he might not have long to wait.

His Majesty arrived at the head table, walked past the members of the Golden Squadron, saying something kind and congratulatory to each, speaking to each by name. He was expert at such things. Maigrey, conscious of the empty chair to her left, knew he was talking to her, but he might as well have been speaking an alien tongue and she with her translator turned off. She didn't understand a word, made some noncommittal answer.

The king moved on, the courtiers trailing behind, laughing and chattering like monkeys. Maigrey's bowels clenched; she was nauseous and dizzy. Swaying on her feet, she gripped the edge of the table and feared for a moment she would have to leave the hall.

Fortunately, the king sat down, which meant everyone else could sit down. Platus hastily moved a chair beneath his sister, or she would have fallen.

"Drink this." He was shoving a glass in her hand. Wine, water . . . it was all the same to her. Maigrey drank it down, never knowing, felt somewhat better. The nausea passed, left her shaking all over.

The royal chaplain rose to his feet, called upon all to bow their heads in worship of the Creator. The assembled multitude did as he asked, most of them discreetly shifting into the most comfortable positions possible, knowing they were in for a long ordeal. The pious king would not have dreamed of eating a meal which had not been prayed over for at least fifteen minutes.

In the quiet that cushioned the chaplain's sonorous voice, Maigrey thought she heard again, very faintly, the sound of an explosion. Thunder. A storm brewing. Shivering, she watched the water condense on the crystal goblet of chilled fruit cocktail, then trickle down the side of the glass, forming a pool on the fine china plate beneath.

The chaplain's voice paused, a disapproving pause. Maigrey raised her head, her heartbeat quickening, looked toward the door along with everyone else in the room except for those among the Guardians who had dozed off during the prayer. The double doors, which had been shut and closed following the entrance of His Majesty, were now—against all custom—opening.

Derek Sagan, clad in battle armor, stood framed by the golden doors. He entered the hall, not to music, but to an accompaniment of murmured wonder and muttered forebodings.

Derek ignored them all. Looking far more like a king than the king himself. Sagan strode down the aisle toward the head table. Maigrey, without knowing that she did so, rose to her feet to be ready. Her squadron followed her example. Sagan's glance flicked over them. He seemed pleased. But his gaze did not linger on them long. His eyes were on the king.

Sagan came to stand before His Majesty. The Guardian stood tall, straight, unbending.

"You do not kneel before us, Lord Sagan," King Starfire said, voice stern. The Starfires had a temper, though it was slow to burn.

"I have no time for meaningless posturing, Your Majesty," Derek Sagan answered, taking command, bringing silence to the hall. Again, the sound of an explosion, louder, nearer. There could be no doubt. "The people of the galaxy are in revolt. At this moment, as we speak, the military base on Minas Tares is under siege by revolutionary forces. There is no doubt but that it will fall, Your Majesty."

The hall was a babble of voices, shocked, incredulous, disbelieving. Sagan's gaze shifted; his eyes met Maigrey's. *Your weapons are beneath the tablecloth.* It was all the signal she needed.

"Down here!" she said to the others. Her bloodsword lay on the floor at her feet. The others found theirs; Platus, Maigrey noticed with sudden irritation, was staring at his as if wondering what in God's name it was.

Action was a stronger wine than any she could drink. Her trembling stopped, the mists parted, everything was clear-cut and sharp-edged. Sagan gestured with his hand, ordering them to take up positions around the king.

Maigrey obeyed, conscious of Danha behind her and Stavros behind him. Glancing back, she saw Platus had not moved, but remained standing, the bloodsword held in limp hands.

We'll be better off without the coward! Maigrey thought angrily. She reached the king's side, shoving courtiers out of her way, Danha deftly handling any who seemed disinclined to move.

Placing her hand on the king's shoulder, Maigrey leaned down to whisper, "Don't worry, Your Majesty. We'll escort you to safety, then crush this rebellion!"

"Thank you, my dear," Amodius Starfire said, his voice soft and filled with sorrow. He shook his head. She could feel the long, wispy white hair brush across the back of her hand.

Maigrey looked to Sagan for further commands. She saw him standing rigid, unmoving, his dark eyes fixed upon the king.

"Your Majesty," he said slowly, "the people have made their will known. They are determined to give up their lives for a cause they believe in, a cause that is just. In the name of the people, as their representative, I call upon you—Amodius Starfire—to abdicate your throne."

"No . . ." Maigrey's hand clutched at the king's shoulder, penetrating the thick fabric of his ceremonial robes, feeling the frail bone and flaccid skin beneath.

His gaze turned to her, and in his eyes the sorrow seemed to be more for her than for himself.

"I'll kill that traitorous bastard!" Danha swelled with fury, seemed to grow six times his height and girth. Foam flecked his lips, the black skin glistened, he was wild-eyed, temporarily insane. Muscles tense, he prepared to leap over the table, throttle Sagan with his bare hands.

Something inside Maigrey had died, some vital part of her. It left her empty, hollow, cold, and calculating as any machine. Like a machine, she functioned. She could still hear her commander's voice.

. . . be brave, my lady. The lives of those you love and have sworn to protect will depend upon it.

Her commander was dead to her, but she would obey his final order.

"Danha, calm down." Removing her hand from the king's she caught hold of Danha's arm. "Pretend to go along with him."

It was her tone, more than her touch, that restrained Danha. Strong as he was, the woman couldn't have stopped him if she had flung her arms around him. But her voice, chill as death, hard as steel, pierced his madness, halted him.

The sounds of battle came through the open doorway, the whining buzz of laser weapons, the cries of the dying, shouted commands, and the confused pounding of feet. The captain of the guard burst in through a side door.

"Your Majesty—" he cried. Light flashed behind him. His chest exploded; he pitched forward on his face and lay in a pool of blood.

All was chaos without, order within. The assembled Guardians might have been politely waiting for their king to dismiss them. A few had risen to their feet, but most kept their seats, stunned, disbelieving. Their eyes were on His Majesty. The king sat in silence.

Sagan pointed at the dead soldier. "Many more will die like

this man, Your Majesty. You can halt this madness. Give up your throne. You will be taken to a place of safety, given a fair trial for crimes committed against the people."

Amodius Starfire stirred in his seat. His back straightened; his head lifted. For the first time in his life, Maigrey thought, watching him through dry, burning eyes, he truly looked a king.

"We hold our rulership through the divine authority of God, Lord Sagan. We cannot give away that which is not ours to give."

No one cheered, applauded, or spoke. Those who heard him were too moved for speech. But, one by one, they shoved back their chairs and rose to their feet in a silent show of respect and support more convincing than noisy clamor.

Support. None of them armed. Trapped . . . like rats.

Slowly, surreptitiously, her movements concealed behind the body of the king, Maigrey inserted the needles of the bloodsword into the palm of her hand. Danha and Stavros did the same. And so, she saw, looking down the length of the table, did her peace-loving brother, his face wincing at the unaccustomed pain.

"I told you he would be stubborn, Commander Sagan."

The voice came from the doorway at the end of the aisle. A man, dressed in a casual business suit, surrounded by numerous armed bodyguards, entered the hall. "I am Peter Robes, Your Majesty, President of the newly formed Galactic Democratic Republic. Interim President, of course, until we hold free elections."

"We have captured the vid station," reported another man, who had apparently entered behind Peter Robes. Due to his short, stooped stature, this second man wasn't visible behind the bodyguards surrounding the President. The guards, whose strange calm and dead eyes caught Maigrey's attention, stepped aside, allowed the man to pass between them. He was clad in magenta robes. Large nodes swelled from the back of a head that appeared too large for his thin body.

"Abdiel!" Maigrey whispered, the sight of the priest striking her an almost physical blow.

"The news has gone out to the planets in the galaxy," Abdiel announced. "The monarchy is crushed. A new order is rising out of the ashes of the old. If you do not want that report to have a literal meaning, Amodius Starfire, I suggest you do as the people require."

"Abdiel!" Maigrey whispered again.

Several years ago, the Order of Dark Lightning had abducted and imprisoned both her and Sagan in an attempt to study the mind-link. The two escaped the priests, finally, but Abdiel—their leader—had succeeded to a certain extent, having forcibly and horribly linked himself to each through the needles he'd had implanted in his own body. Like it or not, a part of each of them belonged to Abdiel, a part of him was within each of them.

Maigrey's eyes, involuntarily, sought Sagan's and his met hers. She knew, in that glance, that he was as surprised as she was to see Abdiel . . . and far more angry.

Peter Robes and the mind-seizer, accompanied by several of the oddly somnambulant guards, proceeded down the aisle toward the head table. Platus hurried to stand beside his sister. He was eyeing the soldiers worriedly, his expression awed and tinged with horror.

"Maigrey—"

"Shhh!" she hushed him.

Sagan had glanced behind him at the approaching group. His face dark, he took a hasty step nearer the king, pitched his voice low. "Your Majesty, do as they ask. If you are reasonable about this, you and your family will come to no harm." His hand clenched in his earnestness. "I pledge you this with my life!"

"We have the feeling you are risking that life in making us this offer, Lord Sagan," the king said with a soft, sad smile. "And we are glad to think you have some regard for the oath of allegiance you took, to know that you are not wholly lost to evil. But we must refuse. We will not submit to the mockery of a trial. As king by divine right, we have only one Judge and it is to Him and Him alone we will answer."

The struggle in Sagan's soul was not reflected in his face, beyond a further darkening of the eyes, a tremor in the muscles of his clenched jaw. Maigrey, who saw within him, was witness to the war, and it was more fierce, more desperate than any other life-and-death encounter she had ever seen. She had been at his side in many another deadly contest; this one he chose to fight alone. The battle came swiftly to an end.

"Then I cannot save you, Your Majesty." Sagan's voice was soft and bitter.

The king nodded calmly. "There is only One who can save me, Lord Sagan, and it is into His hands that I commend my soul."

"May He have mercy on that soul, Your Majesty," Sagan said coldly.

The soldiers, with their strange, dead eyes, were taking up positions around the room. They were human, male and female. Each differed from his or her comrades in height, weight, color of hair, skin, eyes. But they all, somehow, managed to look as much alike as if they'd been born of the same parents. It was the expression on their faces, Maigrey decided at last, studying them carefully, as her commander had taught.

Know your enemy.

"Maigrey!" Platus said urgently. "Do you know what those people are?"

"Androids," she answered, then frowned and shook her head. "No, 'droids have more life. . . ."

"They're alive, Maigrey," her brother continued in a hollow voice. "At least they were. Their minds are no longer their own. They belong to him!"

The horrible enormity of the situation appalled her. What had she said about an ordinary army?

Others in the hall must have arrived at the same conclusion. Abdiel whirled suddenly, confronted a member of the Blood Royal seated in a chair near the aisle.

"It didn't work, did it, Duchess?" the mind-seizer said in the pleasantest possible voice. "Your little mind-games won't work with my people. You cannot seduce them. You cannot captivate them with your charismatic charm. You cannot hypnotize them. You cannot implant subliminal suggestions. You cannot penetrate their subconscious. Why? Because they have no subconscious. Their minds are one, and that one mind is mine."

Abdiel placed his left hand caressingly, palm down, upon the woman's shoulder. The left hand jerked, pressing hard against the woman. The duchess screamed, a high-pitched note of agony, limbs convulsing, nerve impulses disrupted, gone wild. Abdiel removed his hand; the bright light gleamed for an instant on the five needles protruding from his palm. The woman slumped forward on the table, unconscious.

"Anyone else want to experiment on my people?" Abdiel glanced around. "I welcome all challenges."

Sagan advanced a step to stand beside Peter Robes. Maigrey could hear their conversation. Derek was not bothering to keep his thoughts from her now.

"Why did you allow him to come?" Sagan was demanding. "This wasn't part of the plan!"

"But quite an improvement, don't you think, Derek?" Peter Robes asked, with a cool smile. "You yourself were concerned with the possibility the Guardians would resist—"

"Let them!" Sagan was pale with fury. "The palace is surrounded by my troops and those of the revolutionary army. The Guardians can resist all they want, but they have nowhere to go! Minas Tares is completely cut off—"

So he has troops, Maigrey realized, the dull, throbbing ache in her heart spreading throughout her body. The palace surrounded, under siege. It will become our prison . . .

Or our tomb.

Sagan turned on his heel, made a gesture with his hand. A soldier, wearing the insignia of a phoenix rising from flames, entered the room through a side door. He saluted Derek Sagan, awaiting orders.

Sagan said something to him in a low voice. The commander saluted and stood to one side.

The self-proclaimed President and his entourage had reached the royal table by now. Sagan turned to face Robes and Robes alone. Sagan's glance flicked over Abdiel, did not acknowledge the mind-seizer's presence. To do so would have been dangerous, would have given Abdiel power over him that, even now, Sagan was perhaps struggling to evade. Maigrey didn't know. She could no longer penetrate the shadows.

"Your Majesty," Derek Sagan said, dark eyes now intent upon his king, "will you step down?"

Maigrey stood behind the king, waiting for his answer, knowing what it must be, part of her applauding him, part of her wishing it otherwise.

It all seemed unreal to her, reminded her of a time she had attended a performance of *Julius Caesar*. She knew the story before she entered the theater, knew the plot, the tragic outcome. Yet she had wanted—against all common sense and reason—the play to end happily.

"*Listen* to the soothsayer!" she cried silently. "*Don't go to the Senate.*"

But Caesar had gone and would go, every time, because he was Caesar.

"We will not treat with usurpers," Amodius Starfire said

with perhaps more dignity than he had ever spoken in his life,
"and we order you to leave our court on pain of death."

The Guardians cheered in defiance. The mind-dead, who
had posted themselves among the tables and lined the walls,
raised their weapons and brought them to bear upon the
crowd. Silence fell, suddenly, ominously.

Abdiel glided to the President's side. "I believe it is time,
Mr. President, for you to speak to the galaxy's citizens. An
escort is waiting to convey you to the vid station."

Peter Robes turned his head slowly, looked about the hall.
The Guardians—men and women, human and alien, some
young, some old, some wise, some fools, some honest, some
corrupt—all, at the moment, knew what was coming and faced
it with quiet courage. Robes's own must have failed him, then.
Maigrey saw the face, with its plastic good looks, quiver; the
strong line of the jaw began to melt and sag.

"The king—that is, Citizen Starfire and . . . and the
Guardians—are all to be imprisoned," Robes said, clearing his
throat. "Those are my specific orders, Abdiel. Specific orders.
I will convene a tribunal—"

"Of course, Mr. President." Abdiel bowed solemnly,
scratching at his hand, with its decaying patches of skin.

"Remain here to see those orders carried out, Mr. President," Derek Sagan challenged him. "The citizens have waited
this long. They can wait a moment or two longer to know that
the former king and his court are safely imprisoned."

Robes stood, glancing from one to the other, undecided,
irresolute. His jaw worked, but no words came. Sweat beaded
on his forehead, trickled down his cheek. The plastic mold was
beginning to melt.

The attention of the three traitors was focused on each
other. Maigrey took advantage of the opportunity to exchange
covert, meaningful glances with her squadron. She and Danha
drew near His Majesty. If they could convey him safely out of
this room, take him to the royal chambers, they could
barricade themselves, withstand a siege. . . .

The powerful Danha Tusca was detaching the bloodsword,
leaving his hands free to guide and support his feeble king.

A doddering old fool, you called him, Maigrey said to
Danha through the linkage of the sword. *And you'll probably
give your life to try to save him.*

He is my king! returned Danha with fierce pride.

The air crackled. The Guardians were striking, using the

strength of their combined mental powers to disrupt the electricity. Maigrey had a fleeting impression of a blue aura surrounding her, surrounding the courtiers. The lights of the chandeliers flared, then went out, plunging the room into darkness.

All hell broke loose.

Laser fire flashed; Abdiel's mind-dead began shooting indiscriminately into the crowd. The Guardians were on their feet, overturning tables, erecting their own barricades. Some tried to run for the exits, others spoke into commlinks, calling for bodyguards that would never answer their masters' call or any other save that of their Creator.

Maigrey had only an indistinct impression of what was happening in the hall. She and Danha moved swiftly to the king, Stravros and Platus standing guard behind them. The mind-dead had switched on nuke lamps. The harsh, white beams searched through the darkness, seeking out their prey.

"Your Majesty," Maigrey said urgently. "Hurry! We must take you out of here!"

Starfire did not move. He was staring out at the chaos with eyes that were fixed, glazed. His body had gone strangely stiff and rigid; saliva drooled from a corner of ashen lips.

Maigrey and Danha looked at each other helplessly. They dared not lay rough hands on their sovereign, but this was an emergency and it was obvious that their king was ill. Maigrey heard Sagan shouting orders. Fires were springing up throughout the hall. Smoke hung in the air.

"Your Majesty!" She made one more try. Danha was ready, strong arms flexing.

A nuke lamp's light caught them, found them. Laser fire flashed past her, the heat burning the hand that lay upon the shoulder of her king.

The beam seared a hole through the golden crown, penetrated cleanly out the back of the skull. The king didn't make a sound; the expression on his face never changed.

By the light of the nuke, Maigrey saw Abdiel watching with satisfaction. He thought his mind-dead had killed the king. Maigrey, removing her trembling hand from the rigid shoulder, knew differently. She had seen his face. Amodius Starfire had been dead before the beam struck him.

"The king is dead. Long live the king!" Danha's voice roared in her ears.

King. Augustus. Semele . . .

"Semele!" Maigrey activated her bloodsword, jumped off
the dais, and started running for the side door. Her left hand
was badly burned, but she didn't feel any pain. Just as she
didn't feel any pain her heart. She was numb now, and she
concentrated on staying that way. The moment would come
when she would feel . . .

Or maybe not. If she was lucky, she'd be dead.

The fires blazed out of control. Smoke and darkness made
it difficult to see and to breathe. Maigrey had moved so swiftly,
she had left the rest of her squadron behind. She halted,
waiting for them to catch up, knowing she couldn't manage
alone. The bloodsword shielded her from laser blasts. When
her squadron joined her, she started toward the door and had
nearly reached the exit in safety when a voice whispered inside
her head.

Stop her! Stop her, Derek Sagan. She has betrayed you!

Turning, reluctantly, involuntarily, halted by a force she
could not control, Maigrey looked around, saw Abdiel pointing
at her.

"Maigrey!" Sagan's outraged voice rose over the tumult.

She was empty of all feeling, all emotion, even that of fear.
Like her king, she was dead before she had died.

Turning on her heel, she ran, left Sagan behind.

Chapter Five

Mount, mount, my soul, thy seat is up on high . . .
William Shakespeare, *Richard II*, Act V, Scene 5

The revolutionary army had degenerated into a mob, roaming the palace, looting, burning, killing. Most were drunk, either with liquor or power, and were completely out of their officers' control. The Guardians cut their way through these with ease, most of the soldiers reluctant to tackle victims that had the skill and means to fight back. It was far easier and more fun to catch some soft lord in his chambers, butcher him, and then have a little sport with his lady wife.

Maigrey kept her purpose clear in her mind, its light guiding her through the dreadful darkness, shining like the starjewel on her breast. She hoped the soldiers had not yet reached the upper levels of the palace. She and her squad would be able to rescue the crown prince—now king—and Semele.

The palace was a maze of secret passages, built mainly for the fun and amusement of the royal family and their guests. But some of the secret passages had practical uses, such as the one that led from the upper levels of the palace to an underground spaceport. These provided escape for the royal family from the glare of vidcam lights and the constant hounding of reporters. Of course, the secret passages weren't really all that secret; everyone in the palace knew about them. Including Sagan. Maigrey hoped he would be too preoccupied with his massacre to remember them.

Occasionally, the Guardians ran into the men under Sagan's command, soldiers of his new army. The Guardians avoided these. Sagan's centurions were sober, well disciplined, dangerous. They had already taken control of the palace computer center and were rapidly spreading out to seize and hold other areas of strategic importance.

Too late, too late, too late, was the whispered message of Maigrey's heart. Resolutely, she ignored it.

Reaching the elevators to the upper levels, the Guardians slowed, advanced cautiously. This area of the palace was quiet, and they had come to learn that quiet and order generally meant Sagan's troops were in control. The hallway was brightly lit. Either power had been restored to this area of the palace or it had never been lost. Stavros, pressing flat against a wall, risked a look down the hallway where stood the bank of elevators leading to the upper levels. He pulled back swiftly, his face grim.

"Sagan's soldiers, all right. Two of them guarding each lift. There must be twenty of them, at least."

"There's always the stairs," Danha suggested.

"Thirty flights!" Maigrey shook her head. "We don't have time!"

"Maigrey," Platus began reluctantly, "if they've captured the elevators, then they must have gained the upper—"

"Shut up!" she snapped at him. "Shut up and let me think!"

The three men exchanged glances, said nothing. Danha was covered head to toe in blood; his blue robes were sodden with it. He had acquired a lasgun, using it in his left hand. Platus looked gray and ill, held only his sword. He had fought when he'd been forced to, not so much to save his own life as to protect that of his comrades. Mostly he had attempted to keep the enraged Danha from venting his anger in mindless, savage slaughter. Stavros, wielding his sword and another captured lasgun, had been efficient, effective.

"We can fight twenty men," Danha pronounced, the blood-lust burning in his eyes.

"We could, but we couldn't win," Maigrey said. "The swords are draining our bodies' energy and we're probably going to need what we have left when we reach His Majesty. I have an idea. Follow me."

She switched off the bloodsword, though she continued to hold it in her hand, and marched coolly out into the hallway, into the open, in plain view of Sagan's troops. Danha, Stavros, and her brother dashed swiftly after, her plan communicating itself to them through the linkage of the swords.

The centurions appeared slightly startled at the sight of the four Guardians, weapons in hand, blue robes stained black with blood, walking calmly down the hallway. A captain stepped forward, eyes narrowed in suspicion.

"Citizen Maigrey Morianna," Maigrey stated crisply, thanking the Creator she'd remembered at the last moment to change her title, "member of the Golden Squadron. I'm sure you recognize me?"

That was taking a lot for granted, considering how she looked on the vidscreen and what she looked like now. But somewhere beneath the blood and soot and ashes the captain must have seen the woman known to be number two in command of the famed squadron. He saluted, fist over his heart. Maigrey returned the salute, somewhat awkwardly, thinking bitterly to herself that it was like Sagan to have usurped Caesar's homage.

"Commander S-Sagan"—she found it difficult to speak his name, angrily forced herself to repeat it clearly—"Commander Sagan has ordered us to place under arrest Augustus Starfire, formerly known as crown prince. I assume that the elevators have been secured and are safe to use?"

"Yes, citizen." The captain spoke with respect, but he made no move to stand aside. He was looking at their gore-spattered clothing.

"The Guardians in the hall resisted arrest," Danha growled, glowering at the man. "Haven't you heard?"

"We did hear a rumor to that effect," the captain answered. His last doubts appeared to have been erased. He saluted once again and pointed to one of the elevators. "Take that one, citizens."

Maigrey, forcing herself to move slowly and calmly, stepped into the ornate gilded and mirrored lift. Danha, Stavros, and Platus crowded in after her. The captain held the doors open a moment.

"We heard someone killed the king. Is that true? Is the old man dead?"

Maigrey felt Danha, standing beside her, stiffen. She dug her fingernails into his arm. "Yes, the king is dead. More's the pity. We hoped he would stand trial before the people. That's why we are being sent to ensure the safety of the crown prince."

"Good luck," the captain said, releasing the doors. "Though I think you'll find someone's beat you to it."

The doors slid shut. Maigrey gave the lift the floor number—a floor beneath the one on which the private rooms of the royal family were located. The elevator soared upward on jets of air. The four stared at each other in grim silence, tense, alert.

"I wonder what he meant by that?" Stavros asked.

"It doesn't matter," Danha said. "We do the same up there we did down below. That was a brilliant idea, Maigrey, and it will work again. We'll just walk in and, in the name of Derek Sagan, carry our king to safety!"

Maigrey leaned back against the cold glass walls. She didn't feel brilliant. She felt cold and hollow. And it hadn't been brilliance or courage that sent her marching down that hallway under the guns of twenty of the enemy. It had been panic, desperation. Augustus, with his silly giggle, Semele, her baby . . . if it had been born. They were suddenly all Maigrey had, all she was living for.

The elevator slowed. The doors opened. The four pressed back against the walls, weapons ready. The hallway was dark and empty, deserted. Breathing easier, they slipped out.

On this floor were guest rooms, reserved for visiting dignitaries, ambassadors, members of the Blood Royal, most of whom were down below, trapped in the hall. Sagan's guards on the elevators were keeping the looters out—at least until the looters discovered the stairs and decided that whatever wealth was at the top was worth a climb of thirty flights.

"There are passages that lead from this floor to the ones above, aren't there?" Maigrey asked her brother in hushed tones.

"Yes. To almost every room."

Near the same age as Augustus, Platus had spent school holidays in the palace, since he wasn't wanted at home. The two boys had found the secret passages to be great fun and had played in them extensively until complaints from numerous startled and not terribly amused guests had brought the games to a halt. He knew the passages better than any of them. "Where do you want to go?"

Maigrey thought. "Somewhere near the entrance to the royal chambers. We'll have to deal with any guards posted there, and we'll stand a better chance if we can take them by surprise."

"I know of one passage—it's in the Red Chamber, and it comes out in the alcove where that marble statue of the king stands. You know, the one where he's dressed in costume for the royal hunt?"

Yes, Maigrey remembered. That would be perfect. The life-sized marble statue stood on a broad base complete with boar hound. It was huge and would provide cover; about time the silly-looking thing served some useful purpose.

They advanced swiftly but cautiously—two moving, two covering. A blow of Danha's large hand split the door to the Red Chamber. They hastened through the sumptuously furnished rooms, following Platus's lead, and came to a huge walk-in closet. Maigrey shoved aside silken gowns belonging to whoever was currently occupying the rooms—gowns that probably would never be worn again unless it was by the girlfriend of some looter—and found a blank cedar-paneled wall.

Platus studied the panels for only a second, confidently placed his thumb and the little finger of his right hand on two knots in the wood. The wall slid aside, revealing a narrow, winding staircase lit at intervals by electric torches in medieval-style sconces.

Maigrey started to gather up the blue skirts of her robe to climb the stairs. Thinking better of it, she swiftly trimmed the hem of the gown with the bloodsword. The fabric, she noticed, was wet with blood. She paid no attention to it, but hurried after her brother. Danha, bringing up the rear, smashed the plastic torches as he passed them, so that no light would shine out when they emerged.

A short climb took them to a door marked with the royal insignia. Platus, standing above Maigrey, looked around for instructions.

Ready? he mouthed.

Gripping her bloodsword, she nodded, and he put his index finger on the lion's head. Danha broke the last torch, plunging them into darkness. The door slid open silently, for which blessing Maigrey thanked God and the building maintenance crew. Light streamed in from the hallway beyond. Her brother crept out to reconnoiter.

Leaning back against the wall, conscious of Stavros right beside her—one step down—and Danha below him, Maigrey thought of times past when she had been in similar situations. Heart beating rapidly, blood pulsing, excitement mixed with adrenaline had always affected her like strong wine. But the wine was now laced with poison. Fear twisted inside her, the blood flowed sluggishly, she shook with chills.

Platus was gone only a short time. Then he reappeared,

hurrying back down the stairs, speaking to them silently
through the bloodsword linkage. His face, dimly seen in the
light coming from the hallway, was grim. They could hear, in
the distance, a baby's wail.

What's the matter? Maigrey grabbed him, dug her nails into
his arm. *What's wrong?*

*The mind-dead are here. They've killed the royal guard;
bodies are lying all over the hallway. They've got Augustus—I
could see him—and what looks like a doctor—*

The one tending Semele, Maigrey inserted.

*They've sent people to bring her and the baby, apparently.
They're talking about removing them from the palace to a
place that is safer—*

"A prison," Danha growled aloud.

Maigrey shot him a glance, warned him to be quiet.

How many? she asked her brother.

*There were about twenty that I could see. Fifteen just
marched off down the hall. Their leader told Augustus they
were going ahead to secure the area. That leaves five in the
hall, but I don't know how many are inside the royal living
quarters.*

Their backs are to us?

"Yes, but, Maigrey," Platus said softly, urgency giving voice
to his words, "they have the royal family with them! We can't
use the lasguns without risking hitting the king and queen!"

"Set for stun," Stavros suggested.

"A stun setting that would stop an adult would kill a baby.
We'll use the bloodswords," Maigrey said. "They're accurate,
precise. Stab the guards from behind. They'll never know
what hit them. We can take out four immediately. Platus, you
and Stavros grab the king and queen and hustle them into the
passages. Danha and I will deal with whoever's left, then we'll
catch up—"

Maigrey stopped, her breath snatched away. She clutched
at her throat, almost strangling.

"What is it?" Stavros had his arm around her. She had gone
deathly pale.

"Sagan! He's aware of us; he knows what we're planning.
He's on his way to stop us. The swords! He's read our minds.
We should have thought—"

"Too late," Danha interjected. "Let's move! With luck, we'll
be gone long before he can reach us."

They slid out from the passage. Keeping behind the statue,

Maigrey looked into the hallway. The mind-dead were standing in a knot near the entrance to the royal chambers. They did not appear particularly threatening, now that the royal guard was no longer a factor. No weapons were trained on Augustus or the doctor, who stood in the middle of the body-strewn hallway; both were unarmed, so neither was dangerous.

The baby's crying grew louder. Semele emerged from the royal chambers, attended closely by a volubly protesting nurse.

"Her Majesty has had a very difficult delivery! She shouldn't be out of bed! You're endangering her life—"

"Her Majesty's life will be in far more danger if she doesn't escape the palace," one of the mind-dead answered. Maigrey marked him as the leader and her first target. "I beg you to hurry, madam." The mind-dead spoke to Semele. "Derek Sagan has murdered the king. You and your family will be his next victims unless you accompany us to safety."

"Sagan!" Maigrey heard Semele's voice, heard it weak and dazed. "Sagan—a murderer, a traitor?" She looked at her husband, her voice growing firmer as she spoke. She held her baby in her arms. "I don't believe it, Augustus. I don't believe it!"

Maigrey gripped the bloodsword, raised her hand to give the signal.

Augustus went to his wife, put his arm around her.

"Move on, down the hallway," the mind-dead ordered. "We will follow behind, to see that you are safe. You, too, Doctor."

Maigrey breathed a sigh of relief, cast a look of grim exultation at her comrades. Sending the king and queen on ahead would make the Guardians' task much easier. She saw Augustus and Semele started on their way down the hall, Semele holding her baby tightly in her arms, refusing to give him to the nurse, who was fussing over her. Augustus walked with her, his arm around and supporting her. The doctor moved along at the new king's side.

Maigrey crept out from behind the statue and began padding, soft-footed, down the hallway. The mind-dead had spread out, standing in a line in front of her, their backs to her, their attention fixed on the king and queen walking down the hall. Suddenly, acting in concert, as one body, the mind-dead raised their beam rifles.

Not prison! Not taking them to a "place of safety"!

Too late, Maigrey understood. An execution.

She yelled a challenge, a scream of rage that might have come from the throat of the barbaric, savage Amazon woman who, thousands of years before, had defied Achilles on the walls of Troy. Running forward, she screamed again, trying desperately to force the mind-dead to turn their killing blasts on her. Beside her, Danha was thundering like Zeus; Stavros fired his lasgun into the ceiling, filling the hallway with lightning. He dared not fire at the mind-dead, for fear of missing and killing the king.

The mind-dead, acting with one single mind on one single purpose, ignored the fury that was descending on them from behind. Taking deliberate aim, they fired.

Maigrey's shout accomplished something—it alerted Augustus. Looking back, he saw the rifles raising and threw himself in front of his wife and child in a desperate attempt to shield their bodies with his. The blast of several beam rifles, aimed at point-blank range, blew him apart.

The Guardians reached the mind-dead. Maigrey swung the bloodsword, severed the head from the shoulders of one. The headless trunk sagged and toppled to the ground. The returning stroke of her sword caught another of the mind-dead in the back, nearly sliced him in two. Her enemies out of her way, Maigrey didn't pause. She trusted her comrades to deal with the rest, as she had trusted them all her life. Her heart bursting with pain, she ran toward the bloody mass in the center of the hallway.

The doctor lay dead, a hole blown in his back. The nurse was no longer recognizable as a human being. Neither was Augustus. Maigrey, acting in desperation, refusing to let herself think about what she was doing, shoved aside the charred and bleeding chunks of flesh and bone that had been her king in an effort to reach his wife.

Semele lay face-down, her body curled around the baby in her arms. Maigrey prayed to God that the blood on the woman's gown was that of her husband, not her own. Gently, she slid her arm beneath her friend's head and, turning it, lifted it.

Looking into the eyes, she knew her prayer, for some reason passing her mortal understanding, had not been granted. Life flickered in the eyes faintly, but they were already staring far, far away and didn't see Maigrey, didn't recognize her. One thing alone bound the woman to the life she was fast leaving.

"My baby . . ." she whispered. Then her head lolled heavily on Maigrey's shoulder.

"Maigrey!" It was Platus, shaking her.

Maigrey ran her hand through Semele's shining black hair, pressed the head of her friend to her breast. "No, Semele, no! Please . . . no!"

"The baby, Maigrey! The baby's alive!" Platus gently removed the child from the mother's lifeless grip.

Maigrey gazed dazedly at the infant, who seemed to be swaddled in blood instead of a blanket, and saw that the child was crying frenziedly. She hadn't noticed. She held Semele in her arms, hugging the body close to her, rocking the dead mother as the mother might have rocked her child.

Platus peeled back the sodden fabric, gave the naked body a swift glance. "He's all right! No burns." He paused a moment, looked to Danha and Stavros, who had come to stand near. "We can still save the child."

Maigrey didn't move. She clung to Semele, buried her face in the black hair, and wept.

"Maigrey," Platus said to her softly, insistently, conscious of time slipping away, falling like the drip, drip of blood from the baby's blanket. "Maigrey, we can save the child! But we must hurry."

Still she didn't move. To do so, to lay the body down on the blood-covered floor beside the desecrated flesh of Semele's husband, would be to grant victory to death. If only they would leave her alone, let her rest here and stay with her friend. . . .

Danha knelt beside her, put his strong arm around her. "The king is dead, Maigrey," he said, his huge hand reaching out to reverently touch, as a priest might bless, the small, fragile head of the fist-clenched, mewling infant. "Long live the king."

Chapter ·❧❧❧· Six

—. . . wash this blood off from my guilty hand.
　　William Shakespeare, *Richard II*, Act V, Scene 6

Duty called Maigrey back. Through closed eyelids, she seemed to see the light of the Star of the Guardians shining brightly, undimmed by the horror, untarnished by the blood splashed upon it. She kissed Semele's cold forehead, lay the body gently down. Lifting the mother's fast-chilling hand, Maigrey slid from the bloody fingers a ring made of fire opals. She held the ring a moment to the lips that were forever silenced, then tucked it securely into the folds of the gore-spattered blanket that Platus had wrapped tightly around the baby.

"What's the quickest way to the passage that leads to the royal ship?" she asked, speaking and moving briskly.

"His Majesty's bedchamber," Platus answered without hesitation. "There's a door inside the fireplace that leads directly to the launching pad."

"The ship will be guarded," Danha warned, voice grim.

"You can deal with them," Maigrey returned. Her voice was lifeless, without expression; it might have been the mechanical voice of a 'droid. She took a step down the hall, stopped when she felt Danha's hand on her arm. She stared at him with eyes that didn't know him.

"Your sword, Maigrey," he said, holding the bloodsword in his hand.

She stared at it as if she had never seen it before, had no idea what to do with it. She couldn't remember having worn it, couldn't remember taking it off. Nodding, she accepted it back, started to insert the needles into her hand.

"Maigrey, wait," Platus called to her. "Don't you want to take the baby?"

He held out the child to her. Maigrey looked at the infant, who had suddenly ceased to cry and was staring around him with a solemn and uncanny intelligence.

"My arms were meant to cradle the dead," she said. "Not the living."

She activated the bloodsword, and the four Guardians, Platus carrying the child, traversed the hall. The floor was slippery, wet with blood; they moved with as much haste as they dared. Reaching the door to the royal chambers, Platus and the others hurried inside, stopped halfway through the entry hall when they realized that Maigrey wasn't with them.

"Stay here," Stavros ordered Platus, and hurried back to the doorway in company with Danha.

Maigrey stood in the doorway, her body straight and tall, staring into the shadows of the death-drenched hall with eyes that held in them no more life than those of the corpses around her.

"Go ahead," she said to them before they had opened their mouths. "Take the baby someplace safe, someplace hidden. Watch over him. One day the people will come to rue bitterly what they have done. They will be glad to fall on their knees before their king."

"Maigrey, you can't—"

"I can. I must." Her eyes seemed to see them and know who they were for the first time since she'd laid Semele's body to rest. "Sagan's on his way here now. I'm the only one who can stop him. You know that. Go on. You don't have much time."

"I'll stay—" Danha rumbled.

"No." Maigrey shook her head. "As you said, the ship will be guarded. You'll both be needed. Platus can't fight; he has the child. Not that he would be of much use anyway." She smiled slightly. "Don't tell him I'm staying behind. Tell him I'll be joining you soon. You understand, don't you, Stavros?"

"Yes," Stavros answered bitterly. "And Platus will understand all too well. He won't leave you."

"He has no choice. He is a Guardian. Remind him that he has another responsibility now. He must raise up a king." Her fond, sad gaze encompassed both of her friends. "*Dominus vobiscum.* God be with you."

It seemed Stavros would have continued to argue, but Danha clamped his hand around his friend's arm, silenced him. "*Et cum spiritu tuo*, Maigrey. And may the spirit be with you."

Maigrey watched them leave, heard hushed voices in the distance, her brother's raised in protest, Danha shouting him down. Apparently, whatever Danha said convinced Platus to accompany them. Maigrey, though she listened intently, heard nothing more. Her brother, after all, hadn't argued very long or hard.

Platus would be good as both a father and a mother to the boy. He had been gentle as a mother to the little sister who had never known one. He'd comforted her in those first few days at the Academy when she was homesick and lost and afraid. He'd been patient and kind, an eye in the storm of her tempestuous tantrums. He'd been understanding, even when he hadn't understood. All he had ever wanted in return was her love. Would it have cost her so much to have given it to him?

Maigrey stood in front of the door, in company with the dead. The hallway was hushed, silent, the spirits having long since left the frail, mortal bodies to present themselves to God and receive His judgment, His comfort, His wrath. Maigrey heard footsteps, but only in her soul. Sagan wasn't here yet, although he was coming nearer with each breath she drew, each heartbeat. If she could have stilled one or the other, she would have. Her life was worth nothing to her now, but it was worth something to others and so she held on to it, ready to spend it to buy the only thing left of value—time.

··◁■ ■▷··

Nothing was going as it should have. A bloodless coup had turned into a bloodbath. Sagan, who could never remember any time in his life when he had *not* been in control, had lost all control.

"The king is dead, the Guardians are being slaughtered," he fumed aloud to himself. "Abdiel and Robes plotted this between them—genocide, the decimation of the Blood Royal."

Sagan withdrew in a blazing fury from what had been the banquet hall and was now a tomb. If he had been at all sickened and appalled by the mass murders of the helpless, he had sacrificed his better feelings on the altar of his raging anger, watched them blacken and die, leaving nothing but cold ash. The thought had occurred to him that he himself could be in danger, but a glance around the antechamber and the lower hallways of the palace caused him to discard the notion. His troops, whose training he had personally overseen during the last month, were disciplined and organized.

"No, Robes won't harm me. He doesn't dare. He needs me. And he's afraid of me." Sagan considered this fact with regret. He had truly admired and respected Peter Robes; he had believed in the man and in his cause. Admiration and respect were dead now, lying cold and charred upon the altar.

As for the cause, it, too, was dead. Derek Sagan had looked into the faces of the people and had seen nothing to admire. He'd made a mistake; he could admit that to himself. What made the mistake easier to accept was that now he saw how much he stood to gain. The phoenix would truly rise out of the ashes and its wings would be golden.

Sagan was not angry at himself, nor was he angry at Robes, who after all had proved to be weak and fallible and, as such, would be easily used. Derek's anger had now one focus, one object—those who had betrayed him.

"Your report, Captain," Sagan said to an advancing soldier.

"The computer rooms and files and all personnel are secure, sir, as are the elevators to the upper levels. We have also secured the power generator. We were forced to shoot several of the mob—"

Sagan waved this aside as unimportant. "Has anyone tried to reach the upper levels?"

"No one, sir. Except, of course, Major Morianna—"

"What?" Sagan glared at the man so fiercely the soldier felt his skin scorched beneath the burning gaze.

"M-Major Morianna, sir. The men recognized her. She said she was acting by your orders—"

Sagan saw everything, then, saw it through her eyes. He saw the mind-dead in the hallway, saw them raise their rifles, saw fire, blood, struggle, death. And he saw the new life, saw the child, and he saw, suddenly, how it all could work for him . . .

Or maybe not. The royal ship! The one way they could escape! He cursed himself. Why hadn't he foreseen this?

Because he hadn't expected all hell to break loose. Because he hadn't expected chaos. Because he hadn't expected betrayal!

Sagan glanced toward the computer room. He could bypass the security codes, obtain access to the launching bay, but that would take time. He knew from his mind-link with Maigrey that the Guardians were attempting to reach the ship via the secret passages. It was a long way down from the thirtieth level. They were tired, hampered by the need to move slowly and carefully for the sake of the baby. . . .

One obstacle only blocked his path.

Sagan left the stammering captain standing in the hallway and ran through the corridors that were hazy with smoke, littered with bodies and wreckage. He fumed impatiently in the elevator that, had it traveled at light speed, would have traveled too slowly.

She had betrayed him. They had all betrayed him, but hers was the treachery that had entered his body with the force and rending pain of a thrown spear. He had yanked it out, cauterized the wound with the flame of his anger, but he could still feel the bitter pain and would feel it until he had the satisfaction of revenge.

The elevator reached the floor of the royal family's private chambers. The door slid aside, letting him out into the hall of death. He paid scant attention to the bodies, though his gaze was drawn for a brief instant to that of Semele, lying in her husband's blood.

Sagan continued on.

Maigrey was waiting, the only living being in the hall. He bore down upon her, stoking the fire of his rage, feeling it burn hot and satisfying within him. But when he saw her, the flames wavered.

She seemed more dead than the corpses.

The only light that shone anywhere around her was the light of the sword, glowing in her hand, and the light of the jewel on her breast. All else was dark, black as the blood on her gown and in her pale hair.

Sagan activated the bloodsword, raised it. "Stand aside, Maigrey. Let me pass."

She did not answer, did not move. The folds of her gown were not even stirred by her breath—a cold, marble angel with a flaming sword. Sagan moved ahead, muscles tensed to feint, dodge around her.

Her bloodsword, with a quick, deft stroke, was there to block him. And though the gray eyes were dark and lifeless and did not look directly at him, he saw blood flow warm, staining the translucent skin, sensed her mind alert and active.

She did not attack him, but merely blocked his way. He understood her. Getting killed too quickly would thwart her plan. She was buying time.

He hesitated to fight her. Maigrey was a skilled opponent, quick, intelligent, resourceful. They had fought together often for the fun of it and for the practice. Often, she had bested him. Now, she had no care for her own life, which put him at a disadvantage, for he suddenly had a great care for his. Vast vistas of power and glory were opening up before him. And it occurred to him that, without her, he would walk them alone.

"Maigrey"—he lowered his weapon—"don't do this. Come with me."

She made no reply, did not move from her guarded stance.

Sagan's voice softened; he was speaking his heart. "Robes is a fool, Maigrey. The rabble that brought him to power will tire of him quickly. We have but to bide our time and then we can step in and take over. And, in the meantime, together we can raise Semele's child, raise the king."

Maigrey still made no move. But she was listening. He knew. He could tell by the flicker of the long eyelashes, a pulsing of warmth in her cheek.

"Come with me, Maigrey, and I will forgive you."

The eyelashes flickered again, and tears glistened in them. The gray eyes shifted their gaze, sought him, found him.

"But I will never forgive you, Derek," she said, her voice remote and low. "Or myself."

The fire of his anger flared and scorched and consumed him, blinding him with its dark, choking smoke. He struck at her with all the force of his impassioned rage, struck swiftly and savagely. He couldn't see where he struck; he couldn't see her. His eyes burned from the glare of his fury.

He came to himself; the black, blood-tinged mists cleared from his vision. He found her lying at his feet. She had fallen without a sound. He looked to the door, started to enter, but checked himself. He knew he was too late. The child was gone.

Maigrey lay face-down, a pool of blood forming beneath her head mingled with the other blood—the blood of her enemies—on the floor. Sagan stooped down beside her, balancing himself on one knee. She was still alive. He didn't touch her, feel the limp wrist for a pulse, put his hand to her neck. He had no need. He knew she was alive and, in that moment, he knew she was dead to him. The mind-link was broken except for a tiny flickering spark.

Derek Sagan reached down and lifted a lock of the pale, fine hair in his hand. He felt no remorse, no regret. She had betrayed her oath of allegiance; she had betrayed their friendship, their love. She had merited death. And for what? For an aging, inept king whom even God Himself had abandoned.

Sagan felt nothing. His soul was dark and silent as the hall of the dead in which he stood. From now on, he would hear only the echo of his own footsteps walking empty corridors—corridors of power, corridors of glory, but all empty, barren, dark, and chill.

He should kill her, he supposed, his thumb gently caressing the sea-foam-colored strands that lay in the palm of his left hand. The coup de grace, the stroke of grace in which one mortally wounded is put out of his misery. But he couldn't bring himself to do it. To strike her thus, defenseless, unconscious, would be tantamount to murder. Justice had been served. He would place her in the hands of God.

Sagan lifted the strands of pale hair to his lips. "My lady," he murmured, and kissed them, then let them fall. Rising to his feet, he walked away, leaving the empty hall to the dead and to the dying.

··◁▯ ▯▷··

Thirty floors below, Derek Sagan emerged from the dark shadows into the light of flame and battle. Entire sections of the city were ablaze. The hallway was lit by the lurid flare. Looking up, he could see bursts of tracer fire in the skies—perhaps some of the Guardians attempting to escape, or battles between those loyal to the crown against their own comrades turned rebel.

Chaos, confusion. And up there, somewhere, was the royal ship, carrying the tiny king. Sagan considered what it would take to stop them. The Air Corps was under the revolutionary army's jurisdiction. If he could even get through to anyone in command, which he highly doubted, it would be hopeless to try to set them on the trail of the royal spaceship. Danha would be piloting it, and Danha was one of the best, as his former commander had good reason to know.

"Never mind. I'll find them." Sagan swore the oath aloud, to himself and to God. "If it takes years, I will track down those who betrayed me and mete out justice. And, through them, I will find the boy."

A captain, searching the halls for his superior officer, caught sight of Sagan and hurried toward him. Seeing his commander's face, however, the captain paused, hesitated, and appeared reluctant to approach.

Sagan made an abrupt, peremptory gesture, and the captain came forward.

"Pardon me, sir," the captain said, eyeing his commander with concern. "You're not wounded—"

"What is the current status?" Sagan demanded coldly.

"All secure, sir. The fighting in the banquet hall has ended. As you instructed, we are identifying the bodies and entering the names into the computer files. It is certain that several managed to escape."

"We will know who they are. What of the mind-seizer and his . . . troops?"

"They've left the palace, sir. We had a report that they invaded the cathedral. The priests are reportedly defending it." The captain spoke in subdued tones. Perhaps he knew of his commander's background.

Sagan's lips tightened. He could imagine what was transpiring in the sacred precincts. The priests were defending it. Yes, but without weapons other than the Holy Power. And they were forbidden to use that to take life.

Another massacre in the name of the people. Sagan absently rubbed the scars on his left arm, scars inflicted by himself upon himself in the name of God, scars borne only by priests of the Order of Adamant. Abdiel was taking no chances, destroying all opposition. Sagan could do nothing about it now, but the day would come when these dead priests would be avenged.

"What of the city?" he asked, keeping his mind on the business at hand.

"The Army of the Revolution has seized control. We've had reports of looting, rioting, burning. . . ."

Yes, he could see that from where he stood. "The media?"

"They've been escorted off-planet, sir, along with the President."

Good. The holocaust could be glossed over, the truth distorted. In the name of the people.

All was going well—as well as could be expected, considering the chaos.

"Anything further?" Sagan asked wearily. It had been a long night.

"No, sir."

"Then carry on with your duties, Captain."

"Yes, sir." The man saluted, the new Roman-fashioned salute Sagan had instituted among his own command.

His own command. Finally. A fleet of ships, a galaxy to rule. In the name of the people, of course.

Of course.

Turning on his heel, he walked over to a window and stared out into the turmoil and destruction of a city in the throes of revolution. Smoke hung in the air; its acrid smell was in his nostrils and with it the faint, iron-tinged smell of blood.

He watched the flames leap high and saw himself rising up with them on golden wings . . .

Alone.

Book IV

Death Is the Door Prize

O fortuna,
velut luna
statu variabilis,
semper crecis,
aut decrescis . . .

O, fortune!
Like the moon
ever-changing,
rising first,
then declining . . .

Carl Orff, *Carmina Burana*

Chapter ·❖❯❯◗❮❖· One

Nor heaven nor earth have been at peace tonight . . .
    William Shakespeare, *Julius Caesar*, Act II, Scene 2

Thick clouds, dark and sullen and charged with lightning, blanketed Laskar's horizon the next morning. The green sun made no appearance, keeping beneath the covers as if it, too, had slept badly during the night and was loath to rise. Distant thunder rumbled, shaking the ground, stalking the land like vengeful titans.

The rumblings shook Abdiel's prefab house, disturbed the soothing gurgling of the hookah, interrupted his morning's meditations. Just as well to proceed with the day's activities, he decided, removing the pipestem from his cracked, chapped lips and coiling the tube neatly in place.

The door opened noiselessly. Mikael appeared in response to his master's thoughts that had been bent his direction. Abdiel sensed Dion stirring restlessly as well. The thunder had jolted the boy awake from disturbing dreams of a castle in flames. Abdiel sent thoughts that direction, and Dion's subconscious dragged him back down into darkness. Abdiel had arrangements to make, which the boy's presence would render exceedingly awkward.

"The young need their sleep," he told Mikael, who nodded silently in agreement. Drawing up a small table to the sofa on which the mind-seizer lounged, Mikael placed in front of Abdiel the handful of various-colored pills that were his breakfast.

"Sit down, my dear," Abdiel instructed, gesturing with his needle-pronged hand, patting the cushions beside him.

Mikael did as he was told, not lounging, but keeping his body bolt upright, his empty eyes fixed upon the man who gave him inner life.

Abdiel, as was his custom, lifted the first pill, sniffed it, studied its purple hue, licked it, then bit it open to taste the granules inside before swallowing it. He did this with every pill he ingested, treating each as if it were the most rare wine or the most flavorful food. His breakfast, eaten in this fashion, often lasted thirty minutes or more. Dinner could stretch into hours.

The mind-seizer was fond of talking during his meals, which meant that one or more of the mind-dead were often invited to join him. The mind-dead were not noted for their conversational flair. Discoursing with them was, in essence, tantamount to discoursing with himself, since Abdiel put any thoughts they might have into their heads. But it was occasionally useful to him to hear his words come out of another's mouth, just as the text read aloud is often imprinted more deeply in the memory than that absorbed by sight alone.

"Our prisoners?" Abdiel asked, taking up a red pill, holding it to his nose, then putting it down in favor of a black.

"They did not sleep. A guard is posted in the room with them and they attempted to remain awake, hoping the guard would fall asleep and they could steal her key."

Abdiel chuckled, placed the black pill on his tongue, and bit it through. The mind-dead do not require sleep and can remain awake, alert, and functioning until the body itself keels over.

"It is a waste of personnel, master, to keep a guard on them day and night. It would be far more resourceful to kill them now." Mikael made the statement but the thought was Abdiel's. He considered it, then shook his head.

"No. The boy is Blood Royal and has, even for us, an unusually high empathy. Tusca is also Blood Royal, though diluted. The two have formed a bond, unknown to either of them as yet. If the mercenary died, the boy would immediately be aware of his loss. We will kill the mercenary and the woman shortly, but all in good time, my dear Mikael. All in good time."

Abdiel grimaced slightly. The black pills were bitter; he didn't like them. He washed it down with a glass of water and grabbed hastily for an orange capsule, whose flavor he enjoyed.

"I have finalized my plans, Mikael," Abdiel continued, savoring the capsule's faint aroma. "I am now ready to proceed with them. I will rid myself of an ambitious Warlord, a troublesome king, and a perverted Adonian genius. That leaves me with the bomb, the Lady Maigrey, and the star-jewel. And *that*, my dear Mikael, leaves me with the universe."

"The Lady Maigrey will not give up the bomb," Mikael observed.

Abdiel crunched the orange capsule, sucked out the center. He took Mikael's hand, and stroked his palm caressingly. "She will not have a choice. She will be only too happy to give it to me, just as she will be only too happy to die afterward." The mind-seizer considered bonding with his disciple, but decided against it. There was breakfast to finish and work to be done with the boy. He let Mikael's hand drop and turned his attention back to the pills. Abdiel sighed. Still one black one left.

"Do you truly believe the boy is destined to be king?" Mikael asked.

"Destiny!" Abdiel scoffed. "You sound like Derek Sagan, or worse, that priest father of his, who maintained that we are controlled by some omnipotent, omniscient Being who counts the hairs upon our heads and grieves over the fall of a sparrow. Here is your Being." The mind-seizer reached up his hand, needles flashing in the light, and tapped his own skull. "Here is the power that controls and manipulates and determines and decides.

"Faith in this God of his has always been Sagan's weakness and it will be his downfall. You see, my dear, no matter what he may protest to the contrary, Derek Sagan believes in his heart that this boy is his anointed king. He was always a reluctant rebel, was Sagan. He tried to save with one hand what he was destroying with the other.

"If he had devoted himself to conquering the galaxy," Abdiel continued, putting off as long as possible the taking of the black pill, "he could have done so. The part of him that burns with ambition has the skill and intelligence, the wealth, the power to rule. He designed and had that bomb built for just such a purpose. And what does he do? Throws it away in an obsessive search for his lost king! Oh, he has his excuses, made mostly to justify himself to himself. But you will see, Mikael, when it comes to the test, when he is forced to make a choice, he will go with God. And it will be my privilege to hasten him on his way."

"I understand, master," Mikael said, rising, filling the water glass, and returning to his seat.

"This initiation business." Abdiel popped the pill into his mouth, chewed furiously. "A perfect example. I looked into the boy's mind, saw the whole affair. It was as good a performance as any of the old spiritualists used to put on for the benefit of gullible clients. The boy nearly suffocates for no apparent reason. Real spikes, not fake as is supposed to happen, pierce the boy's flesh. Cleansing fire—from heaven, no doubt—heals the terrible wounds."

Abdiel gulped water. Replacing the empty glass on the table, noting with relief that there were only orange, green, and purple capsules left, he wiped his mouth with the back of his hand and selected a green. "What a waste. Sagan has no idea of his own mental power. Not only does he convince the Lady Maigrey and almost convinces the boy that these 'miracles' have occurred, Sagan manages to convince himself! An illusionist who believes devoutly in his own illusions."

"You say 'almost convinces,' master. Then the boy does not believe?"

"Dion believes because he wants to believe, not because he truly does. He was, after all, raised by an atheist and there is doubt and confusion deep within the boy. But instead of accepting and dealing with his internal conflicts, Dion fears them. He seeks desperately to prove himself."

"You have control of his mind, master?"

"No," Abdiel admitted. "He is Blood Royal and of good stock. People denigrated the Starfires, but none of our Order could gain ascendancy over any of them. They were a conceited lot; they thought well of themselves, too well to easily let another take hold. Dion has enough self-love to make him safe from my control, but he has enough self-doubt to leave him vulnerable—not to what I command but to what I suggest. In other words, Mikael, I won't have to force him to do what he will do. He will be glad to do it himself."

Mikael bowed his head in acknowledgment of his master's genius. Abdiel took the last capsule. His repast concluded, he sank back comfortably in the sofa cushions, content to bask in the radiant warmth of the solar heater.

"Bring me the boy," Abdiel commanded.

"Is he awake?"

"He will be, by the time you reach him."

·◄■ ■►·

The storm broke, its fury preceded by a ball of blazing lightning that burst over Laskar with the crack of doom. Lightning flashed constantly, thunder rattled and boomed, rain hurtled from the heavens, hail pounded like fists on the outside of the Warlord's shuttlecraft. The noise did not wake Sagan. He hadn't been asleep. He'd spent the night fighting a revolution, spent the night sharing Maigrey's dream.

He felt this morning as he had felt that morning long ago—drained, exhausted, empty. He could imagine how Maigrey must be feeling and he refrained from touching her mind, as one refrains from touching an open wound that is raw and bleeding. Let it have a chance to heal, the scar tissue to grow over. . . .

"My lord. You sent for me."

"Yes, Marcus. Enter."

The door slid aside. The centurion stood in the doorway.

The Warlord, facing the window, watching the majesty of God's wrath, did not look around.

Marcus remained standing at attention, silent, waiting to be commanded.

"Is my lady awake?" Sagan asked finally.

"Yes, my lord."

"I want to hear directly from you what happened this morning."

"Yes, my lord. I knocked several times on her ladyship's door and received no answer and so, according to your orders, I entered the Starlady's room—"

"*Whose* room?" Sagan glanced around, missing a particularly spectacular lightning strike. "What did you call her?"

Marcus flushed deeply. Thunder shook the shuttlecraft. "The Starlady. Pardon, my lord. It's just a . . . a name we men gave her on board *Phoenix*. We meant no disrespect."

No, that's true enough, Sagan thought. Quite the opposite, in fact. You would die for her in a moment.

Perhaps you will have the chance.

"Continue, centurion," was all the Warlord said aloud.

Marcus cleared his throat. "I entered the Lady Maigrey's room and found her lying on the floor unconscious. I informed my captain—"

"—and he informed me. Go on."

"It appeared, on examination"—Marcus's flush deepened—

"that she was not injured, but had fainted. The captain sent for the base doctor. By the time he arrived, the Lady Maigrey had regained consciousness and refused to see him. She sent us all out of the room and sealed the door shut. The security cameras are on—"

"She's disrupted the signal." The Warlord motioned to his own blank monitor screens.

"I see, my lord." Marcus seemed somewhat at a loss, not quite certain what was wanted from him.

Sagan gave him no help but remained standing motionless, staring out at the storm.

"She's all right, I think, my lord," Marcus continued, feeling called upon to say something. "We can hear her pacing—"

"Thank you, centurion. That will be all. Your watch is nearly ended, is it not?"

"Yes, my lord."

"I relieve you of your duties early. Go get some sleep."

"Yes, my lord. Thank you, my lord. Shall I detail a replacement?"

"No, I will take care of that myself. You are dismissed, centurion."

Marcus did not look overly pleased, but he could do nothing except salute and leave the Warlord's presence. Sagan, watching him obliquely, saw the man glance down the empty hallway toward the lady's room—the Starlady's room—before making his reluctant way aft to where the Honor Guard berthed aboard the shuttlecraft.

The Warlord left instructions with the captain of the guard as to where he could be found, walked down the empty hallway to Maigrey's door, opened it, and stepped in. No door aboard his craft was sealed to him.

Maigrey halted in her pacing, turned her head to look at him over her shoulder. She wore a long, plain, white cotton gown, devoid of decoration. Her pale hair hung down around her shoulders, unbrushed and disheveled. He could see little of her face through the ragged hair, except two eyes, dark as the smoke that swirled through his memories.

"Damn you to hell, Derek Sagan." Her voice was calm, tight, controlled. So might God Himself sound on the day of judgment.

"It had to be done, Maigrey." Sagan was not apologetic, merely explanatory. "Sparafucile told me how you froze when the mind-dead attacked you. That's never happened to you in battle before. I wondered why, and then I knew. You couldn't remember anything about that night, could you? You had blotted out what happened, repressed it. And that repression would hamper your ability to act and respond in any situation where you might meet either the mind-dead or their master again. And you will meet them again, my lady. And soon. For Dion's sake, if for no other, you must be prepared to deal with them."

He had said the right words, touched the right chords; their music was sad, melancholy, but harmonious. That which had driven them apart had—remembered, shared—brought them together. Maigrey leaned her cheek against the steelglass, watched the rain pour down the outside, watched the sky shed the tears that she couldn't cry. Her grief ached and burned inside her, but somehow it was better than that vague feeling of dread and terror, of not knowing, not remembering.

"You're right, my lord," she said softly, her eyes on the flaring lightning, "and in my head I know she's been dead seventeen years but in my heart it seems that she died . . . in my arms . . . just moments ago. . . ." Maigrey lifted her hands, stared at them.

Sagan could almost see the blood that had once covered them, the blood on her blue robes, the pool of blood forming beneath the motionless head.

He walked across the room to the window. Standing behind her, he rested gentle hands upon her shoulders. His sympathy was silent and unexpected, even by himself. Last night, for the first time, each lived through what the other had experienced. Mind-linked, they had once been closer than any two people could possibly come. Pride and mistrust were the barriers that had risen between them; were the barriers that stood between them still. Perhaps, if those barriers had been removed then, things might have been different. Perhaps if they could be removed now . . .

Sagan shook his head, banished the speculation as being wasteful of time and energy. Maigrey remained motionless, watching the retreating storm, relaxed beneath his touch, resting against him for support. Her hand went to her cheek, to the old scar that in her confused mind was an open wound. Her thoughts were much the same as his, or maybe they were his; he couldn't tell anymore. The longer they were together, the more thin and transparent the barriers became. The idea of the barriers falling was both attractive . . . and repellent.

"'Two together must walk the paths of darkness . . .'"

It seemed his father's voice that spoke the words now, as he had spoken them long ago, the only words he had ever spoken since taking his vow of silence. A shiver crept over Sagan, chilling his flesh, until he realized it was Maigrey who had said them.

"I used to think, my lord," she continued, "that we had fulfilled the prophecy, that we had already walked the 'paths of darkness.' But I begin to believe I was wrong. I have walked paths of darkness and you have walked paths of darkness, but we have walked them apart, all these years. And the prophecy says 'Two together.'"

Sagan, understanding, clasped her more tightly, drew her closer to him. Both kept their gaze fixed on the storm, on the lightning dancing between cloud and ground, the hailstones battering the window, the rain that streaked down in glittering rivulets, gathering up and blending their reflections into one, as two streams converge to form a river.

"I look before me," she added softly, reaching up to touch the reflection that reached a ghostly hand to touch her back, "and I see only darkness."

"'Two must walk the paths of darkness *to reach the light*,'" Sagan said, finishing the quote.

Maigrey shook her head. "I see no light."

Sagan did. Sagan saw a light, saw moonlight, bright and shining on a strange planet, saw moonlight gleaming on silver armor, on a knife in his hands, saw moonlight glisten on blood flowing from a mortal wound, on blood on the knife and on his hands, saw moonlight glitter cold in gray eyes that could no longer see the moon or anything. . . .

The vision of Maigrey's death at his hands had come to him often, but never before had it been so clear. It startled him, angered him. He felt constrained, restricted, a prisoner of fate, without a choice. He would see about that, he determined, removing his hands from the woman abruptly.

"We have much to discuss, my lady," he said, his voice cold. "Report to me this day at 1800 hours."

He turned on his heel, stalked through the door that, fast as it operated, barely opened in time to permit him to walk through.

Maigrey, looking around, startled, thought that it wouldn't

have much mattered if the door hadn't operated. In this mood, he would have walked through solid steel.

Sighing, she turned back to stare out the window. The storm was diminishing, its fury spent, settling down into a dull and dismal steady rain.

"You've gone to argue, once again, with God," she said to the absent Sagan, staring at her reflection in the glass, a reflection made of tears. "Why don't you give up? Don't you understand? God abandoned us long ago, my lord. Long ago. . . ."

Chapter ❧ Two

We soon learn that there is nothing mysterious or
supernatural in the case, but that all proceeds from the
usual propensity of mankind towards the marvelous . . .
David Hume, *"The Sceptic"*

The rain continued falling sporadically all during the morning hours. Dion sat with Abdiel most of that time, leaving the
mind-seizer only for luncheon. The young man took his meals
alone, in his room, having little desire for the dubious
company of the mind-dead.

The food cooked by Abdiel's servants was wholesome and
that was about the best that could be said for it. The bland
concoction had a consistency somewhere between porridge
and a meat stew that has been run through a blender. It went
down easily; its uninteresting flavor made no attempt to divert
the boy's thoughts by offering up any new and dramatic taste
sensations.

Being hungry, Dion forked stew into his mouth absent-
mindedly. Alone in his room, away from Abdiel, the young
man discovered to his discomfiture that, thinking back on their
time together, he found the old man repulsive, the bonding
appalling. Looking at the palm of his right hand, seeing the
still red and inflamed puncture marks, and remembering that
rotting flesh pressed close against his, Dion gagged on his
food. Only the insatiable hunger of a seventeen-year-old kept
him doggedly eating.

Painful, disgusting, the bonding had been exciting, too.
Dion began to think of his mind much like Abdiel's strange
house, with twisting, turning hallways and hundreds of locked
doors. Abdiel's mind inside his had opened many of those
doors, introducing the boy to new thoughts and experiences,
new ideas, new ambitions.

The two of them had discussed many of those thoughts and ideas this morning. Strange, but when he was with Abdiel, the young man didn't feel any of the revulsion or disgust that came over him the moment the mind-seizer was out of his sight. Dion recalled, somewhat uneasily, Maigrey's warning to him about strong minds being able to control weaker.

Is Abdiel doing that to me? Dion wondered. Am I under the mind-seizer's sway, as are, obviously, the mind-dead?

No, he decided upon serious reflection, scraping the food from the bottom of the bowl. No, Abdiel has not taken me over. Dion was very much conscious of his own will, knew he still retained it. He vaguely remembered, when Abdiel first entered his mind, a contest between the two of them, a contest that had been extremely painful, a contest the boy had perhaps not won, but which had at least turned out to be a draw.

Dion thought back again to the image of the house. Abdiel tried to seize the house, but I prevented him. I invited him inside, however. He came in and went about opening doors. Light and air flowed into my mind, where once there was only darkness and stifling confusion. . . .

What about that rite of initiation? I asked Abdiel. You saw it in my memory, and you laughed.

"Forgive me, my king." Abdiel laughed again, heartily. "But it was all hypnosis, illusion. Oh, don't feel ashamed. You're not the first to fall for it. Sagan and the lady managed it quite prettily, I have no doubt."

But it seemed . . . so real! I protested. I can still remember the spikes driving through my hands, the fire searing my flesh.

"Of course it did! So did the torture of the Corasians, when they captured you. Yet, they didn't cut off your arm, any more than the spikes on that metal ball pierced your skin. It was all in your mind."

But why? I wanted to know. Why would they do such a thing to me? Why lie to me? All that about God not wanting me to use my power—

"How can you ask, Your Majesty? You know the answer. You've known it all along."

Yes, I guess I have known it. I just didn't want to admit it.

"Precisely," Abdiel continued. "They wouldn't be able to control you then."

You mean, I asked, I can use the power?

"You would need to be trained, but I could do that myself."

Abdiel was modest. "Lord Sagan or the Lady Maigrey could have trained you, but they chose not to."

What a fool I've been! But I trusted, I believed in . . . in her, especially.

"Ah, my king." Abdiel sighed, grew very grave. "I've no doubt that, when you first met the lady after her return from her self-imposed exile, she had only your best interests at heart. But you must remember, Dion, that she has fallen increasingly under the charismatic spell of Derek Sagan. You yourself know how easily he can exert his influence over someone."

Yes, I know.

"It may be possible," Abdiel mused aloud, "that Maigrey is not irretrievably lost. It may be possible to save her. If, somehow, his influence over her could be ended—"

That won't happen until he's dead! I told Abdiel.

"Mmmmmm." Abdiel made no response beyond that soft hum.

Dion put his head in his hands, clasped his hands over his ears. But I can still hear that humming. . . .

And the hum seemed to grow louder and more insistent until it was like the buzzing of thousands of insects inside the young man's mind.

··◁■ ■▷··

Dion fell asleep and was awakened by Mikael, who came to escort the young man back into Abdiel's presence. Escort was necessary. Though Dion had been in the house two days, he continued to be uncertain of his way through the halls and the stairs that all looked alike. And he noted, after making some attempt to memorize a route by counting his footsteps, that Mikael either never took the same path twice or Dion was never lodged in the same room twice.

"I suppose," he said to Mikael as they walked along, "that my friends made it back to the plane safely?"

"I took them myself," Mikael replied. "It was the master's command, since the Warlord is on the planet. I waited to see their plane take off and was informed, by the gentleman known as Anselmo, who has monitoring instruments, that they safely left planetary orbit."

"It's odd," Dion said after a moment, "but I didn't think Tusk would leave . . . just like that."

"Why not, Your Majesty?" Mikael would, to judge by his

words, have registered surprise, had any emotion been able to register itself upon his lifeless face. "After all, you yourself ordered him to go."

Dion laughed ruefully. "I'm glad he isn't around to hear you say that." His laughter trailed off. "He didn't act like he was mad at me or anything, did he?"

"No, not at all. But he did seem to be worried about another friend—a man named Dichter—"

"Dixter," Dion said, cheering up. "John Dixter. Yes, that must be it. I just hope they don't try any wild rescue schemes . . . at least until I get back. I think I should go back," he said, suddenly impatient to be doing something, suddenly overwhelmed by the desire to leave Abdiel.

Mikael said nothing, having nothing to say in reply to such a statement, but led the boy to the master's room. The furnace was going full blast. Dion felt the wave of heat smack him in the face when he entered the door. He held back a moment, experiencing as usual a reluctance to enter. He remained standing in the doorway, fidgeting nervously.

Abdiel glanced at Mikael.

He has been asking about his friends, the mind-dead answered the unspoken question.

And you told him . . . ?

I mentioned John Dixter, as you instructed, master.

Abdiel's lidless eyes flicked sideways and Mikael, understanding, bowed and left the room. John Dixter had been one of many small, assorted bits of information Abdiel had obtained on his expedition into the boy's mental processes.

"Look, sir," Dion began abruptly, "I'm grateful for what you've done for me, particularly"—the voice grew grim—"for showing me the truth about . . . about things. But I think I should be leaving now.

"Let's face it. There's nothing I can do against Sagan. He's surrounded, day and night, by men who would think it the greatest honor ever granted to die for him. Not to mention the fact that he himself could chop me into little pieces without even working up a sweat. Tusk's right," Dion finished bitterly. "I'm just a kid—"

"My dear boy," Abdiel interrupted, voice soft with sympathy, "the great Alexander was in his teens when he fought his first battles and began the conquest of a world. Sagan was no older than you when he fought the cyborgs at the Battle of Star's End. I have not kept you here solely for the love of your company, my king, though your stay has been a sweet pleasure to me. I have a plan, you see."

"A plan? Plan for what?"

"A plan to help you confound your enemy and rescue those you love from his clutches."

"What? How?" Dion demanded, sitting down on the edge of a sofa and leaning forward eagerly.

"Patience, Your Majesty. Patience. All in good time. Two have arrived who will start providing answers."

Mikael appeared at the door to the sauna. "Two gentlemen to see you, master."

"Show them in."

The mind-dead bowed, left, returned, bowed again, and stood aside to permit two people coming along behind him to enter the room.

"May the rain that is falling prosper you as it does the ground. I am Raoul," one said in a mellow, exquisite voice, "and this"—gesturing to his companion—"is the Little One."

Dion stared, momentarily forgetting his own problems in his wonderment. Raoul was certainly the most beautiful human the boy had ever seen. Tall and slender, the man had ivory skin and features that might have been carved by a master craftsman. Hair, long and black and shining, fell from a center part to below his hips. The lithe, well-muscled body moved with the grace of a dancer.

The Little One was aptly named, for he, she, or it came only to Raoul's waist. Whether this personage was child or adult, male or female, human or alien, Dion couldn't fathom, for the Little One was muffled in a raincoat that might have belonged to someone twice the small person's height, topped off by a hat of the style known as a fedora. All that could be seen of the Little One were two large, marvelously penetrating and intelligent eyes, peering out from behind the tips of the raincoat's upturned collar.

"Snaga Ohme has sent us," Raoul said with a fluttering motion of his hand. "I am honored to be in the presence of Abdiel, former Lord Abbot of the late Order of Dark Lightning."

"The honor is mine," Abdiel replied. "Will you be seated?"

"Thank you, no," Raoul answered with a charming smile of regret. "We are bidden not to intrude ourselves long upon your valuable time." The beautiful messenger spoke and looked only at Abdiel. The eyes of the Little One, however, never left Dion.

"We await your words with pleasure," Abdiel said, reaching out his hand and drawing the hookah to his side. He unwound the cord and placed the pipe between his lips.

"My employer, Snaga Ohme, deeply regrets that the business transaction to which you both were parties did not conclude to either his satisfaction or your own. Circumstances beyond the control of both of you intervened and the transaction was consequently disrupted."

"What is your point?" Abdiel sucked on the pipe; the water in the hookah gurgled soothingly.

Raoul brushed aside the black, shining hair from his face with a graceful motion of both hands, as if he were parting a curtain and about to enter center stage. "My employer, Snaga Ohme, wants to make certain you understand that he was acting in your best interests, just as he understands that you were acting in his."

"You may assure Snaga Ohme that I understand him and I am confident he understands me."

Raoul was charmed at the thought of so much understanding floating around the universe. The Little One had never, for an instant, taken the penetrating eyes from Dion, who found it difficult to look anywhere else except at the small, strange figure in the oversized raincoat.

"My employer, Snaga Ohme, is of the opinion that the business arrangement might still be brought to a conclusion satisfactory to both parties. In order to facilitate negotiations, Snaga Ohme would like to issue to you an invitation to attend an Event at his dwelling place. This"—Raoul reached into a pocket of his pale blue, satin-trimmed velvet suit and held out a small silver ball in his fine-boned hand—"will advise you of the time and also secure you admittance. Dress is formal. Weapons will not be permitted inside the hall and may be checked at the door. You will, however, be allowed two bodyguards to accompany you. Guests representing nations, corporations, worlds, and/or systems currently at war with the nations, corporations, worlds, and/or systems of other guests will be required to sign a truce lasting the duration of the Event." Raoul paused to draw a breath, his own having been completely exhausted during the recitation.

Abdiel took the opportunity to respond. "Though I have never had the honor to attend one of Snaga Ohme's galas, I am familiar with the procedure." He made a sign to Mikael, who stepped forward and received the silver ball, then conveyed it to his master. The mind-seizer placed the ball in mid-air, where it remained suspended before him.

Removing the pipestem from his lips, he pointed it at Dion. "I have no bodyguards, only my servant. I have quarrels with none in the galaxy," he added humbly, "but I would like to bring this young man with me. You may assure Snaga Ohme that the boy is worthy. He is of the Blood Royal."

Raoul turned; purple eyes glittered exquisitely at Dion. The messenger extended one leg, placed his hand over his heart, and performed a low dip with his body. "I had the impression most of the Blood Royal were extinct. I am pleased to be informed that I was laboring under a delusion, my lord."

"Thank you," Dion said, flushing to the roots of his hair, feeling extremely awkward and uncomfortable. He was further disconcerted by the fact that Raoul, instead of replying to Abdiel's request, straightened, turned, and looked expectantly at his short partner.

The Little One said nothing; the intently staring eyes did not shift their gaze. Raoul, however, nodded and flipped the long black hair over one shoulder. "The Little One says the boy has feelings of hostile intent but, since they are not directed at Snaga Ohme, the young lord may attend."

Dion gaped, started to speak, but saw Abdiel move the pipestem back and forth, advising silence. The young man held his tongue.

Raoul and the Little One were obviously preparing to take their leave. "My employer, Snaga Ohme, has asked me to ascertain whether or not you would be interested in the property in question should he by chance come by the opportunity to reacquire it."

"Perhaps," Abdiel said, pipestem between his teeth. "Perhaps."

"We will convey your answer to Snaga Ohme. And now, if you will excuse us, we have other invitations to issue and several more to confirm. It has been charming conversing with you, Abbot of the Order of Dark Lightning." Raoul turned to Dion. "Young lord, I am enchanted to have met you. My one regret is that our acquaintance has, of necessity, been short. May the sun soon return to brighten your day."

Graceful, glittering, Raoul took himself out the door. The Little One, without a word, shuffled after, nearly tripping over the hem of the long raincoat, the fedora pulled low over the head, shadowing the searching eyes.

"What was that?" Dion gasped, when he and the mind-seizer were alone.

"What was what?" Abdiel, sucking on the pipe, had been absorbed in his thoughts, appeared slightly annoyed at being interrupted. "Oh, you mean Raoul—"

"Well, yes, but mainly that other fellow."

"The Little One? He's an empath. Raoul is an Adonian and a Loti. Empaths are often paired with the Loti. You know, of course, what the Loti are?"

Dion knew, having been introduced to a few by Link and Tusk during a bar-hopping excursion. *Loti* was the term commonly used for those heavily dependent on mind-altering drugs. When they are high, the Loti never suffer from any "negative" emotions. It would be logical to pair an empath with a Loti, who would generally always be calm and tranquil and would thus never upset the empath or interfere in the empath's ability to ascertain the emotional state of others.

Feelings of hostile intent . . . The more Dion thought about it, the more he resented the fact that everyone around here seemed to be delving into his mind. "When is this Event?" he asked irritably.

"Three days' time, I believe. Let us see." Abdiel tapped the silver ball on its side.

A musical voice responded, issuing the invitation, naming date, place, and time. It further reminded them that the dress was formal, no weapons would be admitted, bodyguards would, truces were to be signed and submitted to Snaga Ohme and would go into effect twenty-four hours prior to the Event and last twenty-four hours after. Champagne at 1800 hours, dinner at 1900, the showing at 2400.

"The showing?" Dion walked over to examine the silver ball that had floated gently down to the table when its message was concluded.

"Snaga Ohme exhibits his wares. That is why only the rich and powerful are invited to this Event of his. All the latest in killing devices will be on display and available for on-site testing—with the exception of some of the larger equipment, battleships, that sort of thing. And the bombs, of course," he added.

"Bombs," Dion repeated in hollow tones, thinking of one bomb, the crystal bomb in Maigrey's possession. He glanced at Abdiel out of the corner of his eye. "That's what Raoul meant by all that business transaction talk, wasn't it? Did you try to get hold of that bomb?"

"Naturally, my king!" Abdiel seemed surprised that Dion could ask such a naïve question. "Knowing Sagan had designed this fearsome weapon and very properly fearing his intent, I took advantage of his defeat by the Corasians to attempt to secure the space-rotation bomb myself. Unfortunately, I could not compete with the Lady Maigrey's offer. I have no precious starjewel to sell."

"I can't believe she did that!" Dion said, shaking his head.

"What better proof could you want of Sagan's dark influence over her?"

Dion stirred restlessly, began pacing the room again. Stopping, he turned to the mind-seizer, who had been watching with eyes almost as intent and penetrating as the eyes of the Little One. "So Snaga Ohme is saying that he thinks there is a chance to get hold of this bomb. How?"

"Ah, my king. Snaga Ohme is not one to be trusted. His ways are nefarious. That Raoul you just met? One of the most skilled poisoners in the galaxy. Never eat or drink anything that man offers you. I fear for the Lady Maigrey's safety. I do, indeed."

Dion stared, shocked, suddenly felt sick and cold with foreboding. "Surely the Warlord would protect her. . . ."

"Would he?" Abdiel was grim, stern. "He's tried to kill her before now, and for less cause. She remains alive because she has been clever enough to make it a condition that the bomb can be released only by her. But she stands alone between two evil men, Dion Starfire. Alone, without help, without protection. Sooner or later, she must fall."

"But what can I do?" Dion demanded, feeling hopelessly young and inexperienced. "I couldn't get in to see her without Sagan having me arrested or maybe even shot—"

"There will be one place you *can* see her and talk to her in relative safety, my king."

"The Event!" Dion murmured. "Will she be there?"

"You may count upon it. Snaga Ohme would not miss such an opportunity. How does that childhood rhyme go: 'Will you step into my parlor, said the spider to the fly'?"

"But perhaps she won't go. Why should she?"

"She will go because her king will be there. Oh, don't look so surprised, Dion. Sagan has spies watching us. He knows you are here with me. No doubt he is gnashing his teeth in rage that not only have you escaped him but you have discovered the truth about him."

"You're saying I should go to the Event and talk to Lady Maigrey. Maybe I can persuade her to leave him— What? What's the matter now?"

Abdiel was laughing. "Ah, the naïveté of youth! You are old enough to understand the ways of men and women, Dion. You've seen the two of them together. Do you truly think *you* can break the hold he has over her?"

Dion flushed with anger and shame. Folding his arms across his chest, he faced Abdiel squarely. "What is it you want me to do?"

The sleepless eyes were like two red suns. "Not what *I* want you to do, my king. What you want to do yourself."

Dion swallowed, said thickly, "Kill Derek Sagan."

"He murdered your uncle, he murdered your father and mother, he murdered the man who raised you and loved you like a son. How many more must die? The Lady Maigrey? John Dixter? You yourself, my king?"

Dion clenched his hands into fists to keep them from shaking. Chills swept his body. He saw again the men falling in that control room, the blood splattering on the walls, on himself. . . . After the slaughter was over, he'd been appalled, horrified, sickened by what he'd done.

It was all for him, he said to himself bleakly. I wanted to prove to him that I wasn't a coward.

But what better way to show him? I won't kill him in secret, like some paid assassin. I'll face him. I'll tell him. In those last few moments of his life, he'll respect me. By the God he believes in, he'll respect me!

··◖■ ■◗··

Abdiel watched Dion, was aware of every thought passing through the boy's head. Perhaps he could have seen them even without his mind-probing skills, for the boy's radiant light shone through the pure, clear crystal of his soul—a paladin upon some holy quest.

The mind-seizer sucked on the pipe, drawing the smoke into his lungs. The drug didn't ease his pain, as he had told

Dion. Rather, it enhanced it. He enjoyed the pain because it was his by choice, a constant reminder of his power.

And there came to him, through the pain, the amusing vision of a boy-king pulling a sword from a stone . . . and promptly impaling himself upon the blade.

Chapter ·◆⊃◯⊂◆· Three

Sors immanis et inanis, rota tu volubilis . . .
Dread destiny and empty fate, an ever-turning wheel . . .
Carl Orff, Carmina Burana

"My lord, guards report that two . . . um . . . personages are being detained outside the base. These two request permission to speak to you. They claim to be sent by Snaga Ohme."

"Indeed. Their names?"

"They call themselves"—the captain grimaced slightly—"Raoul and the Little One."

The Warlord nodded. "Yes, I know them."

"I can show them on the vidscreen, my lord—"

"That will not be necessary. I have been expecting word from the Adonian." Sagan glanced at Maigrey. "This is it, my lady."

"Yes," she agreed quietly.

"Bring them to us here," he ordered his captain.

"Yes, my lord. We have scanned them. They did not come armed."

"Oh, yes, they did. But you would never find their weapons. Don't look concerned, Captain. They are not here to murder me. Send them in."

The captain saluted, left upon his errand.

Sagan kept his gaze on Maigrey, who sat in a chair directly opposite him. The two were in his private quarters aboard his shuttlecraft. They had been together over half an hour and those were the first words they had exchanged, either aloud or silently.

The Warlord's talk with God had not gone well, but he saw no need to share it with his lady. Maigrey had her own misgivings and inner doubts to wrestle and was just as willing

319

to confront them alone. Each was extraordinarily sensitive to the other's touch and, like wounded animals, they both kept hidden in the shadows of their own lairs.

The silence grew loud between them.

"I was told you haven't eaten anything all day," the Warlord said abruptly.

"I was told you haven't either, my lord."

Sagan was about to ask who told her, thought better of it. He knew the answer. His own guards were reporting on him to her now. "I was fasting."

"I wasn't hungry."

"I cannot afford to have you fall ill, my lady."

"When you need me, I will be there. I won't let you down, you know that—" Maigrey recalled suddenly a time when she *had* let him down. Or vice versa. She dropped the subject, and it seemed to fall with an ungodly crash that sent silent echoes reverberating around them.

Sagan rose to his feet. Placing his hands behind him, clasping them beneath the folds of the red cape, he stalked over to the steelglass viewscreen and stared outside. It was night and still raining, a slow, desultory drizzle. Laskar's lights shone as brightly as ever, more brightly, perhaps, reflecting off the clouds.

"We could not have saved the king—His Majesty had sentenced himself to death. But we could have saved Semele and the crown prince, Maigrey, *if* you and I had acted together."

She was up like a blaze of fire, on her feet, standing behind him. "You can't know that!"

"Oh, but I do." He turned, gazed remorselessly down at her. "And so do you."

Maigrey cut short the conversation with a swift knifelike gesture of her hand. "It's pointless to argue. What's past is past, over and done with. What matters is the present. You think Abdiel means to kill Dion, as he killed the others?"

"I do. The Blood Royal will always be a threat to him. He did his best to wipe them out years ago, those that he could reach."

"At least Dion's not dead yet. . . ."

"Of course not. Abdiel prefers to use live bait."

Maigrey shook her head. "I can sense Dion. I know he's alive, but he's indistinct, blurred in my mind. He's drawn very far away from me. From us," she amended belatedly.

"Abdiel's influence. You can imagine what the mind-seizer is doing to him."

"All the more reason to save him."

"First, my lady, it may be necessary to save ourselves. Dion isn't the only member of the Blood Royal the mind-seizer means to destroy. I was always too strong for him to dare to try to touch. He believed you to be dead. Now, the two of us are together again. What greater threat can there be *to* him? What greater opportunity *for* him?" Sagan paused. "We *are* together again, aren't we, my lady?"

Maigrey stirred uncomfortably. "It seems we have little choice—"

"Then take the oath."

"What?" She stared at him in astonishment, uncertain she heard right, the word ringing discordantly in her mind.

"The oath, Maigrey. Retake the oath."

She hesitated, considering, regarding him suspiciously. "What about John Dixter? What about Dion? No, there's too much between us—"

"The hell with Dion! The hell with John Dixter!" Sagan reached out, grasped her tightly, held her fast. "None of that is important now, Maigrey. This is between us—you and me. I learned something last night. Seventeen years ago we betrayed each other, and it wasn't because we didn't trust each other. We trusted too much—in something that wasn't there! Mind-linked, closer than any two beings can come, yet we didn't know each other. Our masters taught us to keep a part of ourselves to ourselves, for the sake of pride. Out of pride, we kept our true feelings—our doubts, our fears—hidden. And that was a mistake. It made us just like any two other humans—never what God intended us to be!"

Maigrey stared at him, caught and held by his words more than his hands.

Sagan drew a deep, shivering breath. "We each took an oath once, long ago—just words to us then. It's not surprising we broke what held little meaning for us. I'm asking you to retake the same oath now. But realize, Maigrey, as I do, that this time the oath will bind us fast. This time the oath will be forged out of steel that has been tempered in the fires—not of heaven, as it was in our youth, but of hell."

She shuddered. He felt her shudder, as though her body had been riven apart. Shaking her head, she tried to pull back away from him. "I can't! Not after . . . not after . . . everything. . . ."

"My lord." The captain's voice came over the commlink. "The two requesting to see you have arrived."

Sagan regarded Maigrey intently. Then he released her.

"Send them in," he said coldly, turning away from her.

Maigrey gathered herself together, picked up the broken pieces, and joined him—momentarily, at least—to meet their guests.

The door slid open, revealing a black-haired charmer in a sky-blue suit and a raincoated companion. Escorted into the Warlord's chambers by the Honor Guard, Raoul glided gracefully, the Little One shambled along behind.

"May night's shadows give you ease, my lady, my lord." Raoul bowed, hand over heart, to each.

"May the moon rise and shed light upon your path." Maigrey offered the proper response among Loti. "Won't you be seated?" But she remained standing, as did the Warlord.

Raoul was so excessively overcome at the lady's politeness and offer of hospitality that for many moments he soared amid flights of effusive gratitude. Maigrey and Sagan contained themselves patiently, waiting for him to descend and come to the point. He finally did so, declining an offer to be seated.

The Little One, on entering the room, resembled very much a man who has suddenly walked head-on into an invisible steelglass wall. The large, bright eyes darted from lord to lady and back again, then narrowed in exasperation.

Raoul, indicating his companion with a fluttering gesture, remarked, "The Little One is considerably impressed at your skill in thwarting his empathic abilities. But then, of course, you are Guardians. The last of the Guardians."

The steelglass wall quivered slightly, but did not fall, though the muscles of Sagan's right hand twitched involuntarily and Lady Maigrey curled her fingers in upon themselves.

"I don't suppose you came here to inform us of that," the Warlord said.

"No, no. Please forgive me. The pleasure of meeting the two of you has rendered me quite overcome. I will hasten on to the purpose of my visit. My lord Derek Sagan"—Raoul bowed—"has received an invitation to Snaga Ohme's Event and has been kind enough to accept. My employer, Snaga

Ohme, is honored, my lord, to think that, once again, your presence will grace his humble dwelling."

"The honor is mine in being invited," Sagan returned, but the ice in his voice chilled the polite effect of his rejoinder.

Raoul bowed again and turned to face the lady. The eyes of the Little One finally focused upon her, never left her, perhaps seeing a tiny crack in the glass. "My employer, Snaga Ohme, regrets exceedingly that he was unaware of the lady's true identity when she last graced his abode. He fears his hospitality on that occasion was deficient—"

"He tried to have me killed," observed Maigrey, smiling pleasantly.

Raoul was astonished, appeared likely never to recover from the shock. "Word has reached the ears of my employer, Snaga Ohme, that you believe the foul calumny heaped upon his defenseless head. Snaga Ohme respectfully reminds her ladyship that Laskar is notorious for its bandits and he wishes only to add his sublime joy over the fact that the lady emerged from her terrifying encounter safe and whole. The lady walks with God."

"And carries a beam rifle," Sagan said coolly. "But please continue."

Raoul's glittering purple eyes danced in amusement. "Yes. Quite true. However, in order to make amends for his deficiencies as a host, my employer, Snaga Ohme, has issued an invitation to the Lady Maigrey Morianna to grace his Event with her presence." The Loti, with a flourish, proffered a small silver ball.

"I would be honored." Maigrey accepted the silver ball, laid it down upon a table, forced it to stay down when it would have risen.

"It is my employer, Snaga Ohme, who is honored, my lady. And now, regrettable that it is to introduce talk of business into anticipation of pleasure, my employer, Snaga Ohme, begs to inform the lady that he would appreciate the prompt return of his property. It is a request with which he is certain she will delight in complying since that property was—undoubtedly quite unintentionally on my lady's part—fraudulently obtained."

"Fraudulently!" Maigrey repeated. "What does he mean by *fraudulently*? He has the starjewel—"

"Ah, my lady." Raoul seemed to retreat before her anger; the empath nearly shriveled up into a ball. "Do not give way to hostile feelings. Snaga Ohme has no doubt her ladyship meant well. But the starjewel, you see, has proven worthless."

"You don't expect me to believe—"

"My lady," Raoul interposed gently, "the starjewel has gone black as coal."

The Little One, eyes on Maigrey, flinched visibly and uttered a small gasp of pain. Maigrey said nothing, made no sound, no movement.

"My lady cannot be held responsible for that," Sagan said. He was startled to feel her ice-chill fingers dig into his flesh like talons, gripping his wrist for support. "The jewel's value is not diminished—"

"A matter of opinion," Raoul suggested delicately. "The jewel is now an object most unlovely to look upon. Indeed, my employer, Snaga Ohme, has discovered that he cannot stand to be around it. He hastens through the room where it is kept to avoid the sight of it. Snaga Ohme was wounded by the fraud, but he bids me say that he has forgiven her ladyship and he will be most happy to return the jewel to the lady if she will return his property to him."

"And you may tell your employer, Snaga Ohme, that her ladyship will see him burn in hell first." Sagan touched the controls, opened the door, summoned the guard with a gesture. "And now I think that you had better leave. Your companion appears to have been taken ill."

The Little One was doubled over in agony, but the large eyes remained fastened upon Maigrey, a gleam of exultation visible through the pain.

"I feel it only right to inform you that my employer, Snaga Ohme, does not take kindly to threats." Raoul grasped hold of his companion's coat collar, seemingly prepared to haul him off bodily.

"I never make threats," Sagan returned, "only promises. My regards to your employer. Inform him that the lady and I will both be pleased to attend his Event."

"May your repose be blessed," the Loti remarked pleasantly, his current state of drug-induced euphoria apparently impossible to upset.

"May yours be eternal!" Sagan muttered, slamming his hand down irritably on the door's operational controls.

Maigrey remained standing near him, her hand grasping the Warlord's arm tightly. She did not look at him. She did not speak. There was no need. He understood. Her soul was laid bare, slashed wide open.

Slowly, she unclenched her fingers, released her hold. Sagan, glancing down, saw four livid marks on his battle-scarred skin, the imprint of her pain. She turned and left him, walking steadily, but moving blindly as one who travels in the thick shadow.

"My lady," the Warlord said. "The night of the revolution, I took the starjewel from around my neck and placed it in its rosewood box. I have it still."

She ceased walking, but did not turn around, stared straight ahead, into the night.

"Maigrey," the Warlord continued quietly. "My starjewel is black. It darkened that evening."

"Is that supposed to comfort me, my lord?"

"Our bond has been forged in the fires of hell. Take the oath."

Maigrey glanced back at him, smiled wanly. "'*Fortune rota volviture; descendo minoaratus . . .*' The wheel of fortune turns; dishonored I fall from grace.'" She looked at him straight on, gray eyes meeting his, no trace of color, of life, anywhere in her. "I will take the oath, my lord."

She left him.

Sagan took no notice of her leaving. He should have been exulting in his victory. The oath would bind them fast. What he wanted, she would want. Thinking and acting as one. Yes, he had been victorious. But Maigrey had managed to rob him of his pleasure.

Her quote had been from *Carmina Burana*, the songs of the medieval goliards. He had not thought of the songs in a long time, and they came back to him now, suddenly, darkening his heart, the voice of the oracle, speaking words of ill omen. He repeated to himself, softly, the closing verse.

"'*Quod per sortem sternit fortem, mecum omnes plangite!*'

"'And since by fate the strong are overthrown, weep ye all with me.'"

Chapter ·····❖····· Four

Questa notte nessun dorma!
This night let no one sleep!
> Giacomo Puccini, *Turandot*

Innumerable dazzling new stars lit Laskar's night sky once the storm clouds had rumbled past. Snaga Ohme's guests were arriving for the Event, and their various shuttlecraft and orbiting ships and planes traced fiery trails across the heavens. Local air and space traffic control was jammed, but they were accustomed, every year, to handling the influx and only the usual amount of crashes and near-misses resulted.

All major luxury hotels, designed for both human and alien species, were booked solid and had been for a year, there being always those who preferred a cramped room with an inadequate supply of towels to the more comfortable but less exotic quarters of their own shuttlecraft. Prefab homes sprang up like fungi after the rains. RV lots were filled to capacity. The locals all turned out, during the mild Laskarian evenings, to stroll about and gape at the fabulous, gleaming spacecraft, the elaborately uniformed guards, the incredibly beautiful mistresses and/or paramours belonging to the galaxy's rich and powerful.

President of the Galactic Democratic Republic Peter Robes did not attend, though he was annually invited. Ohme's Event was not an officially sanctioned function and Robes preferred to keep himself aloof, which always looked good in the press. The President never failed, during the Event, to visit a children's hospital on some impoverished planet and have his photo taken with a young alien, preferably of the small, cute, and fur-bearing variety. His citizen generals were in attendance, however, as well as numerous members of Congress.

In addition came monarchs, military leaders, corporate

heads from all sectors. During the night prior to the Event, the rich and the beautiful and powerful graced the streets of Laskar, a veritable walking encyclopedia of anybody who was anybody. Security, provided by both Snaga Ohme and the city of Laskar, was extremely tight. Tourists were not permitted on Laskar during this time. Of the press, only those commentators with the highest ratings were invited to attend, along with their 'droid reporters and camera crews.

Monarchs and generals at war with other monarchs and generals (and there were many, given the current political turmoil in the galaxy) were often forced into close proximity, either on the street where it was fashionable to take the Laskarian air or at the numerous private parties and gala balls given on the eve of the Event. The warring enemies passed by each other with icy disdain, each affecting not to acknowledge the other's existence. If trouble flared, as it sometimes did among the more hotheaded, brawls were instantly quelled by Ohme's watchful security force, the combatants separated and taken away to cool off.

Generally these outbursts consisted of little more than a barrage of shouted insults and a flurry of gloves tossed contemptuously into faces, but occasionally more serious incidents occurred, as when, seven years prior, the chairman of the board of Allied Galactic Steelglass shot dead the corporate head of Allied Galactic Plastisteel during the soup course at a dinner given by the famous actress Madam Natasa Holoscova. Ever since, party hostesses spent long hours agonizing over their guest lists, scanning the latest computer records to determine who was currently at war with whom and making certain that, if combatants were inadvertently invited to the same party, they were at least seated well out of each other's range.

Military units stationed at Fort Laskar took no part in the proceedings, leaving matters of security, traffic, and crowd control in the capable hands of the Laskarian officials, augmented by the private forces of Snaga Ohme. It was natural, however, that the base should go on alert, considering the number of dignitaries present on the planet and the potential for trouble.

The Warlord did not attend any of the many glittering social functions leading up to the Event, though when it became known that the hero of the Corasian invasion was on Laskar, he was much in demand. The guards at Fort Laskar's main gate turned away a steady stream of liveried, invitation-bearing servants.

Sagan remained on base, inaccessible except to the briga- dier general, with whom the Warlord spent an unusual amount of time. Alert status had quietly been upgraded from yellow to red. The base was sealed off to outsiders. All leaves were canceled. Few in Fort Laskar knew precisely what was going on. But it was easy to guess. From the numbers of troops being mobilized and the equipment they were being issued, the soldiers of Fort Laskar were preparing for some sort of jungle assault. That made it easier still to guess their target, though there were many grim mutterings to the effect that it was impregnable.

Sagan's only other visitor, and the only outsider permitted on the base, was the assassin with the operatic name.

Maigrey and Sagan had neither seen each other nor com- municated in any way since they had parted the night they'd received the invitation. The Warlord had been too busy. The lady had been indisposed. She had borrowed several books from Brigadier General Haupt and shut herself up in her room.

His lordship, when he inquired what her ladyship was reading, was told—much to his disquiet—a book of the collected poems of William Butler Yeats.

Sagan was up late the night Sparafucile arrived to make his report. The Warlord had been studying aerial recon maps of Snaga Ohme's estate, but had long since abandoned his work. Sitting, pondering, he was thinking of Maigrey's choice of reading material. Yeats. He didn't like it. She had probed more deeply into his mind, perhaps, than he had realized or intended. He was half-considering confronting her when the officer on night watch reported the arrival of the assassin.

"Send him in."

Silent as a stalking cat, Sparafucile slid through the door, moving instinctively to melt into the shadows of the Warlord's room until the door was shut and sealed behind him.

"Well?" the Warlord demanded abruptly. "I haven't heard from you." He was tired and irritated at being tired.

"There has been nothing to say, Sagan Lord." Sparafucile stepped into the light, shrugged.

"Abdiel has had no visitors?"

"Only those I tell you before, Sagan Lord. The creatures of Snaga Ohme."

"And the boy?"

"He is with him, Sagan Lord."

"The mercenary and the woman?"

"Them, too, Sagan Lord. But I think they are prisoners, not guests."

The Warlord interrogated him with a glance.

"My instruments show two life-forms always in one place in the same part of house."

"Interesting. I have no doubt you are right. They're not dead?"

"Instrument readings indicate two warm bodies. Sometimes the bodies grow very warm," Sparafucile added with a leering grin. "They find interesting way to pass the time, eh?"

Sagan pointedly ignored this last salacious intimation. Tapping on his desk with a crooked forefinger, he considered the assassin's more pertinent information. "Of course, Abdiel would keep Tusca alive because the boy would know if his friend died. But when Dion is gone . . . or otherwise distracted . . . say, the night of the Event . . ." The Warlord extended his finger, traced a minus sign on the metal. "A pity," he said coolly. "Tusca was an adequate warrior. Something might have been made of him. But he has only his father and the lady to thank."

The Warlord shook himself out of his preoccupation, returned his gaze to the assassin. "Anything else?"

Sparafucile hesitated. "It may be nothing, Sagan Lord, but someone in the house is"—the assassin spread his hands to indicate a guess—"target shooting."

"Target shooting?" The Warlord frowned, stared at him. "How do you know?"

"Don't know, for certain, Sagan Lord. Instrument readings indicate bursts of energy occurring at intervals in lower part of house. Always same place, but different times during day and night."

"It's not a machine of some sort?"

Sparafucile indicated, by a wiggling of his hands, that the Warlord's conjecture was as good as his.

"Target shooting," Sagan reflected aloud. "That presents some interesting possibilities. Continue monitoring, my friend, and inform me through the commlink of any other developments. There will be no more reports in person from now on, Sparafucile. Matters grow too critical. I don't want you to let Abdiel out of your sight."

"Yes, Sagan Lord. I see soldiers on base ready to march, perhaps?"

"You have very good eyes, my friend. Sometimes it might be better to keep them shut, like your mouth."

Sparafucile winked, grinned, and nodded his misshapen head in acquiescence.

"The Event takes place tomorrow night." The Warlord placed the tips of the fingers of both hands together, finalizing his plans. "Abdiel's space shuttle is near the house, I presume? His ship in orbit around the planet?"

"Yes, Sagan Lord."

"The shuttle is guarded by the mind-dead?"

"Yes, Sagan Lord."

"You can handle the mind-dead, can't you, my friend?"

Sparafucile's lips parted, showing sharp-edged, felinelike teeth.

"Very well. Your task will be to prevent Abdiel from fleeing this planet. He will attempt to do so on the night of the Event. How you are to manage this, I leave to you, Sparafucile—"

"I blow him up, then, Sagan Lord."

"No, you fool!" The Warlord's patience cracked beneath his weariness and the strain. He regained control of himself almost immediately. "He may have the boy with him. You will merely keep him grounded until I arrive to deal with him. Do you understand?"

"Not altogether, Sagan Lord—"

"Do you understand what you are supposed to do?"

"Oh, yes, Sagan Lord."

"Return to your post." The Warlord rose, flexed his aching shoulder muscles, rubbed his back.

Sparafucile glided out the door. Pausing as it opened, he turned to inquire, "How is lady?"

"I can't think why her health would be any business of yours."

"You tell lady Sparafucile sends regards." The assassin leered.

"I'll pass that along," Sagan said dryly, "between poetry readings." He paused. "Oh, my friend. If the occasion arises and you can do so without jeopardizing your mission, assist the mercenary Tusca to escape. Then bring him to me."

"What if he not want to come?"

"I said, bring him to me."

"Yes, Sagan Lord."

The Warlord shut the door, hearing as he did so the rhythmic tramp of the centurions arriving to escort the assassin off the base. Sagan was ready for his bed, but he stood long moments in the darkness lit only by the faint night-glow of various instruments and computer screens.

"Target shooting," he repeated to himself, frowning, not liking the inexplicable. He turned it over in his mind, considering. No answers came to him, however, and finally he put the matter aside, put thoughts of rest aside, and continued his work.

···◁■ ■▷···

"Well, what do you think of it?" the mind-seizer asked.

"I'm . . . not sure," Dion admitted.

He held in his hands what appeared to be four small round metal disks, each with a crystal inside, one large metal, crystal-bearing disk, and a small tube that fit inside the palm of his hand. "What is it?"

"A weapon. The gun you will use to kill the Warlord."

"A gun?" Dion appeared skeptical.

"Precisely. These metal disks are cumulators," Abdiel explained. "You place the cumulators on various parts of your body—two on your breast, two at your waist, and one—the largest—over your sternum. When activated by a signal from the gun, each cumulator sends a beam of laser light into the tube in your hand. The tube collects the five beams and concentrates them into one extraordinarily lethal beam that will destroy anything at which you are aiming."

"This . . . this is what I'm to use to kill . . ." Dion left the sentence hanging, studied the gun, trying to appear vastly knowledgeable. "But how do we sneak this into the Adonian's house? Won't his security monitors detect it?"

"His monitors would if the cumulators were activated. But when you enter his house, Your Majesty, the cumulators will be completely drained. Ohme will detect nothing except metal and crystals—your jewelry, my king. The tube you hold now will be encased in a different setting—it will be made to look like a belt buckle."

"But then, how do I charge the . . . the cumulators?"

"The same way you charge the bloodsword, Dion. With your body and your mind."

"Really? Can I? That's incredible!"

"Isn't it," Abdiel remarked coolly. "When the time is right, you have simply to concentrate your thoughts upon the cumulators, which have been designed to work with the particular genetic characteristics of the Blood Royal. Position them over the main nerve bundles in your body, and when you direct your mental energies on them, they will absorb that energy and activate. You have then only to aim and fire."

"Aim and fire!" Dion repeated, studying the gun admiringly.

"You will notice, when you practice firing the gun, that you will feel a warm spot on your skin directly opposite the end of the weapon. A protective coating covers the back of the weapon, prevents the laser beam from doing you any harm. The beam is so powerful, however, that its heat seeps through. Do not be alarmed by it."

"No, no, I won't." Dion barely heard. He was preoccupied in positioning the cumulators on his body.

"You will have no trouble entering the Adonian's," Abdiel continued, "but I must warn you that Ohme has sensors planted throughout his mansion. Once you charge the cumulators, you must act swiftly, or his men will detect you. If you keep to our plan, you should have no trouble luring the Warlord to you."

"No trouble at all!" Dion said, with a flash of exultation. He sobered a moment later, however. "But what about the Lady Maigrey? She mustn't be around—"

"I will answer for the Lady Maigrey," Abdiel said mildly. "Of that, my king, you may rest assured."

A target range was set up in the lower level of the prefab house; the mind-dead removed the collapsible walls to several boxlike rooms and opened them into one long rectangular area. Dion practiced firing the gun at intervals during the day, working an hour or so at a time. In his intense, grim eagerness, he would have worked longer and harder. But Abdiel cautioned against the young man becoming overfatigued, blunting his sharp edge.

Dion arranged the five cumulators over his body for what seemed like millions of times, practiced directing his mental energies toward them. He could have done it in his sleep. He knew because he *had* done it in his sleep—in his dreams, at least—every night since Abdiel had given him the weapon and instructed him in its design, its use. Every night, in his dreams, he used the gun to kill the Warlord.

Down in the target range, on the evening before the Event,

Dion showed off his newly acquired skill for Abdiel and Mikael.

"I can activate the cumulators in only a few moments," he informed them, demonstrating. "Like this. And then—"

Lifting the gun in one smooth, rapid motion, he aimed at his target and fired. The target was a hologram of a man—a tall man with broad shoulders clad in full body armor and helm decorated with the phoenix rising from the flames.

The shot went through the mouth, the one place left unprotected by the man's helm. "Watch this," Dion said. "Mikael, set the target moving."

Mikael did as he was instructed. The hologram began to dodge. Dion turned his back, spun around, and fired, hitting his mark exactly. The target bobbed and weaved defensively. The young man crouched and jumped and hit it solidly from every conceivable angle. Mikael at last shut the target off. Dion, panting, looked at Abdiel. The mind-seizer nodded in satisfaction.

"Excellent, my king. Remarkable, in fact. You are drawing upon the power of the Blood Royal, the power they told you you couldn't handle. An excellent irony. You will use the talent the Warlord denied you to kill him. Mikael, take the gun."

"But I want to keep it with me," Dion protested. "I have to practice. I think I can cut down my time—"

"You are quite fast enough now, Dion. Faster than Mikael. You should rest, my king. Tomorrow night will be a momentous occasion in your life. You must be ready."

Dion was ready to argue, the sensual lips pursed in the stubborn pout that made him resemble his late uncle.

"Good night, Dion," Abdiel hinted.

The young man handed the gun to the disciple with an ill grace and left them, another of the mind-dead appearing on silent command to escort him to his room.

Mikael and Abdiel remained standing in the target range, waiting patiently, hearing the boy's footsteps move far away.

Abdiel reached into the robes that encircled his body, withdrew from the winding-sheet folds another gun.

"Identical," Mikael said, holding the two, one in each hand, comparing them.

"Almost," Abdiel amended. He retrieved the gun Dion had been using and hid it securely in the folds of his robe. "Take this to him just prior to our leaving. Don't give him time to examine it closely. It's difficult to discern the difference, but an astute eye, studying the gun at leisure, could tell."

"How certain are you that he will do this deed, master? It is one thing to shoot at a hologram, another to kill a living man."

"He will. His mind crawls with jealousy, fear, the desire for vengeance. He's killed before this, too. Much as the murder horrified him, he felt secretly exhilarated by the idea of having power over life and death. Besides, what young man does not dream of destroying his father and marrying his mother?"

"His mother, master? I thought his mother was dead—"

"I will explain the concept to you another time, my dear. I am not at leisure to discuss Freudian psychology."

"Yes, master. What about the prisoners?"

"Have them executed," Abdiel said casually, "but not until after we have left for the Event. By then, if the boy senses Tusca's death at all, he will be too excited and keyed up to fully assimilate it."

"I understand, my master."

"Disassemble the house and have my shuttlecraft prepared for lift-off. This planet will be in chaos and, when I return with the bomb, I want to be able to leave immediately."

Mikael bowed in acknowledgment and left to make the necessary arrangements.

Abdiel wended his way back to his sauna. It was nearly time for his bedtime snack—four pills and an injection. After that, an early period of sleep. Tomorrow night's work promised to be strenuous, mentally and physically draining. He would be exhausted for days afterward.

I must look past that, he counseled himself, look to the rewards, the compensations.

Abdiel composed his body on the sofa, lifted the hookah's pipe, and put it between his lips. He summoned up a vision of the boy lying on his bed, hands beneath his head, expending an enormous amount of energy attempting to relax.

"A momentous occasion, my king," Abdiel reiterated, sucking on the pipe. "The most momentous in your life." He drew the smoke into his lungs, spoke to the wisps that curled out of his mouth. "Your death."

··◅■ ■▻··

Dion lay upon the bed, fidgeted and twitched. He knew he should rest, but he couldn't get comfortable. His supper sat untasted on the table in his room. He had tried to eat, but he was so tense the food wouldn't go past the tightening of his throat.

Abdiel had seen inside Dion clearly. The young man could, at this moment, have killed Derek Sagan with the cold-blooded efficiency and dispassion of a professional terminator. In his mind, Dion had moved beyond the murder. The deed was finished, over and done. And it left him standing at the edge of a void.

What would he have accomplished? The removal of his greatest enemy, certainly. The freeing of Lady Maigrey, the ability to rescue John Dixter. But had it taken him one step toward his real, ultimate goal? Had it taken him one step nearer the throne? No, not if things went as Abdiel had them planned.

"And who is he to tell me what to do?" Dion asked himself, sitting up on the edge of the bed. "I'm grateful to him, of course. Without him, I would never have known the truth. But I am king, not Abdiel. And though all kings have their advisers, I'm the one who must make the final decision.

"And I've made it," he announced softly. "I've considered the matter as Platus taught me. I've set the weights in the scale of balance. I know that there are risks to what I plan, but the benefits outweigh them, cause the scale to tip in my favor. Tomorrow night, the most powerful people in the galaxy will be assembled together. I might never have this chance again."

He stared at the five marks on his palm. Abdiel had hinted that he wanted to bond with the boy again, but Dion—remembering all too clearly Tusk's look of shock and revulsion—had pretended not to understand. It had been worth the pain once, to know the truth. But never again. And he would continue to be careful, as he had been for the past few days, to keep the fortress of his mind guarded and secure.

Abdiel might approve what I intend to do, but then again, he might not. I don't want to waste my time, Dion told himself, in pointless arguments.

The truth was that he wanted to take everyone completely by surprise.

···◄■ ■►···

"*Turning and turning in the widening gyre*
The falcon cannot hear the falconer;
Things fall apart; the center cannot hold . . ."

Maigrey paused, and sighed. She had found what she sought. She knew it; the words seemed to spring out of the page as if they'd been printed in red ink, as if dipped in blood.

She should really, she supposed, slip over to the spaceplane and run a simulation. But that would take energy, energy she didn't have. Disrupting the electrical system, forcing open the door, dealing with the centurions both here and those guarding the spaceplane. And all for what? For proving to herself what she already knew.

Maigrey closed the slender volume of poetry, placed it on a shelf. Lying down on her bed, she sought vainly for sleep.

Chapter ·◆>◐◑◐<◆· *Five*

He shall have his fine armor, and every man that sets eyes
on it shall be amazed. I wish I could hide him from death
as easily . . .

  Homer, *The Iliad*, translation by W. H. D. Rouse

Maigrey sat before a mirror in her chambers aboard the
Warlord's shuttlecraft. Brushing her hair, she gazed at her
reflection and it seemed to her as if she had become her
reflection—hard, smooth, cold.

The starjewel was gone, lost to her forever. She might get
it back . . . she *would* get it back (she reminded herself to
think positively) this night. She *had* to. It was the only way to
save John Dixter. But its fire had gone out. Once she imagined
her star would go nova, explode in a brilliant fiery ball, its
death visible to countless generations for light-years after. But
no. Her star had imploded, sunk in upon itself, become a small
dark spot, lost in the vast darkness.

She had failed everyone, it seemed: Sagan, Semele, John
Dixter, Dion. Now add to that list two more: herself and God.
Her intentions had been good. . . . What was it they said?
The road to hell is paved that way. Or did she have the right
to comfort herself with even that poor excuse?

No, Maigrey had to admit it. Her own ambition led her
down this road. She should not curse the darkness when she
herself had blown out the light.

And what of the future? She saw no future. She could see
nothing at all. Though she might grope her way forward, it was
like being trapped in a maze. Reaching out blindly in all
directions, she found herself continually running up against a
blank wall.

Listlessly, she threw down her hairbrush, turned away from
the mirror. She had better start dressing. On the bed lay an

337

evening gown borrowed from some soldier on the base. The
dress wasn't particularly well made or becoming. But it would
do. . . .

A knock on her door interrupted her.

Odd. Sagan usually didn't bother to knock. She unsealed
the door, opened it. The centurion, Marcus, stood at respectful attention.

"My lady, would you come to Lord Sagan's quarters for a
moment?"

Maigrey stared at the man, puzzled. What an unusual
message. Not the formal *His lordship's compliments, and
would you attend him in his quarters?* or even the more
peremptory and impatient *Come to me at once*, as he had been
known to use upon urgent occasion.

"Did his lordship send for me?" she asked.

"If you would come, my lady," Marcus said.

Maigrey shrugged and followed. Entering the Warlord's
quarters, she saw Sagan standing by a far window gazing out
over the base. He looked around at her arrival but let her
know, by his manner and the impenetrable gravity of his
expression, that he held himself aloof from the proceedings.

She turned from him to find the members of the Honor
Guard, drawn up in a line before her. Marcus was apparently
their spokesman, for he saluted her, then said solemnly, "My
lady, we would like to present you with a gift."

Maigrey blinked, startled. The polite response came to her
by instinct through her blank amazement. "I would be honored," she murmured. She cast a quick glance at Sagan. He
had his back to her, his hands clasped behind him.

The centurions parted ranks, moving with stiff precision.
Maigrey had regained her composure, shaken off her surprise.
Expecting roses, perhaps, or a pendant with the regiment's
number and motto engraved upon the back, she was prepared
to be touched and properly grateful.

She was not prepared to be shattered, dazzled.

"This is for you, my lady."

On a form standing at the end of the row of men was
displayed a suit of armor. It was almost an exact copy of the
Warlord's gold and adamantine ceremonial armor. Greaves,
bracers, breastplate, white-feather-crested helm, leather
gauntlets—all were identical to his, yet these had been cast in
a feminine mold and were made of silver instead of gold. A
floor-length cape of royal blue trimmed in swan'sdown hung

from the shoulders, attached by jeweled stars. The Warlord's breastplate was decorated with the image of the phoenix; the breastplate of the silver armor was adorned with an eight-pointed star.

Maigrey saw this much before tears flooded her eyes, transforming the armor into a shining silver blur. She couldn't speak, for the ache in her throat, and was grateful to Marcus for talking to cover for her weakness. And she was aware, confusedly, of Sagan's being almost as shocked and over-whelmed by the sight as she herself.

"Will you accept this gift, my lady? It is presented by us, the men of his lordship's guard, with his lordship's permission and sanction in honor of your valor during the encounter with the Corasians."

His lordship's sanction. Then why the devil was Sagan staring at the armor as if it were being worn by a ghost? Maigrey, mastering her tears, could see him now from the corner of her eye. He had moved forward, almost uncon-sciously, and his face was grim and dark and shadowed.

"This is beyond . . . I am more honored than . . . I can't tell you how much . . ." Words failed her, but it was obvious, by the expressions on the faces of the men, that she didn't need to say anything.

"Thank you, gentlemen," Sagan stated abruptly. "You have pleased her ladyship exceedingly. And now I must ask you to return to your duties."

The centurions filed out, Maigrey doing her best to thank each personally with a silent look of gratitude and a smile. They could never know how much this meant. Stumbling through her own personal darkness, she'd unexpectedly walked into a halo of silver light. When they were gone, she hurried to inspect the armor, eager to touch the cool strong metal, study more closely what she could tell by sight was fine-quality workmanship.

The Warlord stepped in front of her, blocked her way. "Don't wear it, my lady. Don't put it on."

"You can't be serious!" Maigrey glared at him, angry, affronted. "Of course I'll wear it! I can't in honor refuse it. It's a gift. And besides, I *want* to wear it—"

"It isn't a gift, my lady. It has a price."

"I should have guessed as much." Maigrey drew herself up, regarded him with a cool, imperious air. "Name it."

"Your life," he said gravely.

He wasn't being smug; he wasn't blustering or threatening. He was serious, regarding her with a composed, steady intensity that was disconcerting, terrifying.

"I don't understand." The darkness was closing in around her again.

"I have foreseen your death, my lady, at my hands. I told you this, aboard *Phoenix*."

She nodded, vaguely remembering something of the sort.

"Lady, in that vision, you are wearing silver armor. *That* armor." He pointed.

"You ordered it. . . ."

"No!" His denial was vehement. "The men told me what they wanted to do. It did morale no harm and was a logical, practical suggestion. I gave them my sanction, gave the orders needed to get the job done. To be perfectly honest, my lady," he added impatiently, "I took little interest in the project. I had far more important matters on my mind."

Maigrey pushed him aside, moved around him to see the armor. The metal gleamed, shone with a silvery radiance. She drew near, reached out and lifted the helm, smoothing the white feathery crest with her hands. Strong, yet lightweight, the helm was fashioned after Sagan's, covering the top part of the face. Yet she noticed a subtle difference. Hers had been designed, most subtly and delicately, to cover the scar on her cheek.

A tear dropped on the shining surface. She brushed it away swiftly, lest it should spot the metal.

"What are you saying, my lord?"

"That if you accept this armor, you accept your own doom."

Maigrey looked up at him suddenly, swiftly. "And yours!"

"Yes," he said, after a moment's silence, "and mine."

"We have no choice?"

"There *is* a choice, my lady. Cast the armor aside. Throw it away."

"And you would counsel me, out of fear, to renounce this gift that was given to me for my valor?"

"That would be the wisest course, my lady."

"But not the most honorable." Maigrey pondered not her decision—she knew in her heart what that must be—but her reason for it. "I have cast too much aside already, my lord. I thought, in fact, I had nothing left. But I find that I do have one thing remaining to me." She raised her eyes, smiling. "'He shall have his fine armor, and every man that sets eyes on it shall be amazed.'"

"This armor doesn't come from the forge of the gods as did Achilles' armor, my lady," the Warlord said dryly.

Maigrey lightly fluffed the white feathers of the crest, watched them drift softly through the air. "Perhaps it did, my lord," she murmured. "You never know." She replaced the helm on its stand, turned to face Sagan. "And now, my lord, tonight's plan—"

"—does not concern you, my lady. You're not going."

"I'm not." Her voice was calm, flat, like the sea before a hurricane.

"No, you are not."

"And where is the prison built that can hold me, my lord? Where are the walls I can't walk through, if I choose? Where are the men to guard me whose minds I can't turn to butter—"

"Damn it! It's for your own good, Maigrey! It's far too dangerous for you. Remember, my lady, Abdiel wants Dion and me dead. You . . . he wants alive."

"And so do you, my lord. And for the same reason." She came near him, stared up at him. "I *am* going. You can't stop me. I lost the starjewel. I will get it back. I abandoned Dion. I'll do what I can to save him. These are *my* responsibilities. My dying is a risk *you* will have to run, my lord."

"It is not your death that concerns me, my lady. Abdiel has little use for people who are dead."

Maigrey paled, but she remained firm, resolute.

Sagan regarded her with exasperation, then turned away. He strode angrily back to the window, stared out at the base, which had erupted into bustling activity. Troops were mobilizing, hovercraft taking to the air, planes thundering low over the tarmac before swooping into the green Laskarian twilight.

"You will be responsible for acquiring the starjewel, my lady," he said at last.

"Yes, my lord." Her voice was cold and knife-edged.

"And talk to the boy, do what you can to make him understand his danger."

"That will be difficult, my lord."

"It may be impossible," Sagan snapped, watching the organized chaos, seeing very little of what was transpiring. "It's a dangerous game we'll be playing tonight, my lady. If you insist upon playing it."

Ignoring his last comment, she moved nearer him, laid her hand upon his arm. "We could eliminate Abdiel immediately, when we first arrive. Together, we could do it."

"I considered that," the Warlord said, drawing away from

her touch. "But we can't kill Abdiel while he still maintains a
hold on Dion. There's a possibility he could control the boy
from beyond."

"After death? That's ludicrou—" Maigrey began, then bit
her tongue, remembering her brother's ghost appearing to
her. But she couldn't believe Sagan was all that afraid of spirits.
No, there was much more to this game than he was letting on.
The base on full alert, people and equipment mobilizing,
obviously preparing for an assault. Surely he knew he couldn't
take the Adonian's fortress! What did he have in mind? She
tried to enter his thoughts, found them locked, barred,
shuttered against her.

She was suddenly aware of his mind approaching hers and
she immediately slammed and bolted her door. Yes, she would
insist on playing this game. She was planning a few surprise
moves of her own.

"What do we do about Abdiel?" she persisted.

"What we can."

"But if he leaves and takes Dion with him—"

"He won't leave, my lady," Sagan said flatly. "That has been
arranged."

"The ubiquitous Sparafucile, no doubt. He's good, but
Abdiel is far better."

"Sparafucile knows his limits, as do I."

"And so, in essence, my lord, we have no strategy tonight."

"On the contrary, my lady, *my* strategy is perfectly laid out
and prepared."

"You won't tell me?"

"Since when does the commander need to explain his battle
plan to his troops?" Sagan returned with bitter irony. "You
have your orders, *Major*."

"Yes, I have my orders," Maigrey retorted. "But forgive me
if I don't particularly trust you, *Commander*!"

"Forgive, my lady? No, I won't forgive! You betrayed me
once—"

Maigrey turned on her heel, headed for the door.

"Walk out, my lady, and you lose everything! Including
your precious king!"

Her back stiff and rigid, she halted. But she did not turn
around, did not look at him. "What would you have me do, my
lord?"

"If you insist on going tonight, I insist that you take the
oath."

"Which will work to *your* advantage!"

"Perhaps. Perhaps not. Certainly it is a risk *you* should take, my lady."

Maigrey struggled with her anger, paused to consider calmly, rationally, what she should do. She recalled the words of the oath. Yes, it could work to help her, especially if she found herself in trouble. And if not, if all went well and she acquired the starjewel and the boy, the oath gave her room to maneuver.

"Very well, my lord."

She meant to speak coldly, but she had the sudden, frightening impression that the solid bulkhead of the shuttle-craft was falling away from her, that the world was falling away from her, that she was shrinking and shriveling, becoming something small and insignificant and that—tiny and fragile and helpless as she was—she found herself cowering in the presence of a Being terrible and awful in Its divine majesty.

She sank to her knees, and whether it was out of reverence or because her body lacked the strength to stand, she couldn't tell. The Warlord knelt across from her, bending his tall body gracefully, more accustomed to the gesture. But it seemed to her as if he, too, was acting under constraint. Looking into his face, Maigrey saw the Presence and she saw his anger and the battle against it.

God has not abandoned us, after all, she thought, awed and frightened. Perhaps that had just been wishful thinking. If we speak these words now, He will hear and accept our oath and bind us in chains of adamant, forged in the fires of both heaven and hell.

Choice. Yes, we have a choice. We could rise up and walk away and no lightning bolt would blast us, no thunder would split the heavens. Our souls' light—this tiny, feeble candle flame in the universe that, nonetheless, shines brightly as a star in the sight of our Creator, will flicker and dwindle and die.

Two together must walk the paths of darkness to reach the light. So went the prophecy, given when we were young.

What a fool I was to think we'd already walked it! What a fool I was to rail against God for making such dreadful, tragic blunders. Maybe they weren't blunders. It wasn't God who failed us. It was we who failed God. Now He is giving us a second chance.

"Raise your right hand, my lady." Sagan's voice, angry and defiant.

Maigrey understood and could pity him. She had been offered a choice. He, who had made his choice long ago, had been chastised for it, reminded of his duty. Maigrey raised her right hand and held it, palm outward.

Sagan raised his hand, palm outward, the five marks of the bloodsword clearly visible.

"Maigrey Morianna, I hold your life dearer to me than my own. I hold your honor dear to me as my own. This I pledge before the witness of Almighty God." He moved his hand closer to hers.

Maigrey spoke the vow and each word burned itself into her heart. "Derek Sagan, I hold your life dearer to me than my own. I hold your honor dear to me as my own. This I pledge before the witness of Almighty God."

She moved her hand closer to his. Their palms touched; the scars of the wounds pressed together. His fingers closed over hers in a crushing grasp that seemed desperate for the warmth and touch of human contact. She held on to him tightly, no less grateful, and the two remained on their knees, holding each other fast until the Presence left and they knew themselves, once again, alone.

They stared at each other, aware of chill fingers and aching wrists and arms. Each let loose the other's hand, knowing they weren't really letting loose, knowing they couldn't let loose.

"Well," she said, trying to banish a tremor in her voice, "where does this leave us, my lord?"

"My lady, I have no idea," he answered grimly. Rising to his feet, he walked over to the door to his private sleeping quarters, slammed his hand against the controls. "Meet me here in one hour's time!" Pausing before he entered, he turned to face her. "You're wearing that damn armor?"

"Of course, my lord."

"Why?"

Maigrey managed a slight smile. "You would despise me if I didn't."

Sagan glared at her furiously, bitterly. "Which leaves me instead to despise myself for what I am destined to do! I'll have it sent to your quarters." The door slid shut behind him.

Maigrey sighed and stood up, weak-kneed and trembling. Moving past the armor on its stand, she lifted the helm and, brushing the feather crest with her fingers, took it to her room.

Chapter ·◆◦○◦◆· *Six*

". . . two different fates are carrying me on the road to death. If I stay here and fight . . . there will be no homecoming for me, but my fame shall never die . . ."
Homer, *The Iliad*, translation by W. H. D. Rouse

Lord Sagan would have liked to have spent the hour before departure confronting God and demanding to know just what in hell was going on. The Warlord had no time for argument, however. He had to go over his plan with Haupt once again, reassure the brigadier of the likelihood of it succeeding, and bolster the man's sagging courage. Haupt was a good soldier; he was having difficulty being a good traitor.

These machinations took up almost the whole of Sagan's hour, and when they were finished to his satisfaction, he began to don his own ceremonial armor, made of gold and adamant. Ceremonial, but functional. It would turn a knife, deflect the fire of a lasgun, absorb the explosive force of a grenade. It could not, however, stop the blade of the bloodsword, nor would it shield him from a more insidious attack—an attack launched against his mind.

Sagan drew on his gauntlets, smoothed the leather over a forearm marred with the scars of self-inflicted wounds. He had no illusions about his ability to defeat Abdiel in a one-on-one physical challenge. The Warlord had strength, courage, skill in arms. But all that counted for nothing when the mind-seizer burrowed his way into Sagan's skull, carried the battle into realms where even the conscious mind feared to go.

Maigrey and I, joined together, our power totally committed to the defeat of our enemy—we might be able to defeat him. Might.

As for the Adonian, Snaga Ohme would probably drop out of the game tonight. Sagan had that contingency covered.

345

Which left only Dion. The Warlord decided he would have to wait and see. There might be so little of the boy's own will left that saving him wouldn't be worth the bother.

Sagan lifted the golden helm, fit it over his head. He felt better, calmer. He believed that he understood God now and, what was more important, that God understood him. The Warlord picked up the bloodsword, stopped, remembering. Weapons were not allowed.

Let them try to take it, he resolved, and buckled it around his waist.

··◗■ ■▶··

Maigrey, too, wore her bloodsword, with much the same thought. Let the Adonian try to take it from her. Accoutred in the silver armor, she entered the Warlord's quarters just as he was emerging from his room. His gaze flicked over her and she thought she saw the eyes darken, but the helm masking his face kept her from seeing his expression. So did the inner helm masking his thoughts.

His gaze fixed upon her sword. "You know that there are to be no weapons allowed?"

Maigrey looked at the sword he was wearing and smiled.

Sagan nodded, lips parted in a rare, answering smile. Brusquely, he turned to face the Honor Guard, drawn up to send their lord and lady off with fitting ceremony.

"Captain, detail two of your men to accompany my lady—"

Maigrey froze, literally shivering with suppressed fury. "So, my lord!" she said in a soft and deadly undertone. "*This* is the regard you have for my oath! I'm to be a prisoner—"

"Damn it, woman!" Nerves taut, Sagan exploded. "We're each allowed to take two bodyguards!" Shoving his captain out of his way, the Warlord turned to his line of men. "Marcus! Caius! Fall out!"

The two did as commanded, eyes straight ahead, standing at attention.

"You two are, from this moment, no longer in my service."

"Yes, my lord." Both men stiffened, faces paled.

"The Lady Maigrey is looking for two good men to engage in her service. Do you know of two I can recommend to her?"

"Yes, my lord," Marcus said, relaxing slightly, allowing his eyes to shift for a moment to meet hers. "I would be honored, my lord."

"Caius?"

"Yes, my lord. Certainly, my lord."

"My lady." Sagan turned to her with a cold and formal bow. "These two men are willing to enter into your service. Do you accept them?"

"I do, my lord, with my most grateful thanks." She drew near him, murmured, "They will obey my every command?"

"Every command, my lady."

"What if I ordered them to kill you, my lord?"

The dark eyes behind the helm lightened for a moment, glinted with amusement. "I trained them myself, my lady. They are well disciplined. I would trust that, should you order my death, they would obey without question."

"Thank you, my lord," she said. "Just checking."

A signal came over the commlink.

"The staff car has arrived, my lord," the captain informed them.

Turn back, Maigrey. Make some excuse. Pack away the silver armor.

Was it Sagan's voice? Or her own speaking to her? It wasn't urging, tempting, or threatening. It was, once again, offering her a choice.

A choice . . . Achilles' choice—glory or long life.

Maigrey looked into the shadowed eyes behind the golden helm.

You accept your fate, then, my lady?

Maigrey grinned suddenly, her spirits ebullient, her blood burning with excitement. *I chose glory long ago, my lord. Didn't you?*

The Warlord bowed, offered Maigrey his arm. Bowing, she accepted. Silver-gloved fingers shone brightly against golden armor.

Drawing her near him, Sagan whispered softly, "Long ago, my lady. Long ago."

··◁ ▷··

"Dion, my dear boy, you look quite splendid!" Abdiel remarked, gazing at the young man with a critical eye. "Mikael is skilled with his fingers. Turn around and let me see you from the back. Perfect, perfect. No one will suspect a thing."

Dion submitted to the examination with as good grace as possible, considering that inside he was hot as a malfunctioning lasgun, overcharged, building to an explosion. His clothing had been designed to disguise the cumulators and the boy, accustomed to plain jeans and Platus's handmade shirts, thought he literally looked like a fool.

The "jewels" that were the gun's energy source had to be placed on the body directly over the nerve bundles that would activate them. Mikael had designed and sewn a vest whose every centimeter was encrusted with fake costume jewelry, decorated with sequins and garish embroidery. Dion had, at least, been able to decide what pattern he wanted on the vest.

"What was my family's crest like?" he had asked Abdiel, and the young man had frowned severely on being told it was a sun shining down on a lion recumbent.

"But the old has been washed away, hasn't it?"

"Washed away in blood, my king," Abdiel had responded. "Leaving you free to choose your own crest."

Dion had disappeared into his room. Emerging several hours later, he'd handed Mikael a drawing. Mikael had taken it to Abdiel.

A sun with the face of a lion, the sun's flames forming the lion's mane.

Abdiel had sniffed, shrugged. "Ostentatious. Typical of the Starfires. The ancient Greeks would have termed it *hubris*— false pride in oneself which offends the gods. Put it on the vest."

They were preparing to depart for the Event. Abdiel and Dion stood outside the prefab house, the 'copter that was to take them to Snaga Ohme's warming up its engines.

The vest's bright and shining lion-faced sun, done in crystal beads on the back, caught the last rays of Laskar's sinking sun, and both seemed to flame with renewed brilliance. On the front of the vest, two eight-pointed stars, one embroidered on either side of his chest, concealed the cumulators. A medallion, formed in the likeness of a smiling sun with fat cheeks, hung from around his neck. Placed directly over the sternum, it held the largest of the cumulators. A jeweled belt, decorated with eight-pointed stars, fit snugly around his waist and held two more. The gun, devised in the shape of an eight-pointed star, masqueraded as the belt's buckle.

Dion flexed his arms, shifting uncomfortably. The vest was heavy and hot, the medallion thumped on his chest every time he took a step, and the large belt was tightly cinched and seemed determined to cut him in two. He was sweating profusely and reached inside the vest to scratch.

"Your Majesty, really! You mustn't!" Abdiel scolded, holding out a restraining hand.

"It's the heat!" Dion said, almost frantic with nervous energy. "I can't stand this waiting around! Isn't that thing ready to go yet?" he added, referring to the 'copter.

"Patience, Dion. Patience. By the way, Your Majesty, I hope you will forgive me the familiarity of calling you by your name when we arrive at the Adonian's. There will be those in attendance who would not understand."

"I don't mind," Dion said nonchalantly, blue eyes blazing more brilliantly than any sun. Abdiel was wrong. If all went as planned, everyone would understand. But it wouldn't do to say anything about that now.

Dion, to keep his mind occupied and off the itching rash or whatever it was, unclipped the gun from the belt and studied it intently.

"Toying with the weapon—a bad habit," Mikael said, coming up from behind the young man suddenly. "You will make people suspicious."

Dion glanced up, startled. "I just wanted to—"

"Mikael is right, Dion," Abdiel admonished severely. "Put the gun away now, dear boy, and remember—don't draw it again until you are ready to use it."

Dion didn't respond, afraid he'd say something he'd regret. Pretending not to have heard, he stalked over to the 'copter, ducking his head beneath the whirling blades, and climbed inside. What does the old man take me for? he thought. A child? I'm a man, doing a man's job. A knight, riding to do battle to defend the weak and innocent. A king, setting forth to claim my kingdom.

Abdiel attempted to enter the 'copter. But the mind-seizer's magenta robes, decorated with a slash of black lightning, whipped about him in the wind, and he was having difficulty.

Dion extended his hand, took the old man's hand, and pulled him into the 'copter, assisted him in settling himself in the seat. Mikael took the controls, and the 'copter lifted off.

The young man watched the house and the ground fall away from him and was reminded suddenly, forcibly, of the first time he'd ever flown in the spaceplane. He'd been with Tusk . . . the night Platus had died at the hands of the Warlord. Then it had seemed to Dion that his life was dropping away from him.

His gaze left the ground; he looked up at the sky, at the heavens, glittering with stars. Now things were different. Now he was rising to meet it.

The 'copter gained altitude. They could see, in the distance, the bright lights shining from the Adonian's estate.

Abdiel, noticing the boy's rapt face, seeing Dion occupied with inner thoughts, leaned forward and touched Mikael gently on the shoulder.

"That other matter of which we spoke. Is all arranged?"

"All arranged, master," Mikael replied.

Chapter ·◆>○◯<◆· Seven

I'll never get off this world alive.
Hank Williams, from the song of the same title.

"That's a 'copter!" Tusk said, jumping up.

"Yeah, so what?" Nola demanded listlessly, lounging back on the mattress that was the room's only furnishing. "Those zombie types're always coming and going in the damn things."

"Not in the last few days they haven't been," Tusk commented. Restless, he padded over to the door, pressed his ear against it. The whop-whop of the 'copter blades faded fast and he could hear what sounded like hammering, large objects dropping to the ground. Every once in a while, he felt a shudder go through the floorboards beneath his feet.

"Damn!" Frustrated, Tusk gave the doorknob a futile twist, the door an angry kick. "I wish I knew what was going on!"

"Would you stop it?" Nola said, brushing back her sweat-damp hair. "It doesn't do any good, and it'll only bring one of the zombies to warn us to behave. You know what they did to you the last time."

Tusk, grimacing, rubbed his solar plexus. He was still sore, and it hurt to breathe. He guessed he had at least two cracked ribs and probably a bruised kidney. It was, he had to admit, one of the most effective beatings he'd ever taken.

Two zombies had hauled him into another one of the boxlike rooms, bound his hands, and gagged him to keep him from screaming. The mind-dead then proceeded to batter him senseless, delivering each punch with calm, unemotional, ruthless efficiency. And there'd been no emotion in the dead eyes when they'd informed him that if he made any more attempts to escape, they'd give Nola that same treatment—only worse.

It was probably the one threat that could have stopped

351

Tusk. Having spent time in the brig for insubordination (after which he'd deserted the Galactic Air Corps), the mercenary hated confinement and would have gladly risked another beating if he'd been on his own. He was worried about Dion, too, though the first thing he planned to do once he got out of this mess was grab the kid and shake him until his teeth rattled.

"Stupid-ass kid," Tusk muttered, easing himself down on the mattress beside Nola. "Those plans of his he was talking about—he's decided he's gonna try to kill the Warlord."

"You don't know that," Nola said wearily. She was hearing this for about the thousandth time.

"I do, too! I know him. He thinks he's some sort of goddam boy-hero—"

"What did you think when you were that age?" Nola teased, nestling close to him, hoping to change the subject.

"Hell, that was different," Tusk said modestly. "I *was* a boy-hero. I—"

"Shhh!" Nola put his fingers over his lips. "Someone's coming!"

Tusk twisted to his feet, motioning for Nola to do the same. Watchful and wary, they listened to the approaching footsteps. There was more than one person, by the sound of it. The footfalls came to a halt outside the door. Bolts slid aside; a hand pushed the door open.

Four of the mind-dead entered. Two remained standing in the doorway, two walked into the room. The two framed in the door were holding needle-guns, one aimed at Tusk, the other at Nola. The hammering sound was louder and, over it, voices shouting instructions.

"What now?" Tusk growled, eyeing the guns and the mind-dead holding them, weighing the odds, itching to jump the guy and shove that gun down his unemotional throat.

"Come." The mind-dead gestured with the gun.

Tusk decided, reluctantly, he couldn't risk it. While he was lunging, the bastard'd shoot Nola.

"Come? Come where?"

"Outside," the mind-dead repeated, emphasizing his words with the gun. "We're going for a walk."

It's all over, said a voice in the back of Tusk's mind. Dion's gone. They've done with him whatever it is they're going to do and now they can get rid of us. We're gonna take a walk, all right—the last walk. Guess they can't kill us in here, probably don't want to get blood on the walls.

Fight! The temptation flashed through Tusk's mind. His muscles tensed in response. What have I got to lose? He looked at Nola, saw that she knew what he was thinking, saw that she was with him.

By God, I'm proud of her. No tears, no screams. Calm, cool. And, oh God, how I love her!

We'll die fighting, but we'll die. Trapped in this box, we don't have a chance. No room to maneuver, no hope of finding anything to use as a weapon. Maybe once we're outside . . .

Tusk raised his hands in the air, flicking a quick wink at Nola to tell her *Not now!*

The mind-dead escorted them out of the room and through the maze of halls and stairways, one marching behind Tusk, the gun pressed against his back, the other behind Nola.

"That's why you're evicting us, huh?" Tusk said conversationally, looking around. "You guys are packing up and heading out."

The house was being dismantled, the mind-dead swarming over it like ants over a carcass. Walls were being unhinged and taken apart, stacked in neat, numbered piles. Furniture stood on the desert floor, waiting to be hauled into the waiting shuttlecraft. Its lights were on; several mind-dead were working on it, apparently readying it for flight.

Tusk paused, ostensibly to watch the activity. He was, in reality, swiftly scanning the ground, hoping desperately to find a chance for escape.

It was night, but the mind-dead had lit the area with nuke lamps to allow them to continue with their work. The landscape was flooded with glaring white light, almost as bright as, and certainly more appealing than, Laskar's green sun. But, by that light, Tusk could see the prospect for escape was bleak.

More mind-dead than he could count surrounded them, and all of them were armed. The area was wide open; the only cover was a large outcropping of boulders scattered on top of the lip of a gully off to his left. As for weapons . . . well, he could always throw rocks. . . .

The gun poked painfully into his bruised flesh. "Move."

"All right, all right!" Tusk grunted.

He kept his head down, his eyes fixed on the ground. He couldn't face Nola. She'll know, the minute she sees my expression, that it's hopeless, he thought. Hell, probably she knows now.

Warm fingers closed over his hand. He held on to her tightly.

Yeah, she knows.

They were moving toward the boulders. Tusk could see the gully gaping wide, a large crack in the desert floor. The perfect grave. No one would ever find the bodies. Not that anybody'd be looking. He knew, now, as sure as fate, that Abdiel planned to murder Dion after the kid had done the mind-seizer's dirty work and killed Sagan for him. Perhaps the kid was already dead. . . .

I wasn't much of a Guardian, Tusk said to himself. He could see the sad, careworn face of the boy's mentor, the calm, proud, scarred face of his sister. I'm sorry, Platus. Sorry, Starlady. . . . He squeezed tightly the hand clinging to his. I'm sorry, Nola.

At least I'll go out fighting. No one'll find me—*if* anyone finds me—with a hole blasted in my back.

They were circling around the shuttlecraft, heading for the boulders, the gully. I'll wait until we're out of sight of the other mind-dead, wait until we reach the jumble of rocks. If by some miracle we escape, the boulders and gully will offer cover.

Tusk trudged over the hard-packed ground. They had reached the outcropping of boulders—huge red rocks that lay scattered across the desert floor like marbles belonging to some giant's child. The light from the house was partially blocked by the shuttlecraft, which cast long, dark shadows. The gully was wide and deep and, now that they were near, Tusk could hear the faint sound of rushing water—one of those dry creek beds that come to life only when it rains.

Nola tried to wriggle her hand free. Tusk knew why—she was planning to help him fight—and he held on fast. He had a plan himself. We reach the lip of the gully. I give Nola a hard tug, fling her over the edge. Then I'll turn and fight. I hope she's got sense enough to get away. I hope she can swim, he thought, hearing the water gurgling beneath them.

They reached the edge of the ditch.

"Stop," the mind-dead ordered.

So I was right. This is gonna be our grave.

He tensed, drew a breath that would probably be his last, and flashed Nola a quick look that said everything in his heart. . . .

A stabbing beam of light damn near blinded him. Stinging pain tore through his arm. For a moment he thought the mind-dead had fired and missed, then the zombie standing behind him crumpled to the ground.

Tusk blinked, dazed, paralyzed, trying desperately to see what was going on. He wondered if he'd seen the light at all. It had been like a lightning flash on a perfectly clear day. He doubted his senses. But before he could move or react, another deadly beam arced past Nola, and then another . . . and the mind-dead—now really, most sincerely dead—lay on the ground behind them.

"Jump for it, fools!" hissed a voice from the rocks on the other side of the gully.

Tusk was only too happy to obey. He and Nola scrambled and slid down the side of the ravine. It was pitch dark here, out of the nuke lights, and he was still half-blinded. The sound of running water was louder. Tusk came to a halt.

"C'mon!" Nola tugged at him. "What are you waiting for? Someone's bound to wonder why those zombies aren't coming back!"

"You go ahead," Tusk told her. The water thundered in his ears. His ribs hurt like hell; every breath was like sucking in fire.

"Don't be stupid! What's the—"

"Damn it, Nola! I can't swim!"

He was getting his night vision, and he could see her eyes widen. She started to giggle, choked it off. "Tusk," she began, trying to speak calmly, "I don't think the water's that deep. . . ."

"Doesn't matter," Tusk said, breathing heavily. "I've always been afraid of water. Hell, I can't even sit in a bathtub. If it wasn't for showers I'd—"

"What you two waiting for?" A shadowy figure appeared at the opposite edge of the ravine. "Maybe I make mistake. Maybe you want to die."

"Go ahead, Nola. I'll catch up with you. Just give me a minute—"

"No, I'm staying right here with you."

Tusk glared at her. "You can be a real bitch sometimes!"

"I know," she said sweetly. "Well, do we stay here or go across the creek? C'mon. I'll even hold your hand."

"No, thanks!"

And before he could give himself time to think about it,

Tusk stepped into the rushing water, prepared to sink, flounder helplessly. . . .

The water washed over his feet, came to his ankles, and stopped. Nola splashed in beside him. "Want a life raft?"

"Shut up!" he growled, fighting down the irrational panic that had him envisioning black water closing over his head. Grimly, he sloshed forward, reached the other side of the bank, and clambered thankfully back onto dry land.

They scaled the side of the gully with difficulty. The ravine was steep and the loose sand gave way underfoot, while Tusk's bruised and battered body reminded him in no uncertain terms that it wasn't at all amused by the proceedings. Gasping and grunting, every breath a painful effort, he managed—with Nola's help—to make it most of the way. A strong hand snaked down, caught hold of him, and yanked him over the edge. Nola pulled herself up beside him.

Their rescuer grinned at them.

Seeing the deformed face, the cunning, misaligned eyes glittering in the lights of the shuttlecraft, Tusk wondered if they wouldn't be safer back in the bottom of the water-filled ditch. Nola recoiled, her hand reaching for his.

"Who are you?" Tusk growled.

"This way! You come!" The man gestured, leading them into the dark shadow of a gigantic boulder.

Tusk glanced over his shoulder at the shuttlecraft. No one was chasing after them, but it would be only a matter of time. Reluctantly, he and Nola followed the man, who moved with the grace of a snake.

"I am called Sparafucile." The half-breed grinned, white teeth shining in the lambent light of shuttlecraft and stars and a thin, newly risen moon. "That was some nice shooting I did, eh?"

"Lucky shooting," Tusk muttered, looking down at the black hole in his sleeve, feeling acutely the sting of his burn. "Assuming, that is, that you *meant* to miss us. . . ."

"Not luck. Never luck. Sparafucile makes his own luck. And, yes, I mean to miss you." The half-breed's gaze was on Nola. Involuntarily, she shrank away from him, edging her way behind Tusk.

"Why did you save us?" Tusk persisted, eyeing the breed suspiciously. If he was telling the truth, if he was that good a shot, he was probably accustomed to being paid—well paid— for his skill. "What's your price?"

Sparafucile's grin widened. "We understand each other. But do not worry. My price . . . small. Part you pay. Part already paid. Sagan Lord, he say—"

"Sagan!" Tusk sucked in a deep breath and almost gagged with the pain. "Whose side is *he* on?" he demanded when he could talk.

"Sagan Lord?" Sparafucile made a gurgling sound in his throat, apparently an approximation of a laugh. "His own side. Always his own." The half-breed reached out a finger, poked Tusk in the chest. "But this time his side is your side. And your side is my side. I help you. You help me. Understand?"

"No," growled Tusk. "But I don't suppose it much matters, does it, Spara-whatever-your-name-is?"

The assassin shook his head. One eye drooped in a ghastly approximation of a wink at the young woman. Nola tried to smile back, but her smile was strained and she shot an alarmed glance at Tusk when she thought the half-breed wasn't looking.

Scowling, the mercenary rubbed his hurting ribs and flashed her a look of exasperation. I don't like this character any better than you do, but he *did* save our lives.

And while it's not exactly comforting to think of the Warlord as our guardian angel, Tusk decided, I'll take Sagan over Abdiel any day.

"I'll keep an eye on him," he promised Nola, nodding obliquely at the half-breed.

Nola, tossing her head contemptuously, asked the breed crisply, "You mentioned a price to rescue us. What do we do to earn it?"

Sparafucile leered at her. "You shoot? You warrior-lady like Sagan's lady?"

"I'm probably not as good a shot as she is, but yes, I can shoot," Nola answered.

So, Maigrey's with Sagan, just like Abdiel told the boy. Tusk sighed, frowned.

Sparafucile reached into the shadows, lifted what appeared to be a blanket roll, spread it open. It turned out to be a small arsenal. Needle-guns, lasguns, grenade guns, what looked like a hand-held missile launcher, and—in a neat row on the bottom—an assortment of knives. The assassin gazed at his tools with pride, spread his hands over them like a jeweler showing his wares. "You see something you like, warrior-lady?"

Nola looked slightly startled, but—giving Tusk another

glance—began examining the weapons with grave attention. Tusk drew near her. He could feel her shivering in the warm darkness, and he patted her arm in awkward comfort. She found his hand and squeezed it tight.

"The lady'll take that," Tusk said, steering Nola away from the needle-gun that required unerring accuracy, pointing out a disassembled beam rifle.

Sparafucile approved the choice, apparently. He began putting the weapon together with a skill and rapidity that Tusk found impressive. Tusk selected a lasgun and a grenade launcher for himself. "What do you want us to do?"

"Sagan Lord tell me to disable shuttle. I see many dead-ones around and I say to myself: To get close to shuttlecraft, I have to kill one, maybe two or three. The old man comes back. He see the bodies. He get suspicious. He say to himself: Someone has hurt my ship. But then I say to myself: I will help prisoners escape. Then the old man says to himself: It was escaped prisoners that kill my people. He will not think to worry about his ship. Then I say to myself: It will be helpful for me to get close to shuttle if you draw attention of dead-ones away. Understand?"

"Enough." Tusk handed the rifle to a confused-looking Nola. "He wants us to create a diversion so that he can sneak in and sabotage the shuttle."

Sparafucile watched, nodded. "Sagan Lord say you were good warrior."

"Did he, though?" Tusk muttered, not particularly liking having been either the object of Sagan's praise or the subject of the Warlord's conversation. He wondered what it meant.

"What about Dion?" Nola asked him softly.

Tusk looked away, cleared his throat. He hadn't wanted to ask, hadn't wanted to know. He was afraid he'd hear that the boy was down in that dark water. . . .

"Dion? Pretty boy?" Sparafucile, watching them closely, didn't miss a word. "Pretty boy go with old man. Go to house of Snaga Ohme. Big party. Everyone there. Sagan Lord. Warrior-lady. Pretty boy. Old man. Everyone there except you two and Sparafucile, eh? We stay here, have our own party."

Tusk didn't like that either, didn't like it one damn bit. The kid was walking into a snake pit. He was entering a house full of his enemies and blindly taking his own worst enemy in with him. The Lady Maigrey would be there, presumably, but Tusk wasn't certain he could trust her anymore. Somehow, he thought, I ought to try to reach the kid. . . .

"I know what you are thinking." Sparafucile rose to his feet, loomed over Tusk. "But such a thing is not possible. You help boy here. Kill his enemies here."

Or die here ourselves. Tusk heard the unspoken threat. Grimly, he picked up his weapons, stood face to face with the assassin.

"Just what did 'Sagan Lord' tell you to do with us when this little party is over?" Tusk demanded

The half-breed's eyes narrowed to slits. Laughter glinted from between the lids. "He say to take you to him."

Chapter ·❖◦◯◦❖· Eight

> . . . if destiny like his
> awaits me, I shall rest when I have fallen!
> Now, though, may I win my perfect glory . . .
> Homer, *The Iliad*, translated by Robert Fitzgerald

Limo-jets sped down the highway, gliding on soft cushions of air, their occupants quaffing champagne, Laskarian brandy, or the preferred intoxicant of their species. The rich, the beautiful, and/or the powerful were speeding toward Snaga Ohme's like a flurry of gold-tipped arrows. The wealth represented by the jewels they wore alone would have bought and paid for several solar systems.

Crowds of Laskarian natives lined the route, anxious to catch a glimpse of anyone famous, waiting for the inevitable traffic tie-ups that occurred as official arrival time approached and the limos were forced to reduce their speed and settle toward the ground to wait their turn to draw near the gate.

Many of the notables flew in by 'copter, avoiding the crush of traffic, but sacrificing dignity and coiffed hairdos to the wind whipped up by the blades. A few of the more flamboyant chose unconventional methods of arrival. The galaxy's current favorite vid star descended from the heavens in a hot-air balloon, much to her fans' delight. And it was rumored among the mob packed around Snaga Ohme's gate that one barbarian monarch, known as Bear Olefsky, had actually traveled to Ohme's on foot. The Bear had run from where his shuttle was parked in an RV lot—a light jog of about forty kilometers, which he made attired in full battle armor, arriving feeling refreshed and invigorated by the exercise.

The crowd lining the drive outside Ohme's estate numbered into the thousands, many having camped out days in advance. Invisible force fields protected the glamorous from

360

their adoring public while still allowing both glamorous and public the chance to feed off each other.

The major media networks, the only ones allowed, vied with the competition to gain interviews. 'Droid reporters lurked about near the gate, shooting out of the most unexpected places, hanging on to their prey tenaciously until either they were appeased with a "few well-chosen words" or otherwise dealt with. One 'droid made the mistake of attempting to interview Bear Olefsky. Ohme's people had to halt the proceedings for ten minutes to sweep up the pieces.

Lord Derek Sagan emerged from the limo-jet into the blinding glare of light and a roar from the crowd. The Warlord, as he was now being hailed by the press, was a hero and the crowd behind the force field went wild when he appeared.

Maigrey gave her hand to Sagan, who, with dignified, courtly courtesy, assisted her from the car and led her up the walkway to the gate. No one knew who she was and this mystery created an instant sensation. 'Droid reporters, smelling blood, left other victims in mid-sentence and sped toward the fresh meat. The Honor Guard was accustomed to handling the press, however, and kept the 'droids at bay.

The adulation ran through Maigrey's veins, sweet, intoxicating. To this, she had been born. She drank huge gulps of it, enjoying every drop, the persistent 'droids, the swooning teenagers, the plastic phoenixes being waved in the air, the news commentators whose voices could be overheard, speaking into their camcorders.

"Citizens of the galaxy! This is indeed history in the making. You've all heard the rumors that one of the former Guardians, Maigrey Morianna, was discovered alive and was to be brought to trial. You've heard how she turned out to be one of the heroes in the recent battle against the Corasians. We don't know for certain that this woman with Warlord Sagan is, indeed, Maigrey Morianna, but a reliable source close to the citizen general indicates she very well could be. Some of our older viewers may recall that, at one time, the names of Derek Sagan and Maigrey Morianna were linked romantically—"

The Honor Guard forged a path. The crowd screamed for one look, one wave. Proud and majestic, Sagan strolled past them all, glancing neither left nor right, accepting the homage as his due. Maigrey, her hand resting lightly in his, accompanied him, demurely ignoring the vidcams attempting desperately to get a close-up of her face.

Snaga Ohme's remotes guarded the gate. Lord and lady entered, accompanied by the Honor Guard. The excited crowd settled down to await the arrival of their next hero.

Inside the gate, the deadly garden had been romantically lit by a simulated moon suspended inside the Adonian's protective force field. Maigrey paused, feeling buoyant, almost dizzy with excitement and elation. Spreading her arms, lifting her face to the artificial moon, she embraced it and the deadly garden and cheering mobs who had also cheered the day they heard she and her kind were dead.

Maigrey threw back her head and laughed.

The Warlord turned to stare at her in astonishment. Maigrey embraced him, her hands clasping hold of his arms. "It's been a long time, Derek!" she said, laughing up into his eyes. "And I've missed it! Oh, how I've missed it!"

She could see her reflection in the golden helm covering his face, see it—smaller—in the eyes shadowed by the helm. She was beautiful in the silver armor in the moonlight. And he was handsome, proud and burning as the sun. His grip on her tightened. He drew her closer . . .

And then his eyes darkened; her reflection flared in them with silver flame, and was gone. He averted his face, shoved her almost roughly away.

Their minds had touched with their hands and Maigrey had shared with him, in one brief and terrifying moment, the vision of her own death.

The wild intoxicating joy ebbed away, leaving her—for the moment—cold sober. "So," she said quietly to herself, sighing, "not only has the past come between us, but now the future."

The tram car stood waiting to carry them through the garden to the house of the Adonian.

Perhaps there's never been a time for us, she said to herself silently, bleakly, entering the car that had been transformed into a luxurious traveling salon.

A robot, officious and servile, offered champagne to ease the boredom of the trip. Maigrey took a glass, lifted it to her lips, caught Sagan's stern and disapproving eye. Joy bubbled back up inside her, like the bubbles rising up in the hollow stem of the crystal glass.

"There is a time for us, just what it had always been, perhaps what it will always be: now."

··◆━ ━◆··

The crowd outside the gate cheered more of the glittering fortunate, cheered other limos gliding up to the gate, disgorging their contents, spewing forth princes and chairmen of boards and kings and governors and generals and whatever other titles crowned money and success. Later, when the line of limos was drawing near its end and the last of the 'copters were being given clearance to land, a boy with flaming red-gold hair walked past the crowd, whose cheering had about ended for the night.

Some glanced at him curiously, but no one knew him. Bored, they turned away and began to think of going home.

··◁▦ ▦▷··

The Adonian's stately mansion was lit from without and within. Every one of a thousand windows blazed with light; search beams played over the white marble-columned and frescoed walls. The effect was dazzling, and Maigrey resisted strongly the temptation to shield her eyes while walking up the steps that led to the grand ballroom.

A hundred footmen were drawn up in a line on the stairs. Each one bowed from the waist as the guests filed past.

"They're scanning us for weapons," Sagan commented.

"Nice to think we'll provide them with some recompense for their pains," Maigrey returned. Her hand in his, they walked together up the stairs, the Honor Guard following behind.

Sagan glanced at her; the dark eyes smiled. "I am glad you are enjoying this, my lady."

Maigrey smiled back. "I must admit, my lord, I am."

The Warlord's grip on her hand tightened. His expression grew serious. "Maigrey, I—" He paused.

"What, my lord?"

It had been in Sagan's mind to warn her, to remind her of the danger she faced, but looking at her—calm, cool, radiant as the moon on Oha-Lau—he realized that she was well aware of it. She did not walk blindly to her fate. She tread her path with courage, eyes open not only to the light, but to the darkness.

"Nothing." He shook his head. "It wasn't important."

Footmen at the head of the stairs bowed as they entered a perfectly round hall. Armor—silver and gold—gleamed in the lights of a huge glittering chandelier hung not with crystals, but with diamonds. The other guests were being funneled toward a double spiraling staircase carved of rare, highly polished onyx wood. Twisting in upon itself, the two spiraling arms of the staircase swept the guests upward to the second floor, where they stood in line, waiting to be formally announced to those inside the ballroom.

"Pardon me, Lord Sagan, but would you mind stepping this way?"

Raoul, splendid in velvet and lace, and the Little One, who had apparently exchanged his muffling raincoat for a bathrobe which served the same function, insinuated themselves into the Warlord's path. Other guests flowed around them with curious glances, some of the more knowing divining what was going on and grinning at each other.

"My lady"—the Warlord turned to Maigrey—"would you excuse me for a moment?"

"No, no," Raoul said, bowing, "her ladyship must not be inconvenienced by your absence, my lord. Therefore, if she could come as well . . ."

The Little One didn't speak a word, but watched them both with glittering, ever-shifting eyes, peering out over the folds of the bathrobe.

"I will be pleased to accompany you," Maigrey said gravely.

Raoul led them to a doorway just off the hall, the Little One shuffling along beside them, his eyes never leaving them. Maigrey, mental barriers in place, was amused to witness the empath's mounting level of frustration.

Lord and lady were escorted to a small room, comfortably furnished, tastefully decorated, and adorned—they both noted—with the very latest in hidden weaponry.

A footman shut the door behind them.

Raoul turned to face them, a blush mantling his cheeks.

"I am deeply mortified. This has all been a terrible mistake and the fault is mine. But, pardon me, I have been remiss in my duties. May I offer you some champagne? Your ladyship—?"

"I wouldn't drink anything *he* offers you, my lady," Sagan remarked coolly.

"Thank you, my lord. I never cared much for that particular brand."

Raoul shrugged delicate shoulders, waved a perfumed hand. "As I was saying, I am deeply mortified. I was supposed to have told you that no weapons were allowed. Apparently I was derelict in my responsibility. My employer, Snaga Ohme, is most displeased with me and hopes you will accept his humble apologies for the deficiencies of his servant. I assure you, I will be most thoroughly punished for occasioning you such embarrassment, my lord, my lady."

"I trust your master will not be too severe on you," Sagan replied. "You made no mistake in regard to your invitation. You did, in fact, tell us that no weapons were to be allowed and therefore we have not worn weapons. Guards, present yourselves to be searched."

The Honor Guard stepped forward with alacrity. Raoul, blush deepening, didn't even glance at them. "My lord, I beg to differ with you. You . . . and the lady . . . wear the bloodsword."

"The bloodsword is ceremonial, as everyone knows."

"My lord, it was not worn in the presence of the king—"

"When the king arrives, I'll take it off," Sagan said dryly.

Raoul glanced questioningly at the Little One, who scowled ferociously and shook his head.

"My lord," Raoul began, with a flutter of his long, thick eyelashes, "I trust there will be no cause for unpleasantness. . . ."

"None whatsoever," Sagan assured him. "You want the bloodsword, you remove it." The Warlord tossed back the red cape he wore to reveal the bloodsword hanging in its scabbard at his waist.

Raoul started forward, hand outstretched.

"Mind you don't prick yourself on the needles," Sagan continued, speaking in solicitous tones. "The virus injected into the bloodstream is of a particularly nasty strain. It kills, if one is lucky, in a matter of days."

Raoul's lace-cuffed hand halted; the fingers twitched. He darted a swift glance at a mirror hung on the wall. Maigrey followed the line of his gaze, concentrated her thoughts. The lights in the room dimmed momentarily.

The Loti cast another, more urgent glance at the mirror. Nothing happened, and a tiny frown line marred the unblemished surface of his forehead. Apparently some type of negative emotion was able to filter through the drugs.

"There seems to be a problem with the electrical wiring in this house, my lord," Maigrey said. The lights flickered and dimmed again. "I noticed it the last time I was here."

Raoul's hand dropped gracefully to his side. "My apologies for detaining you. Please, continue on into the ballroom."

"We may keep our swords?" Sagan inquired.

"The devil take you both and your swords!" the Loti said, smiling at them both with charming politeness. He opened the door, bowed them out. Maigrey, glancing behind, saw the Little One practically writhing on the floor in fury.

Lord and lady walked to the grand staircase. Couples separated at the bottom of the stairs, each ascending one side of the double spiraling arms, revolving around each other as the stairs carried them upward to jewel-studded doors. An orchestra inside the ballroom struck up a march at just the moment Maigrey set her foot upon the stair. She recognized it.

A pulsing heartbeat of sound. She began climbing the stairs, her eyes on the Warlord opposite. He, too, would know the music. It had been theirs, the squadron's. What coincidence, what chance played it for them now? The melody carried her on a quest, a search for an ultimate truth, tempered by a current of underlying sorrow, knowledge that the answer would never be found. A single trumpet's clear note called her higher. And with the searing note, the drums, a pounding counterpoint to her heartbeat. The trumpet call was stronger, louder, triumphant. She reached the top, the search was ended, sorrow vanquished in hope.

Perhaps some Immortal hand held the baton that had led that music.

Maigrey stood before the jeweled doors. Sagan met her at the same moment. They had ascended step by step, in perfect time, in perfect harmony.

The two of them took their places. The doors swung open, bright light illuminated them, the music swelled louder, and with it rose a hum of voices lifted in laughter and talk, the scent of fragrant candles, perfume.

The herald stood forward. "I present to you the Guardians . . ."

Guardians. The last of the Guardians.

The Immortal hand beckoned them on.

The two stood at the top of the stairs, looked down the vast marble cascade that would carry them into the room, looked down upon a veritable sea of life that had turned and was looking up at them. Silence rose like a wave, drowning even the musicians. Awe, respect, hatred, envy, malice, love, admiration—the silence rose to meet them, the flotsam it had acquired floating upon the top.

The Warlord held out his hand; golden armor flared in the brilliant lights. Maigrey laid her hand in his, preparing to walk down the stairs, preparing—it seemed to her—to walk into destiny.

Sagan turned to her suddenly, the dark eyes seeking, finding, holding her. He brought her hand to his lips.

You are and will ever be my lady.

And you are, she answered him, *and will ever be my lord!*

Chapter ··◀▣◯▣▶·· Nine

Nimis exalatus rex sedet in vertice—caveat ruinam!

Raised to dizzy heights of power, the king sits in majesty—
but let him beware his downfall!

Carl Orff, *Carmina Burana*

Looming head, shoulders, and most of his hairy upper body
above the crowd, the barbarian warrior-king Bear Olefsky
paused in the commission of ravages upon the buffet table to
watch the entrance of Maigrey and Sagan. The Bear's eyes
glinted; a chuckle rumbled deep in his massive chest. Turning
to his two sons, who were both taller and wider than their
father each way and who both went in mortal dread of him,
Bear poked one in his ribs.

"Old Sagan's here, boys," he said in a roaring whisper that
could be heard by at least half the people in the room, "*and* the
Lady Maigrey! By my lungs and liver, I never thought to see
her alive again! I'm glad we came," added Bear, who generally
objected to attending parties such as this, where he wasn't
permitted to grab the women and was forced to drink weak
wine from tiny crystal glasses that always seemed to shatter in
his huge, engulfing hand. "This may turn out to be more fun
than I'd expected!"

··◀▣ ▣▶··

Snaga Ohme, by contrast to his barbaric guest, was resplendent in gleaming white satin formal dress with ermine-lined
cape, white velvet lapels, and white snakeskin shoes. Standing
alone, he formed his own reception line, greeting his arriving
guests. This was his Event, his grand moment, and he saw no
need to share it with anyone.

The Warlord, descending the stairs, sent his gaze sweeping
over the crowd, brought it back repeatedly to one fixed

point—the Adonian. He attempted to keep his mind fixed upon that point as well, but it was difficult. Turbulent inner emotions were robbing Sagan of his concentration. He knew he was in God's eye. It was not a new experience; the Warlord had known he was in God's eye from the moment he was truly capable of understanding the concept of a force, a will greater than his own. But he had never experienced, until now, the feeling that God's eye was intent upon him, watching him with a stern attention that was unnerving and frustrating. It was as if God expected him to do something, and Sagan had no idea what.

Maigrey's hand locked suddenly onto his with a grip like death, brought him back to awareness of his surroundings with a jolting start. Sagan had noted that Ohme, of all the guests present, had not ceased his conversation long enough to pay homage to the Warlord, to a man who was—at this moment— probably the most powerful person in the galaxy. Snaga Ohme had laughed and chatted, eyes flicking briefly to the stairs, to the awestruck crowd. Ohme was aware of Sagan's arrival, obviously, but intended to indicate that he wasn't impressed.

The Adonian turned, finally, to greet the arriving Warlord and his lady and now Sagan understood Maigrey's reaction. Snaga Ohme wore, on a silver chain around his neck, the Star of the Guardians.

Sagan moved his hand swiftly to block her sword arm. "No, my lady!" His fingers closed like a steel vise over her wrist.

"I'll kill him!" Her words seemed wrenched from her. There was no doubting her resolve. "Let go of me—"

"Maigrey! Stop! Think! Not here! Not now!" He wrestled her hand from the hilt of the bloodsword.

Maigrey jerked her arm from his grasp and he tensed, but she was calm again, though her breath came fast and deep, and her eyes, a storm-ridden gray, never left the Adonian.

He was watching them, watching her, saw her struggle, and he grinned appreciatively. Bosk, standing near, had hastened forward, hand darting into the bosom of his formal evening coat. The guests may not have been allowed to bring weapons, but their hosts were apparently under no such stricture.

"Greetings, Sagan, darling," Snaga Ohme said, languidly bowing. "So glad you could come."

"Greetings, Ohme," Sagan replied, standing straight. "Tell your associate to keep his hand where I can see it or he's going to go looking for it in a moment and find it isn't there."

"Bosk, my pet, don't be rude," Snaga Ohme said, perfect teeth gleaming. Bosk removed his hand from the interior of his jacket, opened it, palm out, to show it was empty.

"Lovely lady." Ohme was bowing again. "Delighted you could attend. What a charming game you played with me the other day. I quite enjoyed it, though I will never forgive myself for not deducing your true identity. Ah, you've noticed the jewel." The Adonian placed his hand carelessly on the chain holding the starjewel, flipped it casually up and down.

Sagan noted that the man didn't look at it directly, however. The Warlord found himself unable to look at it without feeling a vague horror creep through his body.

"A remarkable transformation," Ohme was continuing. "My lapidary has studied it and can't explain how it occurred. Sadly, though, there appears to be no reversal to the process. It's quite worthless now, except perhaps as an oddity."

"Then give it back to me," Maigrey said, cold and pale.

The conversation was being carried on in low tones, not meant to be overheard. Most of the crowd—some of whom had witnessed with eager anticipation the small altercation at the foot of the stairs—saw that nothing was likely to come of it and turned back, disappointed, to talk or eat, dance or wait to see who would be announced next. Several, however, continued to observe the Warlord's conversation and a few moved nearer, hovering on the edge of the circle, hoping to catch his attention.

Sagan was aware of them, as he was aware of everything transpiring around him. He knew who they were, what they wanted. And he was prepared to meet them. But not yet, not now.

"*Give* the starjewel back!" Snaga Ohme appeared highly amused, then deeply put-upon. "And I end up with nothing, I suppose," he said, frowning.

"Wrinkles, wrinkles, darling," Bosk scolded, laying a soothing hand upon Ohme's arm.

"I'll pay you our original, agreed-upon price," the Warlord stated, "though I shouldn't. You were the one broke faith with my lady when you attacked her and tried to steal back the . . . property in question. And don't give me that tale about rampaging drug addicts. A man in my employ was there. He saw it all. Your men were recognized. Give my lady her starjewel, Ohme, and I'll transfer the amount I owe you to your account tonight."

"The price has gone up since then, Sagan," Ohme returned, his face smoothing. He glanced at himself in one of the thousand mirrors adorning the walls of the ballroom, perhaps to ascertain if permanent damage had been done. "Doubled, in fact. Your lady put me through considerable mental anguish—"

"—and there's another buyer, isn't there?" Sagan interrupted with imperturbable, terrible calm. "You dared offer what I designed and invented to someone else—"

"Only when it seemed likely I wasn't going to get my money," Ohme returned. "But we shouldn't be discussing business. Everyone's here to have fun!" The charming smile switched on, the Adonian turned away. "If you will excuse me, I must see to my other guests."

"It's cursed, Ohme," Sagan said. And though he spoke softly, some quality in his voice carried, sending a thrill through those nearby who overheard it. Everyone in the vicinity ceased talking, began to watch and listen.

The Adonian paused, glanced back over an elegant shoulder. "What's that you say, Sagan?"

"The starjewel is cursed, Snaga Ohme. Just as if you had taken it from a corpse," the Warlord told him. "It brings death to the one who steals it—a horrible death."

The people on the fringes of the conversation couldn't quite understand, but the Warlord's sternness and grim tone touched them. The gaiety faded; a pall seemed to settle over the crowd.

Snaga Ohme flashed a radiant smile. "The nursery's down the corridor, Sagan. Third door to your left. Go frighten the children."

The Adonian sauntered away, laughing. The crowd, seeing it must have all been some elaborate joke, began to laugh as well. Waiters hurried up, distributing champagne.

"You're right," Maigrey said. "It *is* cursed, and so am I. What have I done?" She shook her head, sighing. The silver flame of her armor seemed to darken, as if a cloud drifted over the moon.

"You did what you had to do, my lady. And if you had not done it, who knows? Abdiel might have the 'property' now."

"Might-have-beens are no comfort. For me, there is no comfort. I did wrong. But," she added, lifting her head, removing her hand from his and placing it on the hilt of the bloodsword, "I will have the jewel back again. And fairly, *not* by murdering the wretch. I'll watch my chance and talk to him. He'll agree to your bargain, my lord."

Sagan's eyes were on the Adonian. "He wears his doom around his neck, my lady. So it will prove."

The Warlord caught sight of those who hovered near, waiting to speak to him. He made a slight gesture with one hand, discernible only to those watching for it. They understood, nodded, and melted back into the crowd.

"Is that Rykilth?" Maigrey inquired.

Sagan looked at her in some surprise, not entirely pleased. "You have sharp eyes, my lady."

"Especially for an old enemy," she said dryly. "I couldn't tell if it was him or not. It's difficult with vapor-breathers, their heads encased in those bubbles, shrouded in that poisonous fog of theirs. He appears quite eager to talk to you."

"He is . . . and I to him. Rykilth's a Warlord himself, now. Quite a powerful one."

"I remember a time when you two— My God, Derek!" Maigrey directed his attention to the jeweled doors, to the top of the staircase. "Look!"

"Abdiel . . ."

The lord and lady were the only people in the room who had noticed the arrival of the new guest. Those who had been paying attention saw only an old man in flashy-colored robes and, not recognizing him as anyone of importance, reached for another glass of champagne. Almost everyone in the room, therefore, missed the first scene of the act that was going to, literally, bring down the house.

Abdiel was announced, using his name and the Order of Dark Lightning. Few in the room knew or remembered what that dread title meant. They paid him no heed. Two people knew and remembered, however. Abdiel sensed their presence immediately. They saw his gaze sweep over the thousand who interested him not at all and focus on the two who interested him a great deal.

Maigrey shivered and rubbed the palm of her right hand. "Where's Dion?"

"There, behind him." The Warlord's voice was grim.

"Why doesn't he come in?" Maigrey asked impatiently, after waiting several moments. "I can't see him! What's going on?"

"It appears that the boy is arguing with the herald. Whatever is happening," Sagan added in some concern, "Abdiel doesn't like it."

Maigrey's gaze shifted to the mind-seizer, who—waiting for his companion—was forced to stand, fidgeting, on the staircase.

"Oh, God!" Maigrey gasped, pressing her hand to her chest as if suffocating. "Oh, God, Derek! I know what Dion's going to do!"

"Yes," the Warlord replied, "the question is now what are *we* going to do?" Bound by the bloodsword to Dion, Sagan knew, too, what the boy intended. The Warlord knew, as well, what God intended. Sagan stood unmoving, the bitter water crashing up against him, pounding on him, sweeping over him in wave after wave of chastisement, retribution.

The herald stepped forward, ignoring the boy. Raising his staff, preparatory to pounding it on the floor to gain attention, the herald was suddenly knocked violently to one side. The staff fell from his hands, clattered down the stairs. The noise and commotion drew the notice of everyone in the room.

Dion stepped forward, his hair a fiery halo, the jewels and beadwork on his vest dazzling in the bright lights. Pale as marble, his hands clenched at his sides, he spoke in a loud, clear, carrying voice that at first crackled with nervous tension but gained in confidence and resolve when he heard his words come echoing back to him.

"I look out on this assembly," he said, "and I see kings and queens, princes and presidents, governors and emperors and rulers of every description. Permit me to introduce myself, since no one, it seems"—with a cool glance at the indignant herald, picking himself up off the floor—"will do it for me. I am Dion Starfire. My parents were Augustus and Semele Starfire, your murdered king and queen. I am their son. I am your ruler. I am your king. I am the king of kings, and this night I claim my throne."

In the first moment following the boy's speech, no one moved or spoke, with the exception of a few, here and there around the room, who were tapping translators, wondering if they'd malfunctioned, wondering if they'd heard correctly.

In the second moment, when everyone decided that they had heard correctly, heads turned, eyes met, gazes crossed, plotting, calculating, speculating. The rightful heir. Found at last. Claiming his own. There was no doubting him. His presence, his looks, the charisma of the Blood Royal. And now what?

A weak and ineffective Congress. A President chafing with ambition. A political system falling apart. It was as if someone had scattered priceless pearls onto the floor. There were those already mentally preparing to grab what they could. . . . They began to edge their way forward.

And then there were those who saw him as a threat, a danger. Certain men exchanged in their glances the knowledge that this king must die as had his father and uncle before him. Die before word reached the populace, die before the royalists could take him to heart, make him a martyr, and that must be soon because already the media commentators were edging their way forward . . . and so these shadowy men began to edge their way forward. . . .

The sound of clapping brought them all to a halt. Abdiel was clapping his hands. The single applause from an audience of one echoed through the hushed and whispering room like the crack of a whip.

"Bravo!" he shouted, his applause increasing in speed and vigor. "A magnificent performance, boy. Don't you agree, honored guests?"

The honored guests weren't so certain. They looked at each other dubiously. Many turned to confront their host.

Snaga Ohme had no idea what was going on, but was happy to take credit for it, whatever it was. He was always pleased when his Events created a sensation, and this one could hardly be topped. He would make vid headlines the galaxy over. ROYAL IMPERSONATOR CRASHES PARTY . . .

Ohme began to laugh, clapping his hands and glancing around at the crowd to make certain all credited him for providing such a spectacular show. People breathed easier, many joined in the laughter, more than a few looked a little foolish, perhaps ashamed for having, momentarily, believed.

Bear Olefsky burst into a roar, caught sight of Sagan and Maigrey. The Bear's laughter died. "Mmmmm," he rumbled deep in his chest. Scratching his bearded chin, he watched and waited.

The room rocked with laughter and applause. Shrill whistles split the air. Many shouted for Dion to repeat his performance. The noted actress Holoscova remarked confidentially that she knew the boy's agent. Bosk was telling the media commentators that Snaga Ohme had discovered the young man acting in a performance of *Henry V* on a cruise liner bound for Star's End.

Dion stood motionless at the head of the stairs. His face was white, drained of life. His eyes had the fixed and glassy stare of a corpse. Every mocking laugh, every shout for an encore seemed a nail driven into his body.

His dream was ending, ending not with a bang but a snicker. Ridicule: the wooden stake through the heart, guaranteed to kill and make certain the victim stays dead. Dion would never rise from this. He was trapped, sealed inside the tomb unless some angel would come and roll away the stone.

"Sagan!" Maigrey turned to the Warlord, grasped his right hand in her right hand, and was amazed and frightened to feel it burning hot and trembling. "Abdiel didn't know anything about this. I felt his fear, for just a moment, and then he devised this means of discrediting Dion. Of discrediting you! The boy is strong, Sagan. He's defied Abdiel. But he's dying now. We have to help him!"

She wasn't certain he heard her. He wasn't looking at her; the dark and shadowed eyes stared straight at Dion, stared at him, through him, beyond him. She caught a glimpse inside her lord's soul, saw the bitter struggle, the most desperate battle he'd fought in his life, and she longed to help him but knew—against this Opponent—her aid was impossible.

Maigrey let go of his hand, fell back a pace as if to give him room to swing his sword arm. She could only stand outside the ring, prepared to go on and battle alone if he should fall. Prepared to take her place at his side if he should win.

The fight was mercifully swift, soon ended. The hand slowly unclenched. The shoulders beneath the golden armor sagged, the muscles of the arm went flaccid, the face beneath the helm aged. "Thy will be done!" He ground the words, spit them out as if they were choking bile in his mouth.

His body straightened, tall and strong. He drew the bloodsword, inserted the prongs into his hand. For the first time, he looked at her.

Draw your weapon, Guardian, he said without speaking. *We must defend our king.*

Sagan activated the sword; Maigrey activated hers. The weapons hummed and blazed with fire. Those standing near them fell back, shouting in alarm. The Warlord stalked forward, the lady at his side. The crowd, murmuring with delighted, horrified anticipation, fell back before them. The two reached the staircase.

Cover me, Sagan ordered silently, and began to climb the stairs.

Dion remained standing perfectly still, but the corpselike eyes had come to life. He watched the Warlord's approach warily, but unafraid. And then his hand moved, moved slowly to the buckle of his belt.

Maigrey turned, ascended the stairs backward, her sword functioning as a shield to guard her partner's back. The Honor Guard, though weaponless, deployed around her and around their lord. Maigrey wasn't really expecting an attack from the crowd, however. She knew, as did Sagan, that their true enemy stood near the top of the stairs. She managed to shift her gaze slightly, dividing her attention between the people below and the mind-seizer above. Abdiel was watching them, a pleasant smile, a knowing smile on the thin, chapped lips.

Sagan reached a wide landing on the staircase directly beneath where Dion stood. The young man had his hand clasped over the buckle of his belt. The blue eyes regarded the Warlord without recognition, without feeling, without emotion. The Warlord's golden armor flared in his eyes like the sun on hard blue ice.

Slowly, gracefully, Sagan bent his great height, knelt down on one knee. The bloodsword's fire flickered and died. Leaning forward, the Warlord laid the hilt at Dion's feet.

"My liege," he said, and bowed his head.

Chapter ✦◦○◦✦ Ten

Hell at last . . .

John Milton, *Paradise Lost*

Dion's hand twitched on the belt buckle, then dropped. He stared at Sagan dazedly, unable to understand or comprehend. It slowly dawned on the boy, however, that no one was laughing at him now. The crowd was silent, stunned, fumbling to grasp the amazing ramifications of what they had just witnessed.

"Pick it up!" Maigrey's voice jolted Dion from his stupefaction.

"What?" he said, staring at the sword at his feet.

Maigrey glided up the stairs, came to stand on the landing just beneath him. "The most powerful Warlord in the galaxy has just made you king! Pick up the damn sword!" Her eyes were still on the crowd, still darting toward Abdiel. "My liege," she added.

Dion reached down.

"Young man, take care!" Abdiel hastened forward, paused when he felt the heat of Maigrey's blade as she turned to face him, keeping her body between him and the boy. "Think what you are doing! You don't know Sagan's motive!"

"I know he didn't laugh at me," Dion returned.

Abdiel's gnarled hands fluttered in deprecation. The lidless eyes narrowed. "I was trying to save your life, Your Majesty! You unwittingly put yourself in dreadful danger. And you'll do so again if you go along with him. He wants you only for his own purposes. He'll make you king, all right! King of puppets!"

Reaching down, Dion carefully lifted the bloodsword and held it in his shaking hands.

This was the weapon that killed Platus. For all I know, it

377

was the weapon that killed my parents. Perhaps Abdiel is
right. What are Sagan's motives? Should I trust him?

No, I can't trust him, Dion decided. But, for now, I can use
him. Perhaps that's what it means to be a king.

"My lord, I— We . . ." he amended, using the royal "we,"
for a king is not one but many, "we accept your service. Take
back your sword and use it to defend our cause."

"Whatever *that* is," Sagan muttered, accepting the bloodsword and rising heavily to his feet.

Dion flushed. He'd sounded ridiculous. He didn't have a
cause, didn't really have anything. It was on the tip of his
tongue to ask "What now?" but he bit the words and bit his
tongue, tasted the blood in his mouth.

"And now, my liege lord," the Warlord began, and Dion
heard—or thought he did—the sarcasm, and smarted beneath
its lash, "I have done for you what I can for the time being. All
those present, whether they think you king or madman, know
you are under my protection. But don't deceive yourself.
Abdiel is right. You've made many enemies. Hasn't he,
mind-seizer?"

Sagan's shadowed gaze flicked to Abdiel, who merely
bowed disdainfully and did not respond. Dion, hearing the
warning in the Warlord's tone, looked to the old man and
found Abdiel looking intently at him, as if to say, Heed *my*
warning!

Frustrated, confused, Dion looked to Maigrey, saw in her
eyes, barely visible behind the silver helm, compassion, pity,
admiration. But her eyes weren't on him. The gray eyes were
on Sagan.

Dion was suddenly angry and glad of his anger; it neatly
covered his fear and confusion.

Abdiel approached him. "And now, my king, if you will
come with me—"

"I'm not going with you or anybody," Dion cut the old man
off. He felt smothered, as if these people surrounding him
were using up all the air. "Just leave me alone, all of you! I
need to be . . . be by myself. I need to think."

The Warlord said nothing, but remained standing where he
was. Abdiel remained standing where he was, appearing to
think Dion had meant everyone leave except him. Maigrey's
eyes were on the young man now, and they were dark with
concern and, oddly, sadness.

It was obvious none of the three was going to budge

without seeing the other two leave first. Dion, exasperated, frustrated, marched off, angrily tromping down the stairs.

"Keep near him," Maigrey ordered Marcus.

The centurion bowed and immediately followed Dion.

"What do you want?" the boy demanded, seeing the guard loom suddenly at his shoulder. "I'm not going back, if that's why Sagan sent you."

"The Lady Maigrey sent me, my liege," Marcus said respectfully. "I am to act as your bodyguard."

Dion turned to look back up the stairs where Maigrey stood, her silver armor shining bright, glittering, cold as the stars. He wanted to talk to her, needed to talk to her, but not around that man. Not around Sagan. And not around Abdiel, either. It seemed she understood, for she smiled at him and nodded.

Drawing a deep breath, trying to ease the tight sensation in his chest, Dion turned to face the staring, whispering multitude. He wished, suddenly, that he was billions of light-years away from this hateful place, from these vampirelike people, who seemed intent on sucking the life from him, feeding off his body. He saw his old home, the drab little house in the outback of Syrac Seven. He pictured himself sitting at his desk, studying with Platus, or playing the syntharp, or digging in the garden. A wistful longing came over him to return to that former life, to go back and be . . . ordinary.

The feeling was overpowering, overwhelming. These people would devour him, take from him everything he had to give, and despise him for giving it. *I will always be alone.* He'd said the words, but only now did he truly understand their veracity and it terrified him. He would always, always, always be alone.

He half-turned, deciding to run away and save himself, but in doing so he lifted his eyes and his gaze caught Sagan's. The golden and adamantine armor flared bright as flame; the red cape flowed like blood. He saw the Warlord standing in the doorway of that small house, saw the expression of contempt twist the mouth, visible beneath the helm, remembered the contempt in the man's voice.

He made you a king! Maigrey's words.

Did he? Did God? Did anyone? Or did you take this on yourself? And if you did take this, do you have the guts to see it through?

"He's afraid," Maigrey said.

"He better be," Sagan returned.

Dion heard them, not in his head, but in his heart.

"Go back to her ladyship, Marcus," Dion ordered. "Tell her, thank you, but I need no one."

He squared his shoulders, shook back the mane of red-gold hair, and walked slowly and proudly down the stairs, walked into the crowd, alone.

··◄■ ■►··

"You've lost him, Abdiel," Sagan said.

"On the contrary," the mind-seizer returned pleasantly, "I've lost nothing . . . unlike her ladyship." He turned to Maigrey. "Is that your starjewel the Adonian is sporting on his breast?"

"If it is or it isn't, it's no concern of yours."

"But I am concerned, Lady Maigrey. I've always had your best interests at heart, my dear. Haven't I, my lord? Sagan and I spoke of you often, dear lady, in those weeks before the revolution. When he and I were such good friends. . . ."

Everything around Maigrey darkened; a shadow stole over her. Sagan had lied to her in the dream! He'd known what Abdiel had intended. He had planned it with him! She could almost see the two of them together, the mind-seizer's hand pressing Sagan's. Perhaps, even now, they were in this together, conspiring against her. . . .

She forced a smile and, with her words, the shadow over her heart lifted. "Long ago you tried to divide us, mind-seizer. You failed then. You fail now."

Abdiel regarded her with grieved sadness. "You persist in willfully misunderstanding me, my dear. My only aim during that unfortunate time to which you refer was to serve you, to open the doors of power to you, as I have opened them for Dion. Yes, I've bonded with the boy. Didn't you know? Couldn't you tell?"

Maigrey could not forbear flashing a startled glance at Sagan. The Warlord gazed at Abdiel coolly, calmly.

"And look where your reckless independence has brought you, my lady," Abdiel was continuing. "To the brink of the abyss. Lower and lower you have sunk. Your starjewel is not only lost to you, it has become an object cursed and defiled. But I see in your heart—for I can see still into your heart, dear lady—that you want it back. I have some influence over the

Adonian. Allow me to intercede for you. I will see to it that he returns the starjewel to you."

"And what do you ask in return for this magnanimous offer?"

"Only that you think of me as a friend, my lady," Abdiel replied humbly. "As I have always tried to be, though you would not let me."

"I really don't care to think of you at all, mind-seizer, if I can help it." Maigrey bowed to him. "Thank you for your offer, but I will act on my own."

The old man's eyes were flat and empty as the eyes of a reptile. Abdiel bowed to her silently; the eyes slid to Sagan. The mind-seizer bowed to him, then Abdiel glided down the stairs to mingle with the admiring and curious throng surrounding Dion.

"You handled him well," the Warlord remarked.

Maigrey shivered, as if she had just avoided treading on a poisonous snake. She could not look at Sagan, attempted to banish the feelings of panic and betrayal the mind-seizer had dredged up from the depths of her being.

"Don't give me too much credit, my lord. I allowed him entry into my mind! I forgot how powerful he was. I let down my guard. . . ." She shook herself free of the memory. "But enough of that. I'll be more careful next time. And now, if you will excuse me, I'm going to try to talk to Dion."

She shifted her gaze to him, smiled. "What you did for the boy was truly noble, truly generous, Derek. I know how much it cost you!"

Sagan shrugged it off coldly. "I did it for myself, my lady. If he had been laughed out of the room, do you think I could ever have promoted him as king? And I don't like the thought of you going off by yourself. We shouldn't separate."

"Don't be ridiculous. We both agreed that I must talk to Dion, warn him of his danger. Besides," Maigrey added with a mischievous grin, "I'm dying of thirst and I'll never get a drink if I'm with you."

"You may find yourself dying of something else, my lady," Sagan said grimly, catching hold of her arm, detaining her. "Abdiel's threat is only the beginning for you, Maigrey. He wants the bomb. He needs the starjewel and he needs you in order to obtain it. I repeat: It's dangerous for us to separate."

"What are you worried about, my lord?" Maigrey leaned near him, suddenly laughed. "If your vision is true, then I'm in danger from only one person—you!"

Sagan released his grip on her, and Maigrey, with a grave salute, left him, running lightly down the stairs. He watched the blue cape flutter after her. The silver armor, catching the light, flared brilliantly, then was lost to sight, its flame almost extinguished by the milling crowd. But here and there, among the multitude, he caught a flash of silver, like moonbeams dancing on a night-dark lake.

"If anyone could cheat destiny, my lady, it would be you. I almost hope . . ." Sagan paused, considering what he had been about to ask. He shook his head. "No, for that would mean we were given over to chaos."

The Warlord cast his gaze upward, to the high, vaulted ceiling adorned with paintings telling the story of—what else—Adonis. The handsome youth was portrayed stalking the wild boar that would be his death. Sagan did not notice the mural, however. He sought higher, beyond mortal boundaries.

"I tested You. You gave me Your answer—with the back of Your hand!" Sagan rubbed his jaw, as if he could almost feel the blow. "But this may yet succeed . . . to both our advantage! Now there is work to be done. Work on behalf of . . ." he paused, shook his head in bemused and wondering resignation, "my king."

Chapter ·◄▪━●═▪►· Eleven

In fortune solio sederam elatus . . . nunc a sumo corrui . . .

Once on fortune's throne I sat exalted . . . I was struck down . . .

Carl Orff, Carmina Burana

Freed of the stern and disapproving eye of her commander, Maigrey was finally able to enjoy a glass of champagne, taking care to pour one for herself from a splashing fountain decorating the buffet table. She had seen Raoul and his diminutive partner circulating among the guests and, recalling Sagan's warning, wasn't about to drink from any glass offered her by anyone. Sipping the wine—champagne went straight to her head; she had learned to drink it slowly—she took time to observe the room and the people in it.

No one disturbed her solitude. The two formidable-appearing centurions warned the media away; few others chose to come near her, though they stared at her with morbid curiosity. Maigrey understood. Perhaps Lazarus, risen himself from the dead, had undergone the same treatment. Not only was she a ghost, she was— How had Abdiel put it—cursed, defiled? Snaga Ohme must be spreading the story of the starjewel. Maigrey downed her glass of champagne at a gulp, poured herself another. Alcohol couldn't make one forget, but it made remembering a damn sight easier.

She saw Sagan descend the stairs, saw him almost immediately drawn into conversation with the vapor-breather, Rykilth. The two moved off and were eventually lost to her sight. Were they talking treason, sedition? Almost assuredly. Rykilth—an ally. Maigrey raised an eyebrow, smiled at the bubbles rising from the glass's hollow stem, remembering the time Rykilth had been an enemy, remembering the time they'd captured and boarded his ship. Their squadron had stumbled about blindly, unable to see in the thick, poisonous atmosphere, afraid to fire for fear of hitting each other, easy targets for the vapor-breathers. Frustrated, Maigrey had opened an air lock . . .

"My lady." Her centurion, Marcus, drew her attention from the bubbles rising to the top, breaking when they hit the surface, and vanishing. "The young man is in trouble."

Maigrey turned her attention to a knot of people near the foot of the stairs. It looked more like a knot of snakes, writhing and twisting about a central object. She could barely catch a glimpse of flame-red hair in the center.

"Go to him, Marcus. Bring him to me. Alone."

"Yes, my lady."

The centurion left upon his errand, slicing through the knot like a steel-tipped spear. Maigrey watched closely, more than half-expecting to see the magenta robes with black lightning hanging over the boy like an evil cloud. Marcus attained his objective, however, and managed to extricate the young man. Maigrey couldn't tell by his expression if Dion was thankful for the rescue or angered at the interruption of his first press conference. At this moment, she didn't care. Despite the champagne, she was in no very good mood herself. She had just spotted Abdiel, conversing with Snaga Ohme. The Adonian was fingering the starjewel. . . .

"You wanted to talk to me, my lady?" Dion stood before her, speaking to her distantly, coolly, as if they'd just been introduced.

Maigrey kept her gaze fixed on Abdiel long enough for Dion to follow the line of her vision, then shifted her gray eyes to him. "I don't much like the company you keep, young man."

Dion flushed, the pale face crimsoning. "I could say the same for you, my lady." He glanced pointedly at the centurions, at the phoenix crest upon their armor.

Maigrey understood, chose to ignore him. "I warned you about the mind-seizers, Dion. I told you how they perverted the power of the Blood Royal." She saw the blue eyes ice over, saw him start to retreat behind the frozen wall. She broke off the direct attack, backed away, hoping to persuade him to come out from behind his barricade. "I'm not blaming you. I'm blaming myself. I didn't tell you enough about them, but that was because I thought they were all dead. I thought Abdiel was dead! If I had known . . ." Her voice hardened, grew grim. She sighed, tried to dispel the darkness of the past. "But I didn't."

Dion regarded her impassively, looking out over the battlements of his chill fortress.

"Perhaps it was just as well you met him," Maigrey continued, trying to sound positive. "He's obviously done you no lasting damage. I saw his face when you revealed who you were. He was surprised, displeased. You resisted him and now you understand the harm he can do—"

"Like what? Open my eyes? Let me see the truth?"

"What truth?" Maigrey asked, feeling his chill steal over her.

"The truth about the power you'd deny me, if you could! The truth about you and Sagan. The truth about that phony magic show you two put on for me—"

"What?" She stared at him, uncomprehending.

"That fake rite of initiation or whatever you called it! Illusion, all illusion. All except the power. And he's going to teach me to use it." Dion lifted his chin proudly, hands fingering the belt buckle at his waist. "He's taught me some already."

Maigrey saw the belt buckle, saw the nervous fingers grasp at it, as if for reassurance. A warning bell sounded in her mind, but its clang was lost in the din of other concerns chiming their discordant notes. Damage *had* been done, perhaps irreversible. Abdiel had probed, discovered the boy's weak vein. He'd been able to inject the poison without his victim feeling the smallest prick of the needle.

Logic. The concrete. Believe only in that which you can see, hear, smell, touch. Platus, her own brother, in his disbelief, his loss of faith, had prepped the boy for the lethal dose. What could she use to counteract it? How could she fight the logical with the mystical?

"And in case you care, my lady"—Dion's cutting voice came to her indistinctly; she could barely hear it through the ringing in her ears—"Tusk is back on Vangelis, making plans to rescue John Dixter. I'm going to join him there tomorrow. We'll be certain to give the general your regards—"

"Tusk . . ." Maigrey heard the name, grasped at it frantically. She'd found, if not an antidote, perhaps a way to slow the poison's effect. "Where did you say Tusk was?"

Dion stared at her coldly, perhaps thinking she was drunk. "I said he'd returned to Vangelis—"

"No, he didn't! He's still at Abdiel's!"

Dion shook his head in disgust. Bowing, he started to turn away. Maigrey caught hold of him, spun him around.

"You fool! Tusk saw through the mind-seizer! He warned you what Abdiel was, didn't he? I tell you, Dion, Tusk and Nola never left the mind-seizer's house!"

"Let go of me—"

"The Warlord has a spy watching Abdiel! Sagan told me. Tusk and Nola are still there. Or they were. Now they're expendable. . . . Dion, look at me. Listen to me! Our minds have been joined through the bloodsword. You *know* I'm telling the truth."

Dion didn't want to look, didn't want to hear. But he couldn't turn doubt's razor-edged blade. It slid inside him. The pain was excruciating, and the boy lashed back.

"Sagan told you that, did he?" he sneered. "When? While the two of you were in bed together—"

Maigrey struck him. A silver-gloved right fist to the jaw, delivered with skill and precision, sent the boy reeling backward into the arms of a gigantic, hairy warrior.

"Ah, laddie," the man said coolly, catching Dion in a grip of iron, "you asked for that one."

Dion's face hurt abominably. He wiped blood from a split and swelling lip, spit blood from his sore and cut mouth. He looked at Maigrey, saw her anger burn in her like a clear bright flame. She smoothed the glove over the knuckles of her right hand.

"Stand up, laddie, and make your apology like a man." The giant hoisted Dion to his feet with such alacrity that he nearly propelled the boy headlong into Maigrey.

Dion stumbled, caught himself, drew himself up stiffly. He put his hand to his jaw, felt it starting to swell. He heard scattered laughter in the crowd, saw people gathering around, felt his skin flush hot with shame. He wanted to apologize, but he hurt too much. Not just the pain of her blow, but the pain inside him. He was confused, furious, and frightened. If what she said was true, he had abandoned Tusk and Nola to imprisonment, perhaps death. Yet Abdiel had assured him they were gone. Who was lying? Who was telling him the truth? Were any of them?

At that moment, Dion hated them all and, above them all, he hated himself.

"If you will, my lady," he said, words coming slowly and

stiffly through the swollen flesh, "tell my Lord Sagan that I want to talk to him. Alone." Turning on his heel, he stalked off, his hand nursing his bruised and bleeding cheek.

"Maigy, Maigy," the giant rumbled, gazing at her in admiration, "you haven't lost your touch!"

"But I shouldn't have lost my temper. I shouldn't have hit him." Maigrey sighed remorsefully, wrung her aching hand. "He'll never forgive me, and I don't blame him."

"Nonsense, Maigy." The giant's bearded face split into a wide grin. "You did rightly. He deserved it."

Towering over her, the warrior-king could easily have made three of her. He was clad in hand-fashioned leather armor, decorated with the tails of animals, dried body parts of various alien species, and long tufts of human hair. His own hair was long and black and curly, trailing down over his back and shoulders to his waist, mingling with a long, black, and curly beard that cascaded down over a broad, well-fed belly.

"A little bloodletting is good for a young one. Releases the evil humors. I should know," the giant added, winking. "You released them from me!" He thumped himself on his round belly. "That sword of yours sent me to bed for six phases! But by my spleen and bowels, lass, it was worth it! That white hair of yours would have made a show in my trophy collection!" He gazed at her helmed head with such fierce admiration that Maigrey's guards took a step nearer, faces set in grim warning.

"There's no need for alarm, centurions," Maigrey admonished hastily, unable to keep from smiling. "The warrior is an old, old friend. Bear Olefsky"—she held out her hands—"it's good to see you again!"

"An old enemy cudgeled into friendship." The Bear ignored her outstretched hands, gathered her into a hug, his large, hairy arms completely engulfing her. "I heard you were dead, lass," he said more somberly, releasing her. "I cut my beard. The shield-wife cut her hair. We made a braid of memory that hangs now in your name-child's room."

"Thank you, Bear," Maigrey replied, her voice soft and sad. "That was a terrible time. . . ."

"But long over now!" The Bear laughed heartily, his booming roar rattling the dishes on the nearby buffet table. "I'll go home, take the wreath, and throw it in the fire! Better still, you come with me, Maigy."

Eyeing her, he shook his head. "You're too skinny. A man wants a woman he can find easily in the dark. Come back to

Solgart with me. The shield-wife will feed you well. You will meet your name-child! You haven't seen her since she was a tiny baby. Though"—he heaved a gusty sigh—"I think she is too much like you. Thin as a young gazelle. I tell her no man will ever want her."

"And what does she say?"

"Nothing. She laughs at me." The Bear tugged at his beard. "Can you imagine that? Laughs at me, her father. If my sons did that—" The Bear clenched an enormous fist, shook it. Then, sighing, he grinned ruefully. "But my daughter isn't the least bit respectful of me."

"She knows you're all growl. How is the shield-wife? Did Sonja come with you?"

"More beautiful than ever!" the Bear said proudly. "But she could not come. She was brought to bed by our sixteenth." The Bear rumpled up his long black curls, shook his head gloomily. "Another boy. Fifteen sons and only one daughter. And she born when you were on our planet for peace talks. Come back, Maigy. You're our luck! And bring old Sagan with you, unless he's too busy plotting treason!"

The Bear laughed again. His voice carried well. Many who had gathered near to eavesdrop quickly left the vicinity.

"I'd like to come, Bear. I'd dearly love to see Sonja and my name-child. But I have other responsibilities." Maigrey looked for Dion in the crowd, couldn't find him. She was worried about him, and her anxiety had pushed back even her desire to regain the starjewel.

The Bear nodded, sobering quickly. "The kinglet? Is it true, lass? Will Sagan back the boy's claim to the throne?"

"He will."

"And you trust him?" The Bear eyed her seriously, black eyes glittering narrowly from beneath thick, curling brows. It seemed he was looking at the scar on her face, though Maigrey knew well enough that it was hidden by the helm.

"Yes." She drew a deep breath. "I do."

The Bear snorted, musing, scratched his hairy chest, visible beneath the leather armor. "If the laddie is truly a Starfire . . ."

"He is, Bear. He's the child I carried from the flames, the child I took from his dying mother's arms." Maigrey's voice broke. The memory was too vivid, too clear. "And Sagan and I performed the rite. That 'magic show' you heard Dion talk about."

Bear appeared even more thoughtful. "My ears and eye-balls. I better be talking to old Sagan about this." He cocked a black eye at Maigrey. "My empire seceded from the Galactic Republic last week, you know, lass."

Maigrey stared, astonished. "No, I didn't! What happened?"

"We received old Sagan's report on the Corasian attack on Shelton's planets. How Robes set us up. It made sense. More than Robes did with his yammering denials."

"Are you at war?"

The Bear was complacent. "I suppose we will be, if the Congress ever gets around to voting to declare it on us. They've been called into emergency session. But I think, when it comes to taking roll call, they'll find more than a few of their members missing."

"But what about the Warlord in your sector?"

The Bear winked at her again. "He's mine. Bought and paid for with the wealth of twenty systems. You think your kinglet could use support like that?"

"Of course," Maigrey murmured dazedly. This was all moving too fast, much too fast.

The Bear made a rumbling sound in his massive chest. "I'll talk to old Sagan. And I'll talk to the lad." Olefsky frowned. "But I'll have to think better of him than I do now before I put him on the throne. Ach!"

The man's gaze fixed on an altercation occurring at the far end of the buffet table, where it appeared his sons had blundered into and inadvertently smashed several articles of furniture and were now involved in a shouting match with Snaga Ohme's hired men.

"Those boys of mine are wrecking the place!" Bear heaved a gusty sigh. "I try to introduce them into society, teach them social graces, and look what happens!"

"Farewell, Bear." Maigrey stood on tiptoe, kissed what she could find of his cheek beneath the beard. "That's for my name-child."

"I'll give it to her, lass." Olefsky gazed at Maigrey, his tone suddenly gentle. "But it would be better if you came to give it yourself."

"Someday, Bear." Maigrey smiled, but there was a sadness in her smile that negated her promise. "Someday."

The Bear watched her walk away, silver armor gleaming brightly, until she was swallowed up by the crowd.

"The memory wreath will *not* go into the fire, Maigy," he said after her, but to himself, "for my heart tells me we would only have to make a new one. It's hard enough for a man to die once; to have to die twice is not fair. You'd think the good God would treat her better. By my beard, lass, I pray your second time will be easier than your first!"

Shaking his shaggy head sorrowfully, Bear Olefsky strode off through the crowd, bowling over waiters, trampling chairs underfoot as he went to knock his sons' heads together, teaching them the finer points of mingling with polite society.

··◁■   ■▷··

"And was it really necessary, my lady, to slug the young man?" Sagan demanded.

"I lost my temper. Our talk went all wrong. It was my fault. I jumped at the boy, leapt for his throat. Of course, he fought back. But still, Dion should never have said . . ." Maigrey paused, not quite knowing where that remark would lead her. "What he said," she ended lamely, feeling her skin burn. "Anyway, he wants to talk to you now. Alone."

The two stood in a far corner of the ballroom, near the orchestra. Rykilth, the vapor-breather, had concluded his conversation with the Warlord, a conversation which had ended satisfactorily for both, to judge by the denseness of the fog generated inside Rykilth's bubble-helm.

"Very well. Where is Dion now?"

Maigrey's flush deepened. "I don't know."

"Damn it, woman! He's in danger! Abdiel has to get rid of the boy, after that pronouncement of his. You heard Olefsky. I've been talking to Rykilth. It's only a matter of time before he and his systems pull out, as well. The political situation is rapidly deteriorating. Dion's claim couldn't have come at a better—or a worse—time."

"I'm sorry, my lord, but he walked off and, to tell the truth, I didn't feel much like going after him. I was afraid I might hit him again. He makes me so mad! He left Tusk there to die. And don't tell me he didn't know what Abdiel was up to!" Maigrey sighed, exasperated, then added remorsefully, "But you're right. I shouldn't have let him provoke me. I'll go with you to talk to the boy. . . ."

Sagan considered it, shook his head. "No. You've done enough harm in that area for one night. I'll find Dion and try to reason with him. If that fails, I'll simply get him out of here.

While I'm doing that, you better have your talk with the Adonian. Snaga Ohme was looking for you. He *claims* he wants to continue negotiations."

"I'll meet with him—"

"Not alone. I won't allow it," the Warlord stated flatly. "And you did take the oath of allegiance."

Maigrey glared at him, at first defiant. Then she realized she wasn't being sensible. The Adonian had already tried once to have her killed. "You're right," she said, swallowing her pride. "I'll arrange a meeting, then summon you."

"You will have your best opportunity of finding Ohme now. He's on the lower levels, opening the target-shooting galleries."

"We're not going to kill him," Maigrey admonished. "The Star is cursed as it is without spilling blood on it. We'll talk to him. When we're finished, I have no doubt he will be glad to return my property to me in exchange for your promised payment."

"Your faith is exceeded only by your naïveté, my lady. Arrange the meeting for at least an hour from now. I have work to do. In the service of my king," he added smoothly.

"This from the man who said he would rather reign in hell than serve in heaven!" She eyed him narrowly. "You're taking this shift in fate far too well, my lord."

"Someone has to reign in hell, my lady, no matter who reigns in heaven." He made her a mocking bow, then started to leave.

"Sagan," she called.

He glanced back at her, impatient to be gone. "Well, what?"

But she couldn't articulate her fears. "Be careful," she said, after a moment's struggle. "Dion's—something about him's not right."

He regarded her thoughtfully, then nodded. "I wouldn't expect him to be, after an encounter with Abdiel. Remember that, Maigrey. The mind-seizer is out there. Waiting. You be careful, as well."

The Warlord left her. Maigrey rubbed the gloved palm of her right hand nervously, prey to a growing sense of foreboding. She confronted herself, examined her fear, and could find no concrete reason for it. She and Sagan would retrieve the starjewel, pick up Dion, and they'd all go home. And after that?

"Perhaps," she said irritably, "we'll spend our time parceling out shares of red-hot real estate. Reigning in hell! What can Sagan be up to now?"

But there was no use worrying about it. She had to keep her mind on the Adonian. Maigrey turned, looked for the exits, and saw that the crowd had thinned considerably. The night's true business was about to commence. Lights flickered on and off three times in the ballroom, a none-too-subtle hint that the entertainment portion of the evening was over. Everyone was now expected to move on to the target ranges, play with the merchandise, and spend money.

Banks of elevators descended to the lower levels. Accompanied by her guards, Maigrey made her way across the empty, echoing floor of the nearly deserted ballroom just as the lights were being extinguished, one by one.

Chapter ❧⟐❧ Twelve

Don't tell me that you love me.
Just say that you want me.

Fleetwood Mac, "*Tusk*"

The desert, by the light of Laskar's moon, took on a faint green tinge that was, to Tusk's mind, particularly ghastly. He hunkered down behind the boulder, blinked his eyes that ached with the strain of watching.

"You'd think someone would've missed those zombies that bird shot by now," he muttered to Nola, "come lookin' for them."

She shook her head. "There's not a lot of brotherly love lost among that group. I bet one zombie wouldn't know another's gone unless they took a head count. What are they doing, anyway?"

"They've about got the house torn down and packed up." Tusk twisted around to look at their ragged companion. "Isn't it time you took off? Wait much longer and the shuttle'll be crawling with those creeps."

"No, no," Sparafucile said, shaking his head and grinning. "You will take care of them for me. Keep them away from shuttle."

The half-breed had been, for the last few minutes, engaged in selecting several tools from an assortment he carried in a chamois skin pouch. Holding each up, he studied every one with a critical eye. The delicate instruments glistened in the lambent light of shuttle, moon, and stars. Tusk recognized them—tools used to work on a shipboard computer's incredibly sensitive and complex microsystems. Sparafucile made his choices, tucked them inside the breast of his tattered clothing, stowed the chamois pouch with the rest of his gear.

"Plannin' to mess up their computer, huh?" Tusk said.

"How the hell are you gonna get inside the shuttle and take the time to do that? They won't *all* be out shooting at us. You gonna tell 'em you're the friendly computer repairman?"

Sparafucile made a noise that Tusk assumed was his version of a laugh. The half-breed suddenly leaned near Tusk, placed his hand on the mercenary's shoulder.

"Sparafucile goes where night goes. Where there is darkness, there is Sparafucile." The half-breed's whisper hissed like the wind among the rocks. Tusk's flesh crawled. He shook off the clutching hand.

"You have time device?" the assassin asked.

"Naw, they took my watch away from me, along with my gun."

"Then you count. Give me one hundred and then open fire. What are you called?"

"I'm Tusk. This is Nola."

"Tusk," Sparafucile repeated thoughtfully. The half-breed rose to his feet, sharp eyes gazing over the edge of the boulder, studying the terrain, watching the movements of the mind-dead. "No-La." He spoke her name in two distinct syllables, turned his malformed head. The cruel eyes glinted. "I like that name. No-La."

"Thanks. I'm kind of fond of it myself." Nola glanced at Tusk helplessly, raised her brows, shrugged her shoulders.

Sparafucile made the odd throaty sound of a laugh again, then slid into the night. Tusk tried to keep sight of him, but lost him almost immediately among the shadows cast by the boulders. He couldn't see the assassin, couldn't hear him. The wind made more noise; the darkness itself seemed to make more noise.

"Jeez!" Nola huddled near him, shivered. "Who is he? Or rather, *what* is he?"

"Professional killer," Tusk said, checking his weapon for the fourth time to make certain it was charged. "Sagan could always afford the best."

"You've heard of this . . . Spara-character, then?"

"No. And I'll bet those who have aren't alive to tell about it."

"But that means us!" Nola said, alarmed.

"You betcha, sweetheart." Tusk patted her hand reassuringly.

"But he said he was supposed to take us to Sagan!"

"He didn't say in what condition. One. Two. Three . . ."

"Oh, Tusk! Let's just leave! Now. No one would know."

"I thought about it." Tusk paused in his count, glanced around. "But we're a long way from nowhere. No transport. No water. No shelter. And you can bet the breed's got a vehicle hidden near here. He'd find us easy enough. Naw, we're better off—"

"—risking our lives, waiting for Dion. That's the real reason you're staying," Nola snapped.

"Twenty-eight. Twenty-nine. Maybe. So what?" Tusk avoided looking at her, focused on a target.

"He abandoned us, that's what! Threw us to the wolves!"

Tusk scowled. "He didn't know we were prisoners."

"The hell he didn't!"

"Damn it, Nola—"

"Aren't you supposed to be counting?"

Women! Tusk seethed. Thirty-one. Thirty-two. She drives me crazy sometimes! It's like . . . like she could see inside me! And she has no goddam business inside me! Fifty-six. Fifty-seven. Or somewhere around there.

"They're moving!" Nola reported, peering up over the boulder.

A zombie had apparently discovered his dead companions and raised the alarm. Other zombies came running. They stood in a knot around the corpses, flashing nuke lamps into the darkness, debating in cool, dispassionate voices what was best to be done.

"You stay here," Tusk told Nola. He strapped the lasgun around his waist. Fumbling in the assassin's bag, he came up with a couple of grenades, thrust them into his pockets. "I'm gonna try to get closer."

Nola's hand closed over his, squeezed it tightly. "I'm sorry, Tusk. I shouldn't have said that about Dion. It's just that I'm scared—"

Tusk stared down at the ground. Then, sighing, he took her in his arms, held her close, rubbing his jaw in her curly hair. "Yeah. Me, too. I got to admit I don't see a way out of this one yet. We got the devil on one side and zombies on the other. But if we do get out of this, Nola Rian," Tusk added, tilting her face and kissing her on the nose, "I may just have to marry you."

"Yeah? Well, I may just have to marry you back! So there. What's the count?"

"Oh, who the hell gives a damn? Ninety-nine. One hundred. Happy? Good, I'm off. Take care of yourself, Rian."

"You, too, Tusca."

The mercenary kissed her swiftly on the cheek, patted her rump, and darted away among the rocks. Nola lifted her beam rifle, balanced it on the top of the boulder, looked down the heat-seeking sight, taking careful aim. The mind-dead had apparently reached a decision. Several were detailed off to search and began making their way into the ravine. Others returned to their work, leaving the bodies of their comrades lying on the ground.

Catching movement out of the corner of her eye, Nola thought she saw a hunched-over shape slip under the belly of the shuttlecraft. She couldn't take her attention from the mind-dead to look more closely, however, and the next time she snatched a glance in that direction, the shape was gone.

She adjusted the sights, brought her first target carefully into focus. This wasn't exactly her idea of a romantic setting for a marriage proposal. And it would be difficult to come back here to celebrate their anniversaries.

But it would certainly make one hell of a good story to tell the kids. . . .

Chapter ···❦··· Thirteen

I am settled, and bend up
each corporal agent to this terrible feat.
William Shakespeare, *Macbeth*, Act I, Scene 7

The below-ground levels of Snaga Ohme's estate were vast playrooms for children fond of deadly toys. Innumerable target ranges allowed potential buyers to observe firsthand Ohme's newest weapons and improvements made on the old. The target ranges varied in shape and size, from small, compact chambers designed for the testing of hand weapons to gigantic, cavernous fields carved out beneath the surface that shook with the simulated blasts of lascannons.

A buyer could not only test the latest models, he could test his own skill. Ohme's ranges were built to accommodate the faint of heart, who could shoot away blithely at rows of holographic ducks, or the more bloodthirsty and daring, who could do battle with robots built to resemble Corasians, vapor-breathers, the barbaric warriors of Olefsky's system, the tentacled aliens of Andares 17, the drug-hyped street gangs of Laskar, or the members of Galactic Democratic Republic armed forces—currently one of the most popular displays.

Steelglass windows permitted viewers the chance to watch the "killings." Soundproofing in the ranges kept the noise level down. It was an eerie sight, thought Maigrey, walking the corridors, surrounded by the flare and flash of battle, and hearing nothing except the laughter or applause of some of the observers.

She paused to view Rykilth, the vapor-breather, doing battle on board a representation of a Corasian vessel. Ohme's set was quite accurate, Maigrey noted, having recently been on board a Corasian vessel herself. She shuddered at the memory and when the fiery orange plastisteel body of a

Corasian appeared, attacking Rykilth from behind, Maigrey's
hand closed involuntarily over the bloodsword.

Rykilth's partner, a Warlady who had been introduced to
Maigrey as Baroness DiLuna, caught sight of the vapor-
breather's danger and shouted a warning. Rykilth turned and
fired his weapon—a new-model lasgun. The Corasian kept
coming, however. Maigrey grinned, though with a shiver.
She'd made the same mistake herself. Rykilth had neglected to
change the polarity on the weapon; the Corasian absorbed the
energy blast, actually increasing in strength. Rykilth "died"
the next moment; a mechanical voice registered a "kill" for the
Corasian. The spectators were noisily appreciative.

"Quite a lifelike simulation, don't you agree, Lady Maigrey?" Snaga Ohme stood at her side.

"Extremely. You appear to be familiar with our enemy.
Some might say a little too familiar." Maigrey glanced up at
him, saw the starjewel, black and ugly on his chest. She
returned her attention to the target range. The Baroness
DiLuna, an extremely skilled shot, had just taken out the
Corasian.

"I have my contacts, my sources. Highly reliable, as you can
see. They should be, of course. I pay them enough. It might
surprise you to know, Lady Maigrey, that our government
comes to *me* for information."

"Nothing about you would surprise me, Adonian," Maigrey
returned. Rykilth, during his "dead" phase, discovered that his
weapon was useless and would be for a full thirty seconds. The
vapor-breather scrambled for cover as the orange glow that
always preceded a Corasian attack lit the target range.

"Not even to know that I am willing to discuss the return of
your starjewel?" Snaga Ohme said offhandedly.

Maigrey folded her arms across her chest, kept her gaze
fixed on the game. "Indeed?"

"I've become bored with it, frankly." Ohme twiddled the
jewel carelessly. It was all Maigrey could do to keep from
throttling him. "It created a nice little sensation this evening,
but that's worn thin. It's abhorrent to look at, and a few people
have been terribly put off by its hideous aspect." Ohme leaned
near her, lowering his voice. "I suppose Sagan's offer still
holds?"

Maigrey was about to reply, but the Adonian nudged her.
"Too many people around to discuss this now. Your boyfriend's
made himself rather unpopular with certain top government

officials tonight and I have numerous defense contracts on the line. We'll talk in private. In an hour, go to Green level. One of the target ranges will be closed and locked, an 'Out of Order' sign posted on it. Four long presses on the entry button and two short will gain *you* admittance, however." The Adonian bowed, with a charming smile. "I look forward to ending our differences, Lady Maigrey."

He left her to join the throng surrounding the victorious baroness, who had just set a new record for number of Corasians killed in a limited time span. The chagrined Rykilth was forced to endure the crowd's jeers, which he took with his usual ill grace, the fog in his bubble turning a noxious shade of yellow. Vapor-breathers were not known for their sense of humor.

"What do you think, centurion?" Maigrey asked Marcus. They moved away from the Corasian target range, proceeding at a slow pace down the corridor.

"I think the last place I'd be in an hour, my lady, is on Green level at a target range marked 'Out of Order.'"

"I agree with you." Maigrey paused, staring at nothing in thoughtful silence. Shaking her head, she sighed. "But, in an hour, that's where we'll be. I *will* have the starjewel back."

"You shouldn't go alone—"

"I won't. I will inform my lord to meet us there. Well, gentlemen," Maigrey added, purposefully cheerful. "We have an hour to kill."

··◁■ ■▷··

Dion nursed the pain of his aching jaw, nurtured the seed of rage. It sent down roots into his darkness, sucked up jealousy and thwarted pride, fed off ambition. The plant grew rapidly, its thick stem twisting and writhing inside him, its fruit sweet to the taste, cloying to the senses.

But the visions it produced appalled and sickened some weak part of him. He firmly trampled that part down, kicked the dirt over it. Absorbed in the care and feeding of his fury, he struggled to free himself from the crush of people who surrounded him, babbling incoherently at him. He couldn't hear what they said, couldn't understand.

Shoving the grasping, greedy hands aside, Dion fled, searching for someplace where he could be alone, where it was quiet and he could breathe. He plunged into an elevator, told it to go up . . . up above the mob, up into the clear air. He had no idea where he was, where he was going. When the elevator stopped and the door opened, he emerged into a hallway and saw that it was empty. Dion could almost have wept in relief.

He sank down on a bench, reveled in the silence. The night air flowed in from an open window, ruffled his hair, cooled his burning skin, filled his aching lungs. He closed his eyes, leaned his head back against the wall.

His rage blossomed, and though the flower it bore was unlovely to look at and foul to smell, Dion reached out his hand to pluck it. The weak part inside him made him hesitate. This wasn't his idea of being a king—murders, lies, double-dealing. But it would all be for the best, he reminded himself. *I'll make it up. Evil is just to get me started. In time, I can afford to be good.*

A voice roused him from his dark dreaming. Glancing down a corridor, he saw the shining armor of the Warlord's centurions.

So, Dion said to himself, *I didn't come here of my own volition. You led me here, drew me here, just as you drew me to you on* Phoenix. *Well, I may not have come here on my own, but I'll leave that way.*

The young man fingered reassuringly the buckle of his belt, rose to his feet, and walked down the hall. He was nervous, but not afraid. Instead he felt eager, elated, excited. He would prove to them all that he was strong enough to be king.

The hallway was long and, in contrast to the rest of the lavish house, was barren and sterile in appearance. Doors on either side of him were shut and locked. He looked through the occasional pane of glass, saw desks and computers and scraggly plants, fizzing drink machines, coffee makers. Offices. Signs on the doors labeled them: ACCOUNTING, BILLING, INVENTORY CONTROL, SECRETARIAL. All closed for the night. Here was where the Adonian conducted his business.

The centurions moved from their positions the moment the boy drew near them, walking farther down the hall. Though they had not glanced in his direction and appeared to be unaware of his presence, Dion knew himself to be under their careful scrutiny, guessed that they were leading him somewhere. The young man's hand clenched painfully over the belt buckle. He'd play their little game. Play it to the bitter end.

The hallway turned at a sharp, ninety-degree angle. Dion left the light of one, entered the darkness of another. This hall was lit only by a purple-blue light gleaming out from a bank of steelglass windows. Halfway down the hall, standing in front of the windows, was the Warlord, the light reflecting off his golden armor. Dion was forcibly reminded of the night Sagan had come to his house, of the night Platus had died by this man's hand.

The nervous, eager excitement drained from the boy, leaving him empty, calm. He could do this.

Dion drew level with the steelglass windows and still Sagan had not turned to look at him. The young man knew the older man was aware of his presence. He followed the Warlord's gaze, looked through the windows. Behind the steelglass were large screens, banks of computers, and other complicated instruments. These rooms, unlike the empty offices, were filled with men and women, monitoring, adjusting.

The Warlord gazed at them intently.

"In there," he said to Dion, starting a conversation as though they'd been talking together for an hour, "is the heart of the Adonian's estate. In there, they control the force field, the sentinels at the gate, the electronic surveillance equipment in the mansion, the murderous devices used to welcome unwanted guests. An interesting room, don't you think, my liege?"

Dion heard the mockery in the man's voice. The sarcastic tone overrode any possible logical sense he could make out of Sagan's words. What does this room matter to me? What does the Adonian matter?

"Whoever controls this room," the Warlord continued, voice low, pitched for Dion's ears, "controls everything."

"My lord," Dion said, "I must speak with you now."

"You arrived late," Sagan replied, withdrawing his gaze from the room, turning to face Dion at last. "I have another appointment. But if you wait here for me, I will return—"

Dion heard—or thought he heard—the sneer in the man's voice. He began to focus his mind, as Abdiel had taught him, upon the weapon. The cumulators responded to the mental stimulation coming to them through the nerves. They began to charge; he could feel them coming to life. Dion slid the gun out of its belt, keeping it concealed in his hand, and aimed it point-blank at the Warlord.

"Your next appointment," the boy said, "will be in hell!"

Chapter ❖◦◦❖ Fourteen

. . . one event happeneth to them all.

Ecclesiastes 2:14

Green level, Maigrey was pleased to note, was swarming with people. Having more than half-expected to find it dark and deserted, she and her bodyguards had emerged cautiously from the elevator, only to find themselves engulfed in a champagne-drinking and laughing mob.

Feeling slightly foolish, Maigrey took her hand from the hilt of the bloodsword and shoved her way through the throng. Ohme's salesmen were circulating, writing orders, checking prices and stock availability, and entering sales and shipping dates on small, hand-held computers.

This was Ohme's museum level, Maigrey discovered. Several of the target ranges offered opportunities to use antique weapons, which always provided amusement. Bear Olefsky and his two beefy sons were having a wonderful time, wielding maces and two-handed swords against an army of robotic knights.

Maigrey walked past the various ranges, looking for the one the Adonian had specified, planning to reconnoiter it before entering. The crowd dwindled in size the farther down the long hallway she walked. Many of the ranges at the end were dark, but none were specifically marked "Out of Order." Turning into another hall, she discovered it to be dimly lit and completely empty. She placed her hand on her sword.

Maigrey and her guards reached the end of this corridor, seeing nothing of the range for which they were looking. They had walked kilometers, seemingly, and left the noise far behind them. No one was around, not even a salesman; none of the target ranges were in use. It was so quiet, now, that they could hear themselves breathe. The ground trembled occasionally beneath their feet; the lascannon demonstrations were apparently still going on.

"This has to be the right level," Maigrey stated, glancing around in frustration. She was tense, nervous, oppressed with an increasing sense of danger. She wondered, too, where Sagan was. He should have joined them by now.

She tried to reach him, touch him with her mind, but his mind was focused, intent on something else. He was aware of her, but he couldn't respond, couldn't withdraw his full and concentrated attention from whatever he was doing. Her sense of danger grew stronger, not only for herself, but for him.

"This is the third hall we've searched. Is there another one we've missed?" she demanded sharply, masking her disquiet.

"No, my lady, not according to the map posted—"

"My lady." Caius touched her arm, motioned with his hand. "Over here."

First glance had indicated that this corridor ended in a blank wall. Caius, on inspecting, discovered that the wall was an illusion, a holographic image. The corridor continued beyond it a short distance. The three, peering through the holograph, could see posted a small white sign, reflecting the light.

OUT OF ORDER.

"That's it." Maigrey drew a breath, felt it catch in her throat. "What time is it?"

"It lacks only a few minutes to the appointed hour, my lady."

Marcus looked at her worriedly.

"We'll wait for my lord," she said to him, knowing what he was thinking, "but only those few minutes."

··◆━ ━▶··

Dion's sweating hand almost slipped off the gun. His mouth was dry; his heart beat so rapidly it made him almost light-headed. His bowels cramped, stomach muscles gripped.

"Do you know what this is?" he demanded, exhibiting the weapon. His own voice sounded strange to his ears, he almost wondered who had spoken.

The Warlord's eyes, shadowed by the helm, flicked over the gun in the boy's hand. "I know. Do you, I wonder?"

"Damn right I know!" Dion sucked in air in a vain attempt to fill his lungs. "I know what to do with it, too. Now start walking, down the hallway."

He and Sagan moved down the corridor, side by side. The guards followed, apparently unaware that anything was wrong.

"No, don't, my lord! Keep your hand away from the bloodsword! You don't dare harm me anyway. You pledged me your allegiance. That God of yours wouldn't like it if you broke your oath, would He?"

"Dion," Sagan said, slowly withdrawing his hand, "the Lady Maigrey needs my help. Yours, too, if you'll come. She's in danger."

"You've made a mistake, Warlord. I'm not the wide-eyed kid who used to follow you around like a puppy with my tongue hanging out. Her only danger is you and I'm about to end that right now. There, this will do." Dion gestured with the gun toward a darkened room, its door standing partially ajar. "Go inside."

"It's not a trick, Dion. Reach out to her through the Blood Royal. You'll know if I'm telling the truth—"

"Yeah, and you'd jump me the moment I so much as blinked! No, my lord. I'll keep my mind on you." The boy was heady with power. The Warlord was actually reduced to pleading with him, trying to trick him. At last, he—Dion— was in complete and total control! "Send your guards away."

Sagan regarded the boy thoughtfully, grimly, then made a gesture with his hand. "Centurions, return to the Adonian's central control room. Wait for me there."

The guards obeyed, leaving them alone. The Warlord entered the room. Dion surged in behind him, slamming shut the door. He glanced around swiftly to make certain the room was unoccupied. Small, windowless, it was furnished with two long tables and numerous chairs. Along a wall stood various food and drink dispensing units, vid and game machines. Obviously, an employee break room.

Sagan strode casually across the floor, came to stand before a game terminal, his back to Dion. Fingers rested idly on the controls. The screen came on, filling the room with a garish yellow and red light that blurred in the boy's eyes.

The young man blinked, endeavoring to clear the film that misted them. He was shaking almost uncontrollably and fought to steel himself.

"So, Dion," Sagan said, "you mean to kill me."

He sounded smug, self-assured, almost amused. Dion went cold, as if he'd plunged in icy water. His vision cleared; his shaking ceased.

"I do," he said steadily, and raised the weapon that had been modeled in the shape of an eight-pointed star.

··◁▫ ▫▷··

Something had gone wrong. Maigrey knew it, knew Dion was involved, but whatever was transpiring with Sagan was murky and confused. She hesitated, toying with the idea of finding them both, of coming to their assistance. But if she left the target range now, she might forever abandon any hope of recovering the starjewel.

Irresolute, she made up her mind. She was here, she would talk to the Adonian. Whatever treachery Snaga Ohme was plotting, Maigrey believed she was equal to it. If he wanted to bargain in good faith, fine. She would do so. If not . . . well, she was ready for that, too.

As for Sagan and Dion, the two would simply have to take care of themselves.

"We're not going to wait for my lord any longer." Maigrey announced her decision to the guards. Drawing the bloodsword, she inserted the needles into her hand. "It's ten minutes past the time. I don't want the Adonian to think I'm not coming."

"I don't like this, my lady," Marcus said, frowning. "It's odd that we haven't seen the Adonian before now, entering the target range himself."

"Quit trying to stall." Maigrey smiled, shook her head. "There's probably another way in and out, a back entrance. Look, I don't like it either. And that's why we're going to be careful. Very careful."

"I wish to God I had a weapon!" the centurion muttered, hands clenching in impotent frustration.

"I wish to God you did, too, but there's no help for that now. We tried our best; there's nothing in these target ranges but toys. At least I have the bloodsword."

Maigrey activated the weapon, motioned the two centurions to fall in on either side of her. By the sword's light, they advanced through the holograph into the deserted corridor. Reaching the target range, they tried to see past the steelglass. It was like staring into a black hole. The darkness was impenetrable, but gave Maigrey the strange feeling that it was luring her inside. She reached out her left hand to the range's control panel, pressed the button that glistened in the sword's light. Four long buzzes. Two short. That had been Ohme's instructions.

A door slid open; chill air flowed out. Maigrey sniffed, caught a familiar scent. The Adonian's perfume. He was in there, then, waiting in the darkness. Maigrey found herself growing suddenly angry. She took a step forward, only to bump into Marcus.

"Let me enter first, my lady."

"Don't be ridiculous!" Maigrey shoved him aside. "You're not armed and I am. Keep a lookout for anything coming up behind us and for God's sake don't let that door close!"

Caius took up position at the door, blocking it with his body, keeping watch down the corridor. Maigrey advanced cautiously into the target range, the sword's light illuminating the chamber. Marcus accompanied her, staying to her left, leaving her sword arm free.

She entered a jungle. A path, cut through masses of artificial vegetation, led into deeper, dense shadow.

"I know this place," she murmured, almost to herself.

"Yes, my lady." Marcus answered her unexpectedly, startling her. "The planet where Lord Sagan found you."

"The planet where I exiled myself."

Marcus drew near. "This is a trap, my lady," he warned softly, urgently.

"Yes. I know."

Maigrey continued on along the path, shoving aside plastic leaves of plants she recognized, plants that grew on only one planet. A planet few people in the civilized galaxy had ever visited. A planet whose image was, however, indelibly imprinted in her mind. The scent of the Adonian's perfume was stronger. He had to be here.

"Very well, Snaga Ohme," Maigrey spoke to the darkness, moved ahead cautiously, "we're tired of playing your little game. The price I'm prepared to offer for the jewel is going down. I—"

Something swung at her head, moving at her from the shadows. Maigrey gasped, ducked involuntarily. Raising the sword to defend herself, she saw—by the sword's light—the soles of two patent leather shoes, dangling in the air above her head.

Something dripped warm on her hand.

Blood.

White trousers, a gleaming white cape, were barely visible among the thick foliage. Maigrey reluctantly lifted the sword higher, and two eyes sprang out of the darkness, stared down at her.

"My God!" she breathed, shrinking back into the shadows, away from the eyes' gaze.

But the eyes couldn't see her. They couldn't see anything anymore. Glassy, empty, only the whites visible, the eyes bulged from a face no longer recognizable, a face whose handsome features were bloated and dark with engorged blood, lips swollen and black, the tongue protruding from the mouth.

Snaga Ohme hung suspended from the limb of a fake tree, his body twisting slowly at the end of a length of silver chain. Wrapped around his neck, so tightly that the chain had cut deeply into the flesh, was the Star of the Guardians.

··◁■ ■▷··

"Yes, Derek Sagan, I mean to kill you," Dion said, feeling the charge build up inside him, burning in his blood until it was almost painful. "Right here. Right now."

"In cold blood? Murder? The king has become an assassin!" Sagan sneered.

"Not murder. An execution," Dion corrected. "I am your king. You've acknowledged as much. As my subject, your life is mine to dispose of as I will. Take off the bloodsword and put it on the floor."

Sagan did not, at first, respond. Then, slowly, he unbuckled the bloodsword from around his waist and, kneeling on one knee, laid it at Dion's feet, as he had done earlier this night in the crowded ballroom.

Dion moved closer, keeping the gun trained on the Warlord, kicked the bloodsword away with his foot. Sagan remained kneeling before him, helmed head bowed.

"Your crimes are these. You came to my home to take me away by force. You murdered the man who raised me. Do you have any defense to offer, Derek Sagan?"

The Warlord raised his head. "I have no defense. What you say is true. But you should consider this, Your Majesty. Perhaps I didn't come to Syrac Seven to capture you, Dion." Sagan's eyes, in the shadows of the helm, flickered with flame. "Perhaps I came to rescue you. . . ."

A tremor seized the young man's hand. Dion gripped the gun harder, willing the shaking to stop. He tried to bring to mind an image of Platus, dying by this lord's treacherous hand.

But all he could see was that house, isolated, hidden away from the world, away from life. His mentor, advising his charge to be . . . ordinary.

"Go ahead, Your Majesty." Sagan spoke almost irritably. "If you're going to kill me, do so now. Or do you plan to talk me to death?"

"Stand up." Dion licked his dry lips.

"Oh, no." The Warlord shook his head. "I remain on my knees before my king. You must kill me as I am, Your Majesty. Kneeling, unarmed, at your feet."

Dion gritted his teeth. "You don't think I can! I can kill! I've killed before!"

"I know. I saw your bloody handiwork aboard *Defiant*. But it's one thing to kill men in battle, when you're fighting for your life, when you're scared. Me, you must murder in cold blood. You must watch me die."

"This is another test, isn't it?" Dion shouted, losing control. Tears of anger flooded his eyes. "Another one of your goddam tests! And what do I have to do to pass? Kill you! That's it, isn't it? I have to kill you because if I don't you'll think I'm weak, spineless, not fit to rule a hill of ants!"

He raised the weapon, aiming at the Warlord's throat, the one place left vulnerable by the helmet and the armor. He could barely see through his tears. Sagan had become nothing to him but a shining blur of gold and blood-red. "Make your peace with that God of yours, Derek Sagan! Because this is one test I will pass!"

Dion summoned the power of the Blood Royal. Electricity surged through his body, danced in his nerves. The energy flooded him, flooded the gun.

He was clearheaded, in control. Carefully, he took aim and fired.

Chapter ⠶⠶ Fifteen

. . . *quod per sortem sternit fortem, mecum omnes plangite!*

. . . and since by fate the strong are overthrown, weep ye all with me!

Carl Orff, *Carmina Burana*

"My fault," Maigrey said, staring at the body of the Adonian, slowly revolving on the silver chain. "All my fault. . . ."

Marcus whispered urgently, "My lady! We've got to get out of here!"

"Too late. We're caught." She shook herself, seemed to come out of a daze. "And I'm not leaving without what I came for."

Detaching the sword from her hand, she caught hold of a low limb of the tree from which Snaga Ohme hung and started to pull herself up. Marcus, realizing her intent, caught hold of her. "Begging your pardon, your ladyship, but let me do that."

Maigrey glanced up at the corpse, at the starjewel dangling just below the left ear. Her stomach wrenched; her hands weakened, nearly losing their grasp. She was thankful for the offer and was tempted to give in. The moment she recognized that temptation, she steeled herself against it, rebuked herself for her weakness.

"It's my responsibility, centurion. Besides, you can't use the bloodsword." Maigrey pulled herself up into the tree until she was level with the head of the gruesome object that had once been the Adonian.

"My fault," she repeated through clenched teeth. Ohme's hands were tied securely behind him. This had been murder, not suicide. Not that she had ever suspected suicide. Adonians think far too well of themselves to leave the universe poorer by their absence.

409

The silver chain had been twisted tightly around his neck
and attached to a hook embedded in an overhanging tree limb.
The Adonian's wrists were wet with blood. He'd struggled
against his fate, the ropes cutting into the flesh of his arms as
the chain cut into his neck. Death had been long in coming, his
own weight dragging him down, strangling him slowly,
slowly. . . .

Maigrey swung the bloodsword. The blade sliced through
the silver chain. The body plummeted to the ground, landed
in a twisted heap at Marcus's feet. The centurion bent over it,
obviously intent on retrieving the starjewel. Maigrey leapt
lightly from the tree, shoved him aside.

Cursed, defiled.

She knelt beside the corpse, cringed at the touch of the
fast-chilling flesh beneath her fingers. The jewel was dark and
slippery with the Adonian's blood. The chain had sunk so
deeply into the flesh it had almost completely disappeared.
Struggling to get a grip on it, she slid her fingers beneath the
chain and finally wrenched it free. She clasped the starjewel
thankfully in her hand, rose to her feet, and very nearly
blacked out. Marcus caught her, held her, steadied her.

"I'm all right," she said thickly, drawing in deep gulps of air.
The sword's light was dimming; her weakness was affecting her
power to wield it. Angrily, she thrust the jewel on its broken
chain beneath the breastplate of her armor. The pointed
crystal pierced her flesh. The pain was welcome, helped her
clear her head. The sword's light grew brighter.

"Now we can leav—" she began.

"My lady!" Caius shouted. "Look ou—"

A flare of laser light, a blast that registered somewhere near
the door.

"A kill," reported a mechanized voice, echoing in the
darkness.

Marcus darted down the path, Maigrey beside him. They
dove through the vegetation and came within sight of the exit.

"Down!" the centurion gasped, reaching out and pulling
Maigrey to the ground. A Corasian trundled into sight,
spinning around, seeking a target. It fired at the sound; an
inoffensive beam of light streaked over their heads.

"Miss," reported the same mechanized voice, which
seemed vaguely familiar to Maigrey, though she couldn't take
time to think why.

"It's only one of the target robots!" Maigrey whispered, almost laughing in relief.

"No, it isn't, my lady," the centurion returned grimly. "Look!" He gestured forward.

Cautiously, Maigrey lifted her head. Caius lay unmoving, his body sprawled in the hallway.

"Your comrade isn't fond of playing practical jokes, is he?" she whispered.

The Corasian's robot head rotated, trying to zero in on the noise.

Marcus shook his head.

"Then we can assume he's dead. . . ."

The door began to close, sliding shut, sealing off their only way out. The robot stood between them and the exit.

"I'll draw its fire!" Maigrey shouted to her guard. "You hold open that door!"

She jumped to her feet, flaring sword in her hand, the bloodsword's shielding device activated. The Corasian robot swiveled to face her. The centurion made a desperate attempt to dodge around it. The robot ignored Maigrey. Its weapons system, built into its body, fired at Marcus. The beam was lethal, blowing up parts of the artificial jungle, showering the centurion with bits of plastic, wire, and polystyrene, but he managed to avoid the hit. Twisting in mid-air, he crashed down among the foliage, uninjured but far from the rapidly closing door.

"Miss." This time, the mechanized voice seemed amused.

Maigrey raced forward, switching her sword to attack mode, and smashed the blade into the Corasian before it could fire again. The robot burst apart, its lights sizzled, its insides smoked, and it went lifeless.

"A kill," conceded the mechanized voice.

Marcus, on his feet again, made a despairing lunge for the door, crashed into it bodily as it boomed shut.

A troillian warrior leapt up out of the jungle undergrowth directly in front of Maigrey. She reacted, but she was too late. The warrior fired at her point-blank. The lasgun's beam struck her in the head.

She was nearly blinded by the bright light, but beyond that, nothing happened. The robot troillian immediately went dark, and sank back down into the fake plants.

"That would have been a kill," the mechanized voice said. "But I don't want you dead, fair lady."

Maigrey gasped for breath, closed eyes that burned from the light. Sweat chilled on her body beneath the armor. The bloodsword's glow dimmed, nearly went out.

"Abdiel . . ."

"My lady, I'm with you!"

Maigrey opened her eyes, tried desperately to blink away the blinding afterimage. "Marcus! Keep down! Don't move!"

The centurion ignored her command, lunged through the jungle to try to reach her side.

A robot Corasian popped out from behind a tree, fired. The blast struck the centurion in the back. He fell heavily to the ground and lay without moving.

"A kill."

The darkness around her was lifeless as the artificial jungle. The target ranges were soundproofed. No one can hear me scream, Maigrey realized. No one had heard Snaga Ohme's scream before the chain cut it off. The door's sealed shut. No way out.

Maigrey felt Abdiel's probe, felt the mind-seizer try to enter her brain.

The bloodsword! Those who use the bloodsword are connected mentally.

Feverishly, she jerked the needles out of her palm, tossed the sword on the ground, far from her. She might have used it to defend herself, but logic told her the sword could be a greater danger to her than a help. Only one weapon would serve against Abdiel—and that was Maigrey's own mind and she wasn't strong enough to wield such a weapon alone.

She tried to establish the link with Sagan.

Abdiel intervened. "Calling for help, are you, my dear? I'm afraid your call can't be completed as dialed. There's no one on the other end. The Warlord is dead. And so is Dion. It's come down to you and me, fair lady. Only the two of us."

Dead! Both of them dead!

The vision came to her of Dion pointing a gun, of the Warlord on his knees before the boy, of deadly beams shooting out of both ends of the treacherous weapon, the murderer dying even as he killed. The vision was real, too real. Surreal. Maigrey burned with shared pain, but she didn't feel the emptiness of death.

Somehow, Abdiel had been deceived, but Maigrey didn't dare concentrate on the Warlord long enough to learn the truth. The mind-seizer believes them both to be dead, she thought. Let him.

But it meant that she would have to face him alone.

Maigrey struggled against the probe that was like a worm trying to bore its way into her consciousness, seeking out weak, soft spots in her defense.

"You have the starjewel with you, don't you, fair lady?" Abdiel continued. "I watched you take it from the corpse."

That horrible moment came back to her: the dead eyes staring at her, the terrible distortion of the bloated face, the blood on the Adonian's wrists.

Maigrey pushed the memory away, deliberately kept her mind dark and empty while she tried to shut down circuits, erase anything in her consciousness that could be used to destroy her.

"Don't waste your pity on the Adonian, Lady Maigrey. He never intended to give the star back to you. It was an ambush. As you suspected, Ohme realized that the starjewel is the missing element—the starjewel arms the bomb. He lured you to this range to murder you, assuming that with you dead, he would be able to recover the bomb. Unfortunately for the Adonian, my disciple arrived on the scene first. Would you like to witness the Adonian's execution, my lady? You will find it most entertaining."

Maigrey saw a vivid picture in her mind, realized she was watching Ohme's last agonized moments of life. The body twisted and jerked as the chain tightened slowly around the neck. He gasped, fought, struggled . . . and then, suddenly, Maigrey was Ohme! She was hanging from the tree. The chain was slicing through her flesh, cutting off her air. The pain was excruciating. She couldn't breathe. Terrified, she gasped, fought, struggled . . .

No! It wasn't happening to her! She was herself, not the Adonian.

Maigrey regained her own reality, but with her success came the numb despair of knowing that it had actually been failure. Abdiel was the one who had succeeded. He had gained entry to her mind. And he knew, because he'd been there before, how to open the Pandora's box Maigrey kept stored in the attic of her subconscious.

"Our host is dead. 'The party's over,' as the old song goes." Abdiel appeared before her, moving out of the darkness. In his hand, he held a nuke lamp; the harsh glare lit his face, shone

brightly in the shadowless eyes, gleamed off the decaying flesh
of head and hand. "I will escort you to your spaceplane, Lady
Maigrey. You will invite me inside and turn over to me the
bomb and the starjewel. And then, if you are very good, my
dear, I might let you join Derek Sagan in whatever afterlife he
finds himself."

Part of Maigrey wanted to fight with her bare hands, to hurl
herself at the old man and claw his face with her nails. But part
of her remained cowering in the attic that had become her
mind, weeping, afraid to move, afraid of so many, many things
that she knew were waiting to reach out and rend her apart.

Abdiel, a pleasant smile on his lips, came closer and
reached out his left hand. Needles flashed. Maigrey shrank
back before him, but he caught hold of her arm, her right arm.
Lifting it, he turned her right hand palm upward. . . .

The centurion, Marcus, lay in the darkness, silent, unmoving, watching. The blast, though it had knocked him down,
had not penetrated the armor. He lay where he fell, feigning
death, waiting for his chance, praying only that somehow God
would put a weapon into his hands.

He had no idea what was wrong with the Starlady, but
obviously this man had some type of mental hold over her.
Marcus willed her silently to fight against it, was shaken and
appalled when he saw her hurl away the bloodsword, her only
means of defense. The weapon hit the ground, slid to a stop
near his hand.

Marcus stared at it. A weapon. God had answered his
prayer, but He demanded a sacrifice in return. The bloodsword could be used safely by only the Blood Royal. Anyone of
ordinary birth and genetic structure jabbing those needles into
his hand would inject himself with death. And there was the
possibility he might do so and still not be able to activate the
weapon. The centurion had been trained by the Warlord in
the techniques of mental discipline, but he doubted if he had
the knowledge and the ability to channel his nerve impulses
correctly, the strength to combat the inevitable pain that must
go with the sword's use.

He heard someone moving through the jungle and knew by
the voice it was the man the Starlady called Abdiel. The voice
had a brittle quality to it. Marcus guessed the man must be

old. Perhaps I won't need a weapon, he thought. My bare hands . . .

But then Marcus heard another set of footfalls, coming—by the sound of it—behind those of the old man. Probably the disciple the old man had mentioned, the one who had killed the Adonian.

Light flared, harsh and white—a nuke lamp. Marcus froze, holding his breath. The beam played over him, flicked past him, leaving him in shadow. The footfalls moved on. Cautiously, the centurion opened his eyes, saw an old man clad in magenta robes. His disciple, armed with a lasgun, walked behind, guarding the old man's back.

The disciple would hear Marcus move. The lasgun—at that range—could blow his head off. It wouldn't help the lady to be killed in her defense, he realized. I have to live . . . at least a little while longer.

Abdiel held the nuke lamp up, shining it on Maigrey. She was like an animal, hypnotized by the light, unable to flee the death that approached. The mind-seizer reached out to her.

Stealthily, Marcus's right hand slid forward, fingertips touching the hilt of the bloodsword. Moving swiftly, silently, he edged it back toward him until he could get a firm grip on it. The centurion hesitated only a moment, long enough to whisper a prayer to the God of his Warlord. Then he jabbed the five needles into his palm.

Searing fire flared through his nerves, tongues of flame licked at his skull, his heart lurched wildly in his chest. Marcus nearly died in that instant. It took every ounce of strength and courage he possessed, adding to it some he didn't know he had, to keep from screaming out in the agony.

But he didn't die. He felt, through the awful pain, the tinglings of energy, saw the sword begin to glow with a weak and feeble radiance. The pain, he realized, was caused by the virus connecting his body with the bloodsword, joining them together, making them one. It had worked! The bloodsword was his to command!

Drawing on the mental discipline his lord had taught him, Marcus used the pain, used it to operate the sword in his hand. The blade flared more brightly. He didn't have much time; the sword's light would be noticed.

Rising, hurling himself forward in the same motion, Marcus swung the sword in a slashing arc, bringing it down on the disciple's hand, the hand holding the lasgun, severing the hand from the body. Mikael did not cry out, but turned toward his attacker, stared at him. The disciple's eyes registered nothing, neither pain nor shock nor fear. Marcus's return stroke slashed Mikael's head from his neck. The head crashed to the floor, the eyes unchanged, looking in death very much as they had in life.

The centurion whirled to face the old man, raised the sword to hack the feeble, bent, and misshapen body in half

Marcus halted, stroke arrested. He was disconcerted to see Abdiel regarding him with almost amused interest, a pleasant smile playing about the cracked lips. The mind-seizer raised his right hand and the centurion found, suddenly, that his arm wouldn't move at his command. But the arm would move, it seemed, for Abdiel.

Marcus watched, shocked, terrified, seeing and feeling his own arm come under the command of someone else. The centurion's right arm, carrying the bloodsword in its hand, offered that sword to Abdiel.

"How very brave. And how very foolish." Abdiel plucked the sword's needles easily from Marcus's bleeding palm, with as much nonchalance as if the guard had been offering him a flower, and tucked the weapon into his belt. "Your use of the bloodsword, centurion, linked your mind to mine, much as the lady and I will be linked now."

Abdiel opened wide his left hand. Marcus saw needles flash in the harsh, white light, needles protruding from the flesh of the old man's palm. The Starlady was staring at the old man as if bound in a riveting trance. Her body trembled. The old man caught hold of her hand. His touch jolted her to action. She fought back, flying into a violent, frenzied struggle to escape him. He gripped her tightly, thrust the needles in his palm deep into her hand.

Maigrey moaned, sank to the floor on her knees, her hand still held fast in the old man's grasp. Abdiel stroked her head as it rested against his thigh.

"There, there, my dear," he said, soothing her.

Then, whispering to her softly, he coaxed her to her feet. Whimpering, she clung to him. As a parent assists a sick and feeble child, the old man placed a gentle arm around her waist, led the stumbling woman toward the door.

Marcus was helpless to act, unable to move.

The door opened. Abdiel, turning, flashed the lamp into the centurion's eyes. "You are a dead man," he said, and released Marcus from his mental grip. Holding on to the Starlady, Abdiel walked through the door and out into the dark and deserted hallway beyond.

Marcus slumped to the floor, like a puppet whose strings are cut. A feverish chill shook his body, a throbbing ache pounded in his head—first symptoms of the disease that would shortly and inevitably kill him.

Chapter ··◈>◯◁◈·· Sixteen

Things fall apart . . .
William Butler Yeats, *"The Second Coming"*

Dion stared in disbelief at a smoking hole burned through the left side of his vest. The cumulator was shattered. The laser beam had struck it, blown it up. Dion's stunned gaze traveled from the destroyed cumulator to the gun in his hand and from there to a hole blown in the wall to the left of the Warlord. A black streak of carbon scoring along the cheek of Sagan's helm indicated how close the deadly, needle-thin beam had come to him . . . and how far.

"What happened?" Dion asked dazedly. Then he began to shake.

He must, Sagan realized, have answered his own question.

"Abdiel happened," the Warlord said, rising from his kneeling stance. Reaching out his hand, he removed the gun from the boy's nerveless grasp, examined it with interest. "A Judas gun. I haven't seen one of these in many years. It fires both directions, front *and* back, betraying its master."

"You—you knew!" Dion stammered, teeth clicking together. The pain of his wound had hit him now, shriveling his stomach. The stench of burned flesh—of his own burned flesh—made him sick.

"I didn't know, but I suspected as much. The Blood Royal occasionally used such killing devices on each other."

"Why didn't you tell me?" Dion put his hand over the wound in a vain attempt to stanch the bleeding. The metal of the cumulator had been driven into his flesh; the crystal had exploded, piercing his skin with tiny, razor-sharp shards.

"Would you have believed me? You had to find out for yourself."

418

"You risked your life—and mine—so that I could prove to myself what a fool I've been!" Dion said bitterly.

"It wasn't much of a risk," Sagan remarked dryly.

"Why?" Dion flared. "Because you didn't think I had the guts to do it?"

"Let's just say, my liege, that it was well God turned your hand or we both would be dead right now."

"God didn't turn my hand!" Dion spoke through teeth clenched against a welling nausea. His body trembled, but not with the pain. It was the intensity of his emotion. "*I* turned my hand! I missed deliberately! I *let* you live!"

"Indeed, my liege. And why?"

Dion straightened, lifted his head, willed himself to stand firm. "Because I can use you. Because I intend to use you. Because you're no good to me dead!"

Sagan eyed the boy silently for a moment. Then the Warlord's lips parted in a rare, dark smile. "I begin to think I've underestimated you, Your Majesty. You may make a king yet!" He held the gun out to the young man. "But you're still a long way from your throne. Next time you use one of these, check the coating on the back. You should find a thick, protective metallic substance. If the coating flakes off with your thumb, like this"—he demonstrated, sending chips of white paint floating to the floor—"then you will feel far more than a 'warm sensation' against your skin when you fire it."

Dion accepted the gun in silence. Tossing it to the floor, he stomped on it, crushed it beneath the heel of his boot.

"What a fool!" he said to himself, tears stinging his eyes. "What a fool!"

"Are you in much pain?" Sagan asked.

"No," Dion lied, swiftly and ashamedly wiping his hands across his eyes. His face was white, his skin cold and clammy to the touch. His breathing was shallow, irregular.

"Good. If you had been," the Warlord continued with a slight half-smile, "I would have suggested you use whatever mental powers Abdiel taught you to block it. I need your help—"

"Maigrey!" Dion remembered. "You said she was danger! What— Is—"

"I don't know." Sagan crossed the room, heading for the exit. "You forced me to expend my concentration on you. And now I can't sense her, contact her. I—" Flinging open the door, barreling through it, he nearly ran down a man attempting to enter.

"Marcus!"

The centurion staggered, collapsed. Sagan caught him. "What is it, Marcus? What's happened?"

The centurion's hands gripped his lord, hanging on to him tightly, determined not to fall. Sagan, supporting his weakening soldier, felt something wet on his arm. Looking down, he saw a thin trickle of red coming from the centurion's right hand. The Warlord turned Marcus's palm to the light. Five fresh needle marks oozed blood.

The Warlord understood. "God help us," he prayed silently. "God help her!"

··◁■ ■▷··

The Lord Abbot of the Order of Dark Lightning spirited his captive through the Adonian's crowded house with swiftness and ease. No one saw them, though they passed many people so close that the old man's magenta robes brushed their skin. People saw Abdiel only when he wanted them to see Abdiel.

Dark Lightning—thus the mind-seizers had named their Order. A sizzling bolt flashing from one mind to another, unseen, unheard, illuminating, devastating. The dark lightning had struck Maigrey, struck her down, seemingly, left nothing in her mind except ashes. She accompanied Abdiel meekly, going where he led her, doing what he told her.

The mind-seizer was surprised at the woman's docile behavior, though every few moments, he injected her with terrors drawn from her own inner being. She was reacting exactly the way he'd hoped she would react. And that made him suspicious. Abdiel didn't trust her. He knew there was a part of her he could never control. He would have preferred a struggle, some small resistance that he could overcome with the pain he knew so well how to inflict, rather than her numb lassitude.

Seated inside the tram car, hurtling toward the front gate, Abdiel studied his victim. The two were no longer bonded; he had removed the needles. He was deep inside her, his poison working. Her face in the bright light of the tram was fixed, immobile, without expression. The gray eyes were like the eyes of the mind-seizer's own mind-dead disciples.

But she isn't, Abdiel said to himself, watching her distrustfully. She's retreated. Hiding in there somewhere. Or

perhaps . . . He sat back, paused to consider. Perhaps not.
Perhaps the Guardian's light has died. Perhaps, inside, she's as
dark as her starjewel. Let's see.

"My dear," Abdiel said aloud. "I want the Star of the
Guardians. Hand it to me."

No emotion on her face, but her right hand trembled.

The mind-seizer knew where and how to hurt her. Leaning
forward, he jabbed a mental knife into her subconscious, saw
her eyes widen, her breath come quick, reacting to a horror
only she could see. Her right hand moved to her breast, to the
place where Abdiel had seen her secrete the starjewel after
she had retrieved it from the corpse of the Adonian. The hand
shook, went rigid, then fell suddenly to her lap. Her eyes
closed; sweat trickled down her face.

So, she isn't quite dead yet, the mind-seizer realized,
feeling almost relieved. But she is close. A few more pricks and
jabs, and she will hand over her starjewel, hand over her life
without hesitation.

The tram car brought them to the front gate of the late
Snaga Ohme's estate. Abdiel was now faced with a problem.
Mikael was dead. The mind-seizer had no one to pilot his
'copter and he couldn't do it himself. His problem was solved,
however, relief coming from an unexpected source. Abdiel
discovered an entire contingent of soldiers from Fort Laskar
digging in, taking up positions around the Adonian's house.

"Sagan, how thoughtful!" the mind-seizer murmured, and
commandeered a 'copter pilot's brain and body on the spot.

They arrived at the base without incident. The mind-seizer
dismissed the 'copter pilot, who, when he came to, had no idea
where he was or how he got there. Escorting his prisoner,
Abdiel slid through the centurions surrounding the spaceplane. Their minds enthralled, the Honor Guard noticed
the mind-seizer and his captive no more than they noticed the
wind or the darkness of the long night.

Abdiel was shivering, both with the chill—though the
Laskarian night was exceptionally warm—and excitement.
He sent Maigrey up the ladder to the spaceplane's hatch,
followed her more slowly, encumbered in his robes, his frail
body unused to the inordinate amount of physical exertion
he'd expended this evening. He commanded her to wait, to
assist him.

She waited, helped him down into the plane's interior with

the gentleness and respect a daughter might have shown a beloved father.

"Thank you, my dear," Abdiel said, and thrust the needles into her outstretched palm, just to make certain she was his and that all went as he had planned.

"Who's there?" a voice called sharply. "Answer me this instant or I'll vaporize—"

"It's me, Lady Maigrey, XJ," the woman responded in lifeless tones.

"Oh, your ladyship!" It sounded as if the computer's circuits were practically melting with relief. "You're back! Does this mean that we can get rid of this infernal bomb?"

Abdiel glanced at Maigrey sharply, saw her waver. The mind-seizer squeezed the needles more deeply into her flesh. She gasped, cried out softly, then said, shuddering, "Yes, XJ, we're getting rid of it."

The mind-seizer led the woman to the cockpit of the plane. The bomb, its gold and crystal sparkling in the light, sat in plain view on the console.

Abdiel removed the needles to allow the woman freedom to use her hands. "And now, my dear, you will release the bomb from the computer's command. First, visual identification of yourself."

"You know me, XJ," Maigrey said.

"I think so." The computer didn't sound convinced.

"You know me, XJ!" Her tone sharpened.

"Yes, ma'am," the computer answered, subdued.

"And now the starjewel," Abdiel breathed, scratching at a patch of decaying skin on his arm in his eagerness. "The starjewel, Lady Maigrey! Show it to the computer!"

Her hand moved to her breast. This time there was no hesitation, no trembling. Reaching beneath the silver armor, she drew forth the jewel, dark and horrible to look at, crusted with the Adonian's dried blood.

"XJ," she said softly, extending the hand with the jewel in it toward the bomb, "you will follow my instructions. . . ."

··◑═ ■◑··

The Warlord looked at Marcus sharply, noticed his skin had an ashen tinge and was covered with sweat. Marcus's fingers clenched over the wounds on his palm. He gently, respectfully removed his hand from his lord's.

"Where's Lady Maigrey?" Sagan demanded.

The centurion straightened, stood on his own, without aid. "A man called Abdiel attacked us—"

"Abdiel!" Dion sprang forward, came up hard against the Warlord's outthrust arm.

The centurion's pallid face was grim, stern. "I'm sorry, my lord. I failed in my trust—"

Sagan's glance went again to the centurion's right hand.

Marcus's face flushed, life returning for a moment to the wan complexion. "It was the only weapon available to me, my lord."

Dion stared. "I don't understand—"

"He used the bloodsword," Sagan said, his voice grating.

"But that means . . ." Dion bit his lip, cast a desperate, questioning glance at the Warlord. "Isn't there anything—"

Sagan shook his head. A spasm of pain convulsed the centurion's body, twisted his face, but, with an effort, he remained standing attentive, alert.

"It was a trap, my lord. The Adonian arranged to meet my lady, ostensibly to negotiate for the necklace—"

"Damn it!" Dion exploded. "We don't need to waste time listening to this! We have to go rescue her! If you won't, I—"

"*You!*" Sagan whirled to confront the young man. "Just remember, my liege, that if it hadn't been for you, I might have been able to prevent this."

The blow struck home. Dion went white to the lips, was shattered into silence.

The Warlord turned back to Marcus. "Continue your report, centurion."

"Yes, my lord. According to what Abdiel told my lady, Snaga Ohme intended to kill her, using robots with live fire inside the target range. Instead, it was the Adonian who died. He was strangled with the chain of the starjewel. My lady cut him down, took the jewel from the corpse—" Marcus coughed, began to choke, gasped for breath.

The Warlord recognized the symptoms: the lungs beginning to fill with fluid, the burning fever, the onset of pneumonia.

"Fetch water!" Sagan ordered Dion.

"No . . . I'm all right . . ." The centurion spoke normally; his breath was coming easier.

"How are you feeling?" the Warlord asked.

"Not too bad yet, my lord," Marcus answered quietly when he could speak.

"It will get worse, I'm afraid. Especially near the end."

"Yes, my lord. I know."   •

Dion made a strangled sound, turned, and bolted down the hallway. The Warlord watched him, prepared to call his guard to chase the boy down, but Dion came up against a wall at the far end of the hall. He slumped against it, his head bent, shoulders heaving.

Marcus followed the young man with concerned eyes, glanced back at his lord. He said nothing, however, stared down at his feet, at the blood dripping from his hand onto the floor.

"You think I'm hard on the boy?" Sagan asked abruptly.

"This can't be easy for him, my lord."

"He has to learn to accept the consequences of his actions," the Warlord returned, "whether he's going to be king or trash sorter on a garbage scow. And while he may be losing a friend, I am losing a trusted, valued soldier."

Marcus raised his head. A semblance of life returned to his fevered face. "Thank you for your praise, my lord. I don't deserve it. I couldn't save her—"

"You did all you could. More than most men," Sagan said, brooding gaze fixed on the centurion's bleeding hand. "Continue your report. It's just as well the boy isn't around to hear it."

"Yes, my lord. The robots opened fire. Caius was guarding the door. He died instantly. The door shut and sealed. Then I was hit and knocked to the floor. I played dead, and I heard a voice talking to the Starlady. The voice told her you had been killed, my lord. You and the boy both."

"She would know that wasn't true!" Sagan protested.

"Maybe she did, my lord. Maybe not. She seemed to die herself when that old man came up to her. Except when he . . . thrust those needles into her hand. Then she fought. I couldn't understand what was wrong with her, my lord, until the old man looked at me." Marcus paled, neck muscles tensed. "He seemed to come inside me, my lord, and he showed me—he showed me my own death. . . ." The centurion swallowed; there came a harsh, clicking sound from his throat. Sweat ran down his face.

"Where did he take my lady, Marcus?"

Marcus struggled to speak. His words came in a choking cough. "To her spaceplane, my lord."

"Damn!" The Warlord swore softly beneath his breath.

"But that's on the military base, my lord. The Honor Guard . . . surely they'll stop him—"

"Abdiel could get past the Portress of Hell's Gate if he chose. How much time has passed since they left?"

"I'm not certain, my lord. I . . . blacked out for a few moments. When I came to myself, I had difficulty finding you—"

"It's been long enough, then. I—"

Sagan stopped speaking, his words interrupted by a voice, a voice only he could hear.

My lord, I can no longer fight Abdiel. But I have found a way to defeat him ultimately and forever. True to my oath, I warn you of what I am about to do. You will have time to take Dion and escape. And, in case you doubt me or my intent, I leave you with this quote: The center cannot hold. *God be with you and my king!*

Sagan stood unmoving, attention strained, trying to catch each word, which came to him more faintly than the one before it. Involuntarily, he reached out his hand, as if to hold on to her. His fingers closed on air, on nothing, and clenched into a fist.

"My lord!" Marcus was alarmed.

The Warlord returned to his surroundings. His eyes flickered with sardonic, grim amusement. "How long would you judge you have to live, Marcus?"

The centurion was shocked, startled by the question. He looked down at his palm. The five wounds were swollen, inflamed, and continued to ooze blood. "I'm not certain, my lord. A few days, perhaps. . . ."

"You are wrong, centurion." The Warlord smiled, thin-lipped, dark. "From now on, those of us on this planet measure our lives in seconds. My lady knows the code. She has the starjewel. She has armed and activated the bomb."

"May God have mercy!" Marcus intoned.

"May He, indeed!" Sagan muttered. He needed to act, act immediately. He could feel the seconds sliding through his fingers like sand, hear the ticking of the clock in every heartbeat. He could do as she told him, take Dion, flee the planet as she advised. That would be the smart course, the wise one.

But to give up everything! Just when it was in his grasp! To lose the bomb! Not only that. To lose Snaga Ohme's arsenal of weapons, the Adonian's computer records. Though Ohme himself was dead, his genius in weapons design and engineering would live on. By now, Haupt would have his troops in position, ready to move in and take over once Sagan gave the command.

This was to have been his power base! This was to have given him the means to rule the galaxy . . . with Dion, of course.

"My lady has beaten Abdiel, and she has beaten me. All without breaking her oath."

The Warlord swore bitterly, softly beneath his breath—a reflexive response; he wasn't even aware he was doing it. He made his decision, realized afterward that there had never been a decision to make.

"Not a word of this to the boy!" he ordered Marcus. "Come with me."

Proceeding down the hallway, the Warlord spoke on the commlink located inside his helm. Ohme's people would be monitoring the transmission, but it was too late for that now. "Haupt! Come in!"

"My lord." The brigadier's response was immediate. Haupt must have been eagerly awaiting word from his commander.

"Alert the base. Have one of the spaceplanes standing by, ready for immediate takeoff. The boy I told you about is in danger on this planet. I want him away from Laskar, away from this system. I'm going to shut the force field down. Send two land-jets to the house to pick us up. Stand by."

Sagan ended the transmission, continued walking. Marcus had made a valiant attempt to accompany him, but Sagan saw, out of the corner of his eye, that the dying centurion was having a difficult time keeping up. Something would have to be done about that.

The Warlord reached the end of the hallway, flicked a glance at Dion, turned his gaze to the connecting hall, to his men standing near the Adonian's control center.

Sagan's eyes suddenly shifted back to Dion. The boy was rapt, staring out into nothing with fixed attention, the full, pouting lips slightly parted, lines of pain smoothed from the face. It occurred to the Warlord that Maigrey might have informed Dion of her intent, but for what purpose—other than frightening the hell out of the boy—Sagan couldn't imagine.

"Dion!" he snapped, and the young man returned to his surroundings with a jolt.

"My lord."

Sagan scrutinized him carefully. Dion's blue eyes were wary, guarded.

"The Adonian is dead. I'm taking over. Whoever controls this arsenal has a good chance of controlling at least a piece of the galaxy. But there's probably going to be fighting. Ohme's people may put up resistance. For your own safety, my liege, I'm taking you off-planet."

The blue eyes were unblinking, their gaze steady and unwavering. "What about the Lady Maigrey, my lord?"

"The Lady Maigrey is beyond our help for the moment. But I wouldn't concern myself with her, my liege," the Warlord added dryly. "My lady can take care of herself."

"We will do what you consider best for the safety of our person, my lord," Dion replied coolly.

Damn! Sagan thought to himself. He's even beginning to sound like his uncle! Something inside warned the Warlord that the young man was taking this much too calmly, but Sagan didn't have time to pay any heed to it. He turned and started down the corridor, heading for the control center. A crash behind him brought him to a halt. The Warlord glanced around.

Marcus, his breath coming in painful gasps, had fallen to his knees.

The Warlord checked his stride, turned back.

Seeing his lord approach him, the centurion attempted to stand, pushing himself up the wall with his hands, the right hand leaving a smeared trail of blood.

"Let me help you," Sagan said, reaching down his strong arm. "You'll travel with Dion. We'll take you to *Defiant*, to Dr. Giesk—"

"What can he do for me, my lord?" Marcus heaved himself to his feet, leaned back weakly against the wall. He burned with fever, struggled against pain, but his armor rattled with his body's agony.

"There are drugs that will ease your suffering—" Sagan began.

"Not this!" Marcus gasped the words. "I know! Abdiel—he showed me my death! My lord!" Reaching out, he grasped hold of Sagan's arm. "My lord, please . . ." His voice broke off in a rending cough.

But the Warlord had seen the dying man's request in the pain-filled eyes.

"I can't, centurion!" Sagan answered harshly, drawing back. "God forbids it—"

"Then let the sin be upon me!"

A hand came from nowhere, brushed against him, shoved him aside. Dion stood in front of Sagan, the Warlord's own bloodsword in his grasp.

Marcus, seeing the sword's light begin to glow brightly, understood. "Thank you, my liege." His lips formed the words; his voice was inaudible.

"Are you ready?" Dion asked.

The centurion's pain-shadowed eyes sought his lord's. "My lord?"

Sagan nodded once, heavily. "God go with—"

Dion struck while Marcus's attention was diverted, driving the sword's flaming blade through the armor, deep into the man's chest. Marcus gave a choking gasp. His body began to sag down to the floor. Dion dropped the sword, caught the dying man in his arms.

The centurion's eyes held the young man in their gaze for an instant, lips forming words that would never be spoken. The right hand clenched in agony, but the body's struggle against death was mercifully brief. Marcus's hand relaxed, slid down to fall lifeless on the floor. The head sagged forward, resting on the young man's shoulder.

"I'm sorry. . . ." Dion whispered, holding the limp body tightly. "I'm sorry!"

He felt a hand touch his shoulder, looked up into the eyes of the Warlord. Gently, Dion eased the body down.

"'*Lux aeterna, luceat eis, Domine, cum sanctis tuis in aeternam; quia pius es*.'" Sagan knelt beside the dead centurion, laid his hand upon the forehead. "'Let eternal light shine upon them, O Lord, with Thy saints forever, for Thou art merciful.'"

Rising to his feet, he turned to Dion.

Whatever Sagan had been going to say went unsaid. The boy was like a clear, crystal votive lamp that guards within it the sacrificial flame. Outside he was smooth, cold glass; within he burned with a devouring fire. His bright clothes, with the lion-faced sun, were wet with blood.

The Warlord was shaken to the core of his being. The awe he had experienced once, during the boy's rite, returned and overwhelmed him. He stood in the Presence, and curse and rail against God as he might, he could not deny it.

The fire in the blue eyes flickered over Sagan.

"It was my responsibility," Dion said, rising to his feet. *My*, the singular, not the royal *we*.

The Warlord did not respond. What the boy said was true, there was no comfort to be offered.

Dion leaned down, lifted the bloodsword, and handed it back to the Warlord. Their hands met. Sagan could have sworn he felt the touch of flame upon his skin.

The young man turned and walked down the hall, never once glancing at the body on the floor.

Chapter ✦⊸◗⊂✦ Seventeen

Mere anarchy is loosed upon the world . . .
        William Butler Yeats, *"The Second Coming"*

"Honored guests and members of the household of Snaga
Ohme, your attention, please." Sagan's voice, deep and cold,
sounded over the paging system like the tolling of the death
knell, instantly silencing the merriment, putting a halt to all
business transactions, bringing everyone to alert, tense attention. "I am Warlord Derek Sagan, speaking to you from the
control center of the Adonian's mansion. Your host, Snaga
Ohme, is dead."

The Warlord paused only long enough to let any astonished
murmurings die down so that he could be heard. "And there
has been an unfortunate accident. One of the nuclear bombs
has been armed and is primed to explode. We are endeavoring
to disarm it, but I would advise all of you to evacuate the
planet without delay. Please remain calm. There is no need for
panic.

"Which warning," the Warlord added, shutting down the
paging system, "should send everyone stampeding madly for
the nearest exits."

The Warlord was inside the central control room. The
bodies of several of Ohme's guards lay on the floor, cut down
by the bloodsword. The takeover had been swift, resistance
minimal. Those manning the control center were already in a
state of confusion. They had received reports of an army
moving into position outside the estate and had been unable to
reach their leader for orders. Most, after witnessing the deaths
of the guards, surrendered themselves to the Warlord.

Now, hearing his announcement about the bomb, they
stood staring at him in wide-eyed terror.

"Get out!" he ordered them, and none hesitated.

Glancing over the equipment, Sagan rapidly located those devices that controlled the force field and the defenses on the estate's outer perimeter. Swiftly, he shut them off.

"Haupt"—Sagan spoke into the commlink—"the force field is down. I've issued the warning to the people inside. Any second now, pandemonium should be in full swing. Move your men into position. You shouldn't meet much, if any, organized resistance."

"My lord"—Haupt sounded worried—"we heard the announcement. About the bomb—"

"A hoax, Brigadier," Sagan cut him off impatiently, "to clear people from the estate. Send in those two land-jets—one for my use and one for the boy. Now!" And he shut down the communication before Haupt could ask more questions.

"You two stay here," he ordered his centurions, who had armed themselves with the dead guard's weapons. "A team from the base will relieve you shortly. Report back to me at the fort. Bring your comrade's body for the rites and cremation."

The centurions saluted, fist over heart, and took up their positions.

We may *all* be cremated, Sagan found himself thinking grimly, if I can't stop Maigrey. Catching hold of the young man, who had observed the takeover with a distant and remote expression on his pale face, the Warlord propelled his king unceremoniously toward the elevators and the lower level.

"Why do I need a separate land-jet?" Dion asked, hurrying to keep up with Sagan's long strides. He glanced at Sagan out of the corner of his eye. "Aren't we going to the same place?"

I would rather reign in hell . . .

"I rather doubt it," the Warlord said.

··◁▩ ▩▷··

The Warlord and Dion entered the ballroom. Sagan looked about him in satisfaction. Pandemonium had been an understatement. People jammed the elevators, some fighting to get in, others fighting to get out. Crowds swarmed up the stairs and through side exits that had been hastily opened, people pushing and shoving each other aside in their haste to flee the doomed planet. Everyone was shouting, using whatever communications devices they had brought with them, ordering their ships readied for immediate takeoff. Sagan noted many of Ohme's people among the fleeing multitude. Their leader's body had been discovered and either they believed the story about the bomb or they didn't want to be around when the authorities arrived to ask questions.

All except one. The tear-ravaged face of Bosk loomed suddenly up in front of the Warlord. "Sagan!" the Adonian hissed, leaping at him, hands going for the Warlord's throat. "You're responsible! You murdered him! I'll—"

The Warlord stiff-armed the man; a knife-handed jab to the neck sent Bosk sprawling to the floor. Sagan kept a tight grip on Dion, stepped over the writhing body, continued past. By now, the media had caught sight of the Warlord and the boy-king and were pushing their way forward. Bomb or no bomb, they intended to get their story.

Sagan shoved and literally beat several reporters out of his path, but the going was slow. The crush of people increased around them, impeding their way. The Warlord cursed. He was beginning to think that he had done his job not wisely but too well when a gigantic form—implacable, immovable as a bearded oak tree—planted itself directly in front of him.

Sagan halted, looked up into a hairy, grinning face.

"My lord!" Bear Olefsky boomed. His laughing eyes sparked, shifted to Dion. "And the kinglet! Well met. You appear to be in need of assistance."

"Get us out of here!" Sagan said shortly.

"With pleasure, my lord!"

Laughing, calm as if he were wading through a stream of water instead of a stream of human and alien life-forms, Bear and his two sons began to clear the Warlord's path. The swelling tide of people pounded against them, but it might as well have washed up against a rock cliff. The Bear moved forward steadily; the masses parted, flowed, and eddied around them. Sagan and Dion surged along in the wake.

They reached the main staircase, Bear catching hold of and tossing overboard those who didn't get out of his way. Once outside of the Adonian's estate, they arrived in time to see a pillar of orange flame shoot into the air—Haupt's forces had blown the power generator. The ground shook beneath their feet. Lights went out, plunging the mansion into darkness, increasing—if possible—panic's reign inside.

Sagan looked above him, saw stars and Laskar's nail-paring of a moon in the sky overhead. The force field was down. He could hear the whine of approaching land-jets. The Warlord took out his bloodsword, inserted the needles into his hand, and activated it. The blade flamed to life. He raised it, signaling to the jets.

"So the Adonian is really dead?" Bear rumbled, coming up to stand next to him. "And who inherits his estate, I wonder?" Olefsky cocked one eye at the Warlord.

Sagan shut off the sword. "I suppose Snaga Ohme left a will."

Bear Olefsky burst out into a laugh that was like another explosion. "And made you executor, no doubt! Or is the word *executioner*?"

"Thank you for your help, Olefsky. You better get off-planet."

"Oh, yes! The bomb!" Bear winked, gave Sagan a slap on the back that nearly knocked the breath from the man's body. "Farewell, Warlord! When you and the lady need me to fight for this redheaded boy-king of yours"—the Bear jerked his head in Dion's direction—"give me a call. I'll be waiting!

"Now, come along, you clumsy oafs! Try not to trample anyone!" Marshaling his two lummoxlike sons, Bear lumbered off into the night. As he left, they could hear the big man repeat, every once in a while, "Bomb!" and chuckle in appreciation.

Sagan stared after him a moment, glanced thoughtfully at the young man. *After all, I might fail*, he thought. *And then Dion would have no one.*

"Bear Olefsky is a good man, my liege," he said to the young man. "You could trust him."

"That would be a change, wouldn't it, my lord?" the boy returned with unconcealed bitterness, blue eyes cool and remote in the moonlight.

The Warlord's lips twitched in a half-smile. Activating the sword again, he guided the jets to a landing.

Dion shouted to be heard over the engine's roar. "Where are you sending me?"

The Warlord frowned. Now that he thought of it, this calm acquiescence was disconcerting. Sagan sensed something behind it, but he didn't have time to try to fathom it.

Perhaps, after all, the boy had simply learned his lesson.

"*Defiant*," the Warlord told him. "To join your old friend, John Dixter. He should be pleased to have company."

"I'm a prisoner, then?" Dion yelled.

"Be any damn thing you can be!" Sagan shouted irritably. He waited only until he saw the boy hustled aboard the jet, then left for his own jet at a dead run.

But it seemed to Sagan that he heard, soft and disquieting, the boy's calm reply: "Thank you, my lord. I will."

Chapter ·◈⊃◯⊂◈· Eighteen

Escape for thy life; look not behind thee, neither stay thou in all the plain; escape to the mountain, lest thou be consumed.

Genesis 19:17

Fort Laskar was quiet, almost deserted, most of its forces involved in taking over the Adonian's estate. Lights gleamed from the HQ and communications buildings. The area around the spaceplane and the Warlord's shuttle was shrouded in darkness.

Sagan stood on the tarmac, cautiously observing Maigrey's plane. No lights. It appeared empty. The guards—his own centurions—posted around it were attentive and alert, chatting and laughing together in low voices, as if their watch had been uneventful.

The Warlord's expression grew grim. He tried, once again, to get in touch with his agent, as he had been trying for the past few minutes.

"Sparafucile." Sagan spoke into the commlink, his voice cracking with impatience. "Spara—"

"Sagan Lord!" The voice was faint, punctuated by what sounded like explosions. "I am here!"

"More to the point, is Abdiel there? Did he return to his shuttle?"

A deafening boom, then the half-breed could be heard: "—he look like all the hounds of hell were chasing after him. He—" Another explosion, a brief interlude of Sparafucile cursing and shouting orders, an answering voice that sounded extremely familiar, though Sagan couldn't for the moment place it. A scrabbling, panting sound, as if the half-breed were sliding into a ditch, and then silence. The link had gone dead.

Sagan tapped irritably at the side of his helm.

Nothing. But at least he could be reasonably certain Abdiel was still on Laskar, since it was undoubtedly the mind-seizer who was attacking the half-breed. And, Sagan thought, eyeing the spaceplane, at least he knew Abdiel was no longer on board. He must have fled when he realized that the bomb had been activated and that he couldn't reverse the process. That would take another code word, one that only Maigrey would know. Sagan wondered, briefly, how Abdiel might have tried to wrest it from her. He wondered in what condition he'd find her.

She was alive, he knew that; he could feel her life pulse within him, as he felt his own. But when he reached out his consciousness to touch her, it was like grasping at the night.

"Captain of the watch!" the Warlord called, striding forward.

The men on duty stiffened to attention.

"My lord."

"How has your watch passed, Captain?"

"Quiet, my lord."

"No one has entered the plane, come near it?"

The centurion, hearing the edge in his lord's voice, looked puzzled, tensed, sensing something wrong. "No, my lord."

Sagan looked again at the spaceplane. No lights could be seen; not a sound could be heard. It appeared lifeless. But inside, a deadly heart beat away the seconds.

"Very well, Captain, I will take over here. You and your men return to the shuttlecraft, prepare it for immediate liftoff."

"Yes, my lord." The Honor Guard saluted, took to their heels.

Sagan hastened to climb the ladder leading up the curved side of the Scimitar. No use reprimanding his men, no use telling them that an enemy had boarded that plane with impunity, strolling right past their very noses, strolling through their minds, leaving no trace of his passage.

The Warlord reached the top, discovered the hatch standing open—a bad sign. He peered down, into the darkness. Sagan eased himself into the gaping hole, dropped down to land soft-footed as a panther inside the spaceplane.

Emergency lights only were operational, bathing the interior in a warm and eerie red glow. Life-support had been shut off. Maigrey must have routed the majority of the computer's systems to the bomb. Sagan inserted the bloodsword into his palm but did not activate it, crept further inside. The air was hot and humid and difficult to breathe, smelling of sweat and fear and the faint, iron-tinged odor of blood.

He found her lying on the deck of the living quarters. She was, to all appearances, dead. Her flesh was chill. His hand on her pulse detected no beat. She was not breathing.

Sagan removed the bloodsword, placed it back in its sheath at his belt, and knelt down beside her. It was all a trick, a sham. She had slowed her body's functions to almost nothing, retreated far back into the inner recesses of her mind.

The Warlord could almost picture Abdiel's terrible frustration. The mind-seizer knew what Maigrey was doing, knew how to bring her out of her self-induced comatose state. But dragging her back to consciousness would take time and, for Abdiel, the minutes to total annihilation were ticking away.

Speaking of minutes. "Computer," Sagan called out. "How much time to detonation?"

The computer's audio clicked on, speaking in a monotone, without a trace of even mechanical life.

"I have been programmed not to respond to any questions or commands."

"Computer, override."

"I have been programmed not to respond—"

"Shut up, then!" Sagan snapped irritably.

"I have been programmed not to respond—"

The Warlord ignored it. Sitting back on his heels, he studied Maigrey. "Oh, you're good, my lady. Really good," he told her. Placing his hands on either side of her head, he joined his mind with hers.

At first it was dark, far darker than the spaceplane, and Sagan edged his mental way forward, moving blindly but unerringly toward his goal. He knew where she'd fled, knew she'd run to a place where only he could follow with ease. And if he never came to find her, it would be a place where she could rest in eternal peace.

··◗■ ■◖··

He entered a chapel, an ancient building, one of the first built on the Academy's grounds. It was night, very late in the night. He found Maigrey, sitting in the back, hidden in the incense-scented shadows that danced to the flickering lights of the votive candles. Sagan seated himself beside her, saying nothing.

In the front of the chapel was a boy—about fifteen years of age. He was well built, strong, muscular. Black hair, uncombed, framed a brooding face. Dark and intelligent eyes watched the flame of a candle he himself had just lit. He appeared to have undergone some recent mental and physical exertion; his hands were raw from rope burns, his hair damp with sweat. He was arguing vehemently with someone.

"Who are you talking to?"

The speaker was a six-year-old girl. She walked up the aisle of the chapel, gazing around it with a solemn air, yet not awed by her surroundings. Her hair was pale and fine and floated around her face like an untidy cloud. She was clad in a white nightgown, the fabric torn and dirty. Her lithe body was thin and tended to run to arms and legs, elbows and knees. Her eyes, especially at this moment, were enormous, luminous in the light of the candle flames.

"They took Stavros to the infirm'ry," she said, stumbling over the long word. She was newly arrived, and still learning the language of the Academy.

The brooding boy did not answer her, refused to look at her. The girl came to stand beside him, glanced up and down and all around the chapel with easy familiarity.

"I guess you were talking to God, huh, Derek?" she said. "Did you ask Him what happened to us tonight?"

"I didn't ask Him 'what.' I *know* 'what'!" the boy responded bitterly, glaring at the child with flashing black eyes. "I was asking Him why!"

Many others at the Academy had quailed before those eyes. The girl remained undaunted. "You mean you asked God why He let us talk together without saying any words? Can't everyone do that?"

"It's called a mind-link and no, everyone can't do it," the boy retorted. "Can you talk to that feeble brother of yours that way?"

"I guess not," the child conceded. "But then, I didn't ever want to." Her eyes were on the wavering flames. "Sometimes, though, I knew what my father was going to say before he said it. I miss my father." Her head turned. She looked at the boy with a new understanding, a sympathy. "Your father . . ." she began, faltering. "I'm sorry. . . ."

"Shut up!" The boy turned on her savagely. "Get away! Leave me alone!" It seemed he might strike her.

The girl stood her ground, her gray eyes wide and fearless

and glimmering with tears. "I know why God did this." She
reached out her hand, laid it timidly on the boy's arm. "It's
because we're both alone."

The boy tensed at her touch, stared at the small, sun-
browned hand on his strong arm. Then he relaxed, as if
something inside him had broken, given way. He bent his
head, seeking to regain control. The child removed her hand,
stood before him in respectful silence.

"You don't have any shoes on," he said to her suddenly, his
voice harsh.

The girl shrugged. "I never wore shoes at home."

"But it's cold here. You'll catch your death. You're shivering. Besides, someone must be looking for you."

"Someone was," the child said, and, reaching out, she took
gentle hold of the boy's hand.

"Maigrey," Sagan said quietly, "it's time to go."

··◁■ ■▷··

She drew a breath, another, and another. Her eyelids
flickered, the long lashes casting delicate shadows over the
scarred cheek. Sitting back, he waited with as much patience
as he could muster, knowing that it would take some time for
her body and mind to reconnect.

"Maigrey," he said after a short while, shaking her.

Her eyes opened. She glanced around dazedly, surprised to
find herself wherever she was, perhaps surprised to find that
she was no longer in the chapel. Awareness returned to her,
and she smiled wanly.

"You decided to come. I guessed you would. You couldn't
bear to give it up, could you, my lord?"

He slid his arm beneath her shoulders. She sat up, too
quickly. The red-washed shadows spun around her. She closed
her eyes, shutting them out, rested wearily against his chest.

"You sent Dion away, my lord?"

"Far away. Can you walk?"

"Give me a moment—"

"We don't have a moment, lady!" the Warlord reminded her
tersely.

Again, Maigrey smiled. The Warlord helped her to her feet.
She paused, to give the plane's hull time to stop moving in and
out. Then she and Sagan made their way down into the
cramped space of the small cockpit. The crystal bomb sat on

the console. Thin beams of light ran from the computer to the bomb. It made a faint sound, as if humming softly to itself.

The Warlord looked inside the bomb, saw the starjewel—or what had once been a starjewel. It had become a grotesque lump, its shape indistinguishable, its eight sharp points clotted with dried blood. Its aspect was hideous, filling the mind with horror and images of tortured death. Sagan looked away from it quickly.

"How much longer?" he demanded.

A smile twisted the corner of Maigrey's lip, twisted the scar that now pulsed faintly with a trace of life. She relaxed into the pilot's chair. Reaching out, she lifted a broken silver chain lying next to the bomb, a chain whose metal was tarnished and dark. Idly, she wrapped the chain around her fingers.

"Oh, I think we'll let that be a surprise."

"It will be," the Warlord said, kneeling down beside her, his eyes seeking to draw level with hers, "to the millions of innocents who will die. One moment of surprise, the next moment one of sheer terror—"

"Don't give me that, my lord." Maigrey's lips tightened; the gray eyes glittered. "You designed this bomb. You caused it to come into being. What is it you tell your men? 'When you pick up a weapon and point it at someone, you better be damn sure in your heart you can use it.' You wouldn't have 'picked it up,' my lord, if you truly cared about those innocents!"

But she was nervous. She wound the chain around and around. Her fingers were black with dried blood. The Warlord probed her mind, but he might have walked into a dark and echoing cavern. Nothing. No fear, no regret, no anger, no hatred. Nothing.

His hand closed over hers. Her skin was like the marble in a crypt.

"You altered the code word needed to shut the bomb off?" Sagan asked. His hand left hers, moved near the bomb, near the keys with their strange symbols gleaming brightly on top.

"Did I, my lord?"

"You must have. Otherwise I could stop it."

Maigrey shrugged. "Yes, you could—*if* I didn't change it. If I did . . . touch that first wrong button, and you *will* get a surprise. Ah, I see you calculating the odds. It would be worth it, I know, in the last few seconds remaining, for you to make the attempt. But you don't know how many seconds remain. It could be five. It could be five million. And who knows, you *might* be able to persuade me to change my mind."

Sagan moved his hand away from the bomb. It was hot in the plane, hot and stuffy. He took off his helm, ran his fingers through the hair that was thick and black but starting to recede slightly from his forehead, graying around the temples. "God will not forgive you, my lady. Your soul will be eternally damned for this."

"Look at my starjewel, my lord, and tell me that my soul isn't already damned." Her gaze, sad and shadowed, went to the crystal bomb. "I wanted it. I wanted it for my own. When I realized I had the means to acquire it, back there on *Phoenix*, I threw away everything for the chance. I deserted Dion, my king. I left John Dixter to die alone.

"Ambition!" Maigrey's fist clenched. "The taint in the Blood Royal. Ambition was what truly led to our downfall, the lust for power that was like the sun in our eyes, dazzling, blinding. The downfall of the Guardians. The last of the Guardians." She sighed. Her bloodstained fingers were entangled in the chain.

Sagan glared at her, frustrated, unable to touch any part of her. He wanted to throttle her. If he couldn't choke the information from her, then at least he would avenge his own impending demise. His hands twitched with the frustrated desire.

But it's difficult to kill someone already dead. Sagan knew then how Abdiel must have felt.

The Warlord threw himself into the co-pilot's seat. God, he was tired! Far too tired. Leaning back, he flexed his shoulders, tried to ease the knots cramping his muscles. If he couldn't figure out some way to stop the detonation, he would be resting comfortably very soon. A very long rest. *Requiem aeternam*.

"Did you know, my lord," Maigrey continued, speaking softly, abstractedly, "that when I knew you were coming to find me on Oha-Lau, when I knew the mind-link had been reforged, I planned to kill myself. Did you know that?"

"Yes," he answered.

"My brother's spirit came to me and convinced me to live. Live for Dion. And I did live. But Dion wasn't the reason. I could see, through your mind linked with mine, the fleet of

ships, the wealth of planets, the power. *That* was why I lived!"
Maigrey looked at the chain binding her bloodstained fingers
together. "And you threaten me with eternal damnation!"

She fell silent. The Warlord said nothing. What was there to
say, except acknowledge the truth? Minutes passed in silence,
counted by each indrawn breath, each heartbeat, each involuntary blink of the eye that might be the last. He could picture
the explosion, a white tongue of fire licking out from the
crystal. His brain would have one split second to react, one
horrible, awful moment of involuntary fear. Then his body
consumed completely, nothing left. . . .

"For one moment," Maigrey said, "we will shine brightly as
a star."

She lifted her head suddenly, glanced around as if she'd
heard a noise. Sagan had the startling impression that she was
waiting for something . . . or someone. He thought, then,
that he'd heard a sound. He turned, looked up into the cabin,
straining to hear.

Nothing. Only the pulse of his own life, beating inside him.
And, above that—the faint, buzzing hum.

"Perhaps I didn't send the boy away, my lady." He hazarded
the throw. The minutes were ticking by.

"You did, my lord. I know. Don't lie to me. I see it in your
mind."

"But he'll be alone now, Maigrey. With no one to advise
him."

"Better for him," she whispered. Her hands twisted the
jewel's blood-encrusted chain, pulled it tighter. "Better for
him. Without any of us to influence him, the taint in his blood
will dwindle, be diluted. Perhaps he'll overcome it—"

"How can I?" The youthful voice was cold, bitter, angry.
The sound of feet came on the deck above them. "How can I
now? After what you've done to me?"

Dion appeared, standing above them at the top of the
ladder leading down into the cockpit. A halo of flame framed
the pale, resolute face, marred by the dark smudge of a
bruised cheek and swollen lip.

The Warlord faced Maigrey, saw her relax, the fingers cease
their twisting. The silver chain slipped unheeded to the floor.
"You should have left, Dion," she advised him quietly, not
looking at him. "You could have escaped."

"I'll leave," Dion returned, "when I have what I came for. My lord, I know how to stop the bomb."

"You do? How?" The Warlord's gaze remained on Maigrey. Suddenly he understood.

"Yes," Dion said, acknowledging his unspoken words. "She told me. She told me what she had done, just as she told you. Only she told *me* how to stop it."

Maigrey's face was pale, sadly smiling. She shook her head, avoided meeting anyone's eyes.

"Tell me the code," the Warlord commanded. He was on his feet, putting his hand to the keys atop the crystal bomb.

"I will, my lord. But first I want something in return."

"You fool!" Sagan snarled. "I don't know how much time is left—"

"Not a lot," Maigrey murmured. "It's too late for any of us now." She pointed to a digital readout on the console. "T minus one minute. And counting."

"I will tell you how to stop the bomb"—Dion ignored the interruption—"in return for . . . the bomb."

Sagan stared at him. "You . . . want what?" He fought a wild desire to burst out into uncontrollable laughter.

"You heard me, my lord. I want the bomb. Give me your word of honor. Swear to me in the name of your God that you will hand over the bomb to me, and I'll give you the code words needed to shut it down. If not—" Dion shrugged.

"T minus forty seconds," Maigrey said, "and counting."

"You expect me to believe that you'd actually have the nerve to stand here and wait to die?" Sagan sneered.

"Try me." Dion was firm, unmoving.

Sagan's eyes narrowed, dark brows coming together. He searched the boy for a crack, a flaw. The Warlord was tense; he could feel sweat running down his neck into his armor. Dion was cool, flawless, perfect as the crystal of the bomb.

"Well, well," Maigrey said, almost to herself, "it seems that our little boy has grown up. T minus—"

"You will have the damn bomb! I swear it, by Almighty God!" Sagan ground the oath with his teeth. "Now tell me the code!" His hand hovered over the keys.

"T minus fifteen seconds . . ."

"The poem's name. 'The Second Coming.'"

"You *didn't* alter it!" Sagan muttered in an aside to Maigrey.

He punched in the words as swiftly as he dared, taking deliberate care.

"No, I didn't." She lifted her head, her eyes fixed on Dion. "I thought it . . . appropriate."

One by one, the rays of light running from computer to bomb flickered and went out. The humming sound ceased.

"Detonation cycle . . . ended," Maigrey said, and softly sighed.

Chapter ❦ Nineteen

And he who at every age, as boy and youth and in mature life, has come out of the trial victorious and pure, shall be appointed a ruler and guardian of the State.

Plato, *The Republic*

Dion drew a deep breath. His knees had gone suddenly weak. He nearly fell, and grasped hold of the ladder's hand railing to catch himself. He was careful not to reveal his weakness, however, or how frightened he had really been. Consequently it was some moments before he considered his voice under control enough to speak.

The Warlord had leaned back wearily against the console. Brow furrowed, he was staring quizzically at Maigrey. She alone seemed unmoved.

"Here we are!" XJ's cheerful voice shattered the silence. "Back again. One big happy family. All together for the holidays. And now I've got something to say. I'd just like to make it known—"

The Warlord came suddenly to attention, listening to a voice on his commlink. "Sparafucile? I can't hear you! The transmission's breaking up. Just a moment. Computer, pick up this signal. Enhance it."

"Yes, my lord," XJ responded; rather miffed at being interrupted.

The half-breed's voice came over the computer's speaker. "He is gone, Sagan Lord!"

Maigrey glanced at Sagan swiftly; their eyes met. Dion remained standing above them, in the living quarters of the Scimitar. He saw them conversing, the thoughts winging from mind to mind. He knew himself to be alone, left out of the world these two shared. For a moment he was filled again with jealousy, anger. Then his gaze went to the crystal bomb. He eased his grip on the railing, stood straight and tall. He supposed loneliness was something he'd better be getting used to.

The Warlord's face had darkened. He looked older, suddenly, and tired. He rubbed his hand over his brow. "Explain."

"We kill the mind-dead, Sagan Lord, and we capture shuttle. But"—the half-breed's voice sounded awed—"when we come close to shuttle, it wasn't!"

"Wasn't? Wasn't what?"

"Just *wasn't*, Sagan Lord!"

"Damnedest thing I ever saw!" added another voice, sounding shaken.

Dion recognized it. "Tusk!" he shouted, elated, the lonely feeling ebbing away. "Tusk, are you all right? And Nola, is she—"

"Yeah, yeah, we're all fine here, kid. You're with the Warlord, huh?" Tusk didn't sound happy.

"Mendaharin Tusca, what's going on?" Sagan demanded, glaring at Dion, stopping the words on the boy's lips.

"Beats the hell outta me, your lordship," Tusk said. "One minute this big mother shuttlecraft was sittin' there, and I go to put my hand on it, and bam! It's gone!"

"Jump-juice," XJ said in gloomy tones.

"XJ? Is that XJ?" Tusk yelled. "Damn it. Look, my lord, I haven't been drinking! I'd swear on . . . on my father's grave that one minute that blasted shuttle was there and the next it wasn't—"

"Calm down, Tusca. I believe you."

"You do?" Tusk sounded dubious. "That's good, my lord, because I'm not sure I believe myself. . . ."

"You saw what he wanted you to see, Tusca. He created the illusion in your mind," the Warlord explained.

"He— Oh, you mean Abdiel. Yeah," Tusk added after a pause, "I guess I can believe that."

"There's nothing more you can do there. Tusca, report back to me at the base."

"Uh, if it's all the same to you, my lord, I'd rather not—"

"Come back, Tusk," Dion cut in firmly, blue eyes on the Warlord. "And you report to *me* from now on. I am your king."

"Shit, here we go again!" Tusk could be heard muttering in the background.

Dion saw the Warlord's dark smile, felt his skin burn.

"You have orders for me, Sagan Lord?" Sparafucile came on.

"I'll be in touch," the Warlord responded briefly.

"Yes, Sagan Lord."

The connection went dead.

"Abdiel escaped," Maigrey said.

"Yes," Sagan answered, and then both were silent. But Dion could almost hear the unspoken conversation filling in the emptiness.

The Warlord picked up his helm. "It's been an interesting night, for all of us. I'm returning to my shuttle. By your leave, of course, Your Majesty."

The sarcasm cut, and Dion would bleed from the wounds inflicted until the day he died. *I have Sagan's loyalty, albeit given under duress,* he realized. *Damn it all to hell and back again, what do I have to do to earn this man's respect?*

"The night isn't over yet, Warlord," he said.

"Not by a long shot, sire."

"There is still much to be done."

"And with Your Majesty's permission, I'll set about doing it," Sagan said, impatience sharpening the edge in his voice.

You'll set about doing it. And I'll . . . I'll . . .

"You're injured, my liege," Maigrey said gently, looking up at him. "You should lie down and rest. I'll call for a medic—"

"No, I'll take care of it myself. The wound's not . . . very deep."

Dion continued to stand, jaws clenched, rigid. He didn't look at Sagan or at Maigrey. He stared fixedly at the crystal space-rotation bomb. "You have my leave to go, Warlord, and continue your duties." *Whatever those are,* he added silently. *You would know. I don't. What am I, after all, but king?* The crystal blurred in his vision. His fingers curled around the cold metal.

"Thank you, sire. My lady," Sagan added, "I'll need to confer with you."

"Yes." Maigrey sounded tired beyond endurance. "I'll join you in a moment, my lord."

There was more to that conversation than there seemed on the surface. Dion glanced down swiftly, suspiciously, saw the Warlord's dark eyes fix on Maigrey's gray ones, saw the shadow in his darken hers.

Sagan nodded, turned, and climbed the ladder leading up out of the cockpit. Reaching the top, he faced Dion, the

Warlord's tall, muscular body looming over the young man.
Gold armor gleamed like flame in the red emergency lights.
"Get some sleep, Your Majesty," he said. "And have that
wound of yours looked at. You'll have a lot to do . . . in the
morning."

Dion didn't reply.

Sagan's expression grew grave. "You should have been
careful what you wished for, Your Majesty. It was granted.
Now we will see what you can do with it." He bowed low,
whether with respect or with mockery, Dion wasn't certain.
He wasn't watching. He waited until he heard Sagan's heavy
tread descending the outer hull of the spaceplane, then the
young man slid down the ladder, coming to stand behind
Maigrey in the cockpit.

She had her back to him, her fingers tracing around the
edges of the blood-encrusted star that was the deadly heart of
the space-rotation bomb.

"Don't go with him, my lady," Dion said, putting his hand
on the back of her chair.

Maigrey shook her head, said nothing.

"Stay here, with me," Dion persisted. "We'll fly back to
Defiant. Sagan will have to free John Dixter now. . . ."

Maigrey shuddered. The pale hair had come undone from
its braid, fell across the scarred cheek.

"The Warlord's right, Maigrey." Dion moved around to try
to see her face, but her hair was a curtain, hiding her from his
view. "I need someone to advise me. I don't know how to be
a king."

"What man does?" she asked. The starjewel's radiance
gone, it was black as a void in space, empty as the vastness
between galaxies. Sighing, she rose to her feet. The spaceplane's red lights gleamed in her silver armor, making it seem
as if she walked in blood.

"There it is, Your Majesty," she said, gesturing to the
bomb. "Yours. Power."

Dion stared at it, frowning, disbelieving. "Sagan actually
walked off and left me with it. I don't trust him. He'll try to get
it back! Maigrey, you must stay with me—"

"You can trust him, my liege," she interrupted him. "He
swore his oath to God."

"An illusionist who believes in his own illusions!" Dion
scoffed.

Maigrey smiled wanly, sadly. "We all need to believe in something."

"Do we?" Dion challenged. "Then tell me this, my lady. That rite you and Sagan put me through. Was that real? Or was that illusion?"

"If you can ask the question, my liege, you aren't prepared to understand the answer." She lifted the silver helm with its white-feather crest. "By your leave, Your Majesty—"

"Riddles! Games! Tests!" Dion shouted, blocking her path. "That's what this was, wasn't it? Another test! You wanted to see if I'd risk my life to attain my goal, my desire, my ambition—that ambition you call the taint in our blood. Well, I did! I was willing to die for it! Does that mean I pass?"

Maigrey gazed down at her own bloodstained hand. She didn't look at him and when she spoke, it wasn't an answer.

"I'm giving Your Majesty my starjewel. You'll need it to arm the bomb. And I'll tell you the code to activate—"

"No!" Dion cried, halting her.

Maigrey lifted her eyes, stared at him. "You don't understand, my liege. Without the code—"

"I understand," he interrupted. "I will keep the bomb . . . as it is. And now," he added tersely, turning his back on her, "you better go. The Warlord will be waiting for you."

She said nothing. Then he felt her arm around him. She held him close. He shut his eyes, longed—for an instant—to lay his head on her breast and sob like a child.

I want to tell you about Marcus, Dion cried silently. He gave his life for you. He died in my arms! I want to tell you about those others I killed. How I dream about them at night. I want to tell you I'm frightened, Maigrey! I don't want to be what I am! I don't think I can! I know I failed the test. I failed you, failed Sagan. I failed myself! I'm ordinary. . . .

"Like Marcus?" she asked aloud.

He opened his eyes, stared at her.

"I must go, my liege. Your Guardians have one last task they must perform." Maigrey reached out to him, touched the necklace he wore around his neck—a necklace bearing a small ring of fire opals. He gazed down at her hand, saw the opals sparkle with myriad lights, a contrast to the dark jewel in the bomb.

Leaning near, Maigrey kissed the bruised cheek.

"Congratulations, my liege. You passed."

·⋅◁▬ ▬▷·⋅

After she left him, he could feel, on his skin, the wetness of her tears. Dion slumped wearily down into the pilot's seat. His wound burned and throbbed.

"She didn't really arm it, you know," XJ-27 remarked.

"What?" Dion was jolted from his pain-filled lethargy. "Didn't arm what?"

"What? The bomb, kid, the bomb! Jeez, where you been all night? It was a trick, to fool that mind-seizer character—"

"—and me," Dion said softly, bitterly. "So that, too, was nothing but illusion."

"We put on quite a show," the computer was saying proudly. "My performance was stunning. 'I have been programmed not to respond to any questions or commands,'" XJ repeated in a flat, mechanical mimic of itself. "We fooled the Warlord completely. And as for Abdiel, you should have seen that old man's face when he heard her give the code and the command. I added a few special effects. Those beams of light were my own touch. He was furious. If looks could kill— But then he thought my lady was already dead.

"You and Tusk better watch how you treat me from now on," XJ continued smugly. "I hear my true vocation calling me. The smell of the greasepaint, the roar of the crowd. Cybernetics Theater . . ."

"All illusion," Dion murmured. Reaching out, his hands closed over the cold crystal of the bomb, this ultimate weapon. He might hurt someone with it . . . if he threw it at them hard enough.

Congratulations, my liege. You passed.

He smiled. Not entirely illusion.

I *am* king.

Acknowledgments

Once again, thanks to Gary Pack, weapons genius, who designed the space-rotation bomb and the Judas gun. (Due to recent unfortunate developments involving his employer, Snaga Ohme, Mr. Pack is currently seeking gainful employment and would be glad to hear from anyone interested in blowing up neighboring planets.)

Thanks again to John Hefter, brother in the outlawed Order of Adamant, for assistance on the Latin translations.

My love to Roger Moore, Georgia Moore, Michael Williams, Mark and Jamie Acres, and my son David Baldwin and daughter Elizabeth who together created Raoul and the Little One and nearly got me tossed out of a PTA meeting!

The Guardians' March is better known in this century as "To the Unknown Man," written and performed by Vangelis on his album *Spiral*, 1977, RCA.

About the Author

Born in Independence, Missouri, MARGARET WEIS graduated from the University of Missouri and worked as a book editor before teaming up with Tracy Hickman to develop the *Dragonlance* novels. Margaret lives in a renovated barn in Wisconsin with her teen-aged daughter, Elizabeth Baldwin, and two dogs and one cat. She enjoys reading (especially Charles Dickens), opera, and aqua-aerobics.

In **The King's Sacrifice**—Volume 3 of *Star of the Guardians* by Margaret Weis—Dion Starfire seems to have truly become king. But, as he discovers in the following scene, there is more to being a king than simply wearing the crown.

The double doors, decorated with the phoenix, closed and sealed. Sagan removed his helm, placed it carefully upon its stand. Hands clasped behind his back, he took a turn about the spacious area of his living quarters, glanced out the viewscreen at the other ships in his fleet, looked to see if there were any messages on his computer screen, then turned to face the boy.

"Well, Your Majesty?" Sagan asked coldly.

Dion's anger was at hand again, sharp and shining with the righteousness of his cause.

"The woman died. The young woman I could have healed! She drowned herself and it was my fault. Never again. Never again will I listen to you or take your advice. You don't want me to discover my true powers because you're afraid of me. I am king and, from now on, I will *be* king!"

Sagan waited a moment to see if Dion had anything further to say. The young man remained silent.

"Is Your Majesty quite finished?"

"Yes, we are."

The Warlord said nothing, did nothing. Dion,

expecting a bitter argument, was taken aback. Not quite knowing what to do, he decided a dignified exit was called for and turned on his heel to make it.

"I have something I think Your Majesty should see," came Sagan's voice.

Dion stopped, hesitated, half-turned, glanced around.

"What is that, my lord?"

The Warlord depressed a button on a console. A vidscreen slid into view. "Computer, bring up exhibit number 221."

A vid appeared on the screen. Blurred at first, it sharpened as the computer adjusted the focus.

The naked body of a young woman, face hideously deformed, lay upon a steel table. The woman's hair was wet, bedraggled, feet and hands were blue, a numbered tag was wrapped around one toe.

Dion made a strangled sound, shock and fury robbing him of his voice. He turned his back, continued walking toward the double doors.

"Look at it, Your Majesty! *If* you have the nerve. Her death was, as you say, your fault. Your responsibility, though perhaps not the way you imagine."

Slowly, hands clenching into fists, Dion faced the horrible image on the vidscreen, faced the impassive, shadowed visage of the Warlord.

"You are right, my lord." The boy swallowed, his throat muscles constricting in his neck. "I have much to learn. I thank your lordship for teaching me."

"You have much to learn, all right!" Sagan snapped.

The cam zoomed in on the body, bringing it closer, closer, studying it from every angle. Dion drew a deep breath, held himself steady.

"Body of Jane Doe," came a voice over the audio, a woman's voice, sounding calm and bored. "Vid taken prior to autopsy for purposes of indentification." The woman gave the planet's date and time, also Standard Military date and time, her own name and official title, adding, "Anyone having information regarding the identity of subject Jane Doe is asked to report to . . ."

The cam lingered for a close-up of the hideous face, traveled more hurriedly over the upper part of the body, moved down the right arm to focus on the palm of the victim's right hand.

"No tattoos. No moles or birthmarks. The only wounds found on the body were discovered on palm of the right hand."

White flesh filled the screen—white flesh criss-crossed with the lines used by fortune tellers to trace a human's destiny, white flesh marred by five, small puncture marks arranged in a peculiar pattern.

Dion let go his inheld breath. Balls of yellow burst before his eyes, he was suddenly sick and dizzy. Dazed, he lifted his right hand, stared down at his palm. Five scars, five puncture marks, arranged in the same pattern. Draw a line between them, connect the dots, and they'd form a five-pointed star.

Sagan ordered the computer to end the vid. It did so, leaving the image of the dead woman's hand on the screen.

"The coroner had a difficult time figuring out what these marks were, by her report," the Warlord continued, regarding the photo with cool, frowning detachment. "She concluded that they were made by five metal needles, pressed into the skin. But for what reason or purpose, she couldn't fathom. She surmised it was some type of drug-use, though she couldn't find any trace of drugs in the body. Admittedly, she didn't spend much time investigating. The young woman had obviously died by drowning, she'd obviously finally suceeded in doing what she'd attempted to do before—kill herself. We know differently, however, don't we, my liege? We know it wasn't suicide. It was murder, cold-blooded, calculating murder."

Dion glanced behind him, saw a chair and sat down before he fell.

"Abdiel." Dion spoke softly. The name conjured up bitter memory. He stared at his hand, curled the fingers over the palm, hiding the marks.

"Abdiel."

"You knew . . . all along."

"I didn't know. I suspected. When I received news of the girl's suicide, I sent Dr. Giesk to examine the body, obtain the coroner's report. He recognized immediately the true cause of death."

"But she drowned! It *was* suicide, the coroner said so." Dion clung to his fragment of hope.

"Yes, death was by drowning. Eyewitnesses reported seeing her jump into the lake. But did she do so of her own volition? I doubt it." Sagan shook his head. "You know yourself how Abdiel can manipulate the mind, especially those with whom he has bonded."

Dion shuddered, grasped his right wrist, nursed his hand as if it pained him. "But she wasn't one of the mind-dead. I would have recognized them."

"Exactly. Abdiel would know that, of course. The girl was probably a new acquisition, one recently obtained. She had probably not given herself completely to him yet."

Dion laughed suddenly, mirthlessly. "What would he have done if I *had* healed her?"

"He had little cause to fear that. He's seen inside you."

The young man flushed, rose to his feet. "What's that supposed to mean? He told me himself I had the power—"

"He told you a lot of things. And then he tried to have you killed," the Warlord interrupted. "What he saw inside you was your doubt, your lack of faith."

"And what is your counsel, my lord?"

"We escaped destruction this time," the Warlord said grimly, "but just barely. We may not be so fortunate again. That is what Abdiel is telling us. That is his warning."

"Warning?" Dion frowned.

"Of course!" Sagan glared at him in exasperation. "Don't tell me that even now, you don't understand. This"—he pointed to the cold, dead hand—"was no blunder on his part. He flaunts his abilities, signs his name to his work."

"But . . . why?"

"Because he knows the debilitating power of fear."

Dion tossed the mane of red-golden hair. "I'm not afraid of him."

Turning, Sagan clasped his hand behind his back, beneath the red cloak trimmed in gold. He walked over to the viewscreen, looked out at the fleet of ships. Dion followed him, followed his gaze. Destroyers, carriers, torpedo boats, support vessels—a vast armada surrounding the Warlord and his king with a seemingly impenetrable ring of steel and fire.

Against all this—one frail old man.

"*I* am, Your Majesty," Sagan said quietly.

He left the viewscreen, crossed the carpeted deck to the computer. Dion noticed, for the first time, that the Warlord was limping slightly, favoring his right leg.

Sagan caught the boy's glance. "A pulled muscle. Nothing more."

He depressed a key on the computer. The dead hand vanished. Dion, staring at the empty screen, thought he could still see it.

"What do we do?"

But he knew the answer, knew the reason why he'd been brought back, knew the reason Rykilth and DiLuna and Olefsky were on board *Phoenix II*.

"We go to war," said Sagan.

THE DEATH GATE CYCLE

Known for their innovation, Margaret Weis and Tracy Hickman reach an entirely new level with The Death Gate Cycle. For this seven-book extravaganza they have developed four completely realized worlds. In the first four novels, a new adventure with both continuing and new characters will be set on each of the four worlds. In later volumes, the realms begin to interact, with the supreme battle for control of all the worlds in the final novel.

Dragon Wing, Volume 1

Generations ago, magicians sundered the world into four distinct realms. Now, few even know of the other worlds. Haplo has been sent through the treacherous Death Gate to explore the realms and stir up dissension. The first visit is to Arianus, a world where islands float in the sky and men travel by enchanted dragonships. The following scene gives us an irresistible taste of the realm of Arianus and the plots surrounding even the most knowledgeable of men who live there.

The captive assassin, known throughout the realm as Hugh the Hand, rode behind the courier, who kept their dragon under tight rein. The courier glanced this way and that in the gloom, as if he had not flown much—odd for a king's messenger. At last they passed over Dandrak's shore and headed out into deep sky. Even here, it was truly dark—as dark as legend held night had been in the ancient world before the Sundering.

Elven astronomers believed that there were three Lords of Night. And though the superstitious thought these were giant men, the educated knew that the Lords of Night were really islands of coralite floating far above them, moving in an orbit that took them every twelve hours in front of the sun.

Beneath these isles were the High Realm, purportedly where lived the mysteriarchs—the most powerful human wyzards. Below the High Realm was the firmament or days' stars. No one knew precisely what the firmament was. There had been many attempts made by both elves and humans to fly up to the firmament and discover its secrets, but those who tried it never returned.

Several times during the flight, the courier turned his head and glanced back at Hugh the Hand, curious to note the reactions of a man who had been snatched from beneath the falling axe. The courier was doomed to disappointment if he thought he should see any sign of relief or triumph. Grim, impassive, the assassin's face gave away nothing of the thoughts behind its mask. Here was a face that could watch a man die as coolly as another might watch a man eat and drink. The face was, at the moment, turned away from the courier, intently watching the route of their flight. A fact the courier noticed with some uneasiness. Perhaps sensing his thoughts, Hugh raised his head and fixed his eyes upon the courier.

The courier had gained nothing from his inspection of Hugh. Hugh, however, appeared to gain a great deal from the courier. The narrowed eyes seemed to peel back skin and carve away bone and would have, in a moment, laid bare whatever secrets were kept within the courier's brain had not the young man shifted his eyes to his dragon's spiky mane. He did not look back at Hugh again.

When the courier noted Hugh's interest in their flying route, a blanket of fog immediately began to drift over and obscure the land. They were flying high and fast and there was not much to see beneath the shadows cast by the Lords of the Night. But all coralite gives off a faint, bluish light, causing stands of forests to show up black against the silvery radiance of the ground. Castles of fortresses made of coralite that have not been covered over with a paste of crushed granite gleam softly in the night. Towns, with their shining ribbons of coralite streets, show up easily from the air.

During the war, when marauding elven airships had been in the skies, the townspeople had covered their streets with straw and rushes. But there was no war upon the Volkaran Isles now. The majority of humans who dwelt there thought this was due to the fear they had generated among the elflords. A few humans in the realm knew the truth—among them King Stephen and Queen Anne. The elves of Aristagon were ignoring Volkaran and Uylandia because they had much bigger problems to deal with at the moment— a rebellion among their own people.

When that rebellion was firmly and ruthlessly crushed, the elves would turn their attention to the kingdom of the humans who had stirred up this rebellion in the first place. Stephen knew that this time the elves would not be content with conquering and occupying. This time, they would rid themselves of the human pollution in their world once and forever. Stephen was quietly and swiftly setting up his pieces on the great gameboard, preparing for the final bitter contest.

Hugh didn't know it, but he was one of those pieces.

Elven Star, Volume 2

Haplo's second journey takes him to the jungle world of Pryan. Here the three races of men, elves and dwarves seem to have already completed Haplo's task of causing unrest—perhaps not even the threat of annihilation can bring these peoples together.

Someone made a whimpering sound. Whether it was Rega or the elf, Roland couldn't tell. He couldn't take his eyes from the giants long enough to find out. He felt Rega's shivering body press against his. Movement in the undergrowth indicated that Paithan, bound like the rest of them, was attempting to wriggle his way over near Rega.

Keeping his eyes on the tytans, Roland saw no reason to be afraid. They were big, but they didn't act particularly menacing or threatening.

"Look, Sis," he whispered out of the corner of his mouth, "keep calm. They don't look too bright. We can bluff our way outta this."

Andor laughed, a horrible, bone-chilling sound. The tytans—ten of them—had gathered around their captives, forming a semicircle. The eyeless heads faced them. A very soft, very quiet, very gentle voice spoke.

Where is the citadel?

Roland gazed up at them, puzzled. "Did you say something?" He could have sworn that their mouths never moved.

"Yes, I heard them!" Rega answered in awe.

Where is the citadel?

The question was repeated, still spoken quietly, the words whispering through Roland's mind.

Where is the citadel? What must we do?

The words were urgent now, no longer a whisper but a cry that was like a scream trapped in the skull.

Where is the citadel? What must we do? Tell us! Command us!

At first annoying, the screaming inside Roland's head became rapidly more painful. He wracked his burning brain, trying desperately to think, but he'd never heard of any "citadel," at least not in Thillia.

"As . . . the . . . elf!" he managed, forcing the words out between teeth clenched against the agony.

A terrifying scream behind him indicated that the tytans had taken his advice. Paithan lurched over, rolling on the ground, writhing in pain, shouting something in elven.

"Stop it! Stop it!" Rega begged, and suddenly the voices ceased.

It was quiet inside his head. Roland sagged weakly against his bonds. Paithan lay, sobbing, on the moss. Rega, arms tightly bound, crouched near him. The tytans gazed at their captives and then one of them, without the slightest warning, lifted a tree branch and slammed it into Andor's bound and helpless body.

The SeaKing couldn't cry out; the blow crushed his rib cage, punctured his lungs. The tytan raised the branch and struck again.

Numb, horrified, Roland summoned adrenaline-fed strength and plunged backward, knocking Rega to the ground. She lay quietly, too quietly, and he wondered if she had fainted. He hoped she had. It would be easier . . . much easier. Paithan lay nearby, staring wide-eyed at what was left of Andor. The elf's face was ashen.

Roland braced himself for the blow, praying that the first killed him swiftly. He heard the scrabbling sound in the moss below him, felt the hand grab onto the buckle of his belt, but the hand wasn't real to him, not as real as the death that loomed above him. The sudden jerk and the plunge down through the moss brought him sharply to his senses. He gasped and spluttered and floundered, as a sleepwalker who stumbles into an icy lake.

His fall ended abruptly and painfully. He opened his eyes. He wasn't in water, but in a dark tunnel that seemed to have been hallowed out of the thick moss. A strong hand shoved him, a sharp blade sliced through his bonds.

"Go! Go! They are thick witted, but they will follow!"

"Rega," Roland mumbled and tried to get back.

"I have her *and* the elf! Now go!"

Rega fell against him, propelled from behind. Her cheekbone struck his shoulder, and her head snapped up.

"Go!" shouted the voice.

Roland caught hold of his sister, dragged her alongside him. Ahead of them stretched a tunnel, leading deeper into the moss. Rega began to crawl down it. Roland followed, fear dictating to his body what it must do to escape because his brain seemed to have shut down.

Dazed, groping through the gray-green darkness, he crawled and lurched and sprawled clumsily head-long in his mad dash. Rega, her body more compact, moved through the tunnel with ease. She paused occasionally, to look back, her gaze going past Roland to the elf behind him.

Paithan's face glimmered an eerie white, he looked more like a ghost than a living man, but he was moving, slithering through the tunnel on hands and knees and belly like a snake. Behind him was the voice, urging them on.

"Go! Go!"

In *Star of the Guardians*, Margaret Weis finally has the chance to go solo on a series years in the making. Fast-paced and action-packed, *Star of the Guardians* is story-telling on an inter-galactic scale.

Read *The King's Sacrifice*, the third volume in the series, on sale November 1991, wherever Bantam Spectra books are sold.

Of course, Margaret Weis will continue to develop new projects with her co-author, Tracy Hickman. Known for their involving stories set on imaginative worlds and peopled with well-drawn characters, the two have reached a new height with their series, *The Death Gate Cycle*. This magnificent series takes place in a world long ago sundered into four separate worlds. It is the tale of the powerful magicians capable of such an act and the men who would repair the damage. Finally, it is the story of those people who live in these four worlds—the realms of sky, stone, fire, and sea—and have only legends to tell them how it all began.

Read *Dragon Wing* and *Elven Star* the first two novels in Margaret Weis and Tracy Hickman's *Death Gate Cycle* series, now on sale in paperback wherever Bantam Spectra Books are sold.

For the summer's best in science fiction and fantasy,
look no further than Bantam Spectra.

SPECTRA'S SUMMER SPECTACULAR

With a dazzling list of science fiction and fantasy stars, Spectra's summer list will take you to worlds both old and new: worlds as close as Earth herself, as far away as a planet where daylight reigns supreme; as familiar as Han Solo's Millennium Falcon and as alien as the sundered worlds of the Death Gate. Travel with these critically acclaimed and award-winning authors for a spectacular summer filled with wonder and adventure!

Coming in May 1991:

Star Wars, Volume 1: Heir to the Empire
by Timothy Zahn

Earth
by David Brin

King of Morning, Queen of Day
by Ian McDonald

Coming in June, 1991:

The Gap Into Vision: Forbidden Knowledge
by Stephen R. Donaldson

Black Trillium
by Marion Zimmer Bradley, Julian May and Andre Norton

Chronicles of the King's Tramp Book 1: Walker of Worlds
by Tom DeHaven

Coming in July 1991:

The Death Gate Cycle, Volume 3: Fire Sea
by Margaret Weis and Tracy Hickman

The Death Gate Cycle, Volume 2: Elven Star
by Margaret Weis and Tracy Hickman

Raising the Stones
by Sheri S. Tepper

Coming in August 1991:

Garden of Rama
by Arthur C. Clarke and Gentry Lee

Nightfall
by Isaac Asimov and Robert Silverberg

Available soon wherever Bantam Spectra Books are sold.